VENGEANCE

by

A.J. Scudiere

To Dan -
Use this as a manual the next time you're off to an assassination.
AJ Scudiere

GRIFFYN INK

Vengeance

Published by Griffyn Ink

For further information, please contact:
Griffyn Ink
www.GriffynInk.com
MediaRelations@GriffynInk.com

Vengeance
A.J. Scudiere
1. Title 2. Author 3. Fiction

ISBN 10: 0-9799510-1-1
ISBN 13: 978-0-9799510-1-1

For Guy,
who is always there for me,
even though I am consistently crazy

There were a handful of people who truly helped make this book what it is:

So many thanks go to Eli, for everything.

The guys at Gun World-Target Range of Van Nuys, California were just fantastic. After I clarified that I wasn't going to hurt any real people, they were tremendously helpful in getting me outfitted for an assassination.

Special thanks go out to David Hughes and particularly to Allen Clark, Jr. of Ernie Reyes World Martial Arts in Gallatin, Tennessee. Thank you for helping us with the design. It made all the difference!

And Sue Koepp, thank you for all you did
and for all the scales you helped tip in my direction.

Chapter 1

The thick smell of blood wasn't a shock. He was used to it. What startled Lee was the woman.

She was sitting at the dining room table, seemingly oblivious to the carnage mounted on the wall behind her. She was working over something, like she was writing, and was deep in her efforts where she didn't acknowledge him.

A large red bow, the kind you would put on a three-foot Christmas present, stole his attention sitting there on the table beside her. She wrote with precision, her head bent low, her rich chestnut hair worked into braids and wound round her head in a style that called to mind *The Sound of Music*.

Lee suppressed the boiling anger in him down to something in the range of a solid simmer and took a step toward her, wondering if she was in shock. Her right hand came up sharply, one leather gloved finger telling him to wait a minute, but the rigid control he saw in her told him she intended for him to wait as long as she wanted.

In that moment he saw what he had previously missed. She wore leather, in several shades of shadow, from her fingertips to her toes. The braids weren't cute, they were cop hair–the kind you couldn't get a hold on and use to yank a person around.

"There." Surprisingly, given the growing stench of death emanating from what Lee was now pretty certain was her handiwork, her voice was musical and held a low note of pride. She stood and turned to face him, holding the bow and what was apparently a large gift tag. And she smiled at him.

As the smile reached her large chocolate eyes, Lee felt the blood drain out the soles of his feet. She was insane. Clinically insane. There was no other reason a person would be truly happy here. Add in that she was armed to the teeth–a short dagger was sheathed at her waist, a pair of matched sais were slid into long, thin pockets down each thigh, strange wood and metal sickles slipped gracefully through lined up loops so they didn't jangle when she walked–and the sweetness he had initially perceived fled like dandelion tufts.

She looked at him like she would a small puppy sitting at the edge of her living room, like he was cute and non-threatening. Lee's hand inched under his jacket to his hip, fondling the warm butt of the 9mm there. Given everything else, he wouldn't put it past her to be fast.

But she didn't say anything, just went about fastening the bow to the body and plumping it a little, like she was Martha Stewart off to a birthday party. The body was held to the wall behind it by serviceable, unadorned throwing knives. At least he was pretty certain they were unadorned, only the last inch of the handle was visible on each of the six blades that had crucified the man to the wall.

Lee thought he had seen lethal in his time, but this looked like the body had been alive when it had been pinned there, and the buried knives were sunk into wall studs. It was the only way that the heft of the large, muscular man wouldn't have come forward, bringing drywall down with him. That took planning.

The face of the man on the wall sagged, eyes and mouth open, blood running in thin rivulets from the edges of each. He had suffered a thousand punctures and surface slices in his final moments, and the woman carried exactly the implements to do it. Although she must have cleaned them thoroughly before sliding them into their leather homes along her lean legs.

Stepping back she admired the tag. And Lee, for the first time, read it.

In payment for murder, rape, and the destruction of families.

One by one, she used claw-like throwing stars to pin obituaries, newspaper articles, and pieces of police reports to dead flesh. After a moment Lee no longer cared what she was tacking to the corpse, he just wondered where in hell the stars were coming from. She would simply produce another and another, like a sick magician.

She turned to smile at him again, and his breath hitched. A wailing started deep at the back of his head.

He'd been wrong. She was just a girl.

The whine grew stronger, and he recognized it for what it was–sirens, more than one. If the girl knew what was coming, she gave no indication, just tipped her head and walked out the back. She moved with a precision that made her look inhuman; he wouldn't have batted an eyelash had she simply climbed the walls or even passed through them. And, though he watched her use the door, Lee heard none of the usual sounds of human movement.

She went down the back steps and flitted away into the woods, an evil sprite or a minion of a vengeful god. Lee wasn't sure.

Beyond the walls, tires squealed and car doors slammed. They didn't call out, but he could hear them out there, gathering steam and numbers. The cops had an idea that something had gone down here. But he was certain they hadn't been expecting this.

His irritation was flaring again, and that was a bad sign. There was no room for emotion in this job. So with a sigh, he pushed the back door open with his elbow, and headed straight for the woods. As much as he would have liked to follow her, his priority was getting out of here.

He walked through foliage he knew too well–deeper and deeper, following the path he had worn over the past week, his focus on the walk, on removing himself from the situation-until he finally emerged. No matter what evidence they found, the boys in blue would know it wasn't his work.

He unlocked the old sedan that was nearly mangled on the outside, but purred like a hot kitten. Climbing in, he slammed his fists against the leather wrapped steering wheel.

Damnit, the bitch had stolen his kill.

*　　　*　　　*

Owen Dunham had everything, and every goddamned little bit of it was sitting at the dinner table with him. His wife looked at him funny, her Russian, tilted eyes knew from the look on his face, even as she passed the buttered corn. Somehow she always knew. Charlotte was painfully oblivious, and he would have to either break her heart or leave it to Annika to foot that bill.

He reminded himself that he loved his job, and that he did good work, and that he could sleep well at night. Other people slept well at night because of him, too. So he reached down into his pocket to fetch the vibrating phone.

Charlotte saw the movement, her bright eyes clouding as the story of having her work held up as an example of some of the best third grade writing the teacher had ever seen faded on her lips. For a moment Owen wondered if Charlotte's 'fiction' had included this.

He offered a repressed I'm-so-sorry-baby-but-I-have-to-get-this smile to his daughter. There was nothing to give to his wife. So he stood and flipped the phone open as he went into his office in his own little version of the separation of church and state. "Dunham."

"Phoenix." It was a voice he knew all too well, even though he'd only once shook hands with the man and saw a face to put to the sound. Randolph just did dispatch. Just spent his time interrupting Owen's family dinners and school plays. "You aren't going to believe this."

Owen rubbed the back of his neck and wondered what the hell had gone wrong this time, because that's all that this could mean. "My kid got an award at school today, she was just telling me about it. This had better be good."

There was a smile in Randolph's voice. "Oh, this is real fucked-up good. Your grudge ninja's back."

"Shit." The ninja had laid low for almost six months. Nothing they could pin on the guy. Sure there were a few things that might have been his work. "Are they sure? Before I leave my family–"

"I've seen some preliminary photos. Open your e-file. If this isn't your ninja I'll eat your socks at the end of the trip."

That was a serious bet, Owen knew. He tucked the cell phone handily against his shoulder, knowing it gave away his age. The move never should have been attempted with a phone this small, certainly not while hacking into his encrypted computer files. The stance was a throwback to a day when the phones had been large enough to cradle in the crook of your neck, back to when he'd first become familiar with the gadgets and had still thought they were pretty cool. Before he'd grown to hate the things.

The photo opened on his screen. As usual, he did a quick once over around the office to be sure that no small eyes had snuck in behind him, that Annika wasn't there looking over his shoulder. His desk faced the door and was back against a solid wall for exactly this reason, but he'd never forgive himself if Charlotte ever saw what he did.

"Oh." His stomach rolled a little at first, just like always. But, God, if that wasn't signature work all over that body. "When's my flight?"

"Half an hour ago."

Knowing and not caring that the dispatcher couldn't see it, Owen nodded at Randolph's standard line. The plane was waiting. He didn't need to pack, because he packed a new bag at the end of each trip, but he did need a few minutes to tell Annika and Charlotte goodbye. It wasn't like the body was going anywhere. "Bye, 'Dolph."

The line disconnected as Owen tried to figure out how the man had been so neatly thumb-tacked to the wall. He should have fallen over and taken the plaster with him. At least the trip would be interesting.

Owen reminded himself of that fifteen hours later.

He scrubbed a hand over his face as his logical brain got away from him. He tried not to calculate how long he'd been awake. But his alarm had gone off at five-thirty the previous morning, putting him at roughly twenty-nine hours up.

He tried to forget the number instantly, and slugged back another cup of coffee. It was too thin. The coffee he was given everywhere was always different, but always equally bad–it was just part of the badge. Cops everywhere hated him, thinking that he tread on their turf, when really it was they who had tread all over his murder scene, so they gave him bad cop coffee. And since good cop coffee was an oxy moron . . . Owen tossed back another shot of it, thinking that if it went straight to the back of his throat it might not linger on his tongue like the socks Randolph wasn't going to have to eat.

Reminding himself that he was nowhere near his record for hours awake, he decided to check out the lab work on their body and their ninja.

In the middle of the night, while still on the scene, he had sent close-up photos of the tag to the handwriting analyst who had opened the file and declared the writing identical to the other tags without even waking up.

The body bore marks of piercings with a long slender awl. Slash marks were cut no more than an inch deep in a handful of non-vital places. Owen had studied the ninja's work before and decided that the knives that held the body had been thrown, the piercings were from sais, and the slashes were the work of kamas. Kamas weren't pretty or flashy. Curved metal knives, mounted sickle-style at the end of wooden, hammer-sized handles, they were all but unheard of beyond the martial arts world. They hadn't hit the movie circuit yet. Given the expert weaponry and use thereof, Owen was certain they had a pro on their hands. He had sighed at this body the same way he had at all the others. The ninja definitely got the job done.

So he had stood in front of the body with the sais he had picked up to match the holes after the last corpse the ninja had left, and this time he mocked poking at it while it still hung on the wall. The cops in the last town had moved the body before he got to play, changing every piece of evidence from certain to possible, and pissing him off no end. He'd been no good to Charlotte and Annika for a full week after that one.

Owen then inserted long metal wires into the many punctures the body bore and he saw something very interesting. Every single one was sticking out a good six inches below his comfort zone in his own natural grip. Blinking, he pulled out a wire and stuck in a sai. Then he replaced the wire and did the same at each hole. Even the angle of the stabs down into the shoulder matched. Owen had smiled.

He smiled again now as he and Blankenship stared down at the body on the slab, still with the long wires sticking out of it as well as the ninja's metal knives. They were overly utilitarian, looking like they'd been cut with a welder from a sheet of thick metal. "Our ninja's about five foot six. Not too tall."

Blankenship snorted. "Of course. Ninjas are little Japanese guys."

There was no comment. Owen had never been sure how Ron Blankenship had gotten into the FBI in the first place. Just as he had never been sure if being the man's senior partner was a blessing or a curse.

Just then, one of the lab guys burst in. Special Agent Nguyen was clothed head to toe in white paper-drape clothing that was catching the sick burning of the fluorescent rays and bouncing them off in all directions. His lips were pressed together as he confronted Dunham. "I got this niggling last time about the hairs we got from the ninja."

"And?"

"I pulled the old samples. They all match." He was clearly upset.

Owen failed to see the issue with that. The hair was about the only evidence they had on the guy. There were no clothing fibers, no fingerprints that could be trailed from scene to scene, and no blood. It seemed no one ever got a wounding hit on the little bastard.

"They match too well."

"Is that even possible?" What the hell was *too well*?

But he was about to find out.

"This hair," Nguyen held a strand up, shaking it, "is old. It is, in fact, the same age as all the other hair we found. The only thing I'll bet on now is that this hair did *not* come off the head of our ninja."

"What?" They had tested it extensively. It was at every scene. But Owen knew. It had been too easy.

Nguyen shook his head. "The scene was salted."

Lee was happy–fate had paid him back for that missed kill. But like all things fate had thrown his way, there was some shit in this one, too. He was going to have to move out.

He'd been staying in a shack in the mountains just north of Atlanta, but that was over now. He'd gotten too close to the city, not that it was really 'city' out this far from the heart, but there were people. And apparently he wasn't suited to be around people anymore. It had been an experiment, and now he was packing the few bags he had.

Tugging his ball cap lower on his face, he lamented that he'd only gotten half his morning jog in today, but figured the adrenaline pumping through his system more than made up for the missed exercise. How many people ever stumbled upon a car accident? Or a robbery in progress? It just didn't happen. But his feet had pounded through the trees on the old trail and so had someone else's–small delicate feet, popping past on bouncy white sneakers. The blonde ponytail reminded him of Samantha. But Sam would never have been stupid enough to be out in the woods oblivious to all but the music piping into her ears. Lee bet this woman wouldn't be that stupid again either.

The man had been wearing jeans and a snarl beneath a heavy beard. Out of nowhere, he chased down the woman while Lee was still too busy staying out of sight to be close enough to do anything. The bastard was almost on top of her before she realized what was happening, and he had her down before Lee was in range.

She'd suffered a few hooks to the face to quell her urge to fight back, and Lee saw then that she was nothing like Samantha, except for being battered. The 9mm Heckler & Koch had come from under his running shirt in a smooth motion. Before his arm had stopped moving he had fired a shot into a tree just over the patch of sunlight-dappled ground where the two were tangled. Both of them had stilled instantly, faces turning to him.

Shit. He turned his head before either could get a good look and motioned with the nose of the gun while he talked. "Lady, roll over and put your face in the dirt."

She shook, but did what he said, even lacing her hands behind her neck like a tornado was coming or she was a police hostage. Grateful for the ball cap serving its purpose, Lee made sure he couldn't see the man's face, and knew from hours at the mirror that the attacker couldn't see his either. The idiot still lunged at him, gun and all.

Lee pointed and took out a kneecap. Out of the side of his eyes he watched the woman jump like popcorn but stay face down. The man screamed and hit the ground on his back.

Fuck. If there was anyone within three miles of this they'd come running at these high-pitched wails that put the woman's own I've-been-attacked yells to shame. Knowing he only had a minute to get the job done, the fact that the man was writhing around holding his knee only made his goal harder.

Lee grinned. Nothing like a challenge. And after a few thwarted attempts he shot the man's balls off with a slick curve gracing his lips.

The bastard had stood as best he could and run at a broken hobble into the woods.

"Ma'am, you're safe now. Best get home."

Lee ran off to his own home, the stupid smile plastered on his face even as he packed up all the incriminating evidence. He had a duffle for rifles, another for guns and ammo and all his spare clips. A smaller one held a thin set of sheets and his clothes, and a fourth had the clothes he wore when he was hunting. All the bags were green camouflage, bought at separate army supply stores, and he had on one occasion had to throw the duffle out into the trees and pray no one found it. The camo had done its job and the clothes had been where he'd tossed them when he came back three days later.

Lee rifled through the cabinets, packed what he could carry, and tossed all the perishable food as far from the shack as he could. Bears and raccoons would destroy that evidence in a matter of hours. Leaving the cans for whomever might find them, he tipped furniture, broke one chair, threw one out into the woods and bowled over the table. He left one cabinet door open and the water pump dripping, not able to completely ruin the cabin for the next person, before lacing the straps of the heaviest duffels across his chest. The other two he carried in his left hand, leaving the right free, just in case.

The half-mile hike to the car wasn't usually made with this much load, but in the past three years he'd bulked up to take it. This didn't wind him though he kept a pace many would be hard pressed to keep up with, even if they were unencumbered. He was at the car in just under six minutes. Although anyone who didn't physically stumble directly onto the object likely wouldn't have known the car was there.

The dull brown color and subsequent rust spots were their own camouflage. When you factored in the tree and branch 'garage' he had built for it, the vehicle became very hard to find. Now he dismantled all his handiwork, scattering the pieces in all directions, and loaded the bags into the backseat. He turned the key and listened to the low hum of a job well done before pulling back a few lengths and getting out. There were tire ruts and a small oil leak, and the slightly worn tracks up to the spot. A shovel from the trunk made short work of the oil-soaked patch of ground, and churned the tire tracks, as well as a few other random pieces of earth, just for effect. Lee tossed the last branches onto the ground, satisfied.

He'd broken a sweat this time. But unless someone stood in the middle of it and knew exactly what they were looking for, they wouldn't find his spot. Twenty minutes after he arrived, Lee started the engine for the second time. Pausing only long enough to slap peanut butter onto wheat bread and pass a thought for Bethany, he waited until the winding two lane road was empty before pulling up onto it, careful to go slowly and not leave tire tracks.

This time he knew where he was going . . . deeper into the Appalachians. He'd go back to where he'd first gone to ground, when only those with crime connections were after him. There was less population and more cover there than anywhere else in America. He'd last longer there, and so that's where he headed.

He linked into I-75 heading north along with the slew of cars who had no idea he was in their midst. The ratty car was camouflaged on the road, too. Utterly unremarkable, no one looked twice at it, or at the man in the t-shirt and plain ball cap.

Five hours, some beef jerky, dried fruit, and a forgettable Big Mac later, he turned off 75. Smaller roads led him deep into the woods, the asphalt becoming broken under the wheels of his car. Poor pavement gave way to gravel and finally no surface at all.

It was only mid afternoon and he was in the middle of nowhere. But he knew exactly where he was. Not wanting to leave the car exposed, he cut branches that would be usable later, and draped them across the sagging roof. It was only partially obscured, but he didn't want to have to do a full break-down if he had to exit quickly. He didn't want to waste the work if someone was here, claiming their twenty acres and no mule.

He pulled the black gun from the side holster, not having noticed it for the whole trip. The metal and plastic were warm from his body heat and he'd carried it so much that it felt like an extension of him–as though he could feel his fingers on the butt from inside the pistol. From the space between the seat and the emergency brake he pulled a silencer and fit it to the muzzle. He then opened his bag and pulled a second Heckler, fitting it with an illegal sixteen round clip, before grabbing a third clip and sliding it between his belt and the waistband on his pants.

Lee felt better with all the heat on him. Just in case.

He pushed aside memories of days where 'just in case' hadn't been anything he worried about, and walked slowly to the cabin he had abandoned nine months ago. It looked empty enough from a distance. It had been here so long that the trees had grown right up to it and over the top, obscuring it from the air and most every side. He sat at the periphery, watching, until the sun went down.

He fetched himself a handful of pretzels when he went back to cover the car more thoroughly. He made another sandwich, this time with honey, and grabbed a small tin can of peaches and a plastic spoon. His cargo pants were full as he made the almost two mile trek to the cabin again. He sat the whole night outside, in various positions around the perimeter, and entered only just before dawn.

Someone had been here.

But from the dust, which he knew from his own experience was hard to replicate, it looked like the visitor had left at least a few months ago. He went through the house, beating anything that would take it–old curtains, the mattress, a sofa that had been much newer and less plague infested the first time he'd arrived. A few mice and spiders scattered at his ministrations, and he locked himself into the back room and slept.

He waited three full days before he emerged and set up shop.

"Whatcha got Dunham? Blankenship?"

Owen wanted to snort, Blankenship didn't have anything. He was like a pinkie toe: people told you it was there for balance, but did you believe them? Unfortunately, the whimsical thought about Blankenship was as far as his humor went. He liked Bean, his agent in charge, which was a good thing for him. Most days.

"We got crap. And we found out that half of what we thought we had was actually crap, too."

"Uhhh." Bean had a way of looking as wounded as you felt. He also looked like the kind of man you expected to pour himself a shot of whiskey or Pepto at any moment. The rounding gut and balding head made you wonder what he'd done to get promoted. But unlike Blankenship, Bean was good where he was. "Better tell me about it."

"The grudge ninja's short." Blankenship offered.

Bean smiled like one would at a retarded child, and turned his attention back to Owen.

"It's true. Cops left the body tacked to the wall this time–"

"Tacked to the wall?"

Owen fought the smile. "It was brilliant, sir." He explained how the knives looked to be thrown to the appropriate points then the victim held in place while they were pounded through. "Into the wall studs, sir. So the body would stay up."

"While the vic was alive?" Bean's eyes were wide.

"Yeah. And given the puncture wounds, and the height discrepancy, the vic had maybe fifty pounds on the perp."

"Son of a bitch." Bean was the only person Owen knew who enunciated every word when he swore. "And?"

"Same as last. Punctures, likely with sais, and slices with kamas." He slid photos across the desk. Bean had other agents to follow and hadn't yet seen the grudge ninja's art this time.

Blankenship put in his two cents. "Looks like the perp took a bat to the vic's nut sack again."

Only Blankenship didn't wince.

Bean tapped a finger on the photo of the victim still on the wall at the crime scene. "The articles?"

"All legit. Even the police reports, from several different precincts around the country. The grudge ninja's good."

"He's also a god damned serial killer." Bean perused the photos again. "Evidence?"

"That's where it gets shoddy sir." Owen explained Nguyen's mad rampage, and how the hairs they had found didn't have consistent curling. When looked at all together, from the four scenes they'd pulled, the hair had all fallen off the head at the same time.

Bean rubbed his eyes, again looking like Owen felt. "So they weren't shed at the scene."

"No sir. The bends and kinks in the hair make it look pretty damn likely that the hair was wound into a brush at one time." His breath escaped him. "It's pretty smart, sir. It got the roots, and Nguyen swears he can tell when it's been yanked. The grudge ninja fooled him up 'til this one. The only thing we are certain now is that the hair doesn't belong to the ninja. He used it to salt the scene."

"Fibers?"

Owen and Blankenship both shook their heads.

"Blood?"

"Just the victim's."

"Anything?" Bean's voice was softer.

"Footprints." Blankenship grinned.

But Owen quelled that when Bean looked to him again. "The same shoes. Men's Skechers, size 10, we know the three designs that use that tread. I'm guessing he only wears them at the scene, because these look identical–*identical*–to the last scene. There's not even any wear on the treads, which would be expected given the length of time since he last struck."

"What else?"

"Jack shit."

Bean nodded and scooted the photos across his desk as though they offended his sensibilities. Still on his feet, Owen just reached out and gathered them.

Bean's hands went down his face, and that meant a truly terrible thought had just passed beneath them, "So we've got a brilliant, ballsy, serial killer on our hands. Crap, this is another Dahmer."

"No sir." Owen had to step up at that. "I'm getting the stats on the victim, and my money says he was as dirty as the last one."

"Doesn't matter. When this goes national news–and sooner or later it will–we are all in deep shit."

It was four months before Lee saw her again.

The Appalachian cabin was serving him well. There was no one within shooting distance. That meant no visitors, which was a good thing. It also meant no roads and no services, which was a good thing, too, if you just looked at it the right way. Lee did.

He'd taken down a crack house he read about at the edge of Nashville. He'd driven the clunker/kitty out to the place and camped out in motels that had way too many roach residents that weren't paying for the room. But no maid service meant no one found the rifles or scopes, or the lead weight of ammo and guns. It also meant no driver's license was required for entry. Lee hadn't had his for about three years. The last thing he wanted was to be identified.

He staked out the house, and watched and waited. Then, when the place was as full as it could be, and the head guy had pulled up in a car that shouted 'I'm in charge and too stupid to keep it to myself,' Lee put his eye to the scope and started picking people off.

He didn't get the women. Didn't really have the heart for it. But he had no issues taking out Mr. White Pimp Jacket, who had kindly worn that bright shoot-me-here clothing. Lee obliged, and enjoyed the red stain that ruined the material as well as the wearer. The others looked up, and a few got away, but a handful lay dead, holes in the sides of their heads. One lucky guy took one right between the eyes. His intelligence at finding Lee's location had only earned him the best looking death wound.

When the outside was silent, Lee left the rifle and pulled out the Hecklers. He went in firing. There were screams and blood, and none of it his. He was badder ass than any of these two-bit crime lords. Some were too high to get their guns lifted before he took them out. Most of the sober people had been outside and stupid.

He fired three rounds into a woman who came around a corner with a rifle trained on him and a scream like a banshee. But the scream warned him she was coming, which was the first bad move on her part. The second was being too uptight or scared, and missing him with the one shot she got off.

He did not hit the woman who cowered in the corner. Nor the man who put his hands up in the air at the first shot, the Magnum still clutched in his right hand. Lee had never considered himself stupid, and he made the guy kick the gun over before he turned his back. The second guy he did that to sat down too docilely and thus, a second after Lee had turned away, he took a quick second look and put a shot dead center in the man's chest. It was a good shot since the dead hands were holding a 9mm almost directly in front of the target. It was aimed at Lee, but like most things it didn't get to him.

In the back room he found a ratty looking girl and a baby. He couldn't pick them up. That would be the end of him. But a beckoning hand made the girl jump up, grab at the half naked and dirty infant who was too scared to cry, and follow him.

If he'd had a heart that might have broken it – that the baby stayed quiet. To be that young and already know that crying did you no good. Or worse.

He gathered guns as he left the house. Weighted down to the point where he could feel it, he pushed back at the hate and despair in him. He was leaving with more ammo on him than he came in with. And that was just the leftovers in the guns. Jesus, he could start a militia with what he was carrying. But he knew better than to leave it for the few he'd left behind to get any stupid bright ideas.

The girl followed him up to his vantage point on the hill, baby expertly balanced on one hip. Lee guessed life was bad when following the gunman looked like a good idea. He pointed to an ear-safe distance and watched as the girl hunkered down and managed to cover both her own ears and the baby's. He didn't look at them again, knowing he wouldn't like what he learned.

Instead he trained his focus on the doors to the house. He planted bullets at the feet of anyone who tried to leave. When he saw the sirens in the distance he started gathering his things, but stayed put until car doors were opening up and bullhorns were put to use.

His hand gestured to the girl to follow him again, and she obeyed, even as he tugged the plain ball cap a little lower. It wouldn't do for her to see his face. He knew what the tale from the house would be. All they'd be able to accurately give was the average mouth and square jaw. His eyes would be described as everything from savior blue to silver to gleaming red. In some descriptions he would quote the bible and in others he'd have horns. Every hair color imaginable would be conveyed and some would say ponytail while others would swear he was bald. Few would get the color of the nondescript ball cap right, or even if he was wearing it.

But if the girl got a good look she could give him away. So he walked ahead and kept the bill low. He thought about packing them into the car, but the car was a piece of work and he couldn't afford to ditch it. Which meant he couldn't afford to put them in it. And he didn't have car seats anyway.

That thought almost made him laugh out loud. Car seats were from another world. Certainly one this girl and the baby hadn't lived in. He led them through trees and along back streets, leaving them at a park. Without making eye contact, he told the girl to wait an hour, pointing out the clock on the bank, then to go into the church across the street and tell them about her and the baby. He told her to ask for sanctuary. Even though she didn't know what it meant, she needed it.

Two months later he had done his research and was in Chicago to take out one of the people who was in the ring responsible for him. Only rarely did he allow himself luxuries, and today he got one. He stood in front of the lot where the house had stood. It was, of all things, a daycare now. No one would move into the house he'd left behind. And no one wanted to put their own home on that site. There was an Indian burial ground feel to the place, he knew.

Regardless, the new daycare buildings denied him the simple moment of looking at the front steps and imagining Sam and Bethy climbing up them, groceries in hand . . . he didn't get any further than that.

He had walked away, thinking that he had gotten a little better, a little further from the pain, or maybe just a little colder.

But now he pushed out the back window of the house he himself had just violated, as close to happy as he got. This last guy hadn't died of gunshot wounds per se. Lee had found a better method, thanks to a nice handful of anatomy books hidden in the cabin in the Appalachians. The first three rounds, fired through the silencer and purposefully sunk into the plaster walls, had effectively corralled the guy and made him scared. But the fourth and fifth, the only two intended for the victim, had punctured lungs.

Lee felt lighter just thinking about it. The man hadn't bled to death, although he had bled more than Lee had expected. He was still pooling in his own living room, having asphyxiated because the bullets had punctured the chest wall. From his reading, Lee had learned that lungs collapsed without an intact chest cavity. If it were only one side, then there was simply a lot of pain and terror, and the lung could be re-inflated at the hospital.

He had enjoyed watching this man who had given the orders, or at least rubber-stamped the massacre of his wife and daughter, suffer the inability to breathe air. Lee hadn't been able to watch as long as he would have liked, because the wheezing and kneeling and chest grasping–the look that life was denied to his victim–hit a little too close to home. He remembered doing just those things himself when he'd found the broken bodies and the blood that had splattered so many directions that everything was red. The cops had later said they couldn't tell what had been his wife's and what had been his daughter's. So, very quickly, Lee had shot out the other lung and watched this asshole smother in open air.

While it had been brutal to relive those moments, it seemed perversely fitting. If he could steel himself a little he might just keep using this method. He hopped to the ground, leaving bent grass beneath his feet. He considered a nice gut shot before deflating the lungs next time. It would require more reading.

Knowing full well that he was leaving blatant evidence of his entrance and exit, Lee continued. What did he care if they knew who he was? They'd have a hard time finding him. He didn't exist. Hadn't since the day he'd found his wife and kid. Well, technically his brother had propped him up long enough to collect the life insurance policies. He'd drunk several thousand of the dollars away, before 'they' had showed up demanding his cooperation.

He'd been smaller then. And he'd agreed. Although the urge to laugh at them had been overwhelming–what else was there for them to threaten? But he'd held it together even though he smelled like a brewery and felt like the mouse in the vat. Then he'd gone to the bar to look drunk while he planned. He cashed out his account about five minutes before he drove his car off a bridge and disappeared. Looking back, it had been a pretty amateur job he'd done of 'killing' himself.

He was much better at these things now.

Which was why it was such a shock to look up and find out he'd run into her. With eyebrows raised, she was standing right in front of him in the dark back alley. He'd spent too much effort thinking and not enough acting.

The houses here were too far apart, trees had been planted along these back roads offering plenty of cover that would only be broken if a car came through with headlights blazing.

The girl was glaring daggers at him and, having seen her work, he wondered if actual metal just might come out of her eyes.

Lee took a moment to look her over. He'd been so startled the last time he'd seen her that he hadn't really seen. She was slim and dressed in her leather shadows again. Her skin was slightly olive and her eyes dark. Even God had made her for blending into the night. He might have called her pretty, but she was much too young. She was actually 'cute'. And that alone was scarier than any demons he could think up.

She was also about six inches shorter than him, which he guessed put her at five-six, five-seven. And she had her little hands clenched on her hips, her body rigid. "Did you kill him?"

Lee let himself look a little taken aback at the demand. "Yes, honey, I did."

"I am not your honey."

He hmphed. "Maybe not, but you owe me one."

She shrugged back into a blue quilted jacket, and slung a red standard high school backpack over her shoulder. "I don't owe you shit." She turned to walk away, but Lee hadn't heard enough.

The Heckler came out from his back and he shot a silenced round into the tree next to her.

She stopped even as the bark still flew, then slowly turned. He had to hand it too her, she didn't look intimidated. Even people with guns were often intimidated by him. He was big, brawny, and bad ass. And he didn't care what anyone did to him. He'd just keep coming 'til he was dead. But this girl looked almost bored with him.

"What the hell do you want? You ruined my evening." The light from the moon filtered through the trees and barely bounced off her. He might have looked past her if he hadn't almost run smack into her.

"Your name." He held the gun trained only a few lethal inches from her.

"Sin."

He laughed. That was perfect for her.

Laughing was a mistake.

She was near enough to take advantage of his momentary change of focus. With swift movements, she grabbed his hand in both of hers so softly that he didn't even realize what she was doing. But she put pressure on the pulse point at his wrist and against the back of his hand, easily turning the gun away from her and almost around to him.

He felt himself jerk with surprise, and in that moment she yanked the Heckler from his grasp.

A quick bite to his tongue was all that kept him from yelling out "Shit!"

With the haughty air of a sheriff punishing a delinquent, she slipped the ammo from the gun, tucking the clip into her pocket before handing the gun back to him with a look that said she thought he ought to be a little more careful with it in the future.

Two could play at that.

With a sigh, he moved his hand along the front of his belt and pulled another clip loose. He casually slid it into the gun and re-aimed it at her.

She should have at least kept the gun, he had three more on him and had been reaching for another even as she had popped the clip out of the one she'd taken. At least then it would have been a fair fight.

She flung her hands out to the side. "Fine then, shoot me already."

She wasn't afraid. Not of him, or his gun, or the fact that the two together could easily remove her from this life.

She looked like a high-schooler-with her backpack and her hair hanging down in French braids this time. There was every possibility that she didn't just *look* like a school-girl but *was* one.

She was also an artist. She'd gotten in his face, although a good part of that was his own fault. But she'd gotten his gun off him, which had never happened before.

The first thing he'd learned about guns was that you never aimed at anything you didn't intend to kill. So Lee lowered the gun.

He couldn't shoot Sin.

Chapter 2

Jesus.

Cyn clamped her teeth. She was pissed.

She'd already gotten the gun off him once. He seemed to realize that as he dropped his arm to the side, the black thing now aimed at the ground. So far only an innocent tree had suffered.

She'd come to Chicago for this one. And now it was gone right out from under her. It wasn't like she could just go get someone else. These things took planning. And here they stood on a dark back street at a standoff.

Still, Cyn felt kind of good. It was enjoyable to face down a man who was much larger than her, and fully armed, and not feel afraid. It had been a long time since she'd been afraid.

"How old are you?"

"Twenty-three." She didn't know why she answered. But there was clearly something kindred here. He would fit well in an exhibit of panthers. He was sleek. Dressed in inky colors, his nondescript dark hair seemed to suck light out of the night. Tanned to the look of meanness, his skin slid over muscles when he moved, telling you what was coiled there waiting. She didn't think panthers would mess with him, and she didn't intend to either.

In fact she had things to do. None of which involved standing around and waiting for the cops. Or worse. There was no telling which silent alarms this doofus had tripped with his shoot-now-ask-questions-never attitude.

She pulled off the backpack and stood on one foot, trading her re-tread work boots for red striped sneakers. Her gloves had never come out. And she was still fully loaded. She would have to empty her well-packed jacket and pants and store everything for the return trip, something she hadn't planned on.

"What?" He taunted. "You've got places you need to be?"

"Yes, as a matter of fact, I do." She needed to be upset, to hang on to her mad for a little while longer. She'd wanted–*waited*–to take this last victim out. He'd been responsible. "Did he suffer?"

"Yes." The gunman's eyes truly looked at hers for maybe the first time. And Cyn saw a human in there.

"Good." This time when she walked away, he let her.

She jogged the distance to her parked car. As she approached, her loose stride altered, taking on the tighter lope and look of a kid. Which was easy enough, because physically she was pretty close to the age. The dull silver sedan was non-descript enough that no one would think twice about it. She headed back to the motel, changed, and went to work packing.

Several teddy bears and a slew of female-looking paraphernalia were spread across the dresser. The offhand look did the task of making the room seem a little more lived-in than it had been. It made her look a little more like the life she lived was normal.

Cyn changed into the more casual clothes she'd brought, emptying the leathers and sliding them into different places in different bags. It wouldn't do for someone to see them all together and get any ideas.

She popped the bottom off her hairspray bottle with a magnet and a twist. Inside she stacked four inches of wickedly sharp stars then plugged the bottom with fiberfill stuffing. Taking a Phillips head to the end of her curling irons, Cyn opened the barrels and fitted her knives cleanly down the large cylinders.

The teddy bears bore the brunt of the remaining weapons. Ripping tiny stitches at the necks of the big bears, she opened them, pushing the now leather tipped sais into one, the kamas deep into the belly of the next, the sheathed dagger went into a third smaller and over-loved bear. She had covered all the metal parts. Moved them so the bears could be hugged and cuddled and the weapons not felt. If she didn't do it right, the weight would shift and, even though all the tips were wrapped, they would prick the handler or push through the soft skins of the bears. Neither of which could she afford to have happen.

With a single needle and a tiny card of thread, she carefully re-stitched the necks, closing the bears for the trip home. She hid the stitches with skill a seamstress would envy, working cleanly and efficiently. Then she threw the hair supplies into her small suitcase and zipped up the hanging bag bearing her leather pants along with two dresses, a skirt, and a blazer she had never intended to wear.

The bears she piled into the front passenger seat of her car and, leaving the room keys behind on the dresser for checkout the next morning, she slipped behind the wheel and headed for the freeway.

The night road was long and dark, which was mostly the way she liked it. She'd planned to drive home tomorrow, after returning to the motel and sleeping off the high. She'd planned to have a high. Instead there was only this deep disappointment and the vague, far-away satisfaction that the man was dead. She was glad the gunman had gotten to him if she hadn't.

Only then did she realize that the gunman had her name but she didn't have his. His crazy laughter had stilted the natural flow of the conversation, and she still wasn't sure what that was about. Her full lips and dark brows frowned into the depths of the car. Not that it mattered.

Trucks passed by, deadly in their speed and careening curves. But Cyn held steady. Lights from the other side of the freeway dulled her senses until someone would come by with brights blazing and clean out her skull. She pulled into a lit-up station for gas and then, a few miles later, got a burger from an all night fast-food joint. The food tasted like the smell in the air: diesel and weeds and loneliness.

Later as the sky was deepest, and even a lot of the trucks had left the roads to her, Cyn pulled off at a spot she knew well. There was cover here enough for her work, and she was both far enough from and close enough to her house. With the dimmest blue light she could find fitted into the caving helmet, she unscrewed the California license plates from the front and back of the car and swapped them with her own Texas plate that had been under the mat with the spare tire. A Tennessee plate was also stored there, just in case. With the quick movements of someone who'd done this before, Cyn put the plate on, stuffed the helmet into a duffel in the trunk, and climbed back in.

In two minutes she was back on the road.

Keeping one hand on the wheel, she untucked the braids and unwound them, making a pile of bobby pins and ponytail holders on the passenger seat in the small bear's lap. She rubbed her head, thinking it all looked so normal. She was headed back to a good piece of normal. She had a shift to work the next night.

Finally, before the sun started its climb, but when the hint of it existed in the not quite absolute night, she pulled up the long driveway just outside Dallas. The house was specifically chosen for a good handful of reasons, the location being a big one. She would have a good drive into the city for work. But that was okay. What was important was that she was far enough out that no one would get the idea to come visit, or think she should ever host anything. It suited.

She opened the door connecting the garage to the laundry room, and stilled. With deep breaths, she listened. On soft sneakered feet, she traced the outline of the house, room by room. Only when she was satisfied that no one was inside, and nothing had been touched, did she take a comfortable breath. Now casual, she returned to the car and though she was dog tired, she carefully unpacked, putting everything in its rightful place.

The leathers were boxed and fitted into a trap door in the back of a cabinet in the kitchen. The shoes went sideways under her bed and into a hollowed out part of the box springs on the almost too frilly white canopied double. The clothes were hung into the closet, looking as pristine as everything else there. The teddy bears were tossed across the pillows, and appeared as innocuous as the rest of the room.

Changing into a set of soft pajamas, Cyn pulled the blackout drapes and climbed in. Her arms, as they did most nights, wound tightly around one of the bears.

There had been another man in Louisville. Lee had taken him out with vicious sniper shots. First kneecapping the man, then working his way to the hands, and the gut. He punctured both lungs again, but it wasn't as satisfying from a distance and Lee didn't let it go on too long. He ended it with a shot through the neck.

He had missed the jugular, not because he had missed his shot–his aim had been true, it was his knowledge of anatomy that wasn't up to snuff yet. But he'd been close enough to something important that blood had come out of the man in changing volumes. Gush then fade, gush then fade, until the eyes had closed, and he had sat back. The man died reclined in his poolside Adirondack chair. Aside from the carnage, mostly just visible blood and the broken drink glass shattered on the imported tile beside him, he looked fairly peaceful.

Lee didn't begrudge the man what he considered an easy death. There had been nothing personal about it. But he knew what strings this man had pulled. How shipments had come into the country under his wing. That those who reported to him were dispersing the stuff to those who would do so again, and then again until it was in the hands of people on the streets.

Looking down the barrel of the rifle with a cleaning scope, Lee checked carefully for cracks and wear. For any part his rag might have missed. He scrubbed meticulously. Damaged equipment was unacceptable. He cleaned like he shot, single-mindedly.

Setting the rifle against a tree next to the others, he stretched his back. The flat-topped rounds of long ago trees served as table tops, and they were littered with implements. Single piece rifle bore cleaning rods, chamois and brushes–most now in need of cleaning themselves. His hands were covered in gun oil, as were his pants and t-shirt. None of them were new to the experience. The bill on his ball cap was pulled low as always. He might have wondered if he would get a permanent edge to his skull where the caps fit, but that would require time. And it had been too long since he had thought of time in any sort of recordable form.

He set to washing out the chamois and brushes. At no time did he kid himself that he was stopping the drug trade. Another head would grow on the monster when the first was cut off. That was inevitable. But there were certain people in certain key places that had to pay for what they'd done, to Sam and Bethy certainly. And there were others who'd been wronged like them, others he'd found out about only later, as interesting bylines in his research, that needed their own retribution. None had been left alive to give it. If he had time, Lee helped.

In Louisville, he'd had time.

But he had his own business to attend now.

It had taken a while to track Leopold down. But he'd done it. The man had disappeared for a while about a year after Lee had gone to ground. Six months ago he'd shown up again. And in that missing time, Lee had learned a lot about one of the mafia's best gunmen.

Leopold didn't seem to have a last name, a family, or a soul. The world would be a better place without him in it. The man would simply end–he couldn't rot in hell, he wouldn't feel it. Leopold had pulled the trigger more times than just on Sam and Bethy. And he'd pulled it plenty on them.

Apparently he wasn't just one for liberating the souls of the mafia's naysayers. He also took their families with ease, as Lee could attest. He also broke bones, threatened, tormented and got cooperation in any way necessary.

Worse, the man seemed to enjoy his work.

Twice Lee had visited the man while he was traveling. Lee had sat with binoculars outside the hotel, he had seen through a crack left in the curtains that the man slept like a baby. Lee was going to make it worse. He would take Leopold out in his own home. Just like the man had done to countless others.

The hotel visits had helped with habits. Lee had carried baggage for the man on one occasion, dressed in an easily stolen bellhop uniform. But mostly Lee had cased the house. Rifled through the closets. And sat outside with a listening dish when the man came home. He hadn't heard any conversations where the hitman told someone his house had been gone through. Didn't mean it didn't happen though.

Lee would either deliver Leopold out of this world, or die trying.

He had no intention of dying. While Leopold might be among the coldest and deadliest, there were others who needed liberating from their earthly bodies as well, and Lee had no intention of failing. Leopold had simply presented himself as a target now. Given his tendencies to disappear, and disappear well, Lee would take him now.

The guns had all been cleaned with Leopold in mind. They shined like new pennies. Tomorrow Lee would fix that problem. More than one shooter had been picked off in the night by the shine off his gun. It was as stupid as striking a match. And Lee wasn't stupid, blacking his guns was the least of what he did.

A convenience store nearby had yielded a box of slightly darker hair color. He hadn't been blonde since Sam. He spent the rest of the afternoon lying in the clearing, soaking up sun, making sure his skin was as dark as possible. His Heckler rested under his loose hand. He only looked like he dozed.

Upstate New York was cold this time of year. Luckily the weather had cooperated and not dropped the slightest precipitation, which worked in her favor. Nothing would stop her from getting in, but if she left tracks, she would have to work doubly hard in the future. She had more work to do beyond this, not ruining it was imperative. However, tonight was big. Leopold was less than one hundred yards away. And he was about an hour from ending his time on earth. Cyn smiled into the cold.

Her breath hung gray and smoky in the air, and she stood and enjoyed it for just a moment. She was only a minute or two early. The sun was just sinking beyond the distant snow-capped mountains. Truly it was breathtaking.

For a moment Cyn regretted not having more time to spend enjoying the beautiful things in the world; she hadn't had much beauty of her own. She got her focus back on the task at hand. The wall loomed tall before her, but trees graciously blessed this side, offering a climb and a view to anyone who wanted.

She'd been here before, more than once. Patting herself down, she did a final check. Everything was in place. Her re-tread boots were on, the stuffed and reinforced steel toes comfortable on her feet. Her leathers were all packed full. A sai handle stuck out of a long pocket just below each hip, and she could loose them faster than an old west gunslinger. Kamas graced each leg just behind the sai, again one for each hand, within easy reach.

Knives she ordered in bulk to a fictional karate school lined the inside of her jacket, under her arms. And throwing stars packed small square pockets along the sleeves. Lastly, her dagger was sheathed at her waist. She'd never had to use it before. She didn't intend to tonight.

Turning her head, she heard the bare branches above her tapping in the slight wind. Her red backpack was tucked under a pile of leaves blown up against a big trunk about ten yards away. She knew what waited inside the house, and she was ready.

Cyn even knew which tree to climb, she'd scoped the whole thing out earlier. Her eyes fell closed for the briefest of seconds while she pushed out all else, and turned for the tree.

Only she didn't even start the turn. An arm clamped around her waist, a leather glove closed over her mouth, and a hot moist voice whispered in her ear. "You don't want to go in there."

Shit.

She knew exactly who it was the instant the arm had come around her.

That she was alive meant that it wasn't Leopold. He would have shot her dead just for being on his property. He wouldn't remember her or hers, probably even when she finished with him. She expected no pleasure from that.

That someone had touched her meant that the person was either retarded or very arrogant. Either option only spelled the gunman.

Cyn stood still waiting for him to release her. The strict tension in his arms telling her how ready he was for a fight. But she wasn't going to give it to him.

At last the hand slowly eased away, and she got to speak. "Go home."

"Nope. He's mine." The gunman's hair was a little deeper hued than last time, as was his skin. She wouldn't have thought either was possible.

She started small. "We're clearly both after the same people. You got the last one. That makes it my turn."

He smiled. That was okay. Cyn hadn't figured he'd take her first offer and just go home. But it had been worth a try.

"You don't want to go up against this guy unarmed. He's mine, Princess."

If she'd thought she was taut from what lay ahead, she'd been wrong. Her muscles cranked to the freezing point. Ice fell from her mouth. "You don't get to call me that."

"Excellent." He didn't care or didn't see. "Now that we've determined you're out of your league, you can back off and let me handle this."

She laughed. Her body shook and her eyes caught fire, but she kept quiet. It was all she could do not to spill it to the brightening stars and give away their point. "I think I've made it clear before that I am not out of my league, nor am I unarmed."

He nodded. His turn to concede one. But he didn't give very far. "How about this? You tell me who you want next and he's all yours."

"Excellent. Leopold." She motioned to the house and smiled–albeit not a happy one.

"I can't." He didn't return the grin. His eyes hardened, and an eerie stillness settled over him. There was a tension she hadn't expected from a man who fought with firepower instead of fists. "It's personal."

She shrugged, feeling his pain, but not giving in to it. "Me, too."

"Did he kill your wife and child?"

He'd asked it as though he was inquiring if she'd remembered to pick up milk on her way home. So she responded in kind. "My parents. I was eleven."

He gave too much away. His expression showed how much he hadn't expected that. His frozen posture thawed a bit and his gloved hand came up to scratch at the back of his loose hair. Loose hair was a mistake, and she focused on that for a second, that and the fact that her carefully timed entry was getting ruined.

His voice was sure, his words were not. "I guess we're at a standoff then."

With a sharp pain in her heart, when she had been so certain she wasn't capable of feeling anymore, she played her trump card. "Did he rape you and your sister in front of your parents? Then execute them in front of you?"

Lee felt the fist in his gut, but thankfully didn't react. She hadn't really thrown the punch, it had just felt like it. He wanted Leopold. He *needed* to take out Leopold. But for all the bullets that had torn through Samantha and Bethany, it had been only lead and avarice that violated them. And no matter how much he might like to think he could have saved them if he had been there, he hadn't had to watch.

He couldn't have saved them, he hadn't known how then. Neither would an eleven year old child have known. Looking at her eyes, he was suddenly grateful that he hadn't been there when Sam and Bethy died. His own nightmares were enough.

He'd seen Sin's calling cards. Leopold would suffer. That was what Lee wanted most. That and to see the man's face when he died.

Sin's chocolate eyes watched him while he decided. Surely she saw the concession before he made it. "Fine, he's yours on one condition: I'm going in, too."

"I work alone."

"Not tonight, Princess." His jaw hardened just in time to catch the right hook he hadn't seen coming. "Ahhhhh!" He managed to keep it quiet, and only barely withheld the return punch. That wasn't because she was a lady–she was so far from it he couldn't imagine her as a woman, but he didn't hit her back.

"You don't call me that."

"Fine!" If she was going to be the instrument of his justice, he'd have to hit her later. She needed to be in top form. Lee decided the matter for her. "Time's a wasting. How were you planning to get in?"

She gave a sigh that was worthy of any teenager facing an unreasonable parent. It made him question her age again. But as he was good at doing with most things in his life these days, Lee ignored it. "The roof."

"There's a big yard between here and the roof and five very large dogs. How are you going to handle those?"

"How would you?" Her eyebrows went up, and it made him wonder if there was some Bruce Lee dog trick that had never made it into the movies. Pulling the 9mm from his side holster, he held it up and smiled.

She snorted, again taking years off her age. "You'd kill an innocent dog?"

"Yes, to get to Leopold." He didn't know where Little Miss Lethal got off being concerned about a dog that he would hardly call innocent. Those were trained killers. "You have to admit that they will have given their lives for a worthy cause."

"True." She smiled a smile that let him know he didn't know much of anything when it came to her. "But why should they have to?"

She started up the nearest tree and he didn't stop her.

"How you gonna do it, Pri–" He stopped himself at the last minute, "Babe?" Although she hardly looked like a babe either, trussed up in those leathers. She looked young and shapeless. But he didn't want to get into a fistfight when he had better things to do.

If she heard the slip, Sin ignored it. "You may not be alpha dog, but I am."

She sat at the top of the wall, looking like a school girl slipping out of the convent. Lee followed. When he reached the top, she clapped her gloved hands and spoke softly "Puppies!"

He snorted, but held the rest back.

All five dogs bounded up and sat beneath her quietly while Lee let a surprised *son of a bitch* roll through his brain but not off his tongue. Sin bounced down on silent, well-trained feet and motioned him to follow. He wondered what the hell twilight zone he'd wandered into, and how that was even possible when he was pretty sure he'd been living in the twilight zone for the past three years.

They simply walked up to the house, staying low and to the shadows, keeping a steady eye on the windows. The dogs trailed behind as though they were hers.

Nothing had happened as they approached. No shots fired from the windows. No lights off or on. That could be just as easily be a bad sign as a good one.

When they slid into the dark of a large old tree growing at the corner of the house, one of the dogs took a disliking to them being so close to the building and started a mean growl low in his throat. Sin turned and growled back, staring the dog directly in the eyes and leaning forward until she was in the rottweilier's face. The dog could have simply opened up and snapped the skin off her head. But it didn't.

Lee reconsidered. He didn't think anyone took skin off Sin without her approval. The dog backed down, and Sin went up the tree.

She was like the night itself. A wraith, she disappeared in between the shadows, and he only ever had the feeling that he caught glimpses of her. Reaching up, he hefted his own muscle along the trunk, disappearing into the branches as soon as he was able.

The leather clad cat above him seemed to have forgotten he was there. He wanted to roll his eyes. But he pushed himself back into control, he wanted to see Leopold dead. And not just any dead: a slow painful dead. So he followed, and did his best to keep his feelings to himself.

She paused at the roofline and stealthily reached out a black clad foot. Certain she was never going to make it without a jump, he watched as she simply stretched a little further and put her foot softly on the roofline, surprising him yet again. Lee vowed it would be the last time.

A finger to her lips told him to be quiet, and just how little she thought of him. God, he'd like to clean her clock. Instead, he gripped the branches in one hand and stepped out as she had. His groin muscles pulled back on him, making him grit his teeth. She must be damn flexible. It didn't even look like she'd been reaching for it, and he had a good six inches on her.

Of course, this wasn't the way he'd have gone in. There was a long silencer on each of the Hecklers; he'd have taken the dogs out one by one, and had a window alarm short-circuited before anyone realized the dogs were too quiet. Then he'd have climbed in and tried out his punctured lungs technique. He wouldn't be skulking up the edge of a roof three stories off the ground, that was for sure.

When she reached the top, she disappeared again into the pitch of night beyond her, somehow it had settled deep and heavy around them while they climbed. The dogs had scampered off to play in the yard, and Lee had to admit that it was better that way. No one would check on missing dogs. And anyone who thought they heard something would look outside and see five very unalarmed dogs and get a very mistaken sense of security.

Sin lay along the top edge of the shingles and scooted until most of her upper body was beyond the ledge. Lee couldn't stop himself, his hand snaked out to grab a firm hold of her ankle. Again she looked at him like she'd forgotten he was there, but she had the good grace not to begrudge his hand.

Reaching under, she yanked at something he couldn't see and slowly came upright with a large piece of wood in her hands. "No one puts alarms on these."

She'd pulled out the roofline vent. He helped her lay it down where it wouldn't slip. Then insisted on going in first.

Her dark eyes flashed in the light of tiny stars and her jaw clenched when he started moving and made it clear he wasn't asking for permission. But then her eyes narrowed as though it was okay to let him go because she was sure she could take him. He wasn't so sure, and he slipped, feet first, as softly as possible into the attic. Sin was less than a full second behind him. She made no noise at all.

Slowly and quietly, they took steps and waited. Took steps and listened. And made their way to the attic door. She knew exactly where it was, and Lee knew she'd been here before, just as he had. He wondered how many times he had barely missed her. If she had stumbled across any of his other kills on her way in. But then he pushed the thoughts from his mind.

One goal. Leopold.

She put her ear to the floor for five or more minutes. This time Lee trusted her implicitly and didn't join her, just listened in the still dusty air of the too grand house. When she felt it was safe, she opened the attic door just a hint. It made no noise, and he imagined that she had oiled the hinges herself.

Sin sat with eyes wide, looking through the crack she had created for about forever. Then she moved it further. For half an hour they did this, finally swinging it open when they could strain to hear the man in the kitchen below.

Lee went down first, hanging by his fingertips and able to just touch one toe onto the polished floor, and let himself to standing. Sin came down next, hanging by a full grasp. Not waiting for him to grab her, she let herself drop, surprised when hands closed around her waist and kept her toes from the ground. Her head snapped over her shoulder as he set her feet down and motioned with a finger to his lips for her to stay quiet.

Clearly neither of them was used to working with anyone else. This was not the best way to pull off the most important kill yet. He almost scrapped it then and there, but immediately talked himself out of it.

Sin wouldn't scrap it. That much was sure. That meant that there were two options. She would succeed, and Lee wouldn't get any part of Leopold's death. That was not acceptable. Or, on the off chance that Sin didn't succeed, she would die. She would also alert Leopold that someone was after him. That, also, was not acceptable. So Lee sucked it up. They might bungle it, but he was all in.

The voice carried up from the kitchen. He'd heard it before. When he'd tracked the man, he listened to his conversations from outside through a dish and headphones. But there was something in the way Sin tensed that reminded him she hadn't heard the voice through gathered air, or over the phone, but that she remembered it from long ago. Though the thought tried to turn his stomach, Lee focused and stopped the churn.

They slunk downstairs, each staying to the sides of the staircase. Not just to remain out of sight, but to avoid the squeaks that grew first in the center of the wood. They hit the second floor, and the single voice became distinguishable as one side of a phone call. It sounded like he was moving around the living room.

Lee would have waited until the call was finished. The worst thing you could do was let the victim alert someone else what was going on. Dead men told mostly the tales you wanted them to. But Sin pushed ahead without his consent, and he didn't dare reach out and grab her. If someone did that to him, they'd likely lose the hand. He had no doubt Sin's response would be similar.

The phone conversation seemed to cover the few sounds they made, and Lee could see why Sin wanted to move while Leopold talked. Aside from them, the hitman was the only one inside. Lee had made certain of it.

They positioned themselves in the back of the house, waiting while the man finished his conversation. But it seemed to last an eternity. By his watch, it was another thirty minutes. Lee had a brief thought that, if he'd known someone else would be here, he would have brought a deck of cards; they could have played War or Go Fish. The absurdity didn't break through his controlled shell to make him laugh. Unfortunately, Leopold was safe as long as he stayed on the phone.

At last the conversation ended, and Sin moved as soon as the phone was back in its cradle. Leopold checked out the window, his tall frame bulked with muscle. The dogs must have been playing, or else he was a brilliant actor. Because he gave no indication if he was aware of the leather-clad death coming up behind him.

Again her metal stars materialized out of nowhere, and she threw two. Jesus, the girl must be off, she hit him in the backs of his arms. With puny little stars. And, as the big man turned, looking like any man at home on an unbooked evening would, Lee thought she had simply baited the bear.

Leopold's face went from looking like he could be someone's dad to the venom Lee would have imagined from the man who had continued to pump lead into Sam and Bethy long after they were dead.

Beautiful blue eyes swung up beyond Sin as Leopold spotted first her, then Lee. Lee offered the man a smile. He had intended to stand in the doorway with his arms nonchalantly crossed and watch the show. But now that Sin had already fucked up, he left his hands by his sides so he could get to his Hecklers as fast as possible. He was prepared to beat her within an inch of her life if she made him shoot Leopold fast just to save her scrawny ass.

But Sin pulled his attention back to her with just a whisper, "Leopold."

Her voice was as smooth as her skin and just as young and gentle seeming. But Leopold wasn't fooled. She was in leather, with sharp instruments hanging from her hips. She stood casually in front of a man she knew to be one of the deadliest in America. And her eyes, which should have been a warm shade, were pure ice. Lee could see that much from where he stood.

Her hands were empty, and Leopold advanced. Lee watched, waiting for her to tense but she didn't. Without his gun or other weapons on him, the hitman was forced into hand combat, and Sin proved herself a worthy opponent. A good hundred pounds lighter than him, she ducked and swerved, and handled the blows he landed with grace. She landed a better set herself. She made his mouth fly open with a gut punch dead center. With the muscles on the man, Lee was certain her hand would hurt. But Sin didn't acknowledge any pain.

She clipped him under the jaw with one fist when the other had looked to be coming, then clipped him again turning the fake-out into a real hit. Her hands quickly grasped his shoulders keeping him from leaning too far back, and she took every advantage of his surprise. With one foot she kicked a leg out from under him, using his own falling weight in her favor as she brought the same knee up and slammed it into his groin. It had all happened too fast for the man to recover before the next hit came.

Leopold let loose of the air in his lungs. But to his credit, didn't go down. Didn't cup his nuts as Lee was fighting not to do just from having watched. He came back with a punch that Sin took only lightly on the shoulder and spun with. She turned, ducked under his arm and let his weight switch their places.

She was behind him and on her feet while he was stumbling forward, following his iron fist that hadn't made the contact he'd wanted. She robbed him of even that.

She hadn't missed with those first stars. She had meant to bait the bear.

Lee no longer doubted her. She had meant to fight Leopold only as much as she needed to get behind him. Her hands quickly and easily found the well between his shoulders and his collarbone and, with the application of well-placed fingertips, apparently touched a prime nerve. As he watched, Lee made a mental note never to let Sin get behind him. The man's arms went slack and his knees lost strength in accordance with the pressure Sin applied. And the Russian mafia's best hitman for the last decade or so, who had managed to come, intact, through any number of onslaughts, had been caught without his gun and brought to his knees in his own living room by a girl. She was nowhere near finished.

As Lee looked, she leaned over and whispered something in the man's ear. He didn't look scared, just mad. But Sin was ahead of him. Her hands moved from his shoulders to her hips, and just as he regained feeling, all of a split second later, he rolled.

She had seen it coming. The sickles she carried had practically flown from their loops and arced at the end of the foot long wooden handles. Leopold was on his ass, facing her now and starting for his feet, but her sickles came down from either side, effectively hooking his ankles. From the sudden jerk, she'd sliced him. As Lee watched, two things happened simultaneously: small red stains formed on the pant cuff at the back of Leopold's ankles and his feet went slack. She'd cut his Achilles' tendons with a very controlled movement, not much more. He wouldn't bleed to death from these wounds.

Before he could think on it, Lee watched the sickles swing again. This time the back of the sickle, the end of the wood handle, found kneecaps and they didn't crush or shatter or break bone. They pushed. Even through the pants you could see where Sin had applied pressure, moving each kneecap from under its ligaments and shoving it to the side. Beyond his hips, his legs were limp and useless.

Leopold was now her toy.

The man sat on the floor in profile to Lee, his jaw clenching tight against the pain. He wouldn't give her the satisfaction of giving it voice. But that didn't seem to matter much to her and Sin stood planted at his feet.

As Lee watched, he thought he saw a flash of something in her eyes, but it passed. It was a fucking good show, that was sure. For a brief moment he wished he'd brought some damn popcorn, but this time he did lean in the doorway and cross his arms.

Slow enough to demonstrate that she knew she was in control, Sin slipped the sickles back along her legs and pulled out the sais. From where he stood, Lee could see the metal warm in her hands. Even with her gloves on, the instruments floated. She didn't hold them–they swirled, seemingly without her. They walked across the backs of her hands and looped around her thumbs. He would have likened it to a baton twirler but it was too smooth, almost ethereal, and too deadly looking.

Leopold didn't sit there and take it, though.

Sin could spin her little sticks all she wanted, the man grabbed the coffee table and sent the small handful of magazines flying as he swung the large furniture at her. Her foot came out and innocuously deflected it. The crash it made was a startling sound, given how each of the combatants had handled it as though it were paper. None of this stopped the movement of the sais in Sin's hands. Leopold grabbed for the next thing, and the next. Sin repeatedly kicked them out of the way, often with her foot high in the air or moving too fast to really be seen. And she never lost her balance.

When he had thrown everything within reach and was starting to scoot backwards, dragging his useless legs along, Sin began playing with him. Using the sais to slash and poke, she took shots to his legs first. And by the little clenches in his muscles it was clear he could feel what she was doing.

She sliced his pants, leaving them in shreds, and showing Lee how sharp the tips of the awl-like blades were, even though they had turned over in her hands a number of times having had no effect. Leopold suffered puncture after puncture as the weapons moved but Sin's eyes didn't. She looked only into the azure that was far too pretty for the man who had pulled the trigger on her mother and father.

Sam and Bethy were getting avenged as well, and countless others Lee would never know of. A slow satisfaction warmed him, an agreeable swell that he didn't get to feel when he did the job himself, at least not until afterward.

Sin punctured Leopold's gut in several places. Then she hit his chest cavity, quickly placing a series of holes in between his ribs. With the wheezing this brought on Lee knew she had hit lung.

Leopold glared. Still pushed up on his hands, he sucked useless air as he looked for something, anything, to use against her. He reached for her sais, although Lee figured that would only get the man a good slice and some severed tendons. It got him no such thing. Sin didn't let those hands anywhere near her laser sharp weapons. Instead as each hand came out, she deftly avoided his touch and poked him in the shoulder.

Then she stood back.

It only took a moment for Leopold's arms to go slack.

He was on his back wracking for air, with no usable limbs. His hair was slick with sweat and tiny beads were breaking out on his skin as his face slowly changed toward gray. Small spots of blood appeared through every tiny hole in his clothing and in places where Sin had bared skin. And still there was anger and fire in his eyes. Still he didn't consider himself down. Lee was glad this bastard was leaving the world.

Sin walked the periphery of the living body in front of her. She should have carried an apple and shined it and taken a bite, as worry-free as she looked. She no longer poked or prodded, just looked down and watched him suffer. She didn't even seem to enjoy it, she was so cold.

What she was watching for or waiting for, Lee didn't know, but the show was fascinating. It was just as interesting as the conversation going on in Lee's head. Why, after three years of practicing and working and waiting for the opportunity, had Lee handed Leopold's kill away in a half second? He smiled a cold smile at the scene in front of him, still at his perch in the doorway.

Because Sin was delivering what he would have. Leopold didn't die slowly, and he didn't die easily. Sin offered pain, just as Lee would have. And she had offered hope, baiting him into a fistfight, then letting him grab and throw whatever he could get his hands on. Then she had taken that hope away, piece by piece. And she had delivered something Lee simply couldn't: humiliation. Leopold would be killed by a small girl.

Still she waited. Staring into blue eyes she had seen close over her own once before a long time ago. There was no rage, no fury, no nothing. Just calculation. Having no idea what she was waiting on, Lee waited on her. The dogs played happily and quietly in the yard. The phone didn't ring. No cars went by on the street. They could stay until Sin decided it was time.

Blood formed quarter sized patches and rusted on the big man on the floor. He didn't move, clearly couldn't control his muscles. His chest heaved with greater and greater effort, small sucking noises attesting to the holes Sin had put in his lungs. As he watched, Lee saw the eyes accept that it was the end. Leopold stopped tracking Sin and looked heavenward, as though heaven would let him near. Lee half expected the body to sink into the earth as soon as it gave up its soul.

Lee didn't see it coming, in fact didn't see it happen, she was so fast. The nonchalance was gone like a memory and her sai stopped spinning, aimed straight down, and the tip was buried into the floor. Leopold's dick was skewered on the blade. Sin let go of the handle.

While his own gut clenched, Lee expected the handle to quiver, given the force of impact. But it didn't. Aside from the red flooding Leopold's face, and the new wracking of his torso, the sai looked like it had always been there.

Sin wore a small smile.

The lone sai in her hand spun as though it had no cares. Sin might have been planting flowers in her garden for the serene look on her face, while Leopold finally began losing a sufficient quantity of blood, from his dick no less.

She started poking at him again, the weapon dancing in her hand as she walked. It just periodically touched the man, leaving tracers and holes. Now he flinched every time. He acknowledged hit after hit. She placed the weapon over his heart. To his credit, Leopold saw what was coming, and he offered prayers in his eyes, but no fear.

Sin still had the upper hand and she held the sai with the tip just touching his chest. Holding it steady, she forced Leopold to puncture himself in order to move his chest and get air. Repeatedly she did this, making hole after hole. Until Leopold finally quit.

Two minutes later he was dead.

Lee smiled.

Sin reclaimed the sai that had been through Leopold's cock. With a calmness too smooth for the victory she had scored, she pulled a yellow car buffing cloth from under her jacket and wiped down the sharp points, before too casually sheathing them in the long leather pockets that traced her thighs.

Then she gulped for air. Thinking she would faint, Lee rushed to get her, but stopped short.

He should have known that Sin wouldn't faint on him.

She turned with fury blazing in her eyes and the wicked, already bloody sickles swinging in her grip at the end of well polished wood handles. This time she cracked the man's knees with the blunt back of the sickle. She sliced his thighs and his belly open spilling blood that didn't pump, but merely oozed out of the skin, already coagulating in his death. But Sin wasn't through. She crossed the handles and leaned over him. When she pulled her arms apart the blades sliced his throat from both sides, meeting in the middle in a single clean cut that shouldn't be possible with two blades and the anger that fueled them. She hacked at his arms.

Lee decided that he'd seen enough.

"Sin." He didn't want to grab her and startle her. He didn't want to have to kill her. She didn't deserve to die with Leopold. On Leopold. Still he risked it. Positioning himself behind her and her deadly blades, his arms came around her waist while her own arms still swung at the body.

As soon as he started to pull her off he was startled by any number of things. She was lighter weight than he gave her credit for. She stopped, her body stilled, the weapons mid-arc and she slumped against him. Somehow Sin trusted him. Probably not any further than she could throw him, although that might be quite a distance. But here, even in that fury, she knew that Lee wasn't her enemy.

He tried to get her back in the game, his voice below threshold. "Got your bow?"

She slipped from his grasp, and he let her, still not anxious for a fight. When she turned, she looked at him blankly, again shedding years from her age.

He tried again. "Gift tag?"

"Oh." She shook her head, a few wisps of hair moving where they'd come loose from the tight French braid. "No. That's for the cops."

"So?"

She shrugged and took out the yellow cloth and began wiping down and shining the sickles. "No cops. Leopold's too high up.

The family will take care of him. I don't want them to know about me."

"Well, I hate to say this." He pointed to the corpse bleeding onto the floor, the whispered conversation almost comical. "But I think there's a body here saying that you came calling."

She arched her eyebrow and went on polishing as though the sickle were the Sunday silver and not the blade she'd just sliced a killer with. "Someone with a grudge against Leopold was here. That could be any of a million people. Clearly two of us even chose the same night."

She walked away, around to the back of the house, slipping the sickles into the hammer loops in her pants as she went. Without looking, she put them through the first loop as well as the second, securing them for the trip back out along the roof.

Lee followed, taking one last look at the man who had shot Sam and Bethy as coldly as Sin had laid him out. If Sin had told no lies about what he'd done to her, then Leopold got off easy, and hell would be too good for him.

They slipped back into the attic, Lee lifting Sin up through the hole, although she showed no surprise this time. They walked the attic quietly even though they weren't worried about it now. They boosted out the open roof vent, holding firm to each other's hands for purchase as the climb up and around was more difficult than swinging down in had been, then popped the wood piece back into place.

The dogs greeted them at the bottom of the tree and walked them out. Sin jumped and caught the top of the tall wall. Wondering how she would do it, he watched as she used sheer muscle to go from a fingertip purchase to pushing her hands down along her waist at the top of the wall and throwing a leg over.

He did the same, although she had already slipped to the ground on the other side before he followed, his feet crunching leaves and making noises he hadn't heard her make before. She was walking out a ways and shaking the silly backpack out from under a pile of leaves. She brushed at it, batting off clinging twigs and maybe a few bugs. But there were no girly shudders or faces, just cold calm.

Lee joined her while she opened the pack and traded out her jacket, folding the leather neatly and putting it into the open space in the pack. She unlaced and removed her boots, slipping easily into the sneakers he'd seen last time. The weapons she slid smoothly from her legs and into the pack. She grabbed something and made her way back to the wall. She tossed it, and only mid-air did Lee see that it was dog biscuits. He smiled. And she was done. Sin started walking away.

She looked like a kid hiking through the woods. Maybe a little too old to be going out for a play date, but the appearance was there nonetheless. She knew he had followed her and she turned, holding out her hand.

When Lee shook it, wondering what the hell for, she spoke.

"Well, I'll stay out of the next one you want. Who is it?"

He sighed, having no idea what to tell her. "I don't know. I plan one at a time. You got someone in mind?"

"Nope. Not yet." She dropped his hand, and stood just for a moment.

"Give me your number, I'll call when I make up my mind."

She laughed, the precious sound of a young woman humored by a man, and a pang went through him that Bethy would not grow to that. The pain the notes in her voice had brought only struck him at random times and since now was not the time to wallow in it, he pushed it aside. Besides, Sin was speaking.

"I don't give my number to strange men. You never know who's a murderer!" She replied cheekily, then she turned serious. "You can tell me now, or not at all."

"I don't know." It was, unfortunately, the best he could do.

Sin nodded, and turned and disappeared into the shadows of the night woods.

Chapter 3

Cyn slept better beneath the frilly white canopy now that Leopold was gone. Her bears were still tight within her grasp each night, and her weapons always tight within the bears. Leopold had been necessary, the other man who had shown up at her house that night when she was eleven had died in a hit when she was seventeen.

While it was fitting that his own people had turned against him and hired someone just like him to take him out, it was also deeply disappointing. Each night Cyn had prayed that Leopold would live until she could get to him. And she was thankful that the gunman had let her have the kill. She wouldn't have wanted to fight him for the privilege. There was something else there, some other thought pushing at the back of her brain, but she pushed it down. She still didn't know his name.

In the six months since she had seen him last, she'd followed her usual routine. She wasn't finished. And, like an athlete, had no plans for what to do when she did finish. So she worked. Leopold had been the big fish to her. But there were others. Higher up. Other hit men. She'd been picking them off, using them as practice.

She'd taken out a Korean man who ran a kidnapping ring, selling boxes stuffed with live children off the docks in Baltimore. There were two boxes and twenty men lingering on the docks the night she'd managed to end it. Winding her way around and through the loaded crates, she'd taken out individual dock workers as she went. None offered any real resistance. All were too surprised by the sudden presence of a girl on the docks, and she had killed each one with cold calculation and a quick precise slice or stab.

A few she had taken from behind. If they didn't turn when she came within three feet of them, she had simply pulled her sai and quickly slipped it between ribs. A downward pressure with her palm used ribs as a fulcrum and opened lungs and heart. The man would be falling, dead, before she could even pull the weapon out. It was also fairly painless. By her count any man working the docks that night could hear the sounds from inside the crates and deserved what he got.

The leader she had toyed with. But he required no serious effort, not like Leopold had. The dark-haired Asian man had turned as she approached, more aware and more wary than his workers had been. He aimed his gun at the girl on the docks with absolutely no remorse. She had taken it off him with just as little.

He had pulled a knife on her then, seeing that she didn't have a gun of her own and that she had tossed his against the black hull of the ship, clanking it against the metal and banking it into the dark water below. Cyn pulled her own knife in response and he seemed startled that she was armed at all. She'd wanted to laugh. The knife was nothing.

And he was a fool with his. She knew it the instant he pulled it, holding the blade upward like a housewife would. Like her mother had tried with her kitchen cleaver against Leopold. Cyn had learned quickly after that to hold the blade out and down. This man wasn't smart enough to see her lethality and run. He swung at her. In three swipes of his knife, she had countered and managed to get her own against his inner arm.

When his tendons severed themselves against her blade, his hand had gone slack and so had his face. He folded, crumpling under his own fear more than anything she had done to him. Yet.

He sold the children into brothels overseas. Cyn knew. Of everyone her blades had ever touched, of every drop of blood she had spilled, none had been innocent.

So she took him out–piece by piece. Her kamas sliced him, as well as the two men who tried to jump her from behind while she worked on the Korean. Bullets had flown at her once, but she'd pulled his still live body in front of her and let him take a few before they stopped. A few knives thrown rapidly in return had yielded more than one grunt and thud.

The others left her alone after that. Their boss wasn't worth it. He was clearly on his way to dead, and part of that was due to bullets from their own guns.

Cyn finished him and fitted him with a tag and bow, before prying open the two crates.

She stayed just beyond the shadows until the cops showed and gathered the children. Then she'd gone home and cleaned, stitched her weapons back into her teddy bears, and slept like a baby.

She'd also, finally, gotten that campus rapist in Oklahoma. She'd read about him in the papers and traveled up every time she had a few days off. She hung out in the parking lots where he struck, driving rentals in and out of the darkened structures at night when there were few cars and fewer people around. She walked with her shoulders and head down. She put in ear buds and turned her music up loud enough that anyone would think she was completely unaware of her surroundings.

It had only taken five months and fifteen tries. But finally, someone had come out at her just beyond the dark empty parking lot exit. A hand had closed over her mouth and dragged her back into the shadows of the nearby trees. He'd even grabbed her by the ponytail she'd hung out like a sign.

Cyn had only struggled enough to make it seem real. It didn't matter that he controlled her head by her hair or that he held a hunting knife to her throat. When he got her down and tried to slit her jeans off her he got something else.

She folded in half, the denim taking a good portion of the brunt of the knife. Her bound hands came together to dig fingers into his shoulder and he lost the ability to hold the blade. She rolled onto it and grabbed it, coming back over and holding the blade straight out from her stomach as he jumped at her. He impaled himself on the knife, and Cyn reminded him that if he had just left, he would have lived. She told him this even as she had pulled upward with the long blade, hot blood gushing over her hands and torso.

She put the bow on him while he was still alive. She set out the tag and tacked the articles into his skin with her stars. She'd done almost too thorough of a job of killing him, as his blood soaked through a handful of the articles, many of which were crime logs from the school paper, and the local police station.

He'd expired while she stood over him, this time using her dusting rag to wipe blood off herself. She'd pulled garbage bags from the trunk of the rental car and changed there in the parking lot before covering the seat with more bags, and climbing in. She'd showered the mess down the motel drain and added the second set of clothes to the garbage bag. She scrubbed out the tub. Washed her hair again. She drove one rental car out to another city and threw the clothes into a restaurant bin then ate a big breakfast at a Waffle House rip-off. She returned the car in a different city from where she'd rented it, and took the train back to campus. She checked out then turned in the second car and took a cab back to the motel. From there she climbed in her own car and headed home. As she drove out of town, the radio was already breaking the story that it looked like the campus rapist had been caught. They didn't mention the bow, just that his face looked like the one on the pictures and that police had strong reasons to believe this was the guy.

Cyn smiled. She held her teddy bear closer, enjoying the dark brought by her blackout curtains. She killed people in her dreams. She planned her next hit. And since she was going after another of the Russian mafia men, she wondered if the gunman would be there.

Owen rubbed his temples. He could hear Bean yelling at him like a skipping CD. "Dunham! Two more!"

Why didn't Bean yell at Blankenship? Owen already knew the answer. Yelling at Blankenship was even more useless than yelling at a brick wall. At least the wall bounced the sound back at you.

And his Agent in Charge had only been stating facts at a high decibel. The grudge ninja was escalating. Serial killers did that. It fit the profile. They got taken over by their urges. The need to kill came more frequently as they broke down psychologically. They got more cocky with each kill. That meant they made mistakes. And mistakes were Owen's friends.

He was going to catch the grudge ninja. But what happened to the ninja once he was caught was anybody's guess. Owen didn't think there was a jury alive that would convict him. The people this guy took down were all far worse than the ninja, but it would be better legally if he left his victims alive. Although Owen had never heard of a serial . . . what? kidnapper? More like bounty hunter. And people who went to court got off with hotshot lawyers or out early for good behavior. Nope, the ninja was doing society a favor. But playing God wasn't allowed–even if you were good at it.

The Korean had been selling kids into prostitution. Then the ninja had gotten the campus rapist. From the evidence it looked like he'd caught the guy in the act. There were long brown hairs at the scene, and it looked like a smaller female form pressed into the ground at one point. But, whoever she was, she was scared or she had developed some serious amnesia about the attack. She hadn't come forward.

Owen stood over the broken ground. Blood had coagulated in a pool in the spot where the body had been. The body had finally been moved, just a little while ago by the lab guys; the cops hadn't touched it. Every officer in America had been told not to move a hair on a body with a big red bow on it. These guys had done their work, even though they'd wanted the capture of the rapist themselves. Little had been touched except by the college joggers who'd found him that morning. They'd actually walked all over the scene and the male had put his fingers to the neck to feel for a pulse.

A sigh pushed out of Owen's throat as he thought of the smears left by the student. What a fucking moron. The body had its belly sliced open. The chest didn't move and he had god damned newspaper articles tacked to his skin with throwing stars. And the idiot checked for a pulse? There was no accounting for what a person would do in shock. At least, that's what Owen told himself to keep from going medieval on the guy's ass.

Yellow tape bordered the scene and little flags stuck out of the ground in several different colors. Four in fact, for each footprint, each tread they had ID'd. There'd be two less if those idiot college students hadn't–

But they had, and there were. It was just the way it was.

Blankenship was interviewing them. Which Owen thought was a good task since the two knew nothing of value. Nguyen was on the scene as well with his tricked out lab semi. He was playing with his broken hair strands in the trailer. The body was laid out on the table in the middle. The FBI would take him away. This was the eighth victim they could tie to the ninja.

There was none of the fake ninja hair here. But there had been some at the scene on the docks. A few strands laid by the body. They still didn't know who it belonged to, but Nguyen swore he was able to identify it on sight. He hadn't been wrong yet.

The footprints were bothering Owen. He just didn't know why.

His phone vibrated in his pocket and he hoped it was Annika. He wouldn't be able to tell her anything while he was here. The line was likely tapped anyway. Owen didn't trust the Bureau not to do it. But he wanted to hear the sound of her voice. To be soothed and comforted and reminded of why he did this.

He recognized the number, but it wasn't home. "Dunham." Speaking his own last name upon answering the phone was another habit that made him a throwback to an earlier time. It was his FBI cell. It lived in his pocket. Who the hell else would be answering?

Bean had already evolved past the need to identify himself. "What are you doing?"

He'd rather his boss had asked what he was wearing. Even something that creepy and twisted would be better than this. "I'm staring at the scene with the body removed."

"Not falling asleep on your feet."

Whether it was intended as statement or question Owen couldn't be sure. He answered. "No. There's something I'm missing." He didn't add, *maybe if I just keep staring at it . . .*

"Go do something else." Bean hung up. He'd checked in. Done what he needed to do. Owen had been slapped around and told to get his ass in gear. Enough said.

Something was wrong. The footprints didn't add up. Four flag colors.

Owen walked the scene.

Nguyen came out and casted all the footprints. As soon as it dried, he picked up the ninja's and showed it off to Owen. Sitting there in his white paper cover-alls he examined it from several angles, a frown marring his perfectly black brows. Nguyen's hair grew stick straight and hung from his head like it was weighted. It was the only thing Owen knew of Nguyen. He didn't think he'd ever seen the man's clothes, he was always covered in sterile disposable lab suits. And for a moment his sleep deprived brain wondered if Nguyen was naked under all that paper.

That would be a laugh. The scientist worked with a handful of field agents, doing lab work and collaborating on cases. They were well trained and truly great detectives. Nguyen would be the best got-you ever if he were naked under there all the time and none of them discovered it. And of course they wouldn't. It wouldn't occur to them to even look for it.

Which made Owen think there was something here at the scene he'd be able to solve if he just thought to look for it.

Still squatting and turning the plaster mold, Nguyen looked up, aiming the captured tread Owen's way. "Something's wrong with it."

"What?"

His head shook, his heavy hair lacking the inertia to move with it. "That's just it. I'm not sure."

"Is this the first time it's been wrong?" Owen scrubbed his hand over his face and wished he was driving Charlotte to school. They would have to abandon the site in a few more hours. They could only maintain it for so long; the location and the price of security was not cost effective.

"No, it's been wrong all along."

"Of course." His brain took off on a different track, denying him the focus he wished. Charlotte was having her first sleepover the next night. He wanted to be home to see it. Three friends were coming. He needed to help ease some of the burden from Annika. Four eight year olds meant no sleep for the weary.

Four.

Four sets of footprints. Two college students. The ninja. The rapist.

Four.

Where were the girl's prints? The one who was attacked. The attack that the ninja thwarted. They had her hair. Fibers from her clothes. But no footprints.

Had the rapist carried her here?

But then wouldn't she have made tracks when she got away?

There were none in the cordoned off area. But then again those two asinine college students had messed a lot of it up.

The girl had seen the ninja.

She would be able to ID the face.

If the ninja showed his face. And Owen would plunk down a good portion of Charlotte's college fund that he didn't. But the girl would have pertinent info.

Nguyen kept examining the scene. It had been vacuumed for fibers. A very few fingerprints had been lifted. They didn't seem to have any from the girl. The ninja had held the blade and probably so had the rapist, but the handle had been wiped clean, the whole thing left sticking out of the man's gut.

Owen was at a loss, and he didn't have any coffee. Nguyen squatted in front of him as good a sounding board as any, and better than most. Better than Blankenship, that's for sure. So he let his voice relay his rambling thoughts. "We need the girl."

That was the name for her, the rapist's victim–'the girl'. When they called her 'the victim' it became confusing whether they were talking about the rapist's victim or the ninja's victim. Nguyen understood. "But she's long gone."

"Can we issue an edict that all female students present themselves to the campus police? We can check under the fingernails of all the brunettes."

Nguyen stood and laughed at him. "Aside from violating the Constitution and several amendments, it wouldn't yield anything. There aren't any scratch marks on the guy."

Owen blinked. "She didn't fight?"

"Not with her nails." He walked off with his plaster casts cradled in his arms like babies. More waited on the ground at Owen's feet, still curing.

Owen turned to go view the unscratched body. This just got weirder every moment.

Lee put the last slug into the man's neck. The bullet made a small, fast suction noise as it left the barrel. Nothing compared to the crack of an unsilenced gun. There was more noise from when it bedded itself in the plaster behind the man, and more a half second later from the man's mouth in protest at the pain.

The blood gushed from the neck wound and Lee wanted to be able to enjoy it, to imagine he could see where the blood level was. As though the man's skin was transparent and you could watch the red drain from him as it came out the hole the bullet had made.

But Lee couldn't watch. Someone had come up behind him.

He knew Michael Norikov could be trusted to die while he turned his back and so he whirled, using his hearing to put a slug into the wall beside the sneak even before he laid eyes on the–

Sin.

"Uh!" Again with the teenage angst. But she didn't protest like a person who had a gun fired three feet from her head and aimed at her. She sounded like he'd just told her no TV tonight.

Lee turned back to the body, the grandson of one of Russia's biggest crime families had expired while he was turned. The moment of death gone.

Damnit.

"Again?" She spoke normally, apparently not at all afraid of him. He admired that even as it pissed him off.

"You know you took several of mine, too. And I *gave* you Leopold." He intended to hold that one over her for a long, long time.

Here they were, having a normal volume conversation in the middle of a house where neither of them had the right to be. It wasn't the dead man's house either. Norikov had only been visiting here, and that made it doubly dangerous that someone would walk in on them.

So Lee turned and left her there, wondering if she'd tack one of her silly bows on the body and mess up his neat bullet holes and blood puddle. He reminded himself that dead was the most important thing.

But she didn't. Even though he was certain that she had her gift tag and bow and neat forty-dollar pen on her. Sin trailed him out the window where he had short-circuited the alarm wire and climbed through. She pushed through the sliced out screen behind him. Even as he jumped down and ruined them, he saw Sin's big tracks under the window, indicating that she'd followed him in this way.

That little faker. She'd known he was here when she came in. What was that 'uh!' for back there? Was she trying to distract him? Itching for a fight?

Lee looked both ways and walked out the back. Two dog carcasses littered the ground not far from the window. Dobermans this time. Yeah, he was alpha dog. Dead was definitely beta. The family had something for guard dogs. And he had to say that Michael had been looking out the window, wondering about his damn dobies when Lee had walked up behind him.

But Michael was still dead.

And there hadn't been time for Lee to make the dogs like and respect him. Michael had only come here on a whim. Lee had barely had time to check it out. Luckily the house three doors down had the same floor plan, and Lee had cased it. That family might have called the cops, but nothing would ever come of it except maybe they got themselves a better security system. Oh, and no more mafia neighbors.

Lee scaled the cheap cinderblock wall at the back of the cookie cutter mansion. It was ten feet high, but a sturdy pool chair put things in his favor. So what if the cops figured out he'd gone over the wall? He was gone.

Sin followed him, dropping to the ground on the outside in her typical silence beside him. But she didn't say anything. Her leather clad butt and braided up hair were all he saw as she walked away.

Lee walked the other direction. The street back here was really only intended as a service entrance, and he pulled a vest and a black watch cap from under an old plastic lawn chair behind the next house. There were doors built into the fences, but the locks were fairly secure. Over the fence had definitely been the way to go. He slipped the clothes on, hoping to look more like the gardener if he was spotted. He'd left his car at the end of the street and had a good quarter mile to walk.

It was only about ten p.m., but the night was dark and deepening. Dogs barked occasionally through the tiny gaps at the back doors in the fences. The gates were all solid, the houses new enough that none of the owners had switched any of them out yet. And that meant no one saw him go by. And no one seemed to believe the dogs when they told their owners he was on the other side. One male voice had yelled "Shut-up, Damnit!" down to some big thing that was giving good solid barks. And someone else made noises in their pool and told something small and yippy not to bark because of what it saw. Lee imagined something illicit was going on there. If they could talk, the dogs would tell tales on him. But they couldn't.

At the end, where the un-named alley made a T with the real street, Lee slid into his car. He made small un-obvious motions, sliding three of the silenced Hecklers out of their hidden holsters under his shirt and popping the clips out before placing them under the front seat. The old car was designed for keeping things there with a well that fit the guns nicely.

He turned over the engine, glad that his kitty didn't make much noise. No one would be able to say when they heard a strange car drive away. He headed back to his motel by way of the scenic route. Just in case he was followed. Although he wasn't sure who would bother. And no one did.

He let himself in with the plastic tagged key, liking places that didn't require ID and didn't care when the residents showed up or left. He put three of his guns into their duffel along with the rifles. He always traveled with a good armory, whether or not he intended to use it. The fourth he took into the bathroom with him. Just in case. Then he popped open a box of cheap hair dye and scrubbed in a lighter color with the latex gloves on his hands and a look of chagrin on his face. He was a little too good at this.

The box required a twenty minute wait to make his hair the appropriate hue. While Lee wasn't concerned with achieving that exact shade of 'praline', he did need a change. Again, just in case.

He'd thought he'd be tired, but he wasn't. And his brain took off while he sat in the grimy bathroom, a slave to the chemicals on his head.

He'd researched Sin. He'd dressed up–meaning clean jeans and a newer T-shirt–and gone into an internet/coffee bar. He'd looked up old newspaper articles on Leopold. None mentioned him by name, but certain hits were definitely his work. Lee had Googled keywords, and found what he was pretty sure was Sin's case. Police reports were public access if you knew exactly where to look. He pulled up a case in Urbana, Illinois where an accountant and his wife had been murdered, leaving behind two daughters. It rang with Sin's brief questioning, and smacked a little too close to his own experience with these guys.

He'd searched everything he could. There were other cases that might be hers. But they were way too old. Or way too new. And there was always something that made the connection wrong, like there had been only male children in the family. While Lee wouldn't put a gender change beyond anyone who'd suffered that kind of trauma, it wasn't Sin.

The Urbana killings had to be hers. The younger daughter was even named Cynthia. She hadn't thought up the name and she hadn't been joking. He'd simply heard the wrong spelling. She was C-y-n. But Lee sure thought his original version suited her better.

There was one problem. She said she was twenty-three. And that her parents had been shot when she was eleven. The dates didn't match. Everything made sense if he afforded her one lie. The report was four years younger than what would match her tale. But the police files did put Cynthia at eleven at the time of the attack, so that was truth. The Urbana murders had happened eight years ago. Which made Sin just nineteen.

Lee checked his watch and climbed into the shower. When he emerged, he took a pair of scissors to the hair around his face. He did a decent enough job shearing off the longish hair that had covered his brows until a few minutes ago. He took off the shag over his ears and evened that into the still-a-little-long hair above it. He also shaved his face clean. He looked enough different from the man who had killed Michael Norikov earlier tonight.

He still wasn't tired, and he really wanted a drink.

So with a sigh, and the deep conviction that no one would find him, he dressed up again. He was in town, and he felt like going out–a rare thing. So he thought he'd go somewhere where broken bottles were accidents and not threats. He put on a new pair of black jeans, the crease still in them, and a different new t-shirt, although it was from the same three-pack as the other.

He decided to forego the ball cap as it would be suspicious in a decent bar and he headed back out in the car. Fifteen minutes later, he'd found himself on a stool in a place with neon out front and a quartered floor. Lee was in the section that served as the bar, behind him were booths and a few tables. To his right was a bank of pool tables and a line of men in untucked shirts and a few women with shirts that didn't reach far enough down to tuck. One of them grabbed a loser before he could start a fight over his lost twenty and she hauled him onto a dance floor littered with sawdust to cover the fact that it was just open cement and an old jukebox that still took quarters. Everything was licked by shadows. Even the few lights that hung here and there were heavily shaded so no one had to see who they were going home with or grinding up against on the floor.

Lee ordered three fingers of half-decent whiskey and nursed the glass. He almost laughed out loud at the thought that this was a 'decent' bar. His old self, the man with the wife and child and closet full of suits and ties, would never have set foot in here. Of course his old self couldn't hold his own in a fist fight and would have cussed someone out in perfect English for breaking his nose.

Now he was probably the riff-raff here. The pool loser was out on the dance floor with his ball cap hiding what he was doing to the neck of the woman in the just-too-tight jeans and his hands sliding around the skin of her bared midriff. Lee wasn't jealous. The woman had nothing on Samantha. Except that she was alive.

An argument was going on between a blonde and someone else. Lee could only see the blonde because her fake platinum hair showed up in the dim light. Her opponent had the sense to stay dark. No one seemed to be getting hurt so Lee tuned it out.

At the end of the bar a pretty brunette was hitting on the man next to her. She hadn't bared the skin at her waist, hadn't stuffed it into the size-too-small denim that seemed to be the norm here. Maybe she hadn't gotten the memo. She was drinking a beer and letting the man next to her slide his hand up an ever more exposed slice of thigh. She tossed a glorious mane of dark curls and giggled as she abandoned her beer on the bar and dragged the man over to the dance floor.

Lee rolled his neck, his attention drawn again to the fools at the pool tables. Money was changing hands despite several hand-lettered 'no betting' signs tacked to the wall. No one was enforcing it, even though it looked like a nice bar fight was shaping up over there. He wasn't getting in the middle of that. Fools with spare change and beer weren't his forte.

He tossed back more of the liquor he wouldn't have deigned to drink three years ago. He'd pretty much quit drinking all together after a one night binge on some homemade Appalachian lightning. Lee was pretty certain it was close to medieval mead, except maybe with a little more paint stripper in it. What he had tonight was the 'good stuff' these days.

The bartender offered to top him off, but Lee refused. It occurred to him that he was drinking Sam's life insurance policy. He lived cheap, so the money would last a good long time. Probably longer than he would. But with a quarter inch left in the glass, his stomach soured. It didn't matter if he could afford it. It was *how* he had afforded it.

And he had to pee. It was time to go get some sleep anyway. He'd pass out in the motel and drive back to the cabin whenever the hell he woke up. He left the glass on the bar and had to walk through the dance floor to get to the john. The couples out here were bordering on necking right there on the floor, and there was nothing romantic about it. A giggle came from red, bee-stung lips where the little brunette was brushing away a hand that had wandered too high. Lee rolled his eyes as he pushed into the only half-way lit spot in the place and relieved himself. He washed his hands and the faucet creaked like it hadn't been used in a while. No one here had a small child they cared about. You became a fanatic hand-washer when you became a parent.

He looked at his somewhat unfamiliar face in the mirror, although the shorter hair and lighter color actually made him look more like his old self. The lines radiating from the corners of his eyes showing how he'd aged ten or fifteen years in the past four, and the cheap t-shirt and bad haircut kept him from believing he was really that same person.

When he pushed out of the john door, back onto the dance floor, he heard a voice saying 'no'. The brunette with too much make-up and too little clothing was pulled out a side door he hadn't noticed before by a large male hand. She protested, although only lightly.

God, sometimes he hated himself. But he hated more to see a woman get hurt. It wouldn't happen if they didn't do that damned giggling and flirting before they said 'no' or probably even if they just said it and were clear about it. With pain and reluctance radiating from between his shoulder blades, Lee pushed open the door. The floor disappeared from under his feet, and two steps down was an alley between two buildings. Only the faintest traces of neon lit walls that corralled three sides of the rough asphalt. It glistened with old rain or old beer, reflecting rainbows and making Lee believe God had a sick sense of humor. An industrial trash bin, spray painted with graffiti and over-stuffed with bags smelling of rancid alcohol, blocked his view of the couple.

But he heard her say 'get your hands off me' with emphasis this time.

And when he looked over the trash bags, he saw two feminine hands held high, pinned against the wall, caught in the grasp of a larger, stronger male hand. That was surely a bad sign.

Lee sighed.

*   *   *

Cyn gave up her struggles after a moment. The man's hand came up and cupped her breast, and she let him. But only for a fraction of a second.

"I said *no*." Her head came forward, cracking into his nose, and letting loose a howl of rage that spurted from his mouth.

Her hands, staying together in his grip, tugged at his, flipping down and under–a move impossible for his grasp to follow. It may have helped that he was backing up from the head-butt she'd laid on him.

Pissed, he hauled back to slug her. But to her practiced eye, the move came with waving red flags: the deep breath, the haul back to gather momentum, the look in his eye letting her know that he was getting ready to give as good as he got. Cyn saw all of it and waited. At the last moment she deftly stepped to the side, letting him throw his massive weight into his own knuckles as he crushed them against the brick where she had stood.

He was open to her now, chest facing her, right foot planted just under the right arm that was experiencing shock waves from the impact, telling Cyn just how hard of a punch he had thrown. Her knee came up to slam between his legs, but with inhuman speed he backed up, looking surprised.

With a quick blink she realized that he hadn't backed up at all, he'd been hauled. Some idiot had come to her rescue–which was the stupidest thing she'd ever heard of. First off, she didn't need rescuing, and second, not a single one of those people in there had looked like a savior.

Her almost-attacker dangled from his collar, blocking her view of whoever held him. But Cyn didn't need to see him when she heard the voice. Even though the words were to the idiot who'd bloodied his own knuckles.

"You'd best stop when a lady says 'no'."

The gunman.

What the hell was he doing here?

The dangling man's toes found purchase on the ground but, instead of running, the moron turned and stared down the man behind him. "She's mine. I'll show her–"

The gunman spoke over him. "Trust me, you don't want to tangle with her."

Cyn thought the idiot didn't want to tangle with the man in front of him either, especially over a lay that he was never gonna get.

But the moron still didn't move.

The gunman rolled his eyes. "She's pulled one over on you."

Thanks, Asshole.

But he continued, "She's sixteen."

"Uh!" The indignant sound fell from her mouth before she could stop it. And in her stupidity she had only added credence to his accusation. So, standing there in the back alley with an angry, would-be rapist hovering between them, she got back at him the only way she could think of. "Dad!"

That was it. The man fled even before the gunman could narrow his eyes.

His voice was cold lead and hit her with the force of the bullets he sent into people so casually. "Is this your idea of sport?"

She didn't answer. She wouldn't have called it 'sport'. Maybe 'clean-up'. But she didn't think the gunman would see it that way. "He's a rapist."

He didn't. "No, he's not. I watched you bait Leopold, which was fine. But you don't bait men with sex then get mad when they want to collect."

She started to open her mouth, but his words came before hers did.

"And don't give me this 'no means no' crap. It only means 'no' when you mean it and I *saw* you in there. You were rubbing up on him and sending out 'yes' as loud as fireworks. You had no right to turn the tables on him out here."

Cyn barely found the good grace to keep her mouth shut.

Cold anger swirled inside her. She stared out from her cooling shell and wished him to hell.

His voice was no warmer. "Something tells me you have no idea what you're playing with." His eyes slid up and down her body, over the small dress with enough rayon to make cling wrap seem baggy. She felt more exposed than she had when the idiot inside had pushed his hand almost far enough up her leg to reach her leathers.

Tamping it all down, Cyn turned to walk away.

His hand grabbed her arm, the heat of his palm pouring into her and surprising her, because he'd seemed so cold. Apparently his skin was the only thing warm about him, his voice was positively frigid. "If I ever catch you doing that again, I will lay you out just like I did Norikov."

She didn't doubt him for a minute. But, when his hand didn't move and her anger didn't simmer down, she did what she'd intended to do, just not to him.

Cyn spun and clocked him one right under the chin.

His head snapped back, but not far enough and, in the instant it took him to register that he'd been hit, his eyes came up with fury in them. His fist came out of nowhere, the warning signs harder to spot than they had been with the bag of untrained mush she'd been up against just a few minutes ago.

All she could do was sidestep and get herself partly out of the way. His knuckles made contact with her shoulder, sending her spinning. But she'd taken enough hits that even as she went around her arm came out, the side of her hand making contact with his neck.

To his credit he didn't cry out. Most men did. The gunman had moved a bit with her blow, robbing her of some of the impact. Even so . . .

This time, when his knuckles came at her face, her hand came up and slapped at it from the side, the feather touch deflecting his aim just enough to make him miss. When he didn't make contact, his bulk came forward, doubling the impact of her fist already headed low on his gut. Cyn had stepped into it, and his muscle didn't absorb any of the blow. His forward momentum changed abruptly to backward.

But his hands were fast and he grabbed her arms. His leg kicked up, maybe by accident, but it was damned effective. The top of his foot made contact with her calf and took the leg out from under her, toppling her onto him as he fell back to the wet cement.

Just before the heavy jarring of impact, Cyn blew out all her breath, beating out the blow that would have stolen it from her anyway. But he did the same thing, the thick *whoosh* from his lungs mingling with her own. The *thud* they made hitting the ground was robbed of any victory in the battle, and Cyn just kept moving.

Her knee came up to catch him where it counted, but she wasn't able to get him with his wits down. His leg knocked her knee out of the way, her only blow a less-than-effective glance off his inner thigh.

Even though he had her upper arms in a bruising grip, he held them out from him at a distance, and Cyn brought both her hands up, jamming the heels simultaneously into his lower ribs. That knocked just a little of the wind out of him, and she used the movement and the moment to shove backwards, landing on her feet between his legs and beating a hasty retreat.

Her retreat was backward though, because she wasn't about to turn her back on this man, and he rocked onto his feet like lightning had blown him up. He shoved her, keeping her from the sideways movement that was necessary if she didn't want her back to come up against the brick for the second time this evening. But that's exactly what she did. Cyn didn't slam her head into it, but he did effectively corral her.

He wasn't stupid enough to take a punch at her. But he also wasn't touching her, so she opted to strike fast and hard. Both hands came out fisted and lightning fast, one into his neck and one at his groin, her shorter stature putting it within her striking distance. He twisted, robbing her of her marks and letting her plow one fist into his hip and the other into his shoulder. Still they were good hits.

Still they weren't good enough. His arms came around her, even as she realized her mistake in coming forward from the wall. His knee came up quickly between where she'd planted her front foot in her forward motion, it lifted her thigh, and the momentum lifted all of her.

Faster than what she'd thought him capable of, he had her off the ground and pinned into the wall, the weight of his body holding her there. She couldn't draw a full breath with him leaning into her like he was. She was the superior fighter, but he was damned good and he outweighed her by a hundred pounds. Cyn bet every one was pure muscle.

Damn the man.

She fought back the only way she knew how.

She buried her teeth into his shoulder.

Or she tried to. Just as she felt the give of skin under the leather her mouth closed over, her head yanked back. His fist was tangled in her loose hair, and shy of yanking it all out of her own head, which she knew to be virtually impossible, she was screwed.

Cyn was grateful that she always went for two strikes at once whenever possible. Her right arm was wrapped around the back of his neck and her nails were poised, digging deep enough into his skin to let him know that she could rip out a handful of flesh and tendon should he do anything.

He didn't move.

Neither did she.

Not that she really could. He had her head held back, completely controlled by the tangle of hair that she really wished she had cut at any time before today. Her left arm was pinned, his elbow pressing into her forearm and her hand unable to reach anything vital on him. Her legs straddled his hips in a position that was making her more uncomfortable by the moment, and left her with nothing to kick except the air behind him. Her non-heeled shoes, so useful for fighting, were now useless for gouging a hole in his hamstrings.

For a minute they stayed there, neither yielding anything except the need to breathe. Cyn refused to gulp for air like her body wanted. She wouldn't give him the satisfaction.

Finally, his voice broke the stalemate.

"You aren't ever going to do anything like that again."

She wanted to ask which he was referring to: laying out rapists in back alleys, fighting with men she underestimated, or getting herself pinned against the wall in a compromising position.

She was about to concede to all of the above, when he clarified.

"No more man baiting."

"No more." The words were a bare whisper of sound across the lips that were hard to get together, he held her head yanked so far back.

"No more." He repeated.

Even as she heard the words, she felt the yield in him. His free hand came against her lower rib cage, but not in malice. He applied pressure there, keeping her from dropping to the ground when he stepped back away.

Cyn complied by loosening her nails and not killing him by digging in and ripping out a third of his neck.

When she was standing, still with her back against the wall, he stepped back and offered an almost gallant nod. "Ma'am." He motioned for her to leave.

It only took a second to turn and walk away. Normally, she'd never give her back to an armed opponent, but here saving face was more important. The insult of showing him her ass and shoulder blades as she walked off was worth the risk. He already knew he could take her, and she knew it too. She didn't have anything else to lose, except that last shred of pride she was clinging to.

Chapter 4

The table was pretty standard. Owen thought it looked like every other conference table he'd ever sat at. It was made of that nice, heavy kind of hard wood that let you know it had cost money. That seemed the only purpose of the quality of the wood. Conference tables didn't get chipped from small children banging knives and forks and god knew what into them. It also had a really nice finish. Again, he couldn't figure out why. This one wasn't in any danger from crayons or Tonka trucks filled with too many Barbies to meet any seat belt safety laws. He sighed. Owen wanted another child.

But it wasn't like he was home enough for the one he had. And his wife would likely wise up and leave him one of these days. He gave more of his time to serial killers than he did to her. What was 'I love you' when his actions spoke otherwise? He was just so tired. He hadn't slept in long enough that he was wondering if a nice pine table would have a noticeable softness difference if he just laid down his head . . . right here . . .

His brain had blocked out the voices. His grudge ninja had thankfully kept him out of town during the last of the 'let's all share' conferences his Agent in Charge insisted on. These meetings were one of the few things that he truly thought Bean was an idiot about.

Brandow's voice was droning as it presented the third of three cases he was working. "Jefferson, I think this body that washed up may be your missing Russian mafia guy. Initial matching of hair and blood type look positive. We're waiting on full scale DNA. We didn't rush it because, well, he's not going anywhere."

Owen heard the slap of photos hitting the table, but didn't look up. He was wondering what he might do if he were home with his wife right now. Charlotte was in school . . . maybe they could make good use of that nice, cheap pine table they had in the dining room.

Brandow's voice cut through again. "He washed up on the Jersey Shore. It's possible his buddies did him in, but this isn't their style."

Another voice–Owen wasn't paying enough attention to recognize it–commented. "Looks like someone went baby-harp-seal on him."

That had everyone standing up and looming over to get a better look. But as the gears clicked into place, Owen practically scrambled across the table to pull the pictures from the hands of whoever held it. He didn't see the agent, only the eight-and-a-half-by-eleven glossy of the bloated body laid out at the morgue.

Even with the wet expansion of the naked skin, and the reality that a photo always lost, puncture wounds were visible everywhere. A particularly large one bored through the man's flaccid dick. The others were neat and small, but you could have fit a quarter through that one. Shit.

But the damning evidence was the slice work. More violent looking than in previous cases, it was definitely his. "This is my ninja." Owen looked up at Brandow and Jefferson for the first time. "Can I get copies of all this?"

"I thought your ninja left bodies with big red bows? Nothing of the sort here. No throwing star marks on the chest, no tiny fibers providing evidence of paper tacked into him. This is a new M.O. then?"

Owen didn't know any of that. It wasn't like his ninja not to mark his kills. "What's the death date?"

Jefferson shrugged. "We're waiting on testing. Like I said, he's mafia, so we aren't about to go after his killer full score. We aren't in any real hurry here."

But Owen was.

Jefferson must have seen it. "Chill, Dunham."

Not bloody likely. He still held the photo clasped tightly in his hand, his half-dead mind now churning like butter. Why would the ninja dump the body? He'd never dumped anyone in the water before. Not even that Korean on the docks. The ninja had left him all of ten feet from the bay, trussed up with a bow. Was Leopold not worthy of a bow?

That couldn't be it. Leopold was worthy of three. Maybe the body just didn't fit all the articles that needed to be clipped to it, so the ninja didn't try. Or maybe the ninja *had* done all of that, and the mafia had found him and disassembled him before dumping their dead comrade into the water.

That was more likely.

Owen discarded that as fast as it came. There were no star marks. The ninja had never done this one up. Was he interrupted? Or had he simply anticipated that the family would get there first? Did he think, like Owen did, that the Russians would have noticed him missing long before the cops got to him?

That would mean that the ninja didn't *want* to leave the bow and the articles for the mafia. Why? Could they ID him if they had the clues?

Owen looked up, only to realize that in his crazed thinking he had left the meeting and was walking back to his office. Startled that he'd done such a thing, and stolen Brandow's photos in the process, he waited to hear Bean's voice yelling down the hall to him. When it didn't come, he opened his door and began jerking open file drawers. He dumped copy after copy of the articles the ninja had tacked to various bodies.

These were his own copies, already transferred onto regular sized white paper, each clearly marked with the date it was found and the name of the victim along with the date of death. Somewhere in here was a clue to who the ninja was. A strong enough clue that it hadn't been left for the mafia to find. Because they would recognize him.

Maybe he was one of them turned traitor. Maybe that was how he knew where to find them, how to get into their homes.

Owen poured over the papers for a few hours before he needed coffee. He hadn't found *it* yet. But he would.

He called Annika to tell her not to expect him for dinner, and he wondered if there was any underlying bitterness in her sweet acceptance. But he didn't have time to dig for it, or try to fix it. Not now.

Ten and a half hours later he sat at his desk staring at the same articles. They'd been arranged and rearranged numerous times. Notes had been made in the blank spaces down the sides.

Owen had searched the names of those who'd been implicated in crimes and, figuring the ninja wouldn't implicate his own work, tried to see who was missing. There were no sounds beyond the door. Not that any could have overcome the roaring in his brain. The office was officially closed for the night. The front desk was no longer manned. Every other light in the hallway was off, and security guards made random checks. Which Owen thought was a hysterical waste of taxpayer money, since whoever broke into the FBI wouldn't be thwarted by a rent-a-cop. Nor were the guards anywhere near as well trained or armed as the men and women they were 'protecting'.

But the man on his floor was nice enough, and Owen said 'hi' as they passed on his way back from one of his too few breaks. His fresh cup of coffee almost sloshed in his hand as he heard the man say 'hello' to Nguyen behind him.

Owen turned. "You're still here?"

"Yeah, your damned ninja prints won't let me sleep."

He didn't have to clarify. The scientist meant footprints. They hadn't gotten a single fingerprint from the guy at any kill. "What about them?"

Nguyen cracked a huge smile.

Owen could only smile in return. He hadn't figured out yet what he was going to get from the articles, but Nguyen had something from the lab for him that should come gift-wrapped, that was for certain.

"Your ninja wears size ten Skechers."

Yeah . . . he waited.

"Only when he's on a job. The weight in the tracks isn't right. He did a good job with it. But that's what was bugging me. He didn't press into the ground right. And that's because the ball of his foot is about three-quarters of an inch further back than it ought to be."

"What the hell does that mean?"

"Your ninja wears a size seven or eight on a regular basis. The ten isn't his regular shoe size. And he's been going to a hell of a lot of trouble to throw us off his tracks. Literally."

* * *

Lee sat back in his car, not tired at all. His lighter hair startled him every time he caught a glimpse of it in the rearview mirror.

Occasionally he cranked the engine and drove around the block. He stopped in a new but equally shaded parking spot each time.

The clunker/kitty had served its purpose, staying unobtrusive and running well. If Sin realized she'd been followed she didn't show it. Lee was unsure until she had arrived at the motel and locked up her car. She'd looked around as she manually clicked the lock into place on the small cream-colored sedan that she drove. She walked to the end of the hall, returning with a soda in her hand, and Lee had to wonder where the hell she'd kept any money on that dress or if she'd just jacked the drink right out of the machine.

Then she let herself into room 113 with no pretense of subterfuge and disappeared behind the deep green door riddled with peeling paint revealing that it used to be orange. The curtains twitched. And, while Lee knew the night would be uninteresting, he was interested.

It was about four a.m. when he circled the block again. This time parking in the spot next to her car. He, too, fetched a soda from the machine at the end of the hall and, returning to his vehicle, he dropped his change beside her sedan. When he stooped to pick it up he stuck a cheap tracking device on the underside of her car.

He'd had good luck using one on Norikov, which was funny because the mafia son should have been sweeping his car every time he got in. But he'd missed Lee's, maybe because it was so cheap and low-tech, and he'd died because of it. Maybe Sin wouldn't see either.

Lee pulled out of the lot and this time parked across the street. He stayed behind trees, keeping to where he could only see the car through a slit in between the massive trunks. He had to have a view of the car. If Sin was smart enough to look for a bug, then she'd also be smart enough to pop it off and leave it there in the parking lot. That way, anyone who was just watching the bug would sit quietly, thinking the car hadn't moved, and only when they got suspicious would they discover they'd been tracking an empty parking space.

Lee wasn't going to be that person.

It was seven hours later that Sin came out. And she looked a hell of a lot more like 'Cyn' to him. Her hair was pulled halfway up in a barrette that had gone out of style before he'd shed his old skin and gone to ground. Sam would never have been caught dead in what the girl was wearing–baggy sweat pants and a red turtleneck that fitted nothing. There was also a large, black-framed pair of glasses sitting on her nose. Lee laughed out loud.

She dumped her stuff in the car and disappeared from view. He frowned until she returned a few minutes later with a small receipt in her hand, presumably from checkout. He wondered if she had paid by credit card and if there was a record of Cynthia May Beller staying here last night. His frown pulled tighter.

Still, when she pulled out of the lot he hung back, then stayed a good distance behind her. There was enough traffic here and enough side streets crossing that he needed to keep reasonably close. The same problem luckily also afforded him cover. So he carefully balanced between too close and too far with the cars. But he didn't think he was in much danger of Sin spotting him.

Flipping the switch on the tracking device, Lee listened as the car was filled with an obnoxious beep beep beep. The speed of the synthetic chirp was correspondent to the receiver's distance from the bug. It got a little longer when she made it through a stop light that he didn't, but he caught up in time to see her take a turn and aim for the freeway on-ramp.

In the past several years he'd often followed people. He'd often stayed awake and alert for days on end. But he couldn't remember ever being this jazzed about following someone he didn't plan to kill.

Sin hit the gas and Lee hung back a little further, allowing the beeping of the bug to space out as he got a little distance from her. Occasionally he got close enough to get a visual, especially when they were approaching exits. She could turn off and he wouldn't know it except that the bug would get very far away very quickly. He didn't want to have to turn around at the next exit and backtrack and play a bad game of 'hotter/colder' at an unfamiliar stop.

Cars in between shielded him from her view, and then there was the forgettableness that he had worked so hard for which worked to his advantage as well. He'd slipped a dark ball cap on his head, and wore it low. She probably wouldn't recognize him if he pulled abreast of her, but he didn't take that chance.

Two hours and no stops later, she exited onto a cross road that was smaller and seemed to lead to better places, but it wasn't a stop, only a turn. A single gas station graced the exit, and the building didn't look as though anyone had graced it in a long while.

She drove until she hit a small town and, much to Lee's surprise, she pulled into a rental car office.

Son of a bitch.

He lost her. She didn't come out of the office. The bug was on the cream colored sedan and would now beep incessantly from the parking lot until the next person rented it. He laughed a bitter laugh from his spot across the street in the shade. Sin didn't know he was following her–what a crock of shit. As usual he'd underestimated her. And she'd shaken him good.

He sat there for twenty-five minutes, waiting for her to come out and wondering if she already had. A handful of cars had pulled out of the lot while he'd stewed. Sure none of the drivers had looked like Sin, but even Sin hadn't looked like Sin this morning. He turned the car around and headed for home, wondering when he'd see her again and how.

As he pulled up to the light, a gray and metal object overtook his rearview mirror. A shuttle bus. Like a spot-on-the-map place like this needed a shuttle bus. But as he blinked he registered that it had just pulled out of the rental car lot, and he wondered if Sin was on it.

What the hell. It wasn't like he had anything better to do. He kept his car slow, letting the bus driver get antsy and pull around him. Then he tailed the rolling metal box down the street. It stopped all of two miles later, purging itself of riders–one of which, he was happy to see, was Sin.

While he was thrilled that he'd made a good guess, Lee was also pretty certain that his little operation was over. Sin had walked into the bus station with the rest of the sheep-people. She had blended right in with her sweats and black rimmed glasses. No one would notice her. Which was certainly not to be said of the other two personas he now knew.

Disgust filled him, to be so close to following her, and yet be so thwarted. She'd disappear in the bus station. He couldn't leave the car here at the curb, he'd have to go find a parking spot, then get inside, re-find Sin, find out which bus she was on, and then follow it. Big mess.

Again the decision was made simply because he didn't have anything better to do. And she hadn't quite sloughed him off yet, though she sure was giving him a good rub. Parking was close to the building but around back from the entrance, and when he finally got inside Lee wondered if she'd already hopped a bus. He grabbed a newspaper and sat down to wait. Pretty much he kept up to speed on the evils of the big world, only he tended to gorge on newspapers and magazines only once every week or more. What happened yesterday was always unknown to him. A few of the articles actually caught his attention, and it was difficult to stay focused on finding his lost cause.

The red shirt saved him. Sin walked across the far end of the terminal, bag in hand, seemingly in response to an announcement. Since he hadn't been paying attention to the garbled wording coming over the speakers Lee had to follow her out to the bus lines. Having no bags, he did his level best to look like he was climbing on one of these busses. Sin got on one that said Raleigh NC.

That raised his eyebrows. Sin had been pretty close all along. He wondered if he'd ever run into her and not known it. Waiting until the bus pulled out, he then went back out the front thinking he'd reclaim his car and pay off his parking fees. In the terminal, amidst all the soft clatter of people, and harsh noise of announcements and busses, he stopped and looked up to see if he could get the route. It was a long way to follow a bus, but if he knew where they were headed, he could get there early.

What he saw, when he finally found the right bus line, burst his little superior bubble. Lee realized that he had never taken the bus–and clearly didn't know what in the hell he was doing. It wasn't like an airplane; the bus stopped along the way. Each city a chance for Sin to exit and disappear.

If he just showed up in Raleigh in two days and greeted the bus, he was likely to find Sin long since gone. Her line was going through Dallas, Little Rock, Memphis and Nashville. Maybe Sin was even closer than he'd just thought. But he was going to have to tail that bus across the country.

It pulled out of the station behind him. Or one of the busses did. He high-tailed it to his car, cranked the engine and shot out of the lot, getting pissed at the wait to pay his measly parking fare. When the bus hit the freeway Lee sent up a prayer that it was the right one and raced to overtake it. Luckily his car was in good working order and the bus was a lumbering beast, slow to get up to speed even though the on-ramp had aimed down to the freeway giving it the help of gravity.

When he was far enough in front, he looked into his rearview and saw Raleigh NC in letters across the front. Slowly it cycled, ticker style, through every stop. With a breath out, relief washed through him head to toe, and Lee was forced to admit that he wasn't following her just for lack of something better to do.

Sin was the most interesting thing to happen to him in a damn long time. She was the only thing besides booze and revenge that had breached his consciousness in three years. She took on grown men in fist fights and won.

Letting off the gas and allowing his car to slip back into the tail stream of the big silver bus, he smiled. Well, she hadn't won against him.

But then again, that was likely only because he had an idea what he was up against. A good portion of her strength came in surprise. She danced around a lot, like small fighters do, ducking and weaving and avoiding the blows that had the power to lay them flat. No one expected her to last past the first one landed on her. But she always did, and she hit back, packing a serious punch in those little fists. But Lee had seen all that in action before he fought her. Leopold hadn't. None of the others probably had either. There was a good possibility that a few had even laughed in her face.

She'd probably gotten off on killing those guys. But even then–even knowing how she fought, that a good solid blow that would KO a big man wouldn't take her down, that he couldn't let her get behind him–the best Lee had been able to get off her was a stalemate. He didn't have to look in the mirror. He could feel the bruises in his neck. They were deep down in there, too. Four purple circles where her fingers had planted themselves and threatened to tear flesh. Lee didn't doubt her capability to rip his throat out, and he didn't trust her to simply leave it as a threat and not follow through.

It had meant he hadn't won the fight. Neither had she. But he was a good hundred pounds heavier and over six inches taller than she.

He kept his eyes on the taillights of the bus.

It was a damned interesting little fix here.

Two hours later, the bus pulled into the El Paso station. The girl in the sweatpants and blobby red turtleneck got off. Her bags were slung over her shoulder. He hadn't seen it before, but she had trouble pushing up her glasses because her arm was wrapped, child-like, around a large teddy bear. Her face stayed mostly hidden. But if it wasn't Sin, then she was getting followed way too often, and he might ought to just butt out and hope he stayed alive.

But it was her. He saw as he circled the parking lot at a discreet distance. He even pulled into a spot and leaned over like he was checking through his luggage or such, while she circled wide like she was lost. Lee didn't buy that for a hot second. Then she keyed open the passenger door on an older model sedan. The finish was a dull silver shade, one hubcap was mismatched, the sides sported a few dents here and there, and Lee smiled. It was an utterly unremarkable car.

He wondered if it was truly hers. Or if she had paid for another rental just to leave it at the lot here.

Sin slipped behind the wheel and started up. Lee exited the lot two cars behind her. He wouldn't want her to look into her rearview and recognize his eyes. After all this, he didn't doubt she'd shake him like a wet dog if she knew he was back there.

They hit the freeway, again aimed for Dallas, and he shook his head. She was still headed in the same direction. He got close. He hung back. He had to pee, and his car actually needed fluid–he was about out of gas. When he reached the point that he was concerned he was going to burst and the car was going to run dry, Sin pulled off at a mildly populated exit.

She gassed her car, paying cash, and Lee had to do the same. Taking a huge chance, but not wanting to lose her if she took off with a full tank and he had nothing but fumes, Lee pulled his cap low and went into the small store. He picked out a bag of chips and a few beef jerky strips to kill the time while she waited at the counter. He turned his back when she went out the door, creating the wicked mechanical chimes that grated his nerves. Although he had to admit that might be due to the fact that his nerves were pretty high strung as it was. He did not need a repeat of the previous night's alleyway last-man-standing here at the gas station. An arrest would only get him in serious shit.

But he knew the same applied to her. So he was taking his chances.

He pushed a few bills across the counter to cover the food and gas. He'd calculated an amount that would pretty much fill up the tank, but not require him to need change. Not being remembered was too important. And if Sin left, so would he.

The guy in line behind him swished a fountain drink that sloshed like the ocean, and Lee gritted his teeth against the need to pee. He shoved back out into the bright light and kept his back to Sin as he gassed up the kitty. She finished when he was still five dollars from done. And that was bad. He couldn't leave the five behind. Someone would think it strange. So he squeezed the handle a little harder, as though he had control of anything to do with the gas, and watched from low under his bill as she pulled into a fast food joint across the street.

She bolted inside, making him a little nervous, until he remembered that Sin didn't run from anything. If she'd seen him, she'd have walked right up and confronted him. Or just clocked him.

He drove over to the same side of the street and packed his car in with a few others down the row from hers. Even though his bladder was about to burst, he took the time to fetch another bug and quickly check the receiver. It let off a loud continuous whine, the bug was so close, and Lee shut it off as fast as he could.

He did the change dropping technique again, and again picked up his quarters. One had actually rolled under her car, and it couldn't get better than that. Except, of course, if Sin saw him. He imagined a foot kicking his ass into Sunday if she spotted him down under her car. So he slapped the device on and got the hell away. He looked inside the store window and saw her.

She was coming from the back. Probably leaving the ladies room and heading for the counter.

Shit. He ducked his head, and made like he was checking out the other restaurant. That was better. His back was to her. The bug was planted. He could pee. The smell of frying fish slapped him in the face when he entered. But, like Sin had, he headed straight for the head. Three minutes later, and feeling three pounds lighter, he washed his hands fingertips to wrists and pushed his way out front. He ordered things that could be eaten with one hand while chasing someone, not caring for the flavor or food quality. Taste was one of those things that had turned to a uniform shade of mid-gray as he had held Samantha and Bethy, limp and bloodless, in his arms that day. He ate to keep active. Alive wasn't the word for it.

So he didn't check his order, and he didn't care what he had, except that lemonade wouldn't make him pee as fast as all that caffeine in soda would. Sin's car was gone by the time he got back in his, and the first thing he did was hit the switch on the receiver. It let off a series of high-pitched blips, each a little further apart than the ones before it.

Twisting the key, he set the car to purring and went back out onto the freeway in the same direction, as it was the best guess to where Sin was headed. The beeping picked up a little speed, and inside four minutes he made visual contact with her car.

Lee ate, drank, and drove. He didn't have CDs to play. He didn't listen to the radio, not that there was much in the way of stations out here in the back beyond of Texas. He didn't watch the scenery go by. Just kept his gaze steady on those little red tail lights, like a man watching a prime piece of ass go by. He listened to the steady static in his head, more like the roar of ocean than a rumble of thoughts or thunder. He gained no wisdom, no insight, no advantage. He simply followed.

He stopped when she stopped, ate when she ate, and stayed as far back as possible. He began to wonder if she'd gotten suspicious of seeing the same car over and over, but there were actually several cars that had kept good pace with them. Being out here between major cities in a big expanse of Texas, it was likely they were all going to the same place, at least for now. He wondered how he would handle it when she stopped for the night and he would need to change cars. He could not successfully trail her another day in the same vehicle. If there was anything Sin wasn't, it was stupid.

Behind him, sunlight was scraping the top of his rear window and he caught the first blinding rays of sunset in his mirror. He stayed well back from Sin, relying on the beeping that had wound him up in a Chinese-water-torture effect early on, but had now grown to the normal rhythm of driving.

It was only when the beeping suddenly began to space itself apart, rapidly showing that he was losing ground on her, that he blinked. He pushed the gas to catch up, but the noises only came further and further apart. With a frown he slowed and listened as the noise slowed, too. Sin was behind him.

But there had been no exits. Or maybe there had been and he'd just had an easy time of it lately and had gotten complacent and not paid attention.

No. He hadn't been complacent. It had been monotonous, but he hadn't missed anything. So how the hell had she gotten behind him? Had she gone all Bat mobile when he wasn't looking and just taken to the sky or some shit like that?

Lee looked for a more earthly explanation. Sin was corporeal if nothing else. When she hit, you knew she wasn't a wraith or anything other than solid. She also wasn't one much for gadgets, he noticed. He had guns and ammo and moving parts. The girl basically played with sharp sticks. So the Bat mobile idea was too far fetched.

Had she just driven off road?

It was the only thing that made sense. She had pulled out into a stretch there where none of the others in their moving pack of cars went with her. Out ahead on her own, she might have taken a sharp turn off.

He was fucked anyway. So he pulled off at the next exit, the beep only coming once every minute or so. It came each time. Just when he was certain the last beep had been the end of it, the machine would cough out another one. It was like listening to a heart monitor and waiting for the patient to just die already. But the beeping didn't die. And about eight minutes into sitting there, it picked up, startling Lee.

"Halleluiah." It was whispered to the interior of the car. It was another notice that he wasn't an uninvolved bystander. That he wasn't just killing time.

The beeping picked up, reached a maximum, and started to slough off again. If he was right, that meant she had just passed his exit on the freeway and was heading on. Hitting the gas for the umpteenth time that day, Lee shot up the ramp, correcting his assumption. All the beeping meant was that the *transmitter* was passing his exit. He wouldn't believe his luck until he saw her car.

He amended it one more time: he wouldn't believe his luck until he saw her car with *her driving it.*

Still, he spotted her tail lights and dull silver finish about five minutes later. He slowly closed distance until he saw long dark hair and a red shirt. That didn't mean it was her. But he wasn't about to get any closer.

He'd either had phenomenal luck today or Sin was going to twist his head on his neck and leave him there for dead the second he got out of his car. It was too dark to see it at first, but about half an hour later he realized what was making that sensation of something touching the back of his brain. Something was different, and he'd finally figured it out. During the time that he had lost her, Sin had swapped out her plates.

Smart girl.

It was deep night when she finally turned off the freeway. Lee sucked in his breath, grateful that he was far enough back to make the turn without riding her tail to do it. He was the only other driver that took the exit. His headlights were burning into her eyes from her rearview, and he had to turn off soon.

He took the first road he saw and prayed it didn't lead to a closed arboretum or the driveway of someone she knew or something ridiculous that would get him killed.

It turned out to simply be a poorly paved road to seemingly nowhere, as much of what was out this way appeared to be. He would have to wait and trust the bug to track her.

After a minute, he turned around, going back out to the road Sin was traveling. The beeping was spacing out, but the road was long and straight. If he drove without his lights he'd alert someone. Or get pulled over–with no driver's license, or any other ID. Lee Maxwell just didn't exist anymore. If another car came along, it would serve as a buffer, and he could pull in behind. But he had no such luck.

Instead he waited until he couldn't see her tail lights. Then he waited that long again, knowing that the small red back lights would be lost to his vision at a much shorter distance than his headlights would disappear to her. He followed the beeping through a small town with three stop-lights, feeling caught in a big metal game of cat and mouse.

Beyond the town he lost her all together. And he wound up playing warmer/colder in the dark, trying out a street here, a gravel road there, all of them wrong until one made the beeping stronger. The driveway curved through overgrowth and Lee thought it would be mighty dumb of him to come out from under the cover of trees and find his headlights shining right on her parked car or something, anything, that would tell her he was there.

So he switched the receiver to vibrate and tucked it into his pocket. It felt odd against his thigh, and there was nothing to be done for the slight buzzing sound that went with the humming movement that replaced the beeps. Checking his guns, he made sure he had one in each holster and his jacket open for quick and easy grasp of the handles, he climbed out of the car.

The overhead light in the kitty didn't come on. The door didn't ding or creak in the hinge. Contrary to looks, the car was pretty stealthy. He even held the handle up, pushed the door into place and let the grip back down. The buzz came against his thigh again. It startled him, but a startle to Lee was quite different than a startle to someone else. Or even to whom he'd used to be. It just engaged his brain, and loosed some adrenaline, until he placed it, then he moved on.

The vibrations came more frequently as he approached. A small glow shone in the distance and Lee went after it like a kid creeping down to the tree before dawn on Christmas. At one point he stopped dead, something catching his vision. It was just the tiniest of glints in the black, but it saved his ass. A strand of barbed wire ran at knee height in front of him. Here in the trees it blended in and was nearly invisible. Slowly checking up and down, he found another right at his neck height. He frowned. Barbed wire to the jugular was not his late night cup of tea.

Just then his mouth slanted wide, a big shit-eating grin lit his face right there in the night by himself. He'd been afraid that Sin had found the bug and he was tracking someone else. But who the hell else would hide two strands of barbed wire to clothesline someone coming through the woods? No one. That's who. This was pure Sin.

Checking again, he ducked and high-stepped through, then walked more slowly. Lee wouldn't put it past her to have another one for any fool who got cocky enough to think they'd gotten through her system. Sure enough, he found a second set, at different heights, too, about eight feet out from the edge of the lawn.

But he didn't go under. He was close enough. The receiver was at such a short distance that it was going off about every second. The buzzing noise and almost itching sensation that accompanied it was a welcome reminder that he'd trailed her to the end point. The transmitter was in that garage. And Sin was in that house.

But it was the house that held him. In the middle of barbed wire and trees and nowhere, was a neat little house with a small yard of lush green grass. Rose bushes lined the perimeter, and he wondered if Sin had read what he'd read before he'd planted Sam all the bushes around their fence–that roses were more effective than the fence at keeping out thieves. No one wanted to carry household objects through a patch of thorns.

From what he could see in the starlight that shone down on her little patch of yard, it looked like the house was a sunny yellow with white paneling around the bottom. Flowers were planted in various beds against the sides, sprays of purples and pinks and yellows were all starting to come into season. There was no light shining around the windows and he wondered if she'd gone straight to bed upon arriving.

Lee couldn't help but wonder if Sin lived here after all. He was beginning to think that maybe Cynthia May Beller did.

He was still standing in her woods, looking at her house, when the spitting sound started. It was all the warning he got. In seconds he was drenched. Sprinkler heads had popped up, fully loaded and firing as they came. The spitting turned to an even hiss as the heads all came into action around the yard and began a night-time, conservation watering.

The sprinklers were all at the perimeter of the yard, meaning each covered grass and woods. It only took Lee a second to understand the seemingly foolish system. He was wearing it. About two pounds of water.

If he'd been about three feet to the right, he would have been blocked by a tree and stayed mostly dry. As it was, no one would want to get close without full rain gear. Anyone coming in under cover of darkness would leave prints and track mud. Lee looked down, although all he could see of his own feet out here in the wet dark was the faintest of outlines. He wondered if she mixed some special mud or such to track him with–if he was standing in it now.

He also realized that anyone caught off guard by the water was about ten times as likely to go right into the barbed wire it was sprinkling through. He shook his head. Sin did not want anyone here who wasn't coming up the drive and waving.

He stepped back a few feet, and turned to go. His eyes failed him. Staring at even the slight glow of the house meant he had to let his eyes adjust to the darkness this way. So he took a breath and waited. Lee did not want to hang himself on her barbed wire.

* * *

It was noticeably warmer inside the house. Unfortunately it was just as dark as the pitch night outside. Annika had left the porch light on for him, but no others. He didn't think she was leaving him one of those typical female messages. Owen was pretty sure she was just saving energy as there was no telling when, or even if, he'd get home at night.

He'd left work early yesterday and picked Charlotte up from school, much to both his wife and daughter's delight. He hoped it made up for the fact that he'd spent all day and into tonight with Nguyen in the lab. Trying, desperately, to find anything on the damned ninja.

He wandered into the kitchen after hanging up his jacket by the door. Neatness was the least of the concessions his wife deserved just for putting up with him. He flipped the light and smiled. Sitting on the stove was a cling wrapped plate. Not only was dinner waiting for him, it was piled high. He shucked the wrap and shoved the whole thing into the microwave, the cycling noise of the appliance already removing his thoughts from home and turning them, machine-like, back to work.

He had other cases. They were fairly simple though. So he solved what he could. He interviewed, he closed. The damn grudge ninja was eating him as thoroughly as he was now consuming his food. He didn't sit to eat. Owen figured he'd done enough sitting on his ass. He also wondered if he had all his hair left. He'd surely pulled fistfuls out or just stressed it all to the point of falling away.

His thoughts took off in frustration. The ninja would kill again. And Owen needed to crack the case. The ninja was methodical, prepared, and lethal. As Nguyen had pointed out, the little bastard was going to a lot of trouble to throw them off track. The shoe thing had been great. Apparently he'd even stiffened the sole to make it break in the right place, looking like the ball of the foot was where it should be. But it wasn't. However, he'd gotten it past Nguyen at a handful of sites before the scientist caught it. Nguyen also suspected the soles had been attached to a different shoe, as none of the sneakers the company carried with that tread offered enough ankle support to allow for the size difference the ninja was sporting.

Owen's plate was clean, and he wished he'd taken the time to enjoy it just a little bit more. Or maybe just a little bit at all.

But even as he rinsed the plate and loaded it into the half-full washer, he thought about his job. He'd joined the FBI to catch the bad guys and to be smarter than everyone else. His own personal jury was still out as to whether the ninja was the bad guy. He was certainly removing seasoned criminals from the pool with alarming efficiency. The FBI, a large, national organization with thousands of employees, didn't seem to be able to take down the mob the way the ninja was. Then again, there was that whole the-FBI-had-to-follow-the-law issue. The ninja had no such constraints and no real compunctions about breaking the rules.

However, if the ninja wasn't the bad guy, then what was Owen doing? Was he in it to be smarter? Because he wasn't feeling much smarter here. He walked into his bedroom, softly closing the door behind him. He undressed to the quiet sounds of the house, doing a good job of it. Between FBI training and too much practice climbing into bed long after Annika had, he was a pro at it.

"Hey, baby."

Her voice surprised him. "You're awake."

"Um-hmmm."

Okay, maybe she wasn't all that awake. But he could see that she held her arms out to him from the faint light leaking in around the doorway and the edges of the curtains. And he could see that he didn't deserve her.

Owen slid into a bed warmed by his wife's slim body and curled her into his arms. This he could do. When she asked him to tell her about the case that was keeping him, he fell even more in love with her. He would say each day that loving her more just wasn't possible, but then she would do something like this, and he would.

Breaking more than one federal law, and knowing Annika was more trustworthy than–clearly–even he was, he told her what Nguyen had found, and how frustrated he was. How he hadn't found the girl's footprints at the scene.

She listened intently. Asked questions that showed him she'd been paying attention, and had been even long before tonight. And then she put her arms around him. "Owen, you need to make love to me."

He smiled. Russian women came in two varieties that he was aware of: the babushka kind, with the warts and facial hair and gnarled fingers, and the supermodel kind. His wife was of the supermodel variety, and even without that, he was insanely attracted to her. After twelve years together, the slightest sexual hint from her still made him hard. Her words put him at attention. But it was the way she said it that made him ask, even as he smiled, "Why is that?"

"Because, when you are done and I am satisfied, I'll tell you what I think."

The chuckle welled up in his chest, "You could tell me now."

"No." She tightened her grip around him and ran long, smooth legs against his own. She was right, he wouldn't hear what she said, his brain was already in his dick. "When I tell you what I think, you're going to get out of bed and go back to your office. So you'll make love to me first."

"That good, huh?"

But she was already peeling her sleep shirt off, sitting up over him. Her breasts were clear in shades of gray now that his eyes had adjusted. "Yes, I am that good."

Thoughts of her thoughts fled his brain, he couldn't hold onto anything but her. He knew where to touch her, how to touch her, what she smelled and felt like. But his memory was always poor compared to reality, and his hands and mouth sought actual sensation. His soul yearned for a connection with her that would tie her to him when he disappeared for days on end.

"Jesus." He hissed when he touched her and found her wet already. He fought to slow down and not just take her, so he turned his attention to kissing her everywhere. On the tide of her second orgasm, he slid into her, knowing and enjoying the way her eyes looked heavenward as he did. She moved with him, biting her lip and fighting back what had once been loud screams before they had a child.

Owen held out as long as he could, then slipped under the pull of his own sweet release and collapsed as gently as he could on top of her. He pushed himself off and to the side even as he gathered her and held her close.

His brain was slipping away into sleep as her fingers found their way through his hair. "Owen, I love you."

"I love you, too, Anni." His eyes were falling closed.

"There are only four sets of footprints at the scene, because there were only four people there."

He sighed. "There were five, we have evidence of the girl the rapist attacked."

She smiled, he could feel it against his chest. “Sweetie, is every agent on this case a man?”

Waking just a little, he thought about that. “I guess so, but that’s not a sexist thing. There just don’t happen to be many women in our division.”

“Fine, but that’s why you’re missing it.” Her hand traced a lazy circle on his chest, and he enjoyed the few moments he didn’t care about the ninja, even if Annika was bringing it up.

“There were only four people. Your ninja is the woman the rapist attacked.”

“Annika–”

He stopped himself even as he said it. Owen sat bolt upright and climbed out of bed buck naked, speaking the words just to try them on his tongue. “The ninja is a woman.”

Annika nodded against the pillow where she still reclined. “She baited the rapist, and when she got him, she took him down.”

He was breathing heavy now. In his mind he could see the scene, see every foot print, and if he overlapped the girl and the ninja the scene played out in perfect sense. Ninja prints led away from the indentation in the ground. It was why no one had come forward. Why the girl didn’t scratch the man, which was most women’s reaction to attack.

He climbed into his clothes with a speed he usually didn’t employ even on an urgent page. He leaned back over his wife who, bless her heart, smiled at him. “I love you, Anni. In ways you’ll never know. I’m sorry.”

But she waved a hand at him to go. “This is why you had to make love to me first.”

Her grin didn’t falter. Or if it did, Owen didn’t see it. He was already out the door.

The ninja’s height. The weight. The quarter-sized hole in Leopold’s cock. It all made a lot more sense if it was a woman. She’d have to be really strong and very well trained. But they already knew that much. Why not a woman?

He paged Nguyen.

Chapter 5

Cyn saw his face on the punching bag. Damned gunman. She kicked out again as the bag swung back toward her, burying her heel into it and sending it up again.

She had worked up a good sweat, but it hadn't loosened any of her aggressions. She was pissed as hell. First Norikov. Then that asshole at the bar. And to top it off, he'd given her that lecture. That 'don't bait a man with sex / you don't know what you're playing with' lecture.

"Agh!" She pushed her fist into the bag where his head would be. She whirled and kicked out behind her as the bag swung back, striking it in what would be the groin region.

She was probably maddest that he was probably right.

No one had ever talked to her that way.

No one had ever gotten the best of her in a fight. She'd always been the one on top in the end. And she practiced damn hard to be sure it stayed that way.

It had been a mistake to let him stay while she took out Leopold. He'd seen her work and she'd lost her element of surprise. Three times in the alley she'd tried to get behind him, and he'd moved each time as though he knew what she was doing. He probably had. Cyn kicked the bag again. Harder.

She hated being honest, but she admitted that if she wasn't honest with herself who would be? She wouldn't have struck Leopold with the stars in his arms and fought him hand to hand if the gunman hadn't been there as backup. She would never have taken the chance. She didn't start fights she didn't know she could win, and she had known she could win because she had loaded guns behind her.

Her honesty didn't change the fact that she was royally pissed.

As always, she let the anger fuel her. A robotic practice dummy sat propped into the corner. Once it had beeped and registered hits and power. She'd shorted two of the blinking lights in the first three days and cracked the casing on its body after just two weeks. So she didn't hit him anymore, just used him the way the Japanese used their wooden totems, as a way of lining up and practicing hits with no force behind them.

Adjusting the dummy upward to a satisfying six-one, Cyn stepped back and decided that it matched his height. Then she rehearsed her aim at targets on the plastic casing, planning where she'd get the gunman the next time she saw him. The nose–fist and wrist in line, thumb side up. The neck–knuckles curled, straight to the windpipe. The kidney–a good strike from the side, down with the elbow. The groin–she drove her foot into it too hard and sent the dummy toppling off to one side.

Setting him back up, Cyn held back and marked the moves again. It had been so hard at first to not just beat at the dummies or the bags she set up, to remain in control and know where she was going. But after that first, flailing, all-out kill, she'd learned quickly. This time she just marked her shots. Her muscles tensed, all held in perfect form. She kicked upward, just touching her foot to the dummy's throat, then did it again, and again, until she hit the windpipe exactly how she wanted to. Then she walked the whole thing again, and again. She practiced faking with one punch and hooking with the other hand. She lined up dual punches, making it so the victim might avoid one, but never both. She tried two fists to the kidneys from the front, but didn't like it. The symmetry allowed the victim to think about both punches as one unit. Two punches after different organs, going different ways, confused people. It made it harder to think quickly, harder to get out of the way. Cyn practiced more and more.

In her mind the practice dummy took on the features of the gunman. Narrowed gray eyes glared down from the plastic face and hair that wasn't sure if it was dark or light topped the head whose chin she kicked at. The other night had been a bitch in more than one way.

The clock on the wall told her it was time to quit.

Obeying, Cyn bowed to the dummy, wanting desperately to kick it in the groin one more time, but not willing to break the ancient code that said the bow signaled the end. The groin kick would be cowardly, the equivalent of shooting someone in the back. She didn't do it.

Instead she hauled her ass out of the large back room and into the shower in the bathroom off her bedroom, closing and locking both the doors as she went. The steam did a little to ease her tension, and she shampooed with the floral fragrance she had. It normalized her a little for work. She used a loofah to scrub herself with another of the floral soaps she got a discount on, then washed her face.

She dried herself and her hair, and went into the bedroom where she pulled pretty, trendy clothing from her closet and stepped into the short skirt and pink top. She set her hair in curlers and applied tasteful makeup. Her shoes matched her shirt, and she pulled a purse from a small collection she had, and packed her wallet and a small makeup bag inside.

Inside an hour she'd gone from lethal to innocuous. She smiled at her reflection and climbed into her car. She had a long drive ahead of her. Looking over her shoulder, she backed all the way out to the street. Once she was out of town, she slipped a CD in and started tapping the steering wheel to the beat.

Wendy would have liked this group. In Cyn's mind Wendy wasn't gone, but was vital and healthy and as strong as she herself was. As far as anyone at work knew, Wendy lived in the house with her, Wendy was her best friend, and they went clubbing on the weekends. Other than her mostly made-up sister, the Cyndy her co-workers knew stayed fairly quiet about her life.

The drive into Dallas was familiar and monotonous and she shut out any temptation of thinking. She couldn't afford to spend time at work with her brain turning to thoughts about the gunman, about Leopold, about who was next. She needed to focus her mind on the spring collection of tees. On lightweight pants. On almost sheer shirts that layered over darker ones.

The city seemed to grow out of the ground in front of her as she approached, but it didn't register in the emptiness of her mind. She pulled in at the mall and parked in a far space, walking to the nearly invisible entrance for employees. Enjoying the slight nip in the weather, she pulled the springy bracelet keychain out of her purse and slipped it around her wrist. Entering the employee hallway by the public restrooms, she turned down a long tunnel that led to back doors to all the shops.

Even in the daytime the tunnel was lit only by fluorescents and was one of those places that you always heard about women being stalked in. More than one horror movie had featured what Cyn suspected was this exact hallway. She was afraid someone would attack her here. Not because anything would happen–she would take down anyone who thought they could get her. They'd have to kill her with a damn quick bullet to the heart or head before anyone got anything off her. But when she took them out she'd have to quit her job and move. She wouldn't–couldn't–stay if anyone knew what she could do. In fact she wouldn't even be able to hang out for the police report. So she walked tall and hoped that no one targeted her.

Reaching the back door of the store without incidence, she used her shop keys to let herself in. Marissa was in the back office, tallying cash drawers and receipts before her shift ended, and Cyn smiled and asked how the day went. Her fellow manager gave numbers then asked about Cyndy's four days off. All she could answer with was there was a guy at the bar that had given her a tangle worth remembering.

Mari laughed. Cyn faked it.

Then she went out and talked to the other girls working the floor. The place was fairly busy for a Tuesday. But the store seemed to be running fine without her. Her eye to detail was what had gotten her promoted, so she did what they expected of her and made a round straightening the store. She refolded shirts, realigned hangers, tugged at a thin sweater on a mannequin, and answered questions from customers. She took her dinner break at the food court with a magazine she'd picked up from the bookstore down the hall. She came back with nothing gained except a full stomach. But the store changed with the waning day, she clocked out the daytime employees and checked in the evening people. The tone in the mall changed around her, too.

More men came by. Fewer moms with strollers. The number of teens had been steadily picking up since two p.m. The place was rolling and they were an hour from closing when Cyn looked up from putting the hanger straps into place on the halters and saw him.

Shit.

She hid her face, even as she reminded herself he wouldn't recognize her figure, or her shoes, or the skirt, or her curly hair.

The gunman was the one person in the whole world she hid from. She had her surface life here and then she had her *real* work. The two had never crossed paths. Until now.

He was in jeans and a plain t-shirt, and his hair *was* almost blonde. She'd seen it two nights ago, but hadn't cared as she'd been too busy trying to kick his ass. Cyn turned back to bury her face in the clothes as he charmed one of her salespeople. She wouldn't have thought he'd have it in him, but he was being friendly and sweet. *Seeming* friendly and sweet, she amended in her head. But Nancy was smiling and helping him.

Feeling her back teeth grinding and the painful pull of the wicked bruise in her shoulder, Cyn made her way back to the office. She wanted to go and help him. She wanted to feel superior and taunt him–if only in her mind–that he didn't recognize her. But she couldn't take the chance. Forget getting attacked in the back hallway, the gunman could take down her life much easier.

She hid in the rear of the store, behind the walls enclosing the office and storeroom, seething until he left. It had seemed an eternity, but her watch told her he'd been there only about ten minutes total.

She bided her time until the store closed, faking her smile, helping customers and the sales floor girls as well, before finally rolling the front gate down and watching as the mall lights went out one by one. Three of them exited the back door and made their way out the long tube of a hallway. It was just as falsely bright now as it had been when she'd come in. Only now she was in a sour mood.

As they spilled into the parking lot, Cyn said goodnight to the girls, watching them as they went in different directions to their cars. They were both older than she was, but didn't know it. And she felt a bit like a mother hen, knowing that if anyone came after one of them in the dark lot, she'd be there and stop it. No matter the cost to her job. Not that these women were her friends. She had no friends.

Eying her car, she half expected to see him standing against it. Only now did she take the time to truly wonder how the hell he'd found her. Or had he just stumbled into her store of all stores?

Was he planning a kill in Dallas? There were a few men here that could use some killing, but Cyn sure wasn't ready to hit so close to home yet. Did he live nearby? And today he just happened into her store? For the first time she wondered if he had a name, and what he did for money, and where he lived.

Realizing that she'd bordered on spacing out, which was a stupid occurrence in a dark parking lot, and an even stupider thing to do with a loaded gunman around, Cyn pushed her thoughts back to the reality around her and scanned the area. Her car appeared absent of any malevolent presence, and she climbed in. Only as she cranked the key did she think about car bombs and how it was a little too late for that. Could he hate her that much? Could he be that mad about the bar? Or was he just pissed that he hadn't taken out the little girl?

She waited a moment longer and thankfully the car didn't blow up. No strange noises or odors came from the engine. No oddly colored smoke poured out the air vents when she turned them on. Then she remembered to check the backseat. It, too, was thankfully void of harmful things. Cyn pulled out from under the halogen light and into the dark. She liked it better under the blanket of night. She didn't like her thoughts.

He hadn't just turned up at her store. There was no way–true coincidence wasn't something she believed in. Worst case scenario: he tailed her and he was going to kill her. Best case scenario: he tailed her and was going to ask her out. Then, when she said 'no,' he'd kill her.

Had he found the store by researching her? God, she hoped not. Anyone with a computer and a Yahoo account could do all the research they wanted these days. Which meant someone else could find her, too. If it wasn't through research, then he had followed her, and that was at least as bad. She'd done so much to shake anyone who thought they could just track her.

Her thoughts turned over and over, none of it good. Halfway home she found a restaurant lot where she could have some light and check out her car. During the ride it had occurred to her he might have bugged the vehicle. She'd also immediately dismissed the thought, as she had switched out cars after Norikov's. But *she* wouldn't have let that stop her and he *was* here. So she'd pulled off as soon as she could.

Cyn slapped the car into park and slammed the door. In seconds, she was on her hands and knees looking under the carriage.

"Do you need help?"

She didn't startle at the voice. Ever aware of her surroundings, she had seen the feet coming and already knew they didn't belong to the gunman. She'd even formulated a good line.

"No, I ran over a plastic bag out on the road and wanted to see if it was caught under the car." She wanted to keep looking without looking suspicious, so she kept prattling. "I'm always afraid anything under the car will just burst into flames." She tossed in a little laugh there at the end for good measure.

"Oh." He thought she was stupid. She could tell from the tone. That was a good thing, she reminded herself. Exactly what she'd been going for, so she had no cause for that tight grind in her chest. He scratched his head and looked at her there on her hands and knees in the parking lot. "Well, you aren't in any danger of the car bursting into fire at all really. That's just a Hollywood thing."

She faked a laugh and continued to search. She didn't know what it would look like. But–

She sure as hell knew it when she saw it. A small metal box, it was stuck into a groove, probably so she didn't risk knocking it off. It had a short antenna that stuck straight out the side, probably also to keep it from damage. Reaching out furiously she yanked it from her car. *God Damnit!!!!*

For a moment she considered chucking it into the restaurant trash bin beside her at top speed, but then she remembered her audience. By force of will, she pocketed the bug, and ran a hand through her hair with a smile. "There's nothin' there. I'll just get going. Thank you."

She slipped into the car and peeled out of the lot before Cletus there could say anything. The night air now slapped at her and her thoughts. As though she couldn't just roll up the windows and breathe her filtered air and live her filtered life. She was reminded again that some things happened to her whether or not she was aware of them.

That son of a bitch had bugged her car! And now she had the bug in her pocket.

Tempted as she was to chuck it out the window, Cyn held on. Throwing it out was a bad idea. The gunman would know as soon as the bug stopped moving that she'd found it and tossed it. The question was how to keep it moving? And moving *away from her*?

Cyn took a turn at the next dirt road, grabbing an expired store flyer from its sprawl on the passenger seat as she went. She folded it, quickly doing her best to make a hat shape while staying on the road. Then she tucked the bug inside. Having no idea how accurate or high tech the bug was, she moved quickly. She'd already stopped once, and the more she kept moving the less likely she was to alert him to his error–which was tracking her in the first place.

Her shoes weren't good for it, but that didn't really matter. The pumps she could replace, thwarting him she couldn't. So she sank her short heels into the mud and didn't wonder if they'd ever recover. With a mad grin, she set the hat down into the water and watched the slow trickle of the shallow creek carry it away. She just hoped her little boat stayed dry enough to keep the thing functioning until she could get to him.

Returning to her car, she popped the trunk and opened the duffle of spare clothes. With a quick look around she decided that she was alone enough to change right here, and already fucked enough that moving to a new state might very well be in order anyway. So it wouldn't matter if she was arrested for indecency. She stripped down to her leather underwear and bra and traded out for the stretch jeans, t-shirt, and sneakers. The sneakers had metal reinforcements in the sole. The shirt and jeans looked casual, but moved with her. She could kick the gunman in the head and not rip a stitch.

She didn't fold the pretty, trendy clothes, just threw them into the trunk on top of the muddy shoes and slammed back into the car. At stoplights she twisted her hair up and put a few ponytail holders into it. It wasn't the tight, sleek style she preferred, but it would have to do.

Cyn took a back road and pulled up beyond her woods, on the opposite side of her house from the driveway. She ran in, jumping through the barb wire she had strung, making very little noise even as she went bounding through the undergrowth. When she approached the edge where lawn met house, she cursed her own paranoia. Blackout curtains hung on every window, and they went a good foot beyond the glass in each direction, making it virtually impossible to see from the outside if a light was on.

She'd done it so no one would ever again know when the last light went out at night. No one would know her schedule to plan by it. But now she couldn't see into her own house. And she was pretty certain that's where he was.

No. Not *pretty certain*. He was in there. Why else would he have bugged her car? Her real car? Because he wanted to find her real house. And he had. He'd followed her all the way from Norikov's. Through two states and three modes of transportation. He'd showed up at her job. And then he'd disappeared. He'd beaten her home.

The only question was, what did he want?

That she didn't know.

Pausing, she tried to think if it made any difference. Did it matter if he was here to kill her? Or to shut her down? Or . . .

Screw it. She knew what was up.

Skirting through the trees, Cyn came up on the side of the house. She stayed low, not tripping the motion sensors, and slunk under the windows to the front door. Slowly, she slid her key into the first well-oiled lock. She turned each one, then crashed through her own front door.

"Hi, Honey! I'm home!"

She yelled it, knowing that no one would hear for miles. Except that bastard in her house. Cyn's eyes darted left and right, checking behind the door even as her brain swept the room to see if anything was out of place. If it was, she couldn't have said what, but she *knew* he was here. She felt it.

She wanted to holler his name out, but again she was startled that she didn't know it.

Even as that thought registered, he sauntered out from her kitchen, a half eaten apple in his hand. *Her* apple. "Hi, Cynthia." He took another bite, thoroughly enjoying the crisp, juicy fruit.

Cyn felt the rage boiling in her. He didn't even look afraid. Or upset that she'd led him off track and lost his little bug. Or angry that she'd known he was here and burst in on him. And he was too far across the room for her to do anything to him without him seeing her come at him and have plenty of time to prepare.

Shit.

He'd called her Cynthia. She steeled herself, it could have been a good guess. Who else went by 'Cyn', but a 'Cynthia'? She took several even, controlled breaths through her nose. She didn't look like she was saving up oxygen for an explosion, but she was.

She neither acknowledged nor refuted the 'Cynthia' remark. "What brings you to my humble home?"

"Just wanted to visit. See how you live." He took another deep bite of the apple and gestured with it, a man without cares in the world. A man in the same jeans and t-shirt she'd seen in the store, only now he had the shirt pulled up and tucked behind the same two black guns she'd always seen him with. He'd probably had them on him in the mall, only the tee had been loose and would have covered them. He wore them as casually as most people wore their clothes. But with the barrels down and the butts up, probably to grab them easier, he would be anything but casual with them. Lucky her.

"Well," She wanted desperately to cross her arms and show how nonchalant she was. But she couldn't. She wasn't stupid enough to get caught with her hands tucked in. "Now that you've given yourself the tour, I'm sure that you know where the door is. Be sure to let it hit you in the ass on the way out."

He nodded, but didn't move, just continued eating what she was pretty certain was her last Granny Smith. "It's an interesting door." He spoke around bites and wiped at his mouth with the back of his hand. "Lots of locks. Locks on all the windows, too, and blackout curtains. But no security system. Why?"

"You'd have gotten in anyway. So why bother?" She shrugged. Also, someone would have had to visit, and someone would respond when the wire was tripped, or show up if it needed repairs. She didn't want that. She didn't need that. But she didn't need to tell him that either.

Slowly she was making her way toward him. Surely he knew it, too.

"True. I can short pretty much any system."

She was close enough now to take a shot. And he was grinning at her, all proud about his alarm system prowess. Cyn decided to go for it.

She reached out for him, fast as lightning, and watched his arm come up to block. But he blocked the wrong place. She wasn't going for a hit, and so he missed. She plucked the half apple from his hand and with a single motion, before he registered it, bounced it off his forehead.

"Ow!" He backed up, leaving the core where it had landed on hard wood floor. "What the fuck was that for?"

"You broke into my house!" *You're here!* She wanted to scream it. Her skin crawled. Her heart squirmed. She *hadn't* put an alarm system on. She'd *known* someone who really wanted to would be able to get in. But she'd wanted to believe the rest would work–the barbed wire, the mud, the bushes, the location, the motion sensor lights, the locks . . .

It hadn't.

What was most disconcerting was how violated she felt.

And that's what made her lash out.

Cyn put two fists out to him at warp speed. But he backed up and side stepped, and she only caught his shoulder. She struck out again, almost pulling the punches she'd already thrown just to send the next ones. She hammered at him, but he blocked and deflected like a pro.

Finally Cyn decided to use her feet.

She threw a punch, leaning out to him as he stepped still further away, leading them deeper and deeper into her kitchen. Even as her fist almost missed, she turned and went for a heel to the solar plexus. It was a dirty shot, but she wasn't above it when the man had taken away all her recent kills, and he was now in her home. As that thought gurgled through her with a mild nausea, she realized her mistake.

He might have taken some of the blow to his midsection, but he had caught her foot in his hands. And he yanked back on it.

Cyn maintained her balance, but it didn't matter, he reeled her in like a fish. He pressed her back against the front of him, wrapping one strong arm tight around her. That, she could have gotten out of. But she was well and truly held. She knew what had happened before she even registered the synthetic zip of metal against nylon. She felt the gun pressed to her neck, even though not enough time had passed for it to move and get there. As she closed her eyes and gritted her teeth against the need to lash out, she felt his chest heave the great sigh he let loose beside her ear. "You really try my patience, Cyn."

She considered kicking him. She could do it from where she stood–a good fling and her left leg would get high enough that, if she flexed her toe, it ought to go right over her shoulder and into his eye socket. That would feel good.

It would feel *great*, for about a hundredth of a second, until she felt the bullet ripping through her neck. Damnit. You didn't fight when there was a gun against your skin. You waited for a better time to make your move.

But waiting was a bitch.

Lee ground his teeth together. Another standoff with Sin. Just where he wanted to *not* be.

He wasn't up for fighting her in her own home. He'd been here alone plenty long enough to find out the place was a well concealed arsenal. Aside from the weapons gracing the walls in the large back practice room, others were hidden around the house, some in plain sight. There was a tiffany lamp with an unusual knob on top in the living room about ten feet from where they now stood. When he'd frowned and tested the knob, it pulled up, metal singing as the sharp sai-like blade slid free of the lamp.

That had only made him curious, so he'd searched the house like he was on an Easter egg hunt. A fire extinguisher graced the wall in the kitchen, and was probably just what it looked to be, but a wooden block held throwing knives instead of kitchen blades. Under the lip of the counter was a small handled dagger. When he'd gotten down and looked, the thing was just velcro'd there out of site. An umbrella in the bin behind the door wasn't all that creative, but the lethal looking blade inside more than made up for its lack of ingenuity. An accidental tap to a very cylindrical looking doorknob had it popping off and spilling into his hand the very sharp throwing stars it concealed. He had several nicks just from putting them back. And he saw that knobs all over the house bore that same slightly unusual shape.

He growled where he stood. One arm was wrapped around Sin's waist and arms, pinning her. And if the hold didn't work, then the gun his other hand kept pressed to her jugular seemed to be doing the trick. No, he didn't want to fight her. Not here where he'd easily discovered a handful of concealed weapons and who knew what he hadn't found. Not here where she was sure to win. And not at all. Once he'd entered the place, he realized he'd come to forge some kind of truce. Maybe even divvy up some of the people that needed to go, so he and Sin didn't waste their planning time only to find the other had come and the kill was done.

He pushed the gun further into her flesh and felt the tension already strung tight within her ratchet up another few notches. To Sin's credit, her voice was steady. He didn't think she was afraid, although if that was because she didn't fear him or just didn't fear pain and death he had no idea. "What is it that you want?"

"Not this." Killing Sin would be like shredding a Picasso because it didn't match the décor.

She took a deep breath. "I realized that I don't know your name."

He laughed. "Are you trying to humanize yourself to me? It's a good negotiation trick."

She heaved a sigh, but he didn't hear it, he felt it. Otherwise she didn't respond.

"My name is Lee. And you and I keep getting in each other's way. I thought a nice Texas girl like yourself might serve some lemonade and we might work out a schedule."

"Yeah, right." She snorted. But in that moment she relaxed in his hold.

"Are you questioning my motives or your own standing as a nice Texas girl?"

"D. All of the above."

Even urging the gun further into her flesh didn't force any of the tension back into her, and he was probably making a barrel shaped bruise on her neck that she'd have a tough job of hiding for her next shift at her rinky-dink job. "Do you promise to not pick a fight if I let you go?"

This time she outright laughed. "Would you trust me?"

Keeping the gun pressed into her neck, he spun her slowly away from him in a macabre version of a waltz. The instant his hand was free, he slid the second Heckler out and trained it on her. He knew she wouldn't get a gun off him the same way she had before, but ten minutes in her house had convinced him that no one knew what was up the sleeves she wasn't wearing. "Should I trust you?"

Her lips pressed together and she sulked. "Yes."

"All right, then." Slowly he holstered both guns, keeping space between himself and her further than either her arms or legs could reach, and hoping that the step she would need to take to get to him would be enough warning. Although it sure as hell hadn't been before. He had bruises to show for all the times he hadn't seen her coming.

She crossed her arms and leaned in the doorway. Lee decided to take it as a gesture of good faith. But her tone was petulant. "You ate my last apple."

"I was hungry." He'd spent too much of the last two days trailing her, and not enough eating.

"How did you find me?"

His eyebrows went up. "Why are you asking? You know about the bug."

Whatever she'd done with it, it kept moving and it sure wasn't parked in the garage. He'd gotten a little too careless, thinking she'd alert him when she arrived. But, as usual, Sin was smarter than that. Lee crossed his arms and leaned against the kitchen counter, consciously mimicking her gesture. "Speaking of, where is it?"

"In the creek."

He frowned at her. "It should stop working if it gets wet, and it's still beeping." He patted his leg where the vibrations were still buzzing against his skin about every forty seconds. Sin was holding out on him.

"It's riding a little paper boat." She smiled. It didn't reach her eyes.

"Very clever."

Her expression didn't change a bit.

Okay. Compliments not working.

Lee held his tongue and thought for a bit. Mostly because he didn't know what to say. He wanted to scratch his head and look her up and down and take the time to figure out how to crack the shell. He just wanted a conversation for Christ's sake.

In that moment he realized just how desperate he was for a real conversation. He hadn't had any in literally years. He'd emailed under assumed names. Asked the dealers about the guns he bought. He'd ordered the occasional food in a diner from a really chatty waitress, but he hadn't had an actual conversation with anyone since . . . his chest deflated. Sam.

He and Sam had talked that morning. He'd gone to work, and stayed in his office. He'd only even said 'hello' to a few people. Then the nosy neighbor had called and said she thought he should come home because something weird was going on. He'd been afraid he was walking in the door to find Sam was cheating on him. He'd been so very wrong.

"How did you find me?" Sin repeated, her voice a blade cutting through his dark thoughts.

Lee sharpened up. "I followed you."

He could see her trying to reason that out. So he held out an olive branch, "And got lucky."

She didn't respond, but went to the fridge and pulled out a bottle of water. She didn't offer him one, just twisted the cap and drank and waited. Watching him.

"I bugged the rental, then when I didn't see you come out of the return office, I took a guess that you were on the shuttle that left a while later." He explained about the bus station and the second bug. Her expression got more foul with every word.

"Anything else?" She asked it through clenched teeth.

"Sure." He smiled. Why the hell not? She was clearly not going to make this easy. "You're Cynthia May Beller."

Her mouth fell open. Hit number two. She tried to pull her composure tighter around her, but it was too late.

"I followed Leopold's old tracks, and what you told me outside his house that night. But I don't think anyone else will find you." As if that would soothe her wounded little heart.

As if she had one.

As if he still did.

"And you're not twenty-three. You're nineteen." He delivered his line and watched her face change into shades of the fury that she was. The water bottle flew past him into the sink, but he hadn't really seen her throw it there. She came at him, fists flying and a little uncontrolled. Sin angry wasn't the cool, collected fighter he was used to. He couldn't tell if that made her more or less dangerous. He blocked a few hits and took a few as well before getting exasperated and pulling the gun from the holster and aiming it square at her–

Sin knocked it cleanly away from herself, but not out of his grasp.

Lee already had his other gun in hand and, as she followed through on the sweep of her arm that had knocked the first gun out of the way, she found the second planted cleanly in the middle of her chest. As she took a tenth of a moment to register that he'd drawn on her again, Lee pulled the first gun back up and laid the end of that barrel flush against the bone on the bridge of her nose.

He'd ruined his own stare down by having the gun in the way. Damnit, staring lost its effectiveness when you couldn't see both eyes. But he gave it his best, as he wasn't quite ready to sheathe the guns again. "Now, neither of us is civilized people, so I'm not going to suggest we sit down and talk like it. But we might try simply not attempting to *kill* each other for a while and see how that helps. *Capisce*?"

Sin gestured to the guns pressing to her as though he was the one at fault for this particular skirmish. "*I* didn't break into *your* house."

"My apologies, but I didn't think you'd let me in if I just knocked."

The looks she was throwing him said he was right on the money, but still he used his thumbs to set the safeties on the guns and lowered them into their holsters for the second time in ten minutes. "Look, I don't think anyone else is going to find you. And I'm not going to tell them."

"Why not?"

He laughed at that one. "Because we each have enough dirt on the other that neither of us has clean fingers to point."

Her face knit back into the calm façade she usually wore. "You know my birth name and my age. If you know that then you know about my parents and my sister." With her hands she gestured to the house around her. "You know where I live and where I work. I know your first name. If you didn't lie to me."

"I didn't." Then he added, "Fair enough."

Lee had to concede some of it, or kill her. Because she'd surely come after him if she felt she was in an inferior position of knowledge. "My name's Lee Maxwell. I live in the Appalachians in a shack that's not on any named street or map. My wife's name was Samantha, and my little girl Bethany was four." He saw the flicker of humanity in Sin's eyes and didn't regret his decision. "Until three years ago I lived in Chicago with my family and was an accountant."

He didn't expect her response. Lee had thought he might get a nod. A handshake? Some concession that he had evened the playing field. He was even prepared for a good dose of Sin's cynicism and a rapid fire round of how-can-I-trust-what-you-tell-me. But he got none of those.

Instead, she threw her head back and laughed. A real, hysterical laugh.

Lee frowned.

When she looked at him again, it was as though he'd told her he ate glue all the way through high school, and there were tears in her eyes. She laughed again. "You were an accountant?"

Owen closed his eyes. His head hurt, but his heart was happy. His kidneys were very angry at him though. He'd been pounding coffee like it was tequila on a bad night.

It had been twenty-four hours since he'd left Annika in bed all glazed and satisfied looking. He'd missed seeing Charlotte off to school, or home, or over dinner. Again.

He'd missed every meal in between and all sleep since yesterday morning. But he was a junkie on a killer high. He'd gotten the profilers out of bed to re-work what they'd given him. And he wanted it ASAP. Everything was different now that the grudge ninja was a woman. Female serial killers were very rare. Successful ones even more so. And, given the method, training, and intelligence that obviously went into each kill, he had something truly one of a kind on his hands.

This could alter the course of his career.

If he cracked it.

Or if he didn't.

Owen still couldn't get used to the idea Annika had thrown him like a steak to a dog. Neither could Nguyen. The scientist kept shaking his head and muttering something like 'it's a damned woman'. Later he'd added that it better be an ugly woman, because he sure as hell didn't want to risk picking her up in a bar.

Owen had laughed at that one. "I'm certain she's very sweet when she's not a psychopathic killer."

Nguyen had growled and bent back over his table. "I'm going to wait until the profilers get back to us on that one." He was re-calculating weights and trying to re-figure what he could out of what he had. Women pressed the ground differently, bore weight in different places. Some of what they'd estimated of the ninja had been based on broad shoulders and lean hips. That was unlikely now.

"Besides," Owen continued, his chin resting in his hand, his brain acknowledging that he was going loopy from lack of sleep and food, "You aren't in any danger from her. She only goes after bad guys. Unless of course you have a dark side the rest of us are unaware of."

Nguyen shot him a dirty look. "I'm a lab geek, I don't have *any* other side, let alone a dark one."

"What I can't believe, what I keep seeing in my head, is the ground where the woman was pressed when the rapist had her down. If that was the grudge ninja, then we had a full body impression of her."

"You make it sound like she was preserved in the La Brea Tar Pits. It was only a little bit of a ground indentation." Nguyen laughed.

Owen needed to go home. "Would you have casted it if we had known?"

"Hell, yes."

"Then I lament the loss of information." He pushed up from where he sat, feeling bad that he had dragged his fellow agent out of bed for this. Probably Nguyen had just fallen into it last night when he'd gotten the call. Owen would bet good money that Nguyen hadn't gotten laid in that time, either. And now, here he was, abandoning the other man to his work while he himself went home to sleep it off. "I was just stopping by to tell you that the profilers aren't going to get back to us until tomorrow."

Nguyen pointed to the clock that read 12:48am. "It is tomorrow."

"Later today then. They are at just as much of a loss over this 'female' thing as we are." Owen grabbed up the coffee cup that was empty again for the umpteenth time today. Only this time he tossed it instead of refilling it. A feeling in the back of his midsection told him his kidneys had breathed a sigh of relief and were praying for water.

"I don't know," Nguyen mused. "I kind of like the whole 'woman' aspect. Then again, maybe I just like that we have her DNA."

"What?"

Nguyen held up the evidence bag. Several broken, long dark strands were barely visible inside. The bag was labeled as being from the grudge ninja's last scene, and belonging to the 'girl'. But the 'girl' was the ninja.

Owen woke all the way up and smiled. Finally, a break.

Chapter 6

She'd slept with a chair propped under the knob of her locked bedroom door. Before she could even think of lying down, Cyn had pulled the seam ripper from her purse and plucked the stitches at the necks of her bears. The weapons were now mostly tucked under her pillow with a few casually hidden around the room. She'd carefully sewn the seams back together on the bears, just as always, just in case.

The windows were locked and barred and she'd stuck screamers on each pane. The small white plastic boxes would register the frequency if the glass broke and set up an ear shattering synthetic wail when it did. She didn't like the screamers usually, in case it was her trying to break in. But before she climbed under the covers last night she'd made sure there was one on each pane in the bedroom.

She'd had trouble falling asleep, her hand slipped under the pillow in seeming relaxation but fisted around the handle of her dagger. After an hour lying there, hyper-alert and waiting, she'd grown bored. And she'd passed out cold.

As she blinked now, she realized it was nine a.m. She never slept this late. She never slept that soundly. The strength and will that had been required to crawl from the depths of her subconscious had been greater than she could remember since she'd been a child in her own bed with her sister in the room and her parents down the hall.

Noises came from beyond the door. They disturbed her more because they existed than because she found them frightening. The noises were responsible for all of it–the screamers, the chair brace, and probably the deep sleep. That disturbed her most of all. The driving need she felt to be honest with herself. He was out there, tooling around in her house, looking it up and down, and finding God knew what. But she was here, sitting on the bed, slowly coming out of her sleep induced grogginess, and she wasn't even suddenly strung tight, ready to bolt. Cyn was willing to sit on the side of her own bed and contemplate the noises.

Lee.

His name rolled around in there, unfamiliar, suiting him. It was a little like finding the gift tag long after you'd received the present and spent time guessing who it was from.

He'd held two guns flush to her skin last night. He'd royally pissed her off with that move. But none of it had compared to when they'd finally called a truce and he'd sighed, slipping the guns back out of their holsters. Her own hands had just reacted, years of training springing up in that instant. Guns came out, therefore Cyn defended.

But he too had trained, and he defended himself against her, his hands and body slipping lithely out of her reach and his mouth forming the words to tell her to back off and not be so damn jumpy, he'd said truce, hadn't he?

Then he'd held the guns up, used his thumbs to push the buttons and she'd watched as the clips had fallen to the floor. His eyebrows lifted at her, his eyes asking her what the hell she thought of that.

Cyn had thought, great, he just gave away his best defense. Not that she hadn't seen him get a fresh clip into a gun faster than she could begin to guess what he was doing, but he'd popped them out and that put him at a decided disadvantage.

She'd been dense enough, or ungracious enough, that he'd had to nod his newly blonded head at the clips there on her kitchen floor. So she'd looked a little more closely and seen that they were empty. Had been empty all the time.

Doing what any self-respecting girl would have done, she stuffed her rage down and marched into her room, furious that she could have taken him, would have, if she'd known that the guns pressed to her skin held no bullets and had been no threat unless he'd decided to pistol whip her. So she'd turned her room into a fortress against him, and gritted her teeth when he announced through the door he hadn't found a guest bedroom so he'd just take the couch. She didn't even bother telling him to leave. Cyn recognized useless when it bit her on the ass.

A part of her brain suggested that she should have snuck out in the night and put him down. Although, there would have been another fight. He wouldn't ever just let her creep up and sever his neck with a kitchen cleaver. There was also the problem that she'd been so deep asleep that if she'd tried it she would likely stumble around in a stupor and wind up dead or tied up herself. Besides, he did good work. She'd stolen his idea about puncturing the lungs and letting the victim suffocate in clear air. He was right. They needed to divide and conquer. This part where they got in each other's way–spent time planning, and then found they had missed the kill by a day or a few hours–was getting ridiculous.

Changing into decent clothes and braiding her hair tightly first, Cyn went around the room and pulled the screamers off the windows before hiding them at the bottom of her tee shirts. She tucked the weapons beneath the edge of the mattress and into the drawers of the bedside tables. When she surveyed it and found the room normal-looking enough she pulled the straight backed chair out from under the knob and returned it to the corner where it lived. When she'd first furnished the place she'd given herself a moment of grief over her paranoia for keeping it in the room. She'd wanted to not have it there, to not need it there. She was stronger now and could defend herself, but the chair was necessary to her sleep. She slept fine most nights with it waiting quietly in the corner. But she couldn't sleep without it at least in the room, because she would lie awake thinking of the times the chair under her knob had saved her when she'd been small and weak. That she had told Wendy what a chair braced there could do and had maybe saved her sister a little grief. And she always wondered what a chair might have meant that first night. If they'd had one.

He didn't appear when she turned the knob, but Cyn had no doubt that the man knew she was up and about. His hearing was keen and he'd certainly know that she was dressed and would possibly even tease her about the shuffling and scuffs he'd heard behind her door last night.

She stalked the corners, waiting for him to jump out at her. But he didn't. Cyn didn't holler out and neither did Lee. Still he managed to shock her half to death when she did find him.

His back to her, he was scrubbing out her heavy-duty blender at the sink. In what looked like fresh jeans–she couldn't be sure because they might have been identical to the ones he wore last night–he wore a bright sky blue tee-shirt and his blonde hair gleamed where he bent over the pitcher. He was more un-stealthy looking than she had ever seen him before. The shirt and his hair were beacons in the daylight. He might as well have painted a target on the back with an arrow and the words 'strike here'.

His voice rose calm over the running water. "I know, the shirts come in three packs and I often throw away the bright ones. But hey, this is the place to wear it, right? You aren't going to miss just because of a darker shirt. I hope you don't mind that I raided your fridge."

Cyn ignored that. She did mind, but not as much as she minded some other stuff. "So, did you bring a suitcase when you broke in?"

He turned and smiled at her, and it occurred to her for the first time that he could–actually smile and have it reach his eyes. That he might have been attractive if she'd known or understood him only made her uncomfortable. Then he opened his mouth and made it worse. "No, I went out to my car this morning and got my bags."

His mouth widened as though he, too, realized she'd slept through someone coming and going from her own front door. But he didn't say it. Which just pissed her off more.

"Well. I have to work today. So you'll have to go, but we can set up a time to map things out and make a phone tree and trade ringtones. All right?"

Leaning back against the counter, he picked up a large plastic tumbler in the pink feminine color she had chosen and swallowed whatever he had blended. It smelled like he'd used a good portion of her fresh fruit and her eyes cut over to the basket to see that indeed the pile there was noticeably lower than it had been yesterday.

He held the cup out to her, mind-reading yet again, "Do you want some?"

Cyn shook her head, although if she was denying that she wanted a taste of her own food, or that he was somehow reading everything on her face, she didn't know.

With a shrug, he began gulping the whole thick drink down.

She waited, arms folded against her chest as though she knew he wouldn't come after her. And she wanted to take a moment to wonder why she knew that. She hadn't known that about anyone except Wendy, and Wendy had been dead for a long time. But Lee didn't give her the luxury of sorting out her thoughts. "Call in sick to work."

"I can't." She threw it back at him as though he had lobbed the keys unexpectedly and just said 'catch!' "I am nothing if not dependable. I never call in sick."

He lowered the cup, the pink color having lost its feminine power in his grasp. Of course this was a man who shot dogs in cold blood. She didn't really need to worry about his sensitive side. Being who she was, she likely wouldn't see it if it slapped her across the face. Lee stared at her. "You are nothing."

Her jaw hit the floor. Of all the insults in all the world–

Her chest closed around the feeling, locking it tight away from her brain, not letting it through.

Lee didn't notice or didn't care. "You don't exist. This house is owned by Cynthia Cooper Macey. You're Cynthia May Beller. Who works at the job?"

Her jaw clenched, but she answered. "Cyndy."

He laughed at that one, only making her arms press tighter against her ribs and her brain wonder where he got off. "Were you ever 'Cyndy'?"

She lobbed that one back to his side of the court. "You were an accountant."

The frown wasn't fierce, but it slammed onto his face. He seemed only mildly disturbed, but something played under the surface, something deeper. Maybe the memory of her deep, deep laughter the night before. "Yes, what's wrong with that?"

"Did you wear a tie every day? Button down shirts? Add your little columns of debits and credits?" She smirked.

"It's no more than 'Cyndy' selling women the right shoes to go with the dress." The frown pulled tighter.

She kept poking at him. "Sure it is. I play at Cyndy. You *were* him. You took your briefcase to work every day and paid your mortgage and wondered if your wife was having an affair with the mailman."

As the words tumbled out of her mouth she saw that she'd pushed something she hadn't meant to. His eyes changed from irritated to irate. She'd hit too close to home, even though she'd only found it humorous that he had been a pencil pusher and she had meant to goad him.

His hand shot out and clamped at her throat. In less than a blink she was slammed against the wall behind her, only barely registering that he held her there tight. That her hands and arms were taut, but she wasn't striking out, wasn't defending herself even though she could. And he wasn't cutting off her air. Merely making what would have been a terrifying point to anyone but her.

No, none of that frightened her.

It was the boiling storm in his eyes that frightened her.

"Yes, I was. All that. And it was my error about the mailman. And I thought I was fine and strong. And I was proud and stupid. And overconfident. What were *you* before they came?!?"

Her chest expanded.

"A child."

The profilers' papers burned holes in his brain. They'd been waiting when he arrived this morning. The profilers Owen was using worked out of a lab two time zones earlier. So his sleeping late–until eight–had hardly been a loss when they hadn't gotten him anything until noon their time.

He'd read every inch of pure scientific speculation. These guys were good. It was why he used them even when he couldn't see them or shake their hands. The husband and wife team was on FBI retainer. Owen could call them if he went through the proper channels, but he wouldn't ever know 'Bob' and 'Dana's real names. The other problem was that they were occasionally wrong. But there was never any way to predict where. Even they had run full analyses on their misses to see if they were consistently screwing up a particular category of information or something they could correct.

So far nothing.

So Owen had to trust what he held in his hands. And later, when he caught his ninja, as he was sure he eventually would, he would be able to look at the profile and say 'they told me so'.

Unfortunately, there was nothing here that gave him new direction. Just confirmation of his own suspicions. Bob and Dana were certain that the ninja was out for revenge.

Duh. Owen figured anyone with Intro Psych 101 and a look at those holes in the victims could tell you that.

They said tags were written because the ninja wanted to be the good guy. So the finder would know that the person had deserved to die. The ninja believed she was doing good work. Probably wasn't religious, as evidenced by lack of ritual of any Judeo-Christian variety. Most of those who murdered in the name of God left something, or performed some cleansing for the soul of the dead. The ninja wanted these men in hell.

Owen read more.

The ninja was likely under forty-five, due to the physical strength and limitations of older female bone structure. Probably a very close family member was murdered by a mafia member as the mafia was the major source of victims. Although the ninja had turned vigilante, the focus remained on the Russian Mafia, specifically the Kurev family. Other killings were of criminals with clear-cut records and evidence of abuse of women and children. When the victims couldn't be ID'd as the definitive bad guys, the ninja often lured them into the crime or caught them in the act. She was careful to never get the wrong guy.

She had possibly lost a child to the mafia. Definitely a husband.

This put her over twenty-eight.

And she had likely been raped or someone very close to her had been. Rape had been listed among the crimes of every man who'd been maimed or injured in his gonads. Each had suffered for that crime specifically.

Owen pulled his brows up for that one.

That made sense. The huge hole in Leopold's cock was different from the other careful, precise, puncture-only wounds he had received. And there had been several bodies where the coroners had made comments about beatings to the gonads. Owen remembered one med examiner saying 'it looked like someone took a baseball bat and knocked his balls into his throat'. He also remembered gulping air and letting out his own gurgled 'Ow' after hearing that one.

But still, besides the age range, which Owen had already had a ballpark guess on, and the rape theory, which he'd been rolling around, too, there was nothing new here. Just a pat on the back to his own deductive reasoning. Maybe he deserved some kudos for paying attention in his 'Psychopathic Killers' course.

He lowered the pages to the desk and his head into his hands. Taking deep breaths, he consoled himself over the lack of usable material here. He rubbed the bridge of his nose. Picked up his coffee cup, which was disappointingly weightless, and set it back down. He rolled his head on his neck several times, and contemplated quitting his job.

The ninja believed she was doing good work.

At no point had they found a body and done anything less than prove that the bastard probably deserved a worse death than he had gotten. Agent Bean consistently reminded him that the FBI had to apprehend the ninja–that the ninja had no right to play God. Owen had to bite his tongue to not ask, 'then who gave the FBI the right to do it?'

Until she started fucking up and taking out good citizens, Owen's personal goal was just to solve the puzzle. But he didn't kid himself that being happy about solving the case would mean he'd be happy about finding the ninja behind bars.

Just then, Blankenship opened the door and handed over some papers.

"The brunette's the real color."

Owen took the words from the other agent, even as he turned over Nguyen's report in his hands. Blankenship wasn't telling him anything that Nguyen hadn't told him last night just from looking at the hair strands. But he thanked his useless partner anyway.

Nguyen was long gone. Off home, to hopefully sleep off his twenty-four hour lab binge. Maybe get laid. Owen sure hoped so. The man could use some loosening up.

Blankenship said something of little to no import and closed the door behind him as he went, leaving Owen with the silence of the room and the roaring of the printouts in his hands. If Annika was right–and she was rarely wrong–he was holding a full DNA report on his grudge ninja. His ninja was female–no male posing as a hapless victim to entice the rapist. The XX genetics had been visible in the hair after two minutes in Nguyen's skilled hands with the microscope.

Now the paperwork spoke to him in weird numbers and told tales that Owen couldn't yet hope to understand. Nguyen had pointed out digits, circling and numbering them in red ink. On a separate page he had typed what amounted to footnotes for his layman friend. Of course they were typed. Nguyen wasn't Owen's age, the man probably didn't know how to operate a manual pencil. The crank sharpener that Owen had mounted on his wall to calm his nerves and give his hands something to do had baffled the younger agent. Nguyen had pointed out that mechanical pencils had been invented long ago, and sharpening was something his own grandfather had done. It, too, should have gone the way of the horse and carriage. The scientist didn't even appreciate the smell of the churned wood shavings. And here were typed notes. It was surprising that the man was even capable of hand-writing the few scribbled jottings on the pages.

But Owen shook off his thoughts and turned toward the knowledge Nguyen had given him. Regardless of the format, the man was full of deductions.

She was blood type O-positive.

That didn't match any they had found, except for some at the scene of the Korean child thief. And he'd been O-positive as well. So Owen's money said that their ninja didn't shed blood at the scene. Ever. She was that good.

She was a carrier for Cystic Fibrosis.

Even Nguyen had pointed out that was only useful in finding her if they had some other leads. Mostly her DNA was helpful in that it could be matched the next time they found it. If they should get so lucky it wouldn't just be evidence at a scene but on a live person.

The telomere quantity on the DNA told them she was young, probably early twenties.

And that made Owen's head snap up. Twenties?? That was way too young. This woman was skilled. Years of practice were required to do what she did. This, coupled with that O-positive info, meant that she hadn't ever taken a serious hit that they knew of – as there had never been O-positive blood found at a scene. No twenty-year-old could have done that. Could a twenty-year-old have the kind of strength that was required to pull off the feats he'd seen the evidence of?

Owen still wanted to believe that the ninja hadn't pinned Leopold with a bow and tag because the mafia would recognize her. Wanting to hang onto the hope that he hadn't been wrong, Owen had altered the theory just a little to fit a female perp. Now, the ninja was a wife. Her husband had been involved. And a wife who'd had time to train like this would have to be, at the very least, in her thirties. Just as Bob and Dana had proposed.

How strong was that 'probably'? How early were those 'early' twenties?

Owen had to call Nguyen.

But the man was likely asleep. And it wouldn't be right to wake him. Not after all the times he'd come in on short notice. Not after all the crimes he'd provided the conclusive evidence for. Not after all the things he'd been able to tell Owen over the years that had sent him searching in the right direction.

So Owen did something he knew he was horrible at.

He set the file aside to wait.

Purposefully he stood and left to fetch a fresh cup of coffee. The hallway brimmed with other agents. As it was just ten a.m. it was no wonder. But they looked at him, and smiled tightly before looking away. He smiled tightly back.

Before, when he was new to the agency, he'd wondered if he was about to get axed and everyone knew it but him. If that was why they smiled those tight-lipped looks at him. But it had been Blankenship, years later, that had hauled him into the bathroom, shoved him at the mirror, and pointed out the look on his face. Owen had been scowling even as he tried to smile at the other agents as he passed. No wonder they looked at him this way. By now he was used to it.

On his rounds, he stopped in the men's room. Then checked in the door at Bean's office, but his superior was on the phone and waved him away. He went into the break room and pulled a clean Styrofoam cup from the dispenser and poured fragrant coffee. For the briefest moment he wondered who had made it, but then he decided to scald his tongue just a touch and took a deep sip. He headed back to his desk.

No one spoke to him the entire time.

He would pick up Charlotte this afternoon. He'd just called Annika to tell her so when Blankenship stuck his head in the door. "We got another one."

* * *

Sin just pissed him off. Lee really wanted to hate her. He wanted to shoot her and remove her from the equation. But he couldn't.

Some humanity remained in him, even if it didn't seem to in her. Not until those moments when she threw her own suffering in his face. And for some reason hers always bested his own. She'd been raped, as a child. Then to add greater trauma, making the rape seem like nothing, her parents had both been executed before her eyes. She was right. She'd been a child.

From the looks of her, she hadn't been anything of the sort from that moment on.

He let her go and flexed his fingers while Sin stood still against the wall where he had pinned her. She didn't change her expression. The flash of fury when she had uttered those two words had vanished as fast as it had come–her face now a mask of calm and irritation all in one look. He wouldn't have believed she'd actually said it, felt something, if he hadn't been able to hear the words reverberating around in his head.

He wanted to concede. To throw, 'you're right' out to her and see if she caught it, if she volleyed it back. Instead, figuring Sin wouldn't give at all, he went halfway. "We need to work something out."

Her eyebrows lifted. "I need to get to work." Her head tilted at him, and he knew that, though he may try, he wouldn't get her to budge an inch. Apparently Cyndy was never absent, never late. And Sin wouldn't let her be.

So he didn't try arguing. "Fine. I'll be here when you get back."

"Hmmm."

Yeah, that didn't sound good. Lee waited.

He didn't have to wait long. Sin shrugged. "Why don't you give me your number and I'll call you and we'll work it out?"

"Because I'm not stupid." He blinked, wondering what the hell she was up to. She was alive after all the kills she'd perpetrated. He'd seen her work. She was smarter than that.

But he was met with a great woe-is-me sigh and Sin's crossed arms.

She didn't speak, and so Lee went for another tack. "I don't even have a phone."

"Really?"

Interesting. Sin was engaged.

"Of course. I live in a shack. I don't exist. So I don't have a phone. Whatever we work out, we need to do it before I go." He shrugged. "Or I could just kill you, and then I don't have to work anything out."

Sin's answer to that was to throw her head back and laugh, a full hearty laugh. The likes of which he hadn't heard since last night when he said he'd been an accountant. "I don't think you can kill me. I think you would have done it already if you could."

As would you. Lee thought to himself. But again he had to admit that she was right. He couldn't kill her. However, if he was smart, he'd use her to his advantage. "So go to work, and I'll be here when you get back, and we'll work something out."

She growled at him. Actually growled.

Lee blinked. He remembered Bethy doing that to him. Usually when she was mad, she would growl and stomp off. But Bethy had been four.

Sin, too, stomped off. Presumably to get ready for work.

There was no way in hell he was going to get a phone, and he sure as shit wouldn't call her. The last thing he needed was a phone conversation between himself and another killer where they discussed who they were going to target next. He might as well dial 9-1-1 on himself before he went in to get his victim. He didn't want *any* phone calls–any record at all–between him and Sin. If he was never connected to her in any way, it would be too soon.

He bided his time, checking out the house and finding a few other weapons as he went. The sink ran, she made noises in her room, something whirred. He didn't look.

Sin didn't emerge. Cyndy did.

Her hair curled softly around a face that any man would look twice at. She looked young, but old enough for any wayward thoughts to be perfectly legal. Her face and mouth were painted, and she even wore a soft, friendly smile that Lee was certain had never graced Sin's lips. A thin skirt swished lightly around long, bare legs, and he was struck wondering what the hell had happened to the Sin he knew.

Or maybe didn't know.

The eyes that were sweet and dark suddenly went to bitter chocolate on him and the full mouth pressed to a lethal line.

There she was.

"You should leave my house while I'm gone."

"Why?" That made no sense.

"Because it's mine." Her voice was Sin's, hard and cold. It came from the depths of her chest, and her feet were rooted solid to the floor. A Mac truck could wrap its thousand pound engine around Sin. Sin would likely walk away.

Lee wasn't a Mac truck. "I know where you live. I could leave, but I'll just come back. I'd like to use the punching bag, and take a shower."

Although he would have thought it wasn't possible, her lips pressed tighter together.

With a sigh, Lee imagined she was ten, and tried reasoning with her that way. "Please? Where else am I going to go? The Days Inn?"

She simply stared at him.

He tried again. "I promise not to play with your toys."

Finally she looked him square in the eyes. "I have to go, and I don't have time to fight with you about it. Be here when I get back, and we'll work things out and then you'll leave."

"Fair enough." He nodded, knowing agreement was the absolute best thing he could do with this lethal, petulant, woman-child.

She slung her purse over her shoulder and headed for the door, looking for all the world like a wife leaving for her job. But at this point he could count seven weapons she passed within touching distance as she made her way to the door. Should she choose, her hand could have snaked out and grabbed any of them. Four could have been flung at him from where she stood. And Sin was fatally accurate. He could be dead before she turned the front knob.

Lee liked to imagine that he would be able to get at least one Heckler out of its holster in time to return the favor. He'd loaded the clips this morning, thinking that he might have led someone here. He'd followed Sin. What if someone had followed him? He'd swept for bugs, but really, he could so easily miss one, it could be anywhere. So he'd put bullets in the bad, black guns this morning, not for protection from Sin, but for her.

Still, even knowing her temper, and knowing what she could do, he couldn't resist. As her hand touched the knob after unbolting all the locks she'd installed, he sang out, "Dear, will you be home in time for dinner?"

Her eyes didn't even narrow as she graced him with a bored look. "I'll be home by seven, and, no, I'm not making you dinner."

Lee smiled then turned away. Let her throw one of her knives in his back. Heckling her was worth it, and he hadn't cared about his own pain or death for three long years. He heard the click and slide of tumblers as she bolted him into the house. Not that that would keep him in. Windows adorned every room, and he'd lift one and go out the way he'd come in. But he didn't want out. He wanted to play.

For an hour he searched the house top to bottom, finding fifteen other weapons. Every closet had a sword and sheath velcro'd to the wall just out of sight. All you had to do was reach in the doorway and tap the wall just inside the frame. Your fingers would close safely around the sheathed blade and a small jerk would let it fall into your hands. Sweet.

Lee had only the slightest pang about going into her bedroom. But he pushed it aside in a heartbeat. It was too interesting, and he didn't believe Sin had any tender feelings for him to worry about. After Samantha had died he'd learned not to waste his concern. It was simply too much energy, and so often misplaced.

He found the sickles under the bed. They were kamas, he now knew. You didn't run into something like Sin and not research it. A few internet videos later and he'd realized that the martial arts tournament winners had nothing on her. They flipped and yelled and flung the blades like a majorette, but in Sin's fingers the weapons floated.

Her sais were tucked under her pillow, crossed in a way that would be uncomfortable to sleep on. But he had to try it. So he laid down on her bed, putting his head where he suspected hers would be and felt the straight blades crossed behind his neck, which turned out to not be all that uncomfortable. When he reached up, one hand to either shoulder, his fingers curled easily around the handles and pulled them out. Even muffled under the weight of the pillow there was a deadly ring as the blades slid across each other.

His Dad had set him up with his first rifle as a wedding present for him. For Sam, a crock pot. But he'd pulled his son aside and given the rifle, told him where to keep it, where to stash the ammo, and that if anyone broke into the house he was to first use the pump action cock, then speak. Anyone who was stupid enough to keep coming was a fool. Everyone recognized the deadly *ch-chnk* of a rifle being cocked. But Lee thought this sound, this *zing* that reverberated even as you readied your blades, was far more deadly. It got even scarier when you were stared down with those soulless brown eyes.

He considered trying to just slip the blades back under the pillow, then considered how embarrassed his soul would be, looking down and seeing Sin discover his body as he'd likely sever his own neck trying to put them back. And Sin would be pissed that he'd bled to death all over her comfy, girly sheets.

So he carefully rolled to his feet and tried to arrange the weapons the way he'd found them. Tilting his head and seeing what he'd done, Lee was certain that he hadn't done it right, he just wasn't sure which part was wrong or how to fix it. Only that Sin would know. And he knew full well he'd not just broken but smashed the promise not to play with her toys. Oh well.

He considered playing with the kamas, but saw that they were dark wood and had the sheen of an often handled tool. He recognized them as the ones he'd seen her kill Leopold with. She'd be pissed if he played with those, especially when he'd seen a practice set on the wall in the playroom. Looking around one more time, Lee spotted the ladder-back chair in the corner. That explained the dragging noise from last night. Smart girl. But then, he'd never thought her anything less.

Not able to resist, he rifled through her drawers a little, pulling up t-shirts and jeans that had obviously come from her store. Like any ordinary woman's bureau. But there were alarms, little high-pitched ones that made noise when glass broke, tucked under the shirts. Sin was not ordinary. His eyes flew wide when he opened the bottom drawer and found leather bras and underwear.

Startled, he just slapped it shut and figured it served him right for looking. He half expected a live rattlesnake to strike him before he got the drawer closed. He hadn't needed to see that.

Lee shook it off the only way he knew how–physically. He went directly into the play room and laid into the punching bag, striking it until he worked up a sweat and felt the resultant zing in his knuckles and wrists. He wanted to hit the practice dummy, but even as he set it up and adjusted the height he spotted the cracks in the casing. Damn girl had really kicked the shit out of the thing.

And those dummies were meant to take abuse. Just not the kind Sin dished out.

When he couldn't resist anymore he pulled the sais off the wall. Getting a firm grip on the handles, he mocked a few of the stances he'd seen on the internet videos. Long mirrors Sin had mounted to the wall told him what an idiot he looked like. So he tried it Sin's way–he twirled them. Or he tried to. Lee found quickly that he couldn't hold onto the damn things. They didn't spin in his hands. He couldn't even flip them and catch the handle with any accuracy. Only his quick reflexes had saved his feet from being pounded or speared.

Putting the sais back on the wall, he pulled down the kamas. These felt better, sturdier. They had more weight, smooth wooden handles he could compare to a hammer–something he'd held before. He didn't even attempt spinning them, just swung them out, checking out his attack radius. He could now slice the neck of a man more than two feet beyond his fingertips. He swung a few more times liking the feel of the movement. Then he tried swinging the sickle in a circle from his wrist, gaining speed and momentum before he reached his arm out and struck.

The slash of air from the metal gave him a sense of certainty he'd only felt before when his fingers closed around the butt of his 9mm guns. He felt a measure of safety holding this weapon. He swung again. Again. Again.

He didn't know how many times he did it. It felt empowering, and he arced the weapon, not even registering feeling as his breath was knocked violently out of him and his stomach clenched with the sudden urge to puke. Only as he hit the floor on his knees did he gain enough sensation to realize he'd done it to himself. Pain radiated all along his left arm, and he curled into a fetal position even as he grabbed his elbow where he'd whacked himself in the funny bone.

Still his stomach tried to purge itself of the protein shake he'd fed it just a few hours ago. His mouth worked like a fish, his eyes wide and glassy, and his one coherent thought from face-down on the mat was to wonder whether or not Sin was standing there behind him. He gulped again and waited for the pain to pass.

What a fucking moron he was. And he'd have a bruise to show for it, too. Sin would laugh eventually. Finally his lungs allowed air into his system and the nausea reduced to a sickening pain radiating from his elbow. The kamas lay gracelessly on the floor where he'd dropped them, only a few inches from where he'd dropped himself.

With the strength of will he acted on but did not feel, he pushed himself to his feet and hung the weapons back on the wall. They mocked him from their point in front of his face. He was tempted to pull a Heckler and shoot them to splinters just for spite, but knew it wouldn't solve anything. He also knew his left arm, luckily not his preferred arm, wouldn't likely straighten all the way for days.

Shaking his head at his own foolishness, he went into the hall bathroom and found there was no soap or shampoo of any kind in the shower stall. There was none at the sink, no toilet paper or anything indicating the bathroom was ever used as such. When he tested it, the showerhead creaked and gave up a trickle of brownish water, confirming his suspicions before it spurted to life and shot clear water out.

No one used this bathroom.

Under the sink various things were stored. But no one ever visited Sin. Ever.

With a raised eyebrow to the wall, he cranked off the water and headed to her bathroom only to frown at the collection of girly, fruity bath products there. This was Cyndy's bathroom. With a shudder, he headed out and searched his bag, pulling out the one bottle of squeeze soap he used for everything. He'd rather brave the unused shower stall than spend a moment in that tub that would leave him feeling like he might as well be wearing a bra and garters. Only at the last minute did he remember to steal a towel.

A half hour later he came out, clean and steamy. A thick fog rolled out into the hallway as he opened the bathroom door, and for a brief moment he wished there was some way to do this when he got face to face with those bastards. It would be nice to appear as if he emerged from hell to kill them. But it would only be that he appeared to emerge from hell. In three years he hadn't emerged once.

Looking down, Lee also realized that he was unarmed, and aside from a thin towel, he was entirely naked. Nope, not worth the smoke effect. He grabbed the Heckler from the cabinet under the sink, the only place he could think of to keep it from taking a bath with him. It folded neatly into position in his palm as he held it, even though he was unaware of the action.

Two minutes later he was dressed, this time in a long sleeved t-shirt that was a bit too warm for the temperature in the house, but the right length to hide his elbow, which was already turning an embarrassing shade of purple.

He sat on the couch for just a moment and saw the shadows in the room were longer than he'd expected. The clock said it was six, and Lee felt his eyes widen. Sin would be home in an hour.

For fifteen minutes he sat there, enjoying the couch. He hadn't had one in a long time. The motel rooms he rented had beds and maybe a straight backed chair or two. He'd pushed the cabin couch out as far away from the small building as he could, and he never sat on it even out in the woods. While he'd enjoy the comfort and the air, the thought of the things scuttering by underneath the cushions, or maybe just biting him in the ass, was enough to keep him off it.

He watched the clock move and sank himself deeper into the cushions. He rested his head against the heavily padded back. For a moment Lee closed his eyes and imagined he was in Chicago. This was the position Samantha would find him in at about this time in the evening. He could imagine her feet were planted not ten inches from his own, and she'd likely have a spatula in her hand as she prepared dinner. "Long day?"

He could hear her voice, crystal clear inside his head. But not outside. And he could see her face full of sympathy and warmth, but when he opened his eyes she disappeared, and he was in the home of a killer, and he was a killer himself. And he was hungry, and Sam wasn't fixing him dinner.

So Lee pushed himself off the couch and decided to raid Sin's kitchen.

She had two four pound chickens still in the bag and a bundle of carrots that sported thin, hair-like roots. A big bag of broccoli tops was pushed to the back of the fridge behind a huge box of blocks of butter. A pound of grated parmesan cheese blocked a jar of applesauce and a tub of spaghetti sauce. The cabinets told the same story. Jesus, Cyndy had to have a freaking Costco card. At least it all looked relatively healthy. He couldn't find a single Oreo or Cheeto anywhere.

Standing in the open door, he let the cold out of the fridge for a few minutes before deciding. Then he pulled a chicken free of its bag. He hacked it to pieces thinking Sin was better suited for this job than he was. She'd fillet the damn thing in seconds.

Laying the chunks he'd made onto a cookie sheet, Lee coated them in spray olive oil and cranked up the heat on the oven. He cooked the way he always did, throwing things together and heating them until they looked done. He cut pears and simmered them in the applesauce, he steamed broccoli and boiled white long-cut rice he'd found in the pantry. He needed an apron with ruffles, he hadn't cooked like this in so long, but he didn't expect Sin to serve him a three course meal. If he wanted to eat, he figured he had to prepare it himself.

He was again enveloped in steam when the locks started clicking and turning on the front door. As it swung open he couldn't resist calling out. "Hi Honey, you're home!"

Water gurgled and hissed in front of him and he couldn't hear her, but by her facial expression she growled at him again. Cyndy's hair was just as neatly in place as when she left, her back as straight, her makeup just as fresh. For all he knew she'd stepped out the door hours ago, freeze dried herself, and thawed just now before she came in.

She marched by making no comment that he'd fixed her dinner.

Lee just kept stirring and checking the oven. He figured he'd feel the knife between his shoulder blades any second. But it didn't come. Instead footsteps stomped into the room and Sin appeared, in cotton leggings with thick socks and a trim long t-shirt that covered her ass only in the sense that it came that low. With her hair slicked up in a high, folded-over ponytail and her face scrubbed free of makeup, she'd taken ten years off her age. She looked trendy enough, not that he knew what was in style right now, but he guessed she was dressed more for kicking ass than looking cool. A looser t-shirt could have been grabbed in fistfuls, no decent hold could be gotten on this one. Loose pants would get in the way. Even the ponytail offered no grip as it didn't swing free.

When she didn't speak, Lee pointed with the spatula, "I made you dinner." He offered a false grin as well.

"Gosh, thanks."

"You're welcome." He scooped the broccoli onto plates he pulled from the cupboard. Sin pulled a water bottle from the fridge and began downing it. She offered nothing except her constant watch until Lee carried the plates to the small table in the corner of the eat-in kitchen. Her only concession was to sit with him and begin to eat.

Wishing she'd say something, and knowing full well she wasn't likely to, Lee chewed for a few moments, enjoying the food and the simple pleasures of a home. Even if it was a lonely one. Even if his present company was everything less than pleasant.

When he was about halfway finished with the meal, he began talking. "I made up a list." He kept the paper on his side of the table, and kept talking. "It's everyone I could think of on short notice that I'd like to take out."

She offered a small nod. "Me, too."

Well, great minds thought alike. She pushed her list at him, and he saw it was on the store letterhead. "You didn't write this on a pad of paper did you?" His alarm skyrocketed and he imagined having to break into the store at night and steal the pad. God, breaking into a mall would be awful.

She gave him a withering look. "What, so the cops can read the impression on the page underneath? Give me some credit. Any seven year old who's read an elementary school whodunit knows better than that, Lee."

He nodded and ate another forkful of chicken smothered in baked pears and sauce. It was good enough to make him want a full stove. He shoveled in rice and passed his list to her, skimming hers as he went. "So we each get the people who turn up only on our list, and we divvy up the duplicates."

"Sounds like a plan, Stan." She pulled a pencil from a stack of note supplies at the end of the table where a phone was perched and began marking up his list.

While he was a little irked at her forwardness, Lee didn't comment. About two thirds of the names were identical. No surprise there. They'd both been hit by Leopold. Both their families had been targeted by the same branch of the same Russian Mafia organization. No wonder they'd been running into each other so much. Sin's father had been an accountant, too. For the first time Lee wondered if maybe he hadn't held the same position her old man had.

She looked up, swallowed the bite she was chewing, and started bartering. "I'd like Winston. I have his tag already composed."

"Fine, give me Dimitri Kurev." The second cousin of the kingpin was wreaking havoc all around the Great Lakes, where it appeared he'd been given free rein.

With a tilt of her head and shake of reluctance, Sin conceded. The meal continued this way with the two of them bartering for who got to kill whom in between bites of broccoli and chicken. It was sick, but Lee found himself enjoying the banter. Sin gave him two hits for one she really wanted to do, although she wouldn't say why.

When the list was done, Lee polished off the last of the chicken on his plate and stood up to get a second helping, offering to fetch more for her. Sin refused. For a brief moment he marveled that his manners hadn't deserted him, and wondered why they had reappeared for this bad-tempered creature.

Sin's voice caught him from behind while he plated up another whole meal. "What if I stumble across someone who needs to go? I took out a Korean selling children into prostitution because I found out about him. It wasn't pre-planned."

Re-seating himself and fighting the urge to put a napkin in his lap, something Sam had always insisted on after Bethany had arrived, Lee sighed. "I don't know. Take them out."

"But what if you're there? Do you ever do that? Just hear about something and go after the person responsible?"

"Of course." He pushed chicken into his mouth, not liking where the conversation was going, but not knowing what to do about it. "Fine, you take the ones west of the Mississippi and I'll take the ones east."

Sin blinked. "You're serious?"

"I don't have a phone. And I sure as hell don't want you writing to me at general delivery and leaving a paper trail about what I'm doing. So no communication. If you want to get yourself caught, be my guest, but leave me out of it."

At that moment, it occurred to him with cold clarity that had just become a complete impossibility. They'd been going after the same people. Certainly not in the same way. But when Sin was caught and they asked if she knew about other mafia deaths what would she say? What would he, if he were the one questioned? Jesus. This was getting twisted, and that was saying a lot from a situation that already had more knots than a macramé convention.

"I'm not going to get caught." She could have been telling a friend that she was perfectly capable of sneaking off to a party after her parents thought she was in bed. Her expression matched exactly that sentiment. But in a moment where the clouds in his head parted and things were revealed, Lee realized that Sin had been denied all those moments. And she'd never reclaim them.

"Look, if you see someone who needs to be taken out of the equation, do it. We'll argue about it when we run into each other."

Setting her fork down she threw another volley at him, even as he shoveled food in as fast as he could. "How will we know when it's time for a new list?"

He liked that about her–the perfect certainty that they wouldn't fail. He pulled at her paper. "I can reach you. I'd tell you where you can find me, but really you turn left at the two big oaks, and go until you see a big boulder . . ." He stopped as he saw her eyebrows rise. "It's a shack in the Appalachians. You'd never find it, and that's the idea. So, why don't you pick someone to do last, and I'll keep an ear to the ground. When I hear that he's gone, I'll be here within three days."

She obviously didn't like that. Gears turned in her head. Lee wanted to hold out an olive branch, but didn't find one to offer. Then he realized he didn't want to hold one out after all. Sin was immature, grumpy, and she could take him down with just a word or two to the wrong people.

By the time she conceded, Lee had the feeling of ants under his skin. He popped up from the table, rinsed his dishes and loaded them into the washer. Grabbing his already packed bag, he slung it over his shoulder and bolted from the door before she could tell him to leave. A quick 'good-bye' was all the concession he gave, as he left Sin at the table with her list.

Breathing a little easier, he sank into the woods, deftly avoiding the strung barbed wire, and crunching undergrowth like an elephant until he reached his car. He cranked the engine and felt his insides begin the same soft growl as the car. With his hand across the backseat, he guided the kitty out of the woods and pointed her to the freeway.

What the hell had he gotten himself into?

He was tied to Sin now, whether he liked it or not. He'd only avoided it in the past because they hadn't seen each other, but from the moment they first made contact they'd been linked. And Lee didn't want to be linked to anyone. Certainly not someone he didn't trust. Someone hard enough to sleep with blades under her pillows. Someone who might be thinking the same thing as him, and be even harder of heart than he was. Who might just have the balls to take out the competition so she wouldn't have to worry about him anymore.

Shit.

He didn't breathe again until he hit the Arkansas/Tennessee border.

Chapter 7

Owen was frustrated as hell, and ready to pull his own hair out. Although that would only add to Nguyen's hair supply. What they had showed the same curled, pulled-from-a-hairbrush look as the others. They matched perfectly to the ones picked up at the previous scenes. They were the same age as the others, confirming that they hadn't fallen off a head in recent history. But there were no brunette, female strands. Not long, not yanked, not broken and short. And the forensics team had vacuumed the whole damn site.

The body bore a big red bow, hand tied, just like the others with wide wired ribbon. They'd checked that out, too, and it was three inches wide, red velvet and sold at every fucking craft store around the nation all year long. No help there. The tag was watercolor paper, stiff and mildly textured. All the same brand, all purchasable at any of approximately two-billion art stores world wide. The pen the tag was written with was a fine quality .3mm gel rollerball, black ink. Nguyen thought it was a Papermate Launch, modeled after the astronauts' pens. That meant it cost thirty or so dollars and was just as generic as everything else that had been used.

Christ, the ninja was on top of fucking everything.

Owen knew he should be grateful. One, few FBI agents got the glory of tracking down a serial killer. Of those who did, most of the serial killers they hunted were impulse killers. Eventually they made mistakes, and got themselves caught. He was tracking a planner, a coordinated killer, a career maker.

The second thing he knew he should be grateful for was the fact that the ninja wasn't taking out average citizens or, worse yet, women or kids. Other agents who tracked repeated murderers operated under the gun. It was worse than being a hostage negotiator, and they'd all had coursework and training on how not to feel haunted about the ones who died while you were still solving the case. If you were tracking a killer and he got to someone before you could stop him, the guilt could eat you alive. Owen had no such feelings. Every time the ninja killed Owen thought, *Way to go, girl.* These men died harsh, painful deaths. And deserved worse. Owen was grateful they were gone, and agreed that the world was a better place without them.

Only Owen now realized he didn't get to live in the better world he was making. He didn't really want this career that kept him raking through the muck of humanity. Finding the ninja would make his place here, because he *would* find her. And then he would leave. He settled back into the uncomfortable chair, making himself at home at the kitchen table, with the latest in the growing pile of dead bodies getting colder just beyond the doorway, and he stared into space, into the better world he was building. In the better world he would pick Charlotte up after school. A different school, because they would move. Far away. Start over. He'd get Annika pregnant again, and be there for more of it. He'd see the ultrasounds while holding her hand. He'd talk to Charlotte about her baby brother or sister.

He took a deep breath and poured himself back into the scene in front of him. The handwriting analysis was back, along with some info from when he'd mailed the actual tag last time. The analyst agreed with the female ID. Owen remembered reading that in each report and tossing the info out as an error, certain that his killer was a man. He mentally chalked one up to the handwriting team. More importantly, though, the ninja was left-handed. The slant, the pressure of the writing was lefty all the way. *Something* to go on. Thank you, God.

Forcing himself up and back into the den, he looked at the body in the chair in front of him. The man was sitting back in his recliner with the TV remote tucked into his hand. His girl had a sense of humor. Although Owen expected that was a certainty as she was obviously very bright. He also suspected that, though she had put the remote there, they wouldn't find a single print on it. So he left that for the crime scene guys to dust and come away disappointed. With a sterile baton he pulled from the evidence van, he lifted one of the legs to check out a suspicion. The leg was heavy as soaked granite, but he was right. The punctures went all the way through into the stuffing of the chair.

Only one look was required to know that this man wasn't a rapist, at least not that the ninja knew of–the groin of his pants was intact. Large pools of blood came from matched, precise wounds to the flanks, indicating that these wounds came earlier in the . . . well, Owen didn't really think it was fair to call it a 'fight'. This guy, trained killer that he was, hadn't stood a chance.

A voice came from over his shoulder, "Ooooh, look at that blood."

Owen's eyebrows went up as that was exactly what he'd been doing. He pointed with the baton, "Indicates that this was an early wound."

"How do you figure that?"

Owen turned to find Nguyen looking at him in a way that suggested the scientist already knew the answer. "More blood. Later, after he'd already lost so much, subsequent wounds just wouldn't be able to bleed like that."

The lab geek nodded, looking even dorkier than usual in his paper shower cap and booties along with the sterile disposable suit he'd donned to investigate the scene. Owen didn't comment, because aside from Nguyen's black rimmed glasses he looked just the same. "It's a nice theory, but not necessarily true."

"Go on."

"Well," Nguyen started, "my money says those punctures didn't go all the way through."

Owen agreed, the holes here were different from the ones that looked deeper. Also, they were elongated, indicating that she had stabbed, then swept the weapon back and forth inside him using the entry wound as a pivot point. They wouldn't know for certain until they lifted the body from the chair, and got the M. E. to open him up, but there was still too much evidence to gather before they started screwing with the scene, so that would have to wait.

The scientist continued, "I'll bet they just sliced through the outer sack of the kidneys and a little ways in. And I'll put just as much money down that's exactly what she intended to do."

"Okay." Owen conceded, but the tone of his voice told Nguyen he needed more.

"Kidneys filter all of the body's blood maybe every three minutes or so, that means the wound would bleed a lot. A lot. Whether it was early or not."

"Damn." Owen looked the body over even as he listened. Puncture wounds adorned the neck square in the front–two, stacked neatly. The arms were pinned, palm up, to the seat, crucifixion style with those same plain-cut throwing knives he'd seen before. And his girl was no slouch, she'd stuck them through the bones just below the wrist as a human could–given the motivation–yank a nail or a knife right through the flesh of the hand between the finger bones. The palm was not the appropriate way to tack someone down. She proved her knowledge again by driving the blades in at an angle toward the victim. This meant that the handles stuck up and away, so the unlucky bastard couldn't simply lift his hand and slide it off the knife handle. The angle made it impossible for him to get his hand that far, given that she'd looped a rope around his neck and twisted it snug but not tight and tacked it firmly into the back of the chair. The rope held him in place, forcing the victim to strangle himself against his already twice punctured windpipe if he tried to move forward. Nifty.

Again Owen slid long wires into all the wounds, and observed the angles at which the man had been stabbed.

He wished fervently that he knew what his ninja looked like. They knew she had dark hair, but with the few broken strands they had all they could do was a best guess. Nguyen said the strands were snapped in such a way as to indicate a ponytail holder, and that meant her hair was six or seven inches longer than the pieces in custody, but that was anywhere from just above her shoulders to down to her waist. That, of course, was still operating under the 'Annika is right' theory. Which Owen was. Given that, the hair was somewhere between milk chocolate and deep, almost black, mahogany. 'Brunette' was the only sure thing, the shade on her head was impossible to tell from a few strands, as Nguyen pointed out that everyone had multiple colors on their head. That was one of the things that made hair dyes look unnatural no matter how good the color was–the single color all over. And since the ninja hadn't colored hers, they couldn't tell.

They had no shed skin cells that they could find, no samples under fingernails, no blood. No one ever got a wound on the ninja. Which made Owen wonder how she accomplished that. Was she so ugly they stood there scared? Was she evil looking? Or was she one of those people that you just had an instinctive reaction to be afraid of? The kind you knew would never hesitate to kill you if it suited their mood? But then again, this man in the recliner had been just like that. What would it take to make him that afraid? Owen re-thought for a minute. Maybe he didn't want to find this woman.

He had to find this woman.

It was the only way to close the book. To go out clean.

As ugly as this was getting–the way the bodies were stacking up–the FBI would put him on this exclusively in another couple kills. That meant when he left, he wouldn't leave loose ends. Which was good. Owen hated loose ends.

He and Nguyen looked at the body with all the wires poking out of it. If he knew what she looked like, he could imagine her killing the man. Instead he paced around the body himself.

Nguyen stood back and just watched. "What do you think?"

"I think she played with him. I want to know how she got him into this chair in the first place. There's no indication of drugs, no needle marks, nothing. But she gets them in some position where they're helpless. His Achilles' aren't slashed like Leopold's, so that wasn't it. She uses a different way every time, I think. I haven't seen this rope around the neck before."

"I like it."

Owen snorted at the other agent. "You would. I think she walked around him. There's plenty of room." He traced the path he imagined she'd taken, and saw all the angles of the wires poking out at him. It was the only way to make sense of the fact that the stab wounds came from all different directions. He was so frustrated. "Not a single damn hair!"

Nguyen rocked back on his paper-bootied heels. "Maybe they'll get something out of the vacuum filter."

"Yeah, right."

His solitude had lost some of its appeal. Lee worried about Sin. All the time. Not about Sin herself, but about the damage she could do to him. He had no fear of death, no fear of pain–as long as it was within the course of action. He didn't mind if one of the assholes he removed from this world took him out, too. As long as it was mutual. But being hauled in by the cops, being interrogated, doing jail time, that wasn't in the books. He'd never been one to live by the Japanese adage of bringing shame upon your family for generations to come, but being jailed would surely accomplish that. Actually, he did like the idea that if he was caught he would at least be 'apprehended'. 'Apprehended' was a verb reserved for the big guys. But otherwise, there was no point. He wouldn't do jail time, because he refused to. His life would be nothing but wasted there. And he was still living now only to amend his error in letting Sam and Bethy die.

He hadn't gotten home in time to save them; he hadn't even had the chance to use the rifle tucked into the top of the closet. At the time, he'd thought that was the greatest shame, although he was now aware that the single action rifle would have been no match against Leopold and his semi-automatics. It would be no use to him in jail either. He'd have to kill himself. While he had no doubt of his capability of making a weapon with what he'd find available in a prison cell, the thought that he would end by his own hand was disheartening. And the thought that Sin held some of his cards was downright depressing. If the cops came at him, he'd just have to put one of those Hecklers to use under his chin, he certainly wasn't going to wait to shank himself in the neck while his cell mate looked on.

It had been four months since he'd seen her. He'd practiced, hauled an old couch into the shack, and purchased a small twin burner gas stove. He'd killed twice, with great satisfaction. Lee couldn't say he'd been happy a day since he'd come home to Sam and Bethany's bloody bodies, but he'd been satisfied.

He was satisfied now, his duffle open on the ugly, brown couch as he packed clip after clip inside. Boxes of ammo sank heavily to the bottom of the bag. Padded cases held the two rifles and sniper scopes, and ran the full length of the duffle, not that he was planning on using them. Silencers were tucked into the only side pocket on the overly utilitarian army luggage. Two of the Hecklers were on him. The other four were in the bag. None were left behind in the shack. Not that there weren't enough shells littering the radius around the place to tell, but he wasn't leaving the guns behind.

He wiped all the surfaces in the cabin with Lemon Pledge and a rag, removing any fingerprints. If he returned and someone was here, they wouldn't be able to tell he was one who'd been here before. Not with any substantial evidence anyway.

Lee made a last check of clothing–jeans, t-shirts, socks, underwear, sneakers, ball caps–way too simple to fuck up. Weapons were far more complicated than the clothing. He had spare holsters, silencers that were machined to each gun, and every one was labeled to match as all the pieces looked identical. But it was all there. He slung the bags crossways over his shoulders and went out the door in a move he'd done many times before. He was on the hunt.

Taking a different path to the now grown over 'garage', Lee kept his quick pace all the way to the kitty. He slung the bags in the back. He'd prefer them on the front seat beside him, but if he got pulled over he wouldn't want to arouse suspicion. He wasn't even sure if the found driver's license he carried for such purposes was still valid. The important thing was not to get pulled over to find out.

Owen stared at the map in front of him. It was the backdrop to his desk and had been for several months. Only rarely did he have maps up. And never before had he needed one that spanned the entire wall or featured all forty-eight contiguous states. He held back the laugh that threatened to burble up from inside him. Several things were causing it to nearly spill. The first of which was the very thoughtful face on Blankenship. Or more what Owen imagined Blankenship believed was a thoughtful face. The man held his chin in one hand, and the elbow of that arm in the other. His eyes were squinted as he stared at pin after pin, and he nodded a lot. He said nothing of real value.

The other thing that made Owen want to laugh was the futility of it all. On TV the FBI put up a map and the agent would come in, look at the pins, and slap a fingertip knowingly onto some spot, certain that was where his criminal was going next. None of Owen's pins formed anything like an arrow. Or even a nice circle to give them a center point.

He had a special set of pins, sixty in all, each a slightly different color ranging from deep purple through the whole rainbow to bright red. He'd filled in the kills he had on record, skipping pins so he could track any later finds and try to place them in the same order that the ninja had taken them out.

So he stared at his map and tried to organize some thoughts.

Serial killers were usually male. This one was female.

Serial killers were usually in their thirties or forties. His might be in her twenties.

Serial killers usually operated within a three hour driving radius of their home base. His was all over the country. She'd even popped into Canada once. And the kills were far enough apart in time that they couldn't triangulate a center of operations by way of back figuring for travel time. With thirteen known victims on the board, and only two of those using the skipped pins and estimated death dates, he was through the purple pins and well into the blue, the most recent of which had a definite greenish tinge. If he hit red he was fucked. And the only thing this map told him with any certainty was that he was heading toward 'fucked' at a fairly rapid pace.

They had everything they needed to nail her. They knew her approximate weight and height and hair color. They had her DNA, not that it would be conclusive in court. They knew she was responsible for these thirteen crimes, or at least had positive proof that she had been present. The gift tags pointed the finger at the same person as much as the M.O. The handwriting, in the hands of an expert, was as unique as a thumbprint or DNA.

The problem was they would have to catch her in the act.

That meant knowing where to look. And where the hell that was, Owen had no earthly clue. He didn't know where she lived, what she did for a living, where she'd trained. If he just had an area, even a general one, he could begin culling, getting rid of those who weren't suspects, narrowing down the list. But he couldn't cull the whole damned US.

If he knew where she was going, then he could just show up. But again, the pins told no stories. She wasn't sweeping the US. She wasn't starting centrally and working her way out. She wasn't going alphabetically through the list of known hit men. She wasn't starting at the bottom of the mafia and working her way up. She was doing other hits as well. Those seemed like they were side gigs, if human death could be referred to that way. The profilers didn't think she was an assassin, in it for money, doing someone else's bidding. The extraneous killings seemed to be evidence of that. But without money changing hands, she got even harder to trace.

If he knew who she was going to hit next, Owen would simply tail the guy. But if a master list existed somewhere, she hadn't left it for him. And, of course, she wouldn't. She was making this extremely difficult.

The only thing Owen could think to do was to go to Kolya Kurev directly. He could tell the man his family was under attack by an unidentifiable grudge ninja, which they probably already knew. Then, together with one of the biggest mafia crime lords in known US history, Owen would pinpoint the members of the group most likely to be hit, and offer them FBI protection.

The taxpayers really wouldn't go for that.

The ninja would continue her work anyway, picking off whoever wasn't protected.

She was too smart to take out someone with an FBI agent on them.

Or, Owen had the sudden thought, she'd kill them right under the protecting agent's nose. She seemed that smart and that well prepared. Oh yeah, the public would love it when that shit hit the fan.

All those thoughts just made the laughter boil a little harder, push a little more against his tightly closed lid, search for release. But he didn't let it out.

He stepped back and memorized his map, so that he would know when he found what he needed. So when he put that last necessary pin in place, his brain would instantly see what it meant. Owen was waiting for his little ninja to screw up.

The drive had been long but, despite the fatigue that was pressing at his body from all sides, Lee had gotten straight to work. He checked into a cheap motel, paying cash and needing no ID. He asked for a room around back with no harsh lights. Looking as road-worn as he probably did, he was a shoo-in for the 'weary traveler–wants to sleep the night away' nod of understanding from the desk clerk. From that nod, Lee gathered that the desk clerk didn't give a shit about who stayed there. Lee barely ranked a once over and the nod. The key was slid across the desk by one hand while the other held the cash and the eyes of the desk clerk were glued to a late night re-run of Oprah. The boy didn't have enough chin hair to be working this late, nor enough sense to be embarrassed that he'd been caught watching Oprah.

Lee had already parked the kitty off in the shadows, not that this guy was in any danger of pulling his eyes away from the trauma on screen long enough to make a positive ID on the car. Exiting the office with a casual walk, Lee fetched the kitty and continued around the building. He unloaded the bags from the back seat, lifting them as though they weren't as heavy as they were. He pulled two steering wheel clubs out from under the seat of the car, as there was a window on either side of the motel room door and it didn't look like the locks on either one were trustworthy. He looked around just a little, only one other car was back here and that might be a good thing or a bad thing, hard to tell at this point.

He bolted the door behind him when he got in and made a quick inspection, his bags still in his hands. The bathroom was a small, windowless cube, as he had suspected it would be. The closet was empty and Lee left the pocket doors to each open as he set the bags on the bed and made his rounds of the room.

He opened the steering wheel clubs and locked them into place to brace the windows closed. As these panes slid sideways he did it at the top where they were least likely to be seen. He had picked up little window screamers like the ones he'd found in Sin's shirt drawer. They seemed like a good idea and when he'd stuck one on a bottle and shot it the little son of a bitch had whined so loud it nearly made him deaf. He couldn't get close enough to work the tiny button to turn it off so he'd left the damn thing on the ground and shot it, too. Then spent the next three days afraid he'd brought some attention to himself even though he was certain he was living in God's own nowhere. Now he stuck one on each of the four windowpanes in the upper corners, again practically out of sight.

He didn't want the room to look fortified. That was a sure sign that he had something to protect. But he stuck the wooden chair under the door handle before he unzipped the bag and started re-arming himself.

He pulled the two Hecklers from the side holsters he wore pretty much continually. That was for 'just in case'. Now he fitted them with silencers and switched out the holsters to ones designed to hold the longer noses comfortably. He strapped another to the inside of each calf, then undid the zipper he'd stitched, hidden, into his pants leg. A good portion of his pants had a slit that he'd put there and sewn the zippers into. This way he didn't have to lift the pant leg nearly to his knee to get to the gun, he didn't have to reach down so far or do that fake shoe-tying thing he'd always seen on TV. So he had a six inch slit just below the knee on the inside of his pant legs. And an open top leg holster. Just reach in and the gun came up.

He rolled his shoulders, selected a ball cap from his bag and pulled it low, he changed jackets. Then he mussed the covers and pillows a bit, left the clothing bag open on the foot of the bed off to one side, and shoved the weapons bag as far into the back of the top of the closet as he could. Then he left.

He cranked the key and the kitty's engine stroked to life. He'd been on the road eighteen hours today, and he was about to take on another three. He was still an hour and a half from his destination, and that was a good thing. The streets were dark with intermittent puddles of ugly yellow small-town streetlights. He drove in and out of their glare wondering how he didn't give himself a seizure from their regularity. Because it was dark and everything was closed down, the freeway looked no different, except the light changed from that mustardy color to a cold harsh blue. Still Lee drove with eyes wide, tired but not yet ready to sleep.

He arrived at Svelichko's a little after midnight. He'd parked two blocks away and walked a large loop around the property, letting the dogs smell him and decide he wasn't a threat. At least not tonight. He climbed a tree and opened the pack he'd slung across his back after pulling it from the tire well in the kitty. Lee snapped the headphones on his head, connected them to the eighteen inch dish and aimed it at the house. It was seriously low tech, but it was impressive what you could gather with a little focused sound.

Svelichko was closing down for the night. Lee heard a late night program, not clearly enough to identify which one, but the canned laughter was discernable even if the rest wasn't. The phone rang, louder and clearer than anything else, and Lee listened to the tones if not the words of the conversation. The quality of the voice told him everything he needed to know. Mrs. Svelichko was checking in to see if her husband was really at home in his own bed. He sounded exasperated and soothing all at the same time.

For a moment, a rush of conscience came to him. She'd be a widow by tomorrow night. Her check-up call would make her an unwitting accomplice to her husband's death. Lee pushed back any stabs of sympathy that threatened. You didn't say 'I do' to a man like Peter Svelichko and think he was a banker. Not of any ordinary variety. The woman knew what she had married. Samantha hadn't. That was the stab that got through.

But he was working, and he pushed that, too, further down inside.

Svelichko hung up. He watched another half hour of TV which yielded nothing of interest to Lee, except that the man had better taste in houses and women than he did in entertainment. Then the light went out and the TV sounds quit.

The silence of the house was a loud roar in Lee's ears. But he listened for another hour before packing up, shimmying down the tree, and skirting his way out of the place. He took a different path back to the kitty, growing tired again as he hiked. The drive back to the motel was accomplished in complete silence, no radio, no music playing, no fingers drumming on the wheel, as his brain went over the plan again and again. He threw himself every 'what if' he could and made a plan for every contingency until he was satisfied with the outcome. The last thing he wanted was to have to think of something on the spot. Worst case scenario, he chose from pre-patterned attacks or escapes.

In his head, every time, Svelichko ended the evening dead.

When Lee arrived at the motel, he parked the kitty in the corner of the back lot under the shadow of the one tree there, and walked across the dark pavement through the dull glow of the one light on the tall fence just beyond his car. He let himself into the room with the provided key, not that it did much good safety-wise, and was greeted by a sub-arctic blast of air. Even though it was colder than the ninth level of hell, Lee swept the room visually, and inspected both the bathroom and the closet before turning off the AC unit. It had been set to come on at sixty-eight degrees, and apparently no one had set it to go off. Maybe it would stop when it iced over, he mused. Punching buttons, Lee re-set the temperature frame and peeled his clothes. He'd be warm enough once he was under the covers.

He threw them back and checked the bed before climbing in. His brain was sucked in to a numb sleep almost instantly.

He awoke at three the next afternoon and went out to find food. He left the 'Do Not Disturb' sign swinging on the knob. Although he was uncertain what that accomplished as there had been a notice beside the bed that, in the interest of conserving energy and water, they weren't going to clean basically anything, ever, unless he specifically requested it. From the looks of the place, even if he did request it, there wasn't much that was going to happen.

The clothing he wore today was clean, but undistinguishable from what he'd had on the day before. His cap stayed low on his head, and no one seemed to look at him twice. He ordered his burgers and ate with his back to the wall at a far table in the fast food restaurant, scoping out the other patrons. After his visit to Sin, Lee had found himself plenty paranoid. He wondered if they knew who he was. Who she was. Where she lived, where he lived. He liked to believe that his cabin wouldn't show up even on satellite photos. But never having seen satellite footage of the area, he couldn't be sure. It wasn't like he could just Google his non-address either. He Googled Sin's place though. And sure enough, there it was, but from the overheads it looked like every other house in the area. You couldn't detect the barb wire or the insanity from outer space.

The people in the restaurant came and went. They ate burgers and no one looked the slightest bit suspicious to Lee. Unless the FBI was hiring mothers with kids or overweight sweaty laborers, no one in there was an investigator. He ate slowly and watched as every car in the lot changed while he was there, so no one had come with him by the time he left. Unless the Feds had wired the Burger King, they weren't on top of him. Not here.

Feeling marginally better, Lee crumpled the waxed sandwich papers with their little pictures of happy cows and chickens and dumped the whole mess in the trash. He shoved the tray onto the growing stack gracing the top of the trashcan and sauntered out to the car. Two 9mm Hecklers had made the entire journey with him. Unsilenced, they were much shorter and therefore easier to stash in the waistband of his jeans. He'd sewn in loops to keep them there, and unless someone hugged him around the hips they'd never know thirty-two rounds were inside live guns on the man at the back table.

He drove to a wooded area outside of town, not wanting to be seen at the motel during the day any more than he had to. Parking in an unobtrusive, out of the way spot, he pulled out the prints of Svelichko's house and studied the layout. He knew it by heart. He'd broken in and walked the floor the last time the man had gone on a trip with his family. A younger man had house sat, but stayed out late partying, and had been too stupid or just too green to get in Lee's way at all. Hell, Lee had even found the wife's calendar with this vacation marked on it.

More than one wife had tipped the hand in his favor along the way. While Lee didn't like leaving widows behind, there wasn't much he could do to change the situation, and he refused to feel bad, when they certainly knew that their spa trips and lavish clothes had been bought with blood money. At least as widows the money would come from the right person's blood.

Light was fading. He'd started his day late and would end it in the deep of night. He waited until it was dark enough that no one at the motel would be able to get a serious look at him. Nothing that would be of any value if they were ever questioned about it later. He drove through another fast food joint, this time getting chicken. He stopped at a convenience store for milk. Soda wouldn't help his stealth one bit. He always imagined an ill-timed belch alerting a mark that someone was in the house. Not good. He took the food back to the room, his usual M.O. on the hunt, and ate in the solitude there. He turned on the TV so he would sound like the average tired motel dweller, and watched as talk show guests got mad and threw punches with no precision or power. They were as oblivious to what was coming as punching bags and they took hits like one, too. After ten minutes he grew disgusted with watching and changed the channel.

Another guest checked in to the room a few doors down. But no one occupied the rooms to either side of him. All he could do was hope it stayed that way. Most people didn't sleep deeply in strange beds, and that meant someone in an adjoining room could pretty much be counted on to know when he came and went. If that person was bored or nosy they might look out the window and see him climb in the car and go . . . so for now he was grateful that no one was there. That it was mid week in a small town motel that didn't see a lot of business even at peak times wasn't a coincidence.

He pulled a Heckler from its home at his hip and lay down on his back on the bed. His hand clutching the gun, all fingers in place but the safety on, he tucked it under his hip so it wouldn't be immediately visible and closed his eyes. Lee couldn't say he slept, but he wasn't awake either. The rest did him good, and parts of his mind wandered through tonight's event. At no point did he think of the 'why'. The 'why' had been decided a long time ago, and Lee knew all he needed to know about this man. More than enough to sleep better after he killed him than before.

When he came fully awake, the light was on in the back parking lot, and dusk had come and gone. Lee stood and changed into darker clothing. He tucked a thin watch cap into his back pocket to cover the brighter color of his hair. He holstered up, checking everything, safeties, clips. He opened and closed all the guns and fitted each with the appropriate silencer. He slid clip after clip onto himself in dozens of places on his clothing that he had designed just for that purpose. At moments like this he remembered that Dahmer had once been pulled over with a body, in pieces, in a garbage bag on the back seat of his car and the cops had written him a ticket and sent him on his way. Lee could only hope he got so lucky if he was cited for anything while carrying enough firepower to probably take out the entire local police force.

But he wasn't pulled over. He parked deeper into the dark than he had last night. Halfway around the back he stopped, waited, heard nothing of significance, and continued. He'd saved his ass on more than one occasion for aborting when he had the idea that he ought to, even if it wasn't solid. So he always stopped and listened. But nothing told him not to continue.

All but invisible in his dark clothes and watch cap, he climbed a different tree, but when he pulled out the dish and listened, he heard strains of the same TV show. He waited until he heard it. A little later tonight. Enough later that his brain had begun to wonder if she'd called remarkably earlier and he'd missed it. But, at a little after one a.m. the phone rang. Again the tones told Lee that Svelichko was soothing his wife, assuring her that he was in his own bed and his dick was in his own pants. When he heard the hang-up and then subsequent silence from the TV shutting off, he set his watch.

A half-hour later he began climbing down the tree. He skirted the fence, fed the dogs, and sent them to their maker happy. They went down quietly with one shot each, the second, with his mouth full, not having enough time to get out a good bark before he, too, fell. Lee climbed the fence, found the basement window he'd planned on using, checked again for screamers and found none. He backtracked and short circuited the wiring in the fuse box, stopping the alarm system. He then cracked the window glass with a padded fist. He reached in and found what he was looking for, a second set of wiring. Svelichko had been a mark before. But he wasn't dead yet.

Lee smiled in the dark, thinking, *you weren't* my *mark before*.

He shorted that wire and slid the window to the side. It moved on well oiled runners, because Lee had oiled them. He visually swept the area behind him, and what he could see of the basement was clear and empty and normal, before sliding through onto plush carpet. Likely he'd leave dirt prints on the creamy weave rug, but still he wiped his feet where he stood, both cleaning his boots so as not to leave more prints and smearing the ones he'd already made. The move was instinctive, and his feet rubbed the carpet while his eyes took in the wet bar and the extensive entertainment set. The curtains were high class silks, even down here. The bar glasses looked like real crystal and the mirrors on the wall made the place look even bigger, and reflected himself back as he committed crimes against a criminal lord.

There was a camera mounted in the corner, but it didn't see the whole room and it didn't scan, although if that was stupidity or arrogance, Lee wasn't sure. What it meant was that it would be much more fun to leave it running than to short it out or cover it. Lee simply hugged the wall, staying out of picture range. It was aimed to catch the bottom of the stairs–the only entry–and the bulk of the room. So he just hoisted himself quietly over the railing. Then scooted up the side of the staircase.

There was no door at the top, but before he looked around corners, Lee paused and listened. Something wasn't right. But he couldn't place it. Telling himself he'd turn around and go out, try again later if he heard anything, he waited. But he heard nothing. Nothing but the usual settling of a house. Svelichko didn't even wake.

So Lee continued.

He made his way around two more camera fields, and was ready to slowly haul himself up and over another railing to the top floor where the master bedroom was, where the mafia man slept, unaware that his dogs were dead and his cameras were not quite placed well enough. Lee's hands were around the ornate iron scrolls of the railing and he'd completed a full chin-up when he saw the feet.

Large, black booted toes stared at him from just outside Svelichko's bedroom door. His eyes lifted upward, knowing how screwed he was before he saw anything beyond the laces, but he had to look anyway.

Sure enough, Sin stared down at him from where she leaned against the wall.

Even as he pulled himself over the railing, Lee swore softly to himself. The next time he got near her with food, he was going to drug her, and while she was out he'd Lojack her. At least then this shit wouldn't happen.

When he was standing square in front of her, he allowed himself to look at the misplaced fury on her face. She motioned with an angry finger, the gloved hand pointing at herself as she mouthed the words 'he's mine!'.

Lee shook his head with a motion he hoped conveyed the full message of 'sorry, sweetheart, but he's on *my* list.'

The little bitch was pilfering his kills now, even after they'd divvied the whole thing up. What a piece of work she was.

Who knew how long she would have argued with him silently? She had to know they were out of camera range. And no matter how erroneous her anger was, she had it in spades. But a small noise, a *snck* from beyond the closed door, had them both snapping their heads. He readily identified the sound as a gun safety coming off. From the look on her face, Sin did, too.

Needing no further communication, Lee opened the door, swinging it wide with his right hand while his left came up, Heckler in firm grasp, his fingers ready. He pulled the trigger, letting fly on the gun aimed at the open doorway before Svelichko could get a shot off. Even as the firearm flew from the man's grasp, Lee saw the knife fly past and hit the left wrist, causing the other shiny thing Svelichko was holding, a silver cell phone, to fall soundlessly to the floor as the arm spasmed and struggled against the blade now embedded in it.

It was a certainty they'd only gotten that done because Svelichko thought he *might* have heard a noise. His gun was unsilenced, a sure sign that he was just making a curious sweep. Had he been certain someone was beyond his door, it wouldn't have been pretty. As it was now, the crime lord looked from one to the other of them, seeing clearly that there were death dealers standing in his bedroom doorway. Lee could watch the thoughts pass through the man's head. His gun was gone from his grasp and his communication stolen as well. He was up shit creek without a paddle.

Svelichko knew it. Lee knew it, and Sin knew it, too.

Maybe that was why she chose that moment to pick a fight. This time, with no one to alert, she spoke, albeit in harsh whispers. "He's mine. What the fuck are you doing here?"

Lee whispered back, knowing as Sin likely did, that in case they were being recorded the whispers were necessary. The sounds might carry better, further, but with no voice, they'd be nearly impossible to trace or place, even with the best technology. "He's mine! You bartered him away."

He wished he'd brought the damn list he'd made that bore her scratch marks and writing all over it, so he could shove it in her face and show her. But he'd memorized it and destroyed it rather quickly, knowing how much it would incriminate him if he were ever caught. Sin most likely had done the same, and they were therefore in a stalemate, as he'd burned his only proof that she was wrong.

Svelichko took these few lost half seconds to turn and run, but he made it no more than two steps before he smacked first his knees, then his open palms, heavily to the carpet. His right ankle was shattered milliseconds after the quick sucking sound of a bullet leaving the silencer of Lee's Heckler broke the air. His left Achilles' tendon was home to a blade, about an inch deep in his flesh, the handle still offering the slightest quiver.

"Just go." She threw the hard whisper at him and turned to Svelichko as though Lee would simply do as she suggested.

He shot at the bed. "No way in hell. You leave."

Svelichko grunted, pulling his hand out from under the edge of the dust ruffle, he was spurting blood as one of his fingers was missing a tip. Lee didn't know what had been under the bed, but he knew he didn't want Svelichko to have it. The man would never have even been able to reach under if Sin hadn't been distracting him.

"I planned this!" As proof, Lee guessed, she pulled white rope out from under her jacket. Then she had the nerve to complain. "You made him bleed."

Both the ankle and the finger he'd shot were pouring blood into the hungry carpet. On the contrary the knives she'd thrown seemed to be stopping their own wounds. They only oozed a little. But Lee didn't get what all the fuss was about. The man had a lot of blood to spare, and since they both planned on making him dead, Lee wasn't sure what hell was wrong with making him bleed.

She huffed, still using the whisper, she pouted. "I wanted him on the bed."

Rolling his eyes, Lee realized he was just screwed. He motioned to Svelichko with the gun. "Get on the bed."

When the man didn't move–Lee hadn't expected him to–he turned back to Sin and shrugged. "He doesn't want to."

"Damnit." But she walked over to where the man was still sitting back on his damaged ankles, nursing his hand and looking over his shoulder at them.

She reached out for the man's collarbone in a move Lee had seen before, but he wondered why she would use it now when Svelichko was already on the floor. At the last minute the man twirled, rising to his knees, and reaching out with bloody hands to grab at Sin. She was faster than that. Still with the rope in one hand, she suddenly produced her kamas and held them at his wrists, the handles holding him back. She didn't injure him at all except for bruises caused by his own force in coming at her. But they were at a stalemate.

With a sigh, Lee hugged the trigger again, the soft *snck* this time heralding a growing stain on the shoulder of the white t-shirt Svelichko had been sleeping in and an instant slackening of his arm.

Sin took the opportunity to rapidly tuck the now unnecessary sickle back into its loop on her pants and in three deft movements she had a rope loop around Svelichko's neck, had it twisted tight, and had painted a look of utter surprise on the man's face.

Lee couldn't suppress a grin. Sin looked pained. Even though he could only see the back and a little of the side of her, she was clearly put out. Still, she hauled the rope up tight, and walked around him, the motion keeping the mafia man at the end of her tether. Still he reached out to her again. Bloody fingers grasped for her ankle, even with the knife still embedded in his wrist that hand was pretty functional. Lee put a bullet through the man's palm even as Sin sidestepped. In a second she had the neck rope staked down to the floor using another magically appearing knife that she pounded with the handle of her sai.

"Damn, that's loud." Lee protested.

Sin shrugged. Then went about tying up and staking out each of the man's wrists. The limp arm didn't offer any opposition but the other did. Until Sin looped the rope one more time just behind the handle of the blade sticking out of that wrist. Svelichko only pulled on it once, and he couldn't hide the flash of pain that crossed his face when he did it.

Sin had those ropes quickly pegged tight, his arms spread wide.

"The dogs will tear you apart." Svelichko spoke calmly, the first time a true voice had cut the air.

Lee shook his head. "Your dogs are dead."

He enjoyed the rush of emotion that the Russian tried to hide. The man had loved the dogs. That just made this a little better.

The expression was quickly masked and replaced with the kind of threats a man makes in his last minutes. "You won't get far. You have to know that. They'll come after you."

Sin even laughed in a whisper. "Put a sock in it."

He tried to twist up, and get a good kick at her. Feeling no pain, or not enough, he tugged from the shoulder at the limp arm thinking he might spring Sin's handiwork free. Lee knew better.

Still standing back, Lee enjoyed sinking a bullet into the kneecap of the leg Sin wasn't holding. The shot elicited a grunt from Svelichko, but nothing more that told of what he suffered. At least some sweat was breaking out on his forehead, and Lee hoped it was from pain and not some sudden onset fever. Still the threats came in even tones. "They'll kill you slowly. They know who you are."

"No they don't." Lee spoke as he searched the laundry hamper he'd spotted at the side of the room. He waited, enjoying Svelichko's silence as he pulled up what he'd been searching for. The silence meant that they didn't know. The mafia man would have been the first to scream names to the heavens had he known them. Lee held up the dirty object as he walked back over to Sin and Svelichko, "Sock!"

He stuffed it into the Russian's protesting mouth wondering if it tasted as bad as it smelled.

"Thank you." Sin smiled up at him even as she pounded the last stake into place.

With all the dignity one could have while splayed out on the floor, Svelichko glared up at them. He twisted against the ropes, causing himself pain in the process. That had been Sin's intent, Lee knew. And he liked the idea. He shot out the other kneecap just to make a matching set.

"Uh!" She cried out, as though he'd taken her dolly. She walked over near the man's head and pulled her sai again. With a controlled stab downward she punctured his windpipe. The mouth worked around the sock and Lee could see the man was fighting hard not to vomit.

Lee almost hoped he would, and he watched and waited, thinking what a fitting end it would be for this man to drown in his own puke, the cut at his throat stinging like a mother-fucker and him not able to do anything about the regurgitation because of the sock in his mouth.

Fascinated, they looked on, silently, for a minute, but the staked man got it together and didn't vomit.

"Damn." Lee whispered softly. He shot a kidney.

The stomach clenched, and blood began to pour out.

"He's bleeding again!" Sin managed to get that righteous teenager sound in her tone even at a whisper. And to her credit she'd staunched most of the earlier blood with her tight ropes at his wrists and ankles. "Fine!"

She pulled her sais and began slicing at him. Just tiny surface cuts intended to wound and cause pain, not to kill. She cut red ribbons into his legs and chest, while Lee shot out a lung. The gasping sound was particularly strong through the dirty sock.

At this point Svelichko started turning just a little ashen although he wasn't giving up quite the responses Sin was clearly hoping for. She cut a little more, but her posture indicated her disappointment. She came back to stand next to Lee.

It was almost done. He decided it was time to concede a little. "I like the staking him out thing."

She nodded. "I staked the last one, kind of." She loosed a smile that was as sweet as any he'd ever seen on the surface, and equally as nasty underneath. "But afterwards I realized I hadn't nearly gone all the way."

She reached into that mystical jacket of hers and produced a slim, plastic canteen. It was clear and Lee could see that it was full of water. What? In case she got thirsty?

Svelichko didn't see it. He'd stopped looking a little while ago. He was too busy trying to breathe. But even still Lee could see him trying to figure a way out of this.

It wasn't going to happen.

Sin opened her little canteen and drizzled some of the water on the dying man. As Svelichko flinched, the smell hit Lee's nose. Rubbing alcohol. Sweet.

He held out his hand. "He's almost done for. Go write your damn tag."

She nodded, and handed over the canteen, leaving Lee to do the honors. He poured half of it, shot the other lung, then poured some of the alcohol into that hole as best he could.

Svelichko breathed his last as Sin stood watch holding her big bow and note tag in hand. She dressed the body with her stars and articles while Lee stood back to watch, wondering if the mafia wouldn't find the body first.

But Sin pocketed the cell phone from the floor before they turned to go.

They didn't speak as they turned in separate directions, Sin up to the attic and Lee about to go over the railing. He tugged at her jacket and motioned for her to follow.

With a put-out roll of her eyes, she did.

He climbed over the railing, lowering himself on sheer arm strength, then reached back up to grab Sin's waist and lower her. They traced the path he'd taken in, avoiding the camera arcs. When the police or Svelichko's mafia friends viewed the tapes, they'd never see who it was.

Lee boosted Sin out the basement window before following. Even as he came up she was scuffing through their tracks. They stayed low and silent through the acres long backyard, but no noises or warnings came to his ears.

Sin paused at the bodies of the dogs and offered some hand motion he was certain was a prayer for their souls. But their souls had guarded evil in life, so Lee had no prayers of his own for them in death.

He and Sin climbed the fence side by side, and she paused just after she hit the ground, her gloved hand dialing 9-1-1, the digital tones shrill and loud in the still night.

With a smile she held the phone away, too smart to put it to her ear as she waited for a voice to come on the other end of the line. When it did, she tossed to phone casually over the fence where it would land somewhere near the dead dogs.

They traipsed through the woods, making far less sound than two humans ought to. It was nearly a full mile before they reached his car. With pressed lips, Lee opened the passenger door and half handed, half forced Sin into the seat. He held the handle up and closed the door, letting go of the catch just as it reached the closed position. Even a nearby deer didn't flinch.

Lee gave it a look before heading quickly around the back of the car, knowing full well there was nothing keeping her in that seat. He wasn't equipped with child safety locks and it had never occurred to him to outfit the kitty for kidnapping. Sin could just open the door and bolt if she so chose.

But she didn't.

Lee opened his own door, and slid sharply into the driver's side. He closed them in with only the tiniest of *click*s before he turned to face Sin. Her countenance was calm, and she was clearly wondering what he would say, her eyes wide, searching his face.

Lee spoke in full voice for the first time since checking into the cheap motel the previous evening, but this time he practically yelled. The deer even jerked and bounded away as he let fly. "What the fuck was that?!?!"

Chapter 8

Cyn blinked as Lee's words rushed over her full of hot air. She yelled back, the deer was long gone and anyone who might have cared to hear them had already heard. "What the fuck was that?! That was me being gracious! You horned in on my kill!"

"That was mine!" He yelled back, before sucking in enough air to fill the Hindenburg and visibly trying to contain himself. After several deep steadying breaths and an insulting, under his breath count to ten, he spoke more calmly this time. "Svelichko was mine. You thought he was yours. It was a mistake."

She folded her arms across her chest, knowing it was immature, but hell, he'd already done his count-to-ten crap, why not? "I don't make mistakes. It's how I'm still alive."

He was looking out the front windshield now, staring at trees, his gloved hand resting on the steering wheel as though he were driving. "Clearly, neither do I. And, clearly, at least one of us, if not both, made a mistake here."

His right hand reached down, and before she realized what he was doing he started the engine and began reversing out of the woods. They were moving and she was sitting in the car with him, something she'd had no intention of doing. That alone spoke volumes about how slow she was on the uptake around him. Maybe she had made a mistake. With a sigh, Cyn gave her best shot at concession. "I memorized my list and shredded it. I left it in four different dumpsters in three different counties."

He laughed, a hearty laugh that poked at her brain for some reason, but Cyn ignored the feeling. "That's paranoid. I just burned mine."

"Yeah." Her voice sounded as glum to her ears as she felt about that one. "I realized that as I left the second dumpster. By then the pieces were too tiny to burn without getting my fingers, and I just decided to finish what I started."

Lee didn't speak as he drove. He pulled the watch cap off his head with one hand while the other steered. That meant there were no hands to smooth the blond strands that were matted and sticking out in every direction. He tucked the cap under the seat and produced a ball cap. Starting to put it on his own head, his right hand swung with the easy motion of too much practice simply pulling the hat down into place, but a quick sideways glance had him passing it to her instead. Cyn took the cap and had to adjust it to fit her head. Hers apparently wasn't as inflated as his and she popped the plastic tabs two notches smaller before she could wear it without it slipping down and striking the bridge of her nose.

Figuring the point of the cap was to keep them from looking like the people who'd left Svelichko's just minutes ago, and to be as obscure as possible, she pointed at his head. "If you don't want to get noticed, you might want to fix that."

"Oh, shit." He moved his head to see in the rearview, and for a brief moment both hands left the wheel to rake through the mess and bring it to enough semblance of order that he wouldn't get any stares. Luckily, they were still on deserted two-rut paths that cut through trees and private property and the ruts were fairly straight. A few seconds later his hands clasped the wheel again as the woods cleared and he looked left and right before pulling out onto a paved road with a few cars smattered here and there to account for 'traffic'. No one paid any attention to them.

Taking a moment, Cyn checked out the interior of the car. It was nicer than she would have expected from the outside. She'd first noticed rust spots and the occasional place where the rust had graduated to a full-on hole in the body. That, of course, was after she noticed the car itself, and they'd been practically on top of it before she even saw what it was. But for all the obvious age and damage, it didn't clink or rattle and the engine hummed with easy life. "Where'd you get this thing? Rent-A-Wreck?"

His mouth quirked up at her remark, even though his eyes didn't leave the road. "Rent-A-Wreck doesn't have them this good. The engine in this thing is top notch. I keep her tuned up myself. No records. And you have to admit, she's practically invisible."

Her eyes flew wide. "This is *your* car? You didn't rent?"

"It's mine. I can't rent. I don't exist." The twist of his lips didn't register even as rueful, and his eyes hardened even as he said the words.

Again with the being slow on the uptake. Why was she only just now thinking of this? "Where are we going?"

That time the smile reached his eyes. He knew she was being slow, and he thought it was funny. She'd have been mad if it wouldn't have to be at herself.

"We're going to drive through somewhere because I am suddenly hungry. Then we'll park somewhere else and talk. We've got to figure this shit out–better than we did last time."

Or one of us is going to have to kill the other. Cyn thought it but bit her tongue to keep it from passing her lips. She didn't want to kill him, and he didn't have the heart to kill her. The empty clips. The missed opportunities. And the damn sympathy, because she'd told him. No, he couldn't do it. She sighed and settled back, knowing that, no matter how hungry he was, they weren't stopping anywhere near here.

With discrete movements, she pulled sais then kamas from the pockets and loops on her pants. Without leaning too far forward, she slid them one by one under the seat, grateful for the old design of the car. There was a slight well under the cushion to keep the weapons from sliding forward if Lee hit the brakes. She pulled the remaining knives from her jacket, counting as she went, and mentally chalking up each one she'd left behind, making sure none were unaccounted for. Surgeons got sued for leaving gauze in people. Cyn figured if she left a knife behind randomly, she just might get the electric chair. So she recounted events until every blade added up. Then she bound them with a ponytail holder she plucked from the end of a braid and tucked those, too, under the seat. Next was the dagger and sheath. By the time she pulled the stars out and very carefully, so as not to slice it, wound the other pulled ponytail elastic around those, she could see Lee was trying very hard not to stare.

"How many fucking weapons do you have on you?"

"You know, you shouldn't say things that you don't want someone to overhear."

He frowned. "The car's not bugged and I wanted you to hear."

"No," She smiled and still didn't answer his question. "Sometimes people in the other cars are deaf and they lip-read. You don't want them to call the cops and tell them you asked me about implements."

He sighed into the night, a deep sound of exasperation that was sweetly satisfying to her ears. She couldn't kill him, but pissing him off was certainly a pleasing substitute.

"There are no deaf people in the cars around us. And how the hell will they call the cops if they're deaf? They can't have one of those typing things in the car with them. And they can't read my lips from the other lane." He rolled his neck as though to work out the kinks she was putting there.

Her smile was small but sure. "I only say it because I read of a case where a man was caught exactly that way. He was bragging to his friend about robbing a liquor store while they were driving. A deaf woman in the car in the next lane read his lips, memorized the license plate and called when she got home. The cops showed up and arrested him."

He sighed again, unable to come back to that one.

Cyn managed to enjoy silence for all of thirty seconds before he started shooting off that mouth again.

"So, I saw a news report where a guy stole a prescription pad and wrote himself prescriptions for Vicodin and Percocet and all the good stuff to sell on the street, and he was caught before the doctor even knew the pad was missing."

Cyn waited.

But it didn't come. What was the damn point of that? She was forced to voice it. "So?"

This time Lee returned that small sure grin, as he clearly thought he had her. But she was going to wait and see. He hadn't had her anywhere near as often as he'd expected. "See, the pharmacist called the cops. Why?"

"Pray tell."

"Because she could read the writing on the prescription, and she thought that was suspicious that it was so clear. Sure enough, while the guy was waiting to have the drugs filled, the cops called the doctor, the doctor counted the pads and realized one was missing, and the cops showed up and arrested the guy." His smile widened and he took a left turn a little sharply, throwing her into the door for punctuation.

Glad she'd automatically strapped herself in, Cyn glared. But nothing came of it. Lee, too, was belted. He probably realized, as she did, that a car accident injury, even a minor one, could send them to prison. While her brain processed that and the story he'd told, which she still didn't get the point of, her fingers began untwisting her hair. By the time she had it down, now a big ruffled mass of kinks from the tight braid job, she hadn't figured it out.

She turned in the seat, looking at his profile. "So what's the fucking point of the story? You might have gotten caught if someone lip-read you asking me about the w-word, but I have never stolen a prescription pad." Her shoulders were knotted from trying to figure him out, and she needed a moment of Tai Chi to center herself. Of course that was best accomplished in a grove of trees, with sunshine and blue skies, and as far away from Lee as possible. He totally screwed with her Chi.

He grinned, screwing it up a little further. "The point is, your handwriting can get you caught."

That was no damn point at all. "So?!"

"So," he turned his head and looked square at her. Although she wasn't pleased with that, as he looked incredulous, like she was being far too dense to see the obvious, but she didn't see it. "You've left your handwriting on those tags at every scene. You've been beyond cautious about fingerprints, hair, everything, but you've left a handwriting sample at all but one place I've seen."

Even as she gulped for air she saw the concerned look on his face. The small frown that pulled tighter and tighter. Air filled her lungs even as she fought off the reaction. He was worried for her.

But that didn't matter.

Cyn let out a peal of laughter that had tears springing to her eyes almost instantly. Her arms wrapped around her waist as, moments into the fit, her sides were already hurting. She sucked air to fuel the next sound, which could only be described as a very unladylike guffaw. She cackled, she wiped at the tears, she looked up and saw his now confused face, and laughed some more.

Not wanting to draw attention to them or the car in any way, she fought to get some composure. Luckily they were on the freeway now and probably no one had noticed a thing. Cyn was extremely grateful that he hadn't sprung that on her in the city. The cops would have pulled her over for being on drugs.

With deep even breaths she slowly got herself together.

Lee drove on. His face now a wealth of disbelief. He hadn't known what to do with or about her before, and now it was only worse. "You're going to have to explain that, because the way I see it, you fucked up leaving those notes."

"You're worried about me." She was starting to add 'that's sweet', when he interrupted, making her glad she hadn't.

"I'm worried about *me*. We know too much about each other." His lips pressed into a thin line. "Your clinical insanity is a threat to my freedom."

Her head tipped, acknowledging that he was part right. They each had the power to bring the other down, in more ways than just in combat. So she attempted to soothe his worry, "But I'm not insane."

He didn't say anything, just kept driving into the black night, further and further from where her car was parked. As always, it would be good where it was until at least noon the next day. Cyn wasn't going to let delays or a need to head the opposite way lead to her being brought down by a parking ticket. She'd never needed the contingency before, but tonight she was glad she'd planned for it. What was disconcerting was that she wasn't in control of the situation. What was more disconcerting was that she wasn't truly bothered by that.

She couldn't take him in a fair fight. Or probably even an unfair one. He was armed to the teeth, and, while she'd slid her weapons under the seat and out of immediate reach, his were still in holsters. He was fast enough to make her wonder if he'd been a wild west gunslinger in a past life. At any moment, he could have a bullet in her before she literally even knew what hit her. But she was fairly relaxed for having just come off a kill and being in a car headed very much the wrong direction.

After a few beats she realized he wasn't going to comment on her 'I'm not insane' remark. So she continued, "I'm also not left handed."

"What?" His head whipped around to look at her, then he snapped his eyes back to the road as soon as he realized what he'd done.

"I'm not left handed." And she was still ahead. "I wrote all those notes with my left hand. I practiced for years to make it look natural, but that's not *my* handwriting. The notes only link one note to another, and it's not like the crime scenes aren't all linked with my handiwork already. I don't leave evidence behind."

"What about all the times you practiced? If they find out who you are, they might find some of those old pages."

She shook her head. She'd been thinking ahead for years. "I burned or shredded and flushed every single practice sheet. I also practiced in ink that would run when it got wet, further destroying any evidence."

He still shook his head. "What if someone remembers you writing with your left hand?"

"They'd have to have been spying on me very furtively. I made a point to always be alone, and to immediately destroy anything I did. Even the early stuff that was too pitiful to link to anything."

"Jesus, Cyn."

She shrugged. So she was single-minded? So were a lot of girls. They were bent on getting married or having a career. She truly made the world a better place. And she was getting those bastards back for what they'd taken from her. "Those notes are the only remaining samples of that writing. And you're the only one who knows I can do that."

"Why'd you tell me?"

Why had she?

Cyn shrugged again. "Because that isn't going to be the thing that puts it over the edge. You already knew enough to call the feds on me if you wanted. And you were worried that I'd left evidence behind. I didn't. So you can sleep better."

They were off the road now and he was pulling into a drive thru and asking her what she wanted. She hadn't been hungry before, but suddenly as he spouted off two orders–which apparently were both for him, because he turned and looked at her like *what-did-she-want?*–her stomach growled at her. Nothing was healthy, but she ordered a combo with a grilled chicken breast and decided to screw it and have the fries and soda.

Five minutes later she had a hot, heavy paper bag on her lap and had already sucked down a third of the bathtub of soda and almost half her fries.

Lee watched her sneak bites of food, but didn't say anything. "Look, forget finding a place to park. Your motel or mine?"

Her eyebrows rising, Cyn stopped mid chew, "I'm assuming that isn't a come on?"

"No, not a come on. When were you planning to leave town?"

A shrug slid across her shoulders, as usual, she'd leave whenever she woke up. "Somewhere just after first light."

"Me, too. That means we need to figure this out fast." His hand snaked into the bag and pulled out hot fries that he shoved into his mouth all at once with no grace.

"Where are you staying? Out this way?"

"A half hour further." He pointed along the freeway lights, the direction they'd been headed. His eyebrows raised. "Twinsburg."

"I'm the other way entirely."

He sighed. "How seedy is your place? Did you need ID to check in?"

"Of course." He didn't?

"That's what I figured. That means my place is less likely to remember us coming in, and more likely to house low level thugs than someone who does what we do. We should bunk at my place. Which means we need to head to yours." It was braced with a soul weary sigh as it had already been a long night. But with a roll of his neck and a twitch in his seat, Lee visibly shook it off and sat up straighter, ready to face the haul.

Cyn didn't shrug out of it so easily. "Back the way we came then. And I'll need my car."

"Unwrap my sandwich for me?"

Lee tried to work the crick out of his neck without being obvious. No one was around the back of the motel at three a.m. when they finally arrived. The other patron back here was still out.

Lee had suggested they leave her car in a spot in town for the remainder of the night. There were a few other cars gracing the street where it sat, but the little silver sedan screamed rental and probably would have stuck out like a sore thumb pulling in here. Sin hadn't protested.

When he closed the door behind her, each of them let the bag they'd carried slide off their shoulder and onto the bed. She snorted with disgust. "I had two beds."

"You also checked in with ID and into a room for one. That place was far more likely to look at us than anyone here would be." He shook his head. "I saw a security camera in the lobby. What were you thinking?"

She frowned at him, that same *I-don't-make-mistakes* look she'd given him earlier. "For your information, I didn't give the camera a decent look at me at any time. The only person who saw me was the clerk at check in. Furthermore, I was thinking, that since I used another fake ID, if anyone came looking for me it would have to be with a photo in hand and at that point it would be a little too late to worry about the camera."

She didn't add *so-bite-me* but he read that in her face, too.

Lee refrained from saying anything. Mostly because she was right. She used IDs but she did seem to have enough different ones that anyone looking for her wouldn't find her by paper trail. They'd have to be looking for *her*. And he didn't know how they'd find her without knowing what and who she was.

"Are we sleeping in shifts?" The question came at him from out of the blue, and he was totally unprepared for it. The last time he'd slept in shifts was when Bethany had been a baby and she'd been sick. There hadn't been anyone to takes shifts with in so long. He blinked a few times, wondering how to answer.

"Why? Are you a heavy sleeper?"

Something crossed her face, but he couldn't identify it, and wasn't sure he wanted to. "No. Can we discuss this whole thing in the morning? I'm tired now. We were on the road forever."

She yawned and stretched, looking a little like a sleepy kid and a little like a killer. Kinky hair exploded out from under the too big ball cap, her large liquid eyes could have suckered a cocker spaniel puppy, but the leather get-up and the bag of weapons next to him were pure pro.

"Yeah. Can you share the bed or do you want me to take the floor?" He didn't know where the manners had appeared from again. She could just as easily sleep on the floor as he could. Hell, she was the only person on earth who was harder than he was. The concrete under the old carpet probably felt downright squishy compared to her.

But she yawned again, "We can share. As long as you know that if anything touches me, I'm skewering it."

"I figured as much." He laughed again and felt the lead creep into his bones as he finally admitted how exhausted he was. He leaned back on the side of the queen that he already occupied, peeled his jacket, kicked his shoes off and slid under the covers. He decided to sleep in his jeans in deference to Sin's odd sensibilities, anyway he was too tired to change them even though he thought he might still be wearing microdroplets of Svelichko's blood.

Figuring he'd be out as soon as his head hit the pillow, Lee was surprised to hear Sin shuffling around in the bathroom. She scrubbed at something, and he heard the sandpapery noises of her toothbrush followed by splashes of water.

Owen had walked off the plane and onto the night-cooled tarmac at Mitchell Air Force Base around four a.m. It would be another forty-eight hour crime scene binge. So naturally it had begun at the end of an already long day.

Why the hell the ninja couldn't kill someone in the early morning was beyond him. Blankenship was more of a cross to bear than a help of any sort at these times. His partner had sat beside him in cushy seats on the Task Force Lear Jet they'd been given this time, throwing out comments about the case while Owen looked at faxes as they came in. Special Agent Blankenship had hogged some of the pages as they'd spit out. He'd pointed and talked, mostly stating the obvious and putting the 'special' in Special Agent.

Owen was definitely quitting once this case closed. He wouldn't be able to work with anyone who actually had a decent thought after this. He was too used to running the show with Blankenship around. And he wouldn't be able to put up with this for much longer. Period.

Hauling his bag over his shoulder and not caring if his partner kept up, Owen headed to the car that awaited them. The local Agents had just pulled up to give updates, stating they'd secured the scene and swept the police out. Of course the cops had responded en masse to the 9-1-1 call that had tipped this one off, and in doing so they'd contaminated almost every room in the house and certainly the scene. Owen had expected no less.

What he still prayed for were long brunette strands of hair.

That would show that the ones already in custody belonged to the ninja. It would almost certainly make the ninja female–as it would be heavy circumstantial evidence that a fifth person, an attacked woman, didn't exist at the scene of the campus rapist. And it would place the owner of the hair at both scenes.

He prayed for a fingerprint–one of those knives would hold a nice one. If he was going to dream, then he'd wish for a full set. Owen had practiced with throwing knives at the range a few times, talked to the FBI expert, and taken a quick lesson from the weapons man. The correct grip wasn't a fist but more the way you would tightly grasp the edge of a paper. All the fingertips would touch the handle, and her knife handles were smooth metal.

He prayed for a fiber or a tool that only came from one place in the world. Something they could trace. He doubted they'd get anything of the sort.

Instead he listened to the briefing, then quickly flipped open his cell phone and left a quick message for Annika. After all these years of him leaving at the drop of a hat, she didn't always pick up the phone when he called to say he'd gotten in safe. She said she trusted he'd gotten there, and that she needed to sleep through the night as she was going to be a single parent for the next few days. Even as he thought the outgoing message he got was clearly a sign from the Gods Of The Obvious that he needed to leave the job, he thought about the fingerprints he was leaving on his phone. The ones he'd left all over the plane, in this car, there was even a smudge on the window. And, given his propensity to push car doors open with his palm, he had to assume there was at least a partial there. How could the ninja ever leave a scene that perfectly free of fingerprints and fibers?

It had to be very well planned.

When he got back home, he'd spend his days working that angle with Nguyen.

Agent Nguyen seemed to read his thoughts from the facing seat in the back of the short limo. There were no lights and no foiled bottles of champagne back here, this was strictly a working vehicle. If things went as Owen expected, there wouldn't likely be anything to celebrate. They weren't even close. With a sigh the lab agent looked at him, "Are you looking for your own fingerprints?"

Owen nodded.

"Well, if you ever do anything illegal, just cut out a few big arrows and point them at yourself. You are the easiest man to track that I have ever seen. You touch fucking everything."

At that moment, Blankenship looked at his own hand clasping the door grip beside him and released it, as though it might do any semblance of good. Owen fought not to roll his eyes.

But Nguyen continued with the razzing, "It would be harder to track a shedding dog that had just walked through a mud puddle."

"Thank you." Owen made no effort to keep the wry tones out of his voice.

The local agents looked back and forth at each other. Their eyes told the story that they were sizing up the agents on the case, and Owen concluded that they'd read it right. Their looks held respect for Nguyen and bewilderment at Blankenship. How that man had even gotten into the Bureau in the first place had to be a marvel of family connections.

The Agents spilled out of the car without speaking as they reached the scene. Uniforms held the perimeter, and to their credit they looked discrete and quiet. The dark shirts and pants blended into the night, only small silver glints off their badges gave away their positions. Yellow crime scene tape had been used sparingly, just across the gate to the yard and the driveway. Two patrol cars sat in the cordoned off drive more silent than the dark around them.

Good.

Blankenship flashed his badge, but Owen and Nguyen didn't bother. They simply shook hands and Owen introduced all of them. "I'm Special Agent Dunham, this is my partner Agent Blankenship. And Special Agent Nguyen, who runs our mobile lab. The local mobile FBI crime scene lab will be arriving for him in a short while. If you could do us the favor of keeping the scene quiet, we'd very much appreciate it."

The local mobile lab was likely to be just as discrete as their own, but you never knew. And it didn't hurt a bit to make friends with the local cops. These guys got all the coolest scenes taken away from them, and likely their own homicide guys were already in a snit. Owen made sure to remember names and spend Bureau money ordering coffee and food for the cops.

After repeating back each of their names and committing faces to memory, Owen walked up the pretty stepping stones that led to the grand house. It was a misleading sunshine yellow, with pretty white gingerbread trim. A plastic child's playhouse sat off to the side looking well used and loved with a little sprig of silk flowers adorning the front door. They were a smaller version of the ones on the heavy steel mesh door on the front of the house. The steel door offered far better protection than a flimsy screen, but it had decorative scroll work and was painted to match the pretty trim. Several of the neighboring houses had the same type of measures in place, so there was nothing out of the ordinary here. Nothing that said 'fortress' or 'mafia'. Nothing that told of the people that lived, or now didn't, behind the door.

With the white linen handkerchief he always carried for such things, Owen tugged at the top edge of the steel door. It had been left slightly ajar by the local police so that no one would need to touch the knob again, thus salvaging any fingerprints that hadn't already been rubbed to oblivion. He pushed at the heavy inner door with its leaded glass inserts and cautiously stepped over the threshold.

The living room spoke of wealth and what passed for taste. Svelichko's wife, the daughter of Russian immigrants herself, had grown up with far less money than this. While she hadn't gone Graceland on the place like some nouveau riche were prone to do, she had fallen too far to the safe side. Everything was in shades of cream and white. Lights blazed throughout the entire house, but Owen already suspected the only actual color he would find would be the rust brown of blood in the upstairs bedroom.

As he and Nguyen followed the commanding officer on the scene up the stairs, Owen noted that another set leading down into the basement was tucked underneath it. Given the lush carpeting on the stairs and the style of the remainder of the place, he suspected the downstairs was just as lavish and pale.

The police officer spoke as he led the agents up, offering the same few trite phrases that Owen had heard at every ninja scene. Things to the effect of 'couldn't have happened to a more deserving bastard,' 'we left it as clean as we could,' and 'man, that shit is fucked up'.

Owen so desperately wanted to tell them it was a woman. Just to see the looks on their faces. But he couldn't reveal that. Only a small handful of Agents under Bean's supervision knew of that little probability. And it needed to stay that way.

At the doorway to the bedroom, another man in blue stood guard. To his credit, he stood straight, not leaning on the wall, and he seemed alert. Owen had looked for, but hadn't seen, any tread marks or footprints on any of the carpeting up to here. Nothing they could identify beyond the usual 'people had walked here' marks. He looked up at Nguyen as he pointed discretely to the floor, and Nguyen shook his head 'no'.

"It's like blowing snow, man." Nguyen had already started donning the sterile paper over-suit that they would wear into the bedroom to get a good, up-close look at Svelichko. "The carpet's too thick, it absorbs everything and leaves nothing."

Owen pulled his suit on, too. He tried to not look into the room, but he'd already seen enough to know that the mafia man was in his jammies, the body cold but not old. And he was staked out like a tent. Worse than the last one. Also, this one had been phoned in by Svelichko's own cell phone. No one had spoken to the 9-1-1 operator, just left empty silence. Officers had come to check out the scene and found the dead body. Given the empty call, they had looked for the offending phone, although Owen had thought it only logical that the man couldn't have made the call himself. Neither hand looked able to retain any tension, and he was clearly dead in a bad way. So they'd stepped their officer footprints all around the scene and shed invisible strands of true blue poly-cotton blend all over the victim. But at least they'd ultimately found the phone outside by the dead bodies of the dogs.

That meant that the ninja had most likely made the call herself. Damn. She'd been right here. She'd held that phone and alerted them. She was likely still in the area. But the neighbors had already been questioned and had seen nothing. As they had no idea what her name was or what she looked like, unless someone phoned in saying that a brunette woman was throwing knives at them, it would be like finding a particular piece of straw in a haystack.

Taking a fortifying breath and letting go of the desire to turn tail and try to trace her, Owen pushed his sterile-papered self through the doorway. As he'd suspected, Svelichko's eyes were wide and glossy, his skin was the ashen color of the departed. Given the number of holes in the lung region, he was pretty certain the man had been close to this particular shade of gray even before he was dead.

There were small pools of blood in varying spots on the floor, indicating that he'd been wounded before he'd been staked, while he was still mobile. One came out from under the dust ruffle and even left a smear on the hem of the cream colored silk. With his sterile baton, Owen leaned way down and lifted the edge of the fabric. After a moment where his eyes adjusted, he made out a dark shape attached to the underside of the frame. It looked like a .357. But Svelichko clearly hadn't gotten it.

Another gun lay off to the side of the room. Certain that it didn't belong to the ninja, Owen figured Svelichko had pulled it on her and she'd knocked it from his grasp. And with some force, too, as it was a good distance from the body and there was no evidence of a struggle on that side of the room.

Nguyen's eyebrows went up. He pointed. "Sock." He grinned.

The bastard had a sock stuffed in his mouth. Owen fought back his own corresponding smile, and wondered if the man had gotten too mouthy for his girl. Nguyen padded across the room and lifted the hamper lid with his own sterile poking stick. "Looks like it's one of his own. Fifty bucks says it's dirty."

"I ain't taking that one. I'm with you."

Even without the money riding on it, Nguyen bent over the open-eyed face, without touching anything, and sniffed. "Oh yeah, it's dirty. Niiiiiice. Wait."

Owen looked up at the lab agent as he sniffed again. "Isopropanol."

"That uncommon?" Owen asked.

"It's rubbing alcohol, doofus."

"Thank you." Owen didn't think he'd been called 'doofus' since about third grade. But if it was rubbing alcohol, then he probably deserved the title. Of course it wasn't something they could trace. It never was.

Blankenship's voice hollered up the stairs, and Owen only hoped that the moron didn't wake the neighbors. They didn't need any interference. Any. "Point of entry is in the basement, we got broken glass."

"Out or in?" Owen asked in a fairly normal tone, as Blankenship was at the top of the stairs and visible through the doorway now.

"In, and it looks like out as well. Hard to tell." He went off to check the rest of the place. The only good thing about Blankenship was that he'd learned to stay out of the way. And he made really great useless statements to the media. If they didn't want anything usable said, but didn't want to use the 'no comment' line that only riled the media, they sent Blankenship.

The man could talk reporters into a near coma and give nothing of value.

Owen turned back to the body. As he looked closely he would see stains at the edges of where the alcohol had been. "Looks like she poured it over the cuts, after they were made."

"Bitch!" Nguyen smiled as he said it though. "That had to hurt."

Owen pointed with his little baton. "Look how tight the ropes are, he struggled there at the end. Probably against that pain. That's just plain mean."

"No one ever made the mistake of calling this one 'sweet'. She was out for suffering even at the beginning." The lab agent was gathering small samples with spatulas and baggies even as he reminisced. "Remember the hole in Leopold's dick? That was just for sheer pain."

"As a male, I'll still remember that when I have Alzheimer's and no longer recognize my own children." He shook his head, his eyes still tracking along the body as they looked for anything new. "I already woke up in a dead sweat one night with a nightmare based on that one."

Nguyen gave a rueful smile and held up fingers, "I've had that dream three times already. Ex-girlfriends wielding ninja weapons. It is not fun."

Owen laughed, even as Nguyen frowned. He'd never taken his eyes off the body, but now he focused on the hand, and then the foot. He wandered a few feet away and bent over to look at the carpet, where a few blood splatters defined a point. "Dunham."

That was all he needed to say. With the look on his face giving urgency, Owen came right over to where his friend was pointing.

"Look."

A hole in the carpet surrounded silver. A slug.

"Holy shit."

"A bullet." They said it at the same time.

Nguyen said something coherent first. "Do you think it's Svelichko's?"

But Owen was already wondering, and Nguyen was heading back to the body, the sock stuffed in its mouth not doing a damn thing to prevent it from telling tales. It was suddenly screaming them.

"The bullet is facing that way. Given the embedding and the angle, it was shot from about . . . there." Owen followed his own finger through the doorway. "Do you think Svelichko hit the ninja?"

Nguyen's usually even voice sounded excited. "Svelichko has bullet holes in him."

"What?" The grudge ninja didn't use bullets. Did she? Then again, she'd never staked anyone down until a year or so ago when they'd found the one man tacked to the wall. She'd been evolving. The alcohol was new. So were the bullet holes. "Son of a bitch. Are they from that gun?"

Nguyen went back over to the gun, leaned over, and sniffed it. "No. No powder smell. This thing hasn't been fired in recent history. If the gun that fired those is here, then we haven't found it yet."

Blankenship appeared at the doorway again. Unfortunately, he was speaking again. Owen forced himself to listen.

"The cell phone that made the 9-1-1 call was next to some dead dogs. It looks like it was tossed over the fence, so we have an exit point from the yard. No prints on the phone except what the Crime Scene guys say look like Svelichko's."

Owen nodded. He'd expected nothing less. This night had been far too long. The sun was coming up beyond the rich cream sheers and while he hadn't expected the place to be a wealth of answers, he sure as hell hadn't expected so many new questions.

"Oh, and the dogs were shot, point blank."

Later, as Lee blinked at stark sunlight fighting its way around the edges of the cheap curtain, he realized he'd passed out cold last night. He sucked in air, wondering what time it was. Judging from the sunlight, he'd slept later than he'd planned.

Sin was curled up facing away from him, at the far side of the bed. Her hair had lost most of its fuzzy kink, plastering itself down her back as he peeled the covers up and away. He waited for her to jump and lunge at him with something sharp, or at least offer a bone-breaking fist to his face as she woke. But Sin did none of it. She breathed deeply in long, chest moving inhalations.

Lee pushed at her shoulder, his eyes blinking, denying reality, as he saw what she was wearing for the first time. Beneath his fingers was soft flannel, pink with black-outlined fluffy white sheep jumping fences and cavorting all over the men's style cut. Jesus, she looked like a girl.

But as he pushed her shoulder again, he felt the bra she wore underneath. She was Sin. No vulnerability, no give. She might as well have worn a sign that said 'keep out'. "Wake up. It's late."

"Huh?" She rolled onto her back, and therefore crowded him on the bed that wasn't really all that large to begin with. She pushed long hair out of her face as she squinched eyes at him that weren't quite awake.

"We need to get going."

He didn't say anything else, just slid out of his side of the bed and headed to the shower. He scrubbed up with his one bottle of shampoo/soap that he always used, rubbing his head and face at the same time and wondering what the hell he was going to do. Bracing his hands against the tiled stall wall, he planted his feet behind him just wider than his shoulders. This meant his feet were almost in the opposite corners. Hot water sluiced over him and he let it do what it could for the cricks in his shoulders. What the hell was he going to do about Sin?

He couldn't keep an eye on her from Appalachia. And they'd screwed up this one, big time. If they did it again, they might end up in jail, or in side-by-side electric chairs. He didn't trust her. He trusted her to act like Sin, but that meant that he could count on her to fight to the very end. Whether that meant she'd throw him out as a bone to someone trying to get her, he didn't know.

She was a loose cannon, and you had to keep an eye on those.

Lord knew she probably felt the same way about him.

But what he was actually going to *do* about it, he didn't know.

He patted himself with the motel towel, but it was so much the opposite of fluffy that it less absorbed water from him than it just scraped his skin dry. Emerging from the bathroom with the towel around his hips earned him a glare from Sin, and it occurred to him that she was standing, pink flannel and exuberant sheep and all, between him and his Heckler. He hadn't even thought to take it into the bathroom with him like he usually did. His clothes were draped over a towel rack that the motel hadn't seen fit to leave a towel on, and he didn't have Sin's moves.

He was as vulnerable before her as he had ever been.

She stared, as though the sight of him was an insult to her nature, then tromped past him into the bathroom. In one hand she clutched a case of toiletries that left a trace of perfume as she marched by.

That was odd. Sin surely didn't have any sensibilities to offend. But he was glad to have a clear line from himself to his gun again.

Hearing the door click behind him as she locked herself into the bathroom, he waited for the telltale *shoosh* of the water in the shower before peeling off the towel and sliding into clean jeans and a t-shirt. He picked his navy ball cap off the side table where Sin had left it just a handful of hours ago and tried to fit it to his head. It took a moment as she had adjusted it a few sizes down.

With the shower droning on behind him, he couldn't resist. After sliding the Heckler, unsilenced, down into the side of his jeans, he lifted the pillow she'd slept on to find her sais. This time both handles pointed to the edge of the bed, where her hands would have been as she'd been curled to that side.

He almost smiled. What a pair they made. Sleeping with weapons under their pillows. Ready to take all comers.

It was the sais under the pillow, and the large fluffy teddy bear sitting on top that he hadn't noticed before, that made him realize something for the first time. He actually liked Sin. And she liked him for the same reason.

She was the only person he knew of in the whole world who understood him.

His brother Todd didn't know if he was alive or dead. He'd helped with cashing out Sam's and Bethy's life insurance policies, and then Lee had left his remaining family behind. He'd just felt so removed from all of them–his parents, his co-workers, the couples he and Sam knew from Bethany's school. They all had become spirits to him, not on the same plane, not speaking his language. He had wandered his own world for years now, making real contact with other humans only before he killed them.

Aside from Sin.

Of course, the obvious answer to that was that she wasn't human either. In fact she was worse than him. He had to wonder if she'd been at it from the moment Leopold had left her house and left an eleven-year-old-girl alive.

Lee thought all this as he packed his bags, repositioning the rifles, shifting the ammo. He was only seven rounds lighter than when he came, but his load was noticeably lessened.

He had only the faint tick of the bathroom door handle turning to warn him she was behind him. He hadn't seen her take any weapons in with her, but then again David Copperfield only wished he had a jacket as cool as hers. Lee wouldn't put it past her to sleep in cheesy flannels that were not only cute but loaded to the hilt.

Her voice didn't startle him, but what she said did. "I slept like a rock last night. You?"

He nodded as he turned and looked at her. She again looked like her nineteen-year-old self. She wore tight jeans and a tighter t-shirt. Her hair hung in wet ropes around her face.

"Yeah, me, too." He had to admit to that. One–he hadn't woken up until late. There was no excuse for that if he hadn't been sleeping like a rock. Two–if he lied to her, she'd likely kill him.

Her eyes looked at the wall off to the side, "I never sleep like that."

He just nodded and went back to packing. He was done quickly and sat on the edge of the bed in awe as she ripped at her three teddy bears and shoved the sais, kamas, and dagger down their gullets. With the quick sure movements of a quilter, she rapidly put the bears back together without leaving any obvious marks of tampering. He was impressed, and found it all too fitting that the girl with the drawer of leather underwear had pink sheep jammies and teddy bears that were as lethal as she.

She packed the remainder of her things into a small handful of carry-on size bags. And before she finished, Lee began a dialogue that would change things one way or another. He wasn't sure when he opened his mouth if she would agree or kill him.

"We fucked up."

She grunted and wiped down her shampoos and shower lotions before packing them into a purple plaid zipper case.

"If we fuck up again we could wind up dead."

"Yup." She agreed, but just went about packing, not helping the conversation at all.

"We need to operate out of the same place." She paused a beat, and he kept talking before it got into her mind that he was crazy or dangerous and she decided to rip open a teddy bear on him. "So we don't get in each other's way. So we can take out whoever whenever."

He didn't know what to say after that, so he shut up and waited.

Sin kept packing.

It was a full minute of her shuffling around the room, pulling things out of the closet and folding them in the way that spoke of working in a clothing store, before she finally replied. "You want to move in with me?" She didn't quit moving and her body language said nothing other than did-you-remember-to-check-under-the-bed.

"I can't."

"Oh, well." She shrugged as though he'd been talking about a box of cereal.

"I can't shoot at your place. You're too close to civilization. Like you, I practice all the time."

Sin nodded, this time looking at him, as she zipped up the last of her matching luggage and gathered up the teddy bears in her arms, before plopping on the bed.

Lee took another breath. "You should come out with me."

She squinted. "I have a job. A life. I can't just leave."

"Sure you can." He shrugged. "You don't have those things–Cyndy does. You're not Cyndy. Quit the job."

She stared at him like he was nuts. And he probably was. Only as he spoke did he feel the tug of missed human communication. Even the fight over Svelichko last night had been more than he'd spoken to another single human since the last time he'd talked to Sin. He tried another tack. "Do you need the money?"

"No." She shook her head, still looking square at him with confusion plain on her face.

"Then why do you have to keep the job?"

"It's cover." Like he should know that.

"You don't need that kind of cover. You can just go to ground."

Probably unconsciously, she hugged the bears tighter. "But I have a house, a car, a . . ."

"We'll lock up the house. Sell the car. You quit your job, dying mother or something-"

She laughed at that. "Aunt. I'm visiting her now, helping her through another round of chemo."

"You can move your practice gear out, there's plenty of room. You can devote yourself to whomever you want, know I won't get in the way, and spend the remainder of your life not worrying about getting permission from your boss to do what you need to do." Lee made perfect sense to himself. But the incredulousness that crossed her face told her he'd struck something and it probably wasn't good.

"The remainder of my life?" She physically withdrew, pulling back even as she was already out of reach. "Are you suggesting that there isn't much of it?"

He was just as flummoxed by that as she apparently was by him. "You can't be serious. I don't expect to last more than another year or two in this business. Do you think you'll go on living like this?"

Her jaw worked, lush lips trying to form words, the teddy bears' necks bending as she squeezed them until they gave. Sin stared out of wide eyes, looking like he'd said he wanted to unleash the plague.

Great–his only human contact was a moron. She wasn't a fool, but did she really think she could grow old like this? People like them had a limited life span. It wasn't anything he'd really put to thought, and God knew he hadn't talked to anyone about it before, so he didn't really know how to go about doing it. But his truncated life was just a fact he had accepted as he'd stood bloody and lost in his own living room. He'd held Sam and Bethany, one limp body in each arm, as though he could bring them back by loving them enough. By being sorry enough. By something, anything. And he'd known then that he was starting on his own path to join them.

But Sin seemed to think this was a career of sorts.

By the time he'd formulated something to say, she was looking at him with pity rather than horrified bewilderment. Her working jaw made sounds and his brain strung them together into intelligible phrases.

"I can't come live with you. Not if you're planning on dying. I'm not."

"I'm not planning on it." She twisted every damn thing around. He sighed. "I just figure it's an inevitability in this business."

"No."

Sin stood up as though to leave, then plopped back down on the bed. He had seen the gears shift in there, and watched as it had clicked into place that he would have to drive her back to her car.

With an exasperated sigh, one he had used on Bethy the night before she died when she wouldn't clean up her room, Lee cocked his head. "Well, then, how do you propose we solve this problem? The lists sure didn't cut it."

"I don't know." She practically yelled it at him as she stood again, this time flinging the teddy bears onto the bed behind her. They landed with fluffy precision, her years of practice evident even here, even as the one bear bounced just a little oddly, not squishing exactly right, and giving a little sign of the weapons inside him.

Sin was breathing rapidly, and only then did Lee realize what he was asking. He had no issues with abandoning the shack–he'd twice simply abandoned lodgings on a moment's notice in the past several years. If he lost the kitty–probably the thing he loved most–he'd shrug and find a way to get another car. His clothing, his practice bottles, even the Hecklers, were all manufactured items, and utterly replaceable.

Lee's eyes put together the story the pieces told right in front of him. Sin would sooner rip his arm off than let him rip the arm off one of the bears. She'd likely painted the walls in her home herself. Maybe she'd said it was for security, so no one saw what she had, but she'd chosen colors. Decorated. Probably designed the lamps and a good handful of the hidden weapons herself. She was attached to her life.

He sighed. "Is there someone there you can't leave?"

She shook her head too fast to be lying.

No, it wasn't the people Sin was attached to. She'd likely learned that lesson the hardest way she could. At gunpoint. But she was sewn tightly to her things.

He tried again. "You can bring all your stuff. Don't sell the house. We can keep it as another base." She couldn't sell the house anyway. No one could ever know what was there. The real estate agent would call the CIA after just a walk-through. "We can try it and see if it works. Maybe we come up with a better solution. I can buy you another car if need be."

She shook her head, shaking off his offer. Lee had to wonder for a moment if he really needed humanity this much, to try to forge some bond with this girl who was everything less than human. Only as he thought it did he see that the bond had already been forged. And he, the more human of the two, was the one who saw it for what it was.

Her voice was haughty. “I don’t need your money. I don’t need the paycheck from my job. When I turned eighteen I got access to my parents’ life insurance policies. And they’d been heavily insured.”

He nodded. The stories were just too similar. “So tell me about it in the car.”

Chapter 9

Cyn pushed the uneasiness down to where she didn't have to deal with it. The move didn't feel wrong per se. It just didn't feel right, either.

But logically she knew she and Lee had to keep each other's backs. If he was caught, then there was a good possibility that so was she–it had been that way from the moment she'd first seen him. They were cut of the same cloth. Committed the same acts. Were a danger to each other, just by knowing the other existed. They were far too much alike for all that she was certain they weren't alike at all.

She had made the decision to move while sitting in the overly comfortable seat of the 'kitty', as Lee referred to his car. She got it. The thing really did purr, but she kept having those disconcerting moments where things didn't match. As a kid, her sister had come home one day and pitched a head-sized piece of granite at her. Cyndy had screamed, but it had bounced right off, causing no damage except the mental. It had been a convincingly painted chunk of foam that Wendy had thought was cool. The kitty was like that. Her brain said the seat should be lumpy, that the wheels should waver, and she should feel every ridge in the road. She was almost made more uncomfortable by the fact that she was comfortable.

The air conditioning kept her at a perfect temperature even though sunlight was streaming in the front windshield and the car had no trouble pulling the small U-haul trailer that Cynthia Ellen Winslow had rented just outside of Boulder. When they'd gotten it, so far from Dallas, Lee had stacked it with cinderblocks and slowed his pace, as though he was hauling something more important than empty metal.

Cyn could only be grateful for the twenty-four hour reprieve the trailer had given her from him. They'd have drawn attention had she followed the kitty at the sedate speed Lee kept it at. So she went on ahead, knowing that he knew exactly where to find her, a fact that had bothered her from the start. Her consolation was that in a short while she would know exactly where he lived. On the downside, she'd live there, too.

She'd dumped her car and rented another as early in the day as possible. Once she got to her house, Cyn used the space of time before Lee arrived to pack what she needed, cover what she didn't, and figure out what the hell she could leave behind. She stored a few things in the attic, put slipcovers on the furniture, and fought the tightening in her chest as she looked around her increasingly alien house. She cleared the back room of anything that looked even vaguely martial arts related, surprised to find that when she bundled her entire sword collection together, she had more than she could lift, and a handful that she'd forgotten she even had. After a moment of thought, she divided the bundle into two parts and grabbed another tarp to wrap the second bundle. She packed the swords jelly-roll style in the blankets, rolling tightly then adding another sword, so that none of the blades or even sheaths ever touched.

Clothing was bagged and left behind or packed to go. Her eyes rolled and she re-packed when she realized that she'd included heels and nice blouses. She didn't need work clothes anymore. She called the office from her cell, as she had no land line to trace, and quit point blank. She offered all the explanations about her dying aunt. Said she was out of state and wouldn't be back. Apparently, she lied very convincingly, if the amount of gushing Marissa did and the sympathy she expressed, were any indication.

Out in the back woods, in the bright sun of afternoon, she took a break to play on the tall balance posts she had set up by sinking slim logs upright into the earth. Jumping ninja style from one small top to the other, she maintained her center and pushed down the soft bubbling inside that told her she'd have to destroy this, and she only now realized that it had been pride she'd felt when she'd come out here to practice. The tops were only just larger than the ball of one foot, and they weren't true ninja practice poles. Those swayed more the higher they were. Hers had been built just a little too sturdy for her weight.

She'd given herself a five foot span on two of the tallest ones. The seven foot height had caused countless bruises and the need to grit her teeth and ignore a lot of pain when she had started. But that was months ago and now she could make the jump easily. Her brain simultaneously swept her surroundings, finding them empty, and focused on the five inch circular top of the sawed wood where she'd be landing in a moment. Almost without input, and certainly at this point she needed none other than 'go', she pushed off her right foot and leapt. Her left toes hit square in the middle, taking the impact as her right leg came in, the spare motion absorbing some of her forward momentum. The ball of her right foot tucked in behind the left, using what little space there was to the best of her advantage.

Cyn turned, keeping her hips square over her tiny chunk of standing space, and in a heartbeat went over to another pole top. She pushed off with her left foot this time, striving to be truly ambidextrous, and landed a half foot lower than the pole she'd just left. She altered the heights in her poles so she could practice, and therefore remain stable, on changing ground.

Now she pushed herself again, to do what needed to be done. Lee couldn't stay here. The police would be out in a heartbeat if he fired rounds out of her back yard. Even if the noise didn't cause trouble, sooner or later someone hunting deer in the expanse out beyond her home would get one of Lee's bullets in him. Accidentally didn't matter. That the person would be trespassing wouldn't matter. It was Texas, everyone but Cyn owned a gun, and you just didn't shoot your neighbors.

She spotted the ground and hopped down with ease, even though her feet had been well over her own height to start with. A deep sigh settled into her chest even though she fought it and she pulled on work gloves before picking up the shovel and hacking at the dirt around the tallest pole. She'd worked so hard to sink these.

"I can get that."

A hand appeared over her shoulder, startling her, but she didn't let it show. Giving herself a swift mental kick for not knowing he was there, she spoke. "I can do it."

"I know you can. But I can probably do it faster and you need to finish up inside. I can't sort your things for you." He plucked the shovel from her fingers and went to work bare-handed.

Cyn hadn't protested. It wouldn't have done any good anyway. She went back into the house where the air was cooler and less disconcerting. She berated herself again for letting him sneak up on her, and promised herself she'd be hyper-vigilant. Now was not the time to become lax, what with the move and the new partner, all of which might very well spell more trouble. In any case, it was a new M.O., and that alone created a need for greater awareness. New was when you were likely to make a mistake.

She had packed and stored and made several trips in her rental car, carefully putting throw away items in a series of dumpsters that made a circle around a central point fifteen miles away. Her house lay just outside the circle. She then swung by her post office box, in the small town almost twenty miles the other direction. She'd chosen it specifically because it didn't have video surveillance. She spoke to an employee for the first time since she'd opened the account two years ago, and picked up the large cardboard box that had been delivered for her. She played dumb and sweet, thinking she'd make less of a scene if she allowed the nice man to carry it to her car for her than if she just threw the thing over her shoulder and hauled it off herself. After it was situated in the backseat, she headed home for maybe the last time.

Many of her bags were missing when she returned, and Lee's car was nowhere to be seen. Lee himself was gone, but she just couldn't work herself into believing that he'd stolen her stuff. She'd feel like a Class A fool if that was indeed what had happened, but she wasn't even going to consider it for another, what? eight to ten hours. There was no way the man talked her into moving then ran off with what she'd packed when her back was turned. Also there was the problem that he knew she would hunt him down and kill him with the very weapons he'd taken, if that were the case. No, he'd be back.

Only fifteen minutes later she spotted him walking up to the house through the woods. He passed the spot where her poles had been and, to his credit, he'd flattened the earth back and covered it with the usual smattering of leaves. You would never guess what had been there. The choking sensation threatened her again, but Cyn ignored it, which was easy to do–she'd been ignoring everything that bothered her for so very long.

Lee was halfway across the grass, just a shadow in a yard of shadows created by the deepening dusk, when the spitting noise came.

"Shit!" He yelled it loud enough for her neighbors, none closer than a mile, to hear, and bolted for the house.

Cyn laughed even as he barreled into her. He knocked her off her feet because she simply hadn't reacted, and made it in the door only after the sprinkler heads had popped up one by one and started spraying. He beat the water by a hair.

"Oh yeah, laugh it up." Lee pushed to his feet from where he'd toppled them both.

"I'm guessing you made friends with my sprinklers before."

"Yeah." He nodded, still brushing imaginary carpet fibers off his t-shirt in an attempt to regain some dignity. "Out in the woods, too. I didn't see that coming."

"Well, then it did its job."

He had conceded a little. "It's brilliant. It looks stupid rather than fortified, and no one wants to steal anything through a soaker."

After she pointed out the final things to go into the trailer, including the new box, they'd eaten the last of the food in the fridge and camped out. Lee took the white sheet draped couch and Cyn used a sleeping bag on her now bare mattress. Her room wasn't the same, everything was gone except her traveling weapons–they were here, unstitched from their bears and under her pillow–and the straight backed chair that she tucked under the knob.

She hadn't been sure that she'd needed it. Her feelings now were that she needed protection from what was outside the house, rather than what was in it. The screamers would have done far more good stuck to the windows, but she'd packed all but three thinking that would be the maximum necessary for any hotel room, but it wasn't enough for her room. And not enough was the same as none, so she hadn't stuck them on.

Still, she'd slept soundly, and they'd left before first light, Lee downing the last of the milk straight from the jug. They'd tossed their trash in a restaurant dumpster two miles away and then officially hit the road. They stopped for lunch in a little mom-and-pop that was too busy to chat them up or remember anything about them, and too small to have any kind of video surveillance going.

What should have been an eighteen hour drive looked like it would be closer to twenty-four. Night was creeping up and they'd decided to drive straight through, as a U-haul at a motel was not only going to be memorable, but would prove tempting for anyone wanting to steal a wad of stuff already loaded and ready to go. The real problem was that if this U-haul was stolen, they were in deep shit. It was full of weapons, and leather outfits, and all kinds of things that could tie Cyn definitely, and Lee maybe, to a handful of homicide scenes. Driving straight through was the way to go.

They stopped at a rest area to stretch and walk a little and do anything but rest, then exited for the next drive-thru that offered something other than burgers identical to what they'd had for lunch. After the fruit and yogurt was gone, and her sandwich carefully and silently chewed, Cyn started the first conversation of the day.

Her roiling feelings about being talked into picking up stakes and moving with someone she knew both far too well and not at all had kept her quiet to this point. "Am I going to have to ask to borrow the car?"

He laughed and sucked down the last of his coke, having refused to order water because he thought it would be just another thing someone might remember, and there was nothing they wanted like they wanted to be invisible. "Can you drive a stick?"

She snorted. "Of course I can. I bought an old car and ground the gears to dust until I learned."

"Why did you do that?"

"This boy in high school was teasing me saying that girls couldn't drive a manual."

Lee nodded, as though the machinations of high school were something from his distant past, like they were in hers. "You showed him."

"Not really." She started in on the fries while she talked. "I got access to my money when I turned eighteen. That's when I bought the car and finally started doing what I needed to. I had already dropped out of high school by then."

Lee shook his head a little like it was all just a bit too much to digest. “You dropped out of high school?”

“Sure.” She shrugged and swallowed the fries she was chewing, although she wasn’t really sure why she was still eating them since they tasted like salted cardboard. “Look, Mr. CPA, not everyone needs to attend Trigonometry through to the last day in June.”

“But how’d you get your job without a diploma? Don’t you need that now, even in the mall?”

“I got my GED.” She laughed. “I took that fucking test four times.”

He frowned into the night ahead of him. “It doesn’t seem like you to go do something and fail it.”

“Who said I failed? I’ve got four GEDs under four different names.” She shook her head, as though that might dispel why she’d felt so compelled to actually test each time. “I’ve got driver’s licenses in all the names by using forged birth certificates, but for some reason I felt it necessary to take that test each time. The birth certificates are the only things that are fakes.”

“That’s kind of crazy.”

“It keeps me alive.” Cyn tilted her head and went back to eating the cardboard fries. She figured if she was hungry enough to chew them, then she ought to do so. There was no telling when they’d get to stop again.

With no warning he changed the subject. “I still don’t see why we didn’t sell your car.”

“I don’t need the money. My folks’ life insurance policies were big. Millions. And selling the car makes us memorable.” The last fry came up covered in visible granules of salt, but since the salt only improved upon the lack of flavor, Cyn ate that one, too.

“When they find the car and trace it to the owner of that house, then we might just be screwed.”

She sighed. She’d gotten rid of the car before he returned and had rented another for just the previous day. “Look, I spent a long time dumping that car. It isn’t going to come back and bite me in the ass, and therefore isn’t going to bite you in the ass either.”

He hugged the right hand side of the freeway, gearing up for the long exit onto I-40 as they left Little Rock. Because darkness had descended, they hadn’t seen anything of the town, just an abundance of exits and a few extra tall lamps lighting their way. The kitty’s high-beams cut through the gradually opening country as they made their way out the sprawl that was nearly identical to what they'd driven through on the west side of town. After a minute of following road signs Lee picked up his previous thread. "All that car has to do is get linked to the owner of that house, or the girl who works in the mall, and all is fucked. Royally."

"Not gonna happen. Do you think I didn't think of that?" She crushed the fry box and sucked down the last of her soda, pushing all of it down into the now empty food bag and shoved that to the side of the foot well. There wasn't room in the back, it was crammed with suitcases and the things they had gathered this morning. Normally she would never have traveled with so much visible, but the U-haul was stuffed, and the trunk had other suitcases, and if they were–God forbid–pulled over, the search would yield nothing in the car and it would look normal to have all the gear as they were clearly moving.

Cyn situated herself almost sideways in a desperate need to keep her legs and ass from going to sleep. For all the training and practice that she'd done, she'd never learned how to prevent that one. "The car isn't registered to the same person who bought the house. I bought it three states over. The night before, I pulled the Texas plates off and packed them in the trailer. The car is wearing a set of Utah plates that go to a car of the same make and color and model year. When I registered the car, I got those Texas plates under a third name, then I pulled the vehicle ID numbers off and replaced them with some from another car of the same make and model year that I got from a junkyard in Florida. And yesterday I sank the car in deep water, long before the sun came up, just outside of Amarillo. I took the bus to Lubbock, where I rented the car to go to Dallas. So even if they see the tracks leading into the water, which I think I covered pretty damn well, and they pull the damn thing up, I just don't think it's going to get traced."

He blinked a few times. "I had no idea you were that paranoid."

"Sure you did. I'm alive." She turned back to face the front, "And you're not one to talk Mr. I-live-in-a-shack. I looked this car up and down and you seem pretty paranoid about your kitty getting traced back to you. What I did was really no more effort than your I-practically-built-my-own-car-so-there-would-be-no-records, you know."

* * *

Lee sighed, they were on the way back from the third army supply store they'd hit in the five days since he'd brought Sin to his shack. He'd known when he packed the U-haul that he couldn't handle her. But more what he couldn't handle was the look on her face when they'd arrived.

She'd accepted the generator and the fact that there were only four rooms with grace. She'd looked at the pump by the sink like it was quaint, and maybe to be treasured. But she'd looked at the U-haul trailer and seen that everything would not fit into the shack. Her room was piled high with boxes and bags, and he couldn't just add another room onto the building.

They'd worked their butts off, making things fit. So Lee had been surprised at the warmth that had suddenly begun to permeate the small log cabin. It wasn't a shack anymore. Sin cleaned, dusted and washed, and acted incredibly female. She practically nested. He'd had to stop her before she made the place look too lived in, or made it too difficult to abandon.

That was another thing. He'd had an entirely mobile life up until this point. When he'd taken the attacker out that morning on the trail, he'd simply gone back to where he was staying and he'd been out, and out without a trace, inside of a few hours. There were traces everywhere now that Sin was here. She lived a planted life. She had no ties to family, but the girl clearly put down roots. Jesus, if he wasn't careful there'd be ironed curtains hanging in the windows.

His only consolation was that, aside from the weapons, the place didn't look like it was inhabited by killers. Still. They'd had to make trips out three times. Sin didn't want to stay behind, and she didn't know the area well enough herself to go alone. And they really did seem to function well together. They'd stood shoulder to shoulder in the Army Surplus Store and looked at tarps, tents, and camouflage netting. They'd seen what was there and worked out a plan that they both liked.

In a few hours, the kitty was unloaded and they'd cleared a few small key trees out in a twelve foot by twelve foot space, leaving older taller growth to provide canopy. They laid ground cover for cushioning then used plywood and the cut trunks to construct some crude flooring. They wrapped standing trunks of the large trees in the army green canvas tarps and tented it with waterproof sheeting in the dullest brown color they could find. Then they skirted the whole thing with the camo netting, making it impossible to see until you were nearly on top of it. It was simply a bigger, better constructed version of his 'garage'.

Sin had worked like a dog. Aside from insisting that she wear leather work gloves constantly, which Lee hadn't bothered with since he'd hit the road three years ago, figuring the pain of blisters and the toughened hands were both good for him, Sin had done just as much work as he had.

While he stood back to inspect the lean-to, looking for flaws or ways to improve it, Sin was already hauling things inside. He'd seen her weapons collection before, but continued to be impressed by the sheer volume. This was even after she'd gone around with some wicked epoxy and the biggest wad of Velcro he'd ever seen and hidden daggers, swords, and throwing knives all over the inside of the cabin. She wedged a few in key, hidden places on the outside as well, and stuck screamers on all the windows. But even with all that already placed, she unrolled sword after sword. Knives were bound with what looked like ponytail holders. When unpacked, throwing stars clattered in great heaps to the crude floor where she knelt. And Sin looked happy, like a kid at Christmas, even though she was opening all her own stuff.

He would never have tangled with her in his past life. He would never have gotten past the leather outfits or the penchant for weapons. He'd been used to women with careers or kids on their minds, not death. But here she was, not only in his house, but he was building rooms for her and altering his life around her. Because this child with her toys could bring him down.

Because he wasn't living his old life. It had been ripped out from underneath him. And when he'd opened his eyes from his alcoholic haze after Samantha and Bethany's deaths, he'd seen that this was the life that had always been lingering just under his own.

While his life had been solitary for years, he realized now that it had been that way because there hadn't been anyone else to bring into it. But he was human, he craved company. Sam had read him an article once about abused children; she'd said they thrived, while it was neglected children that died. Humans needed contact, even if it wasn't favorable, and he had to wonder if he'd been neglecting himself and had maybe moved into the 'abuse' category by bringing Sin here. But there'd been nothing else for it–this was the human contact he was getting.

And maybe it could work. Although this was turning out to be a damn lot of work for that 'trial period' they'd discussed it as. Still, he was determined, even if he wasn't sure if he was making a friend or simply keeping his enemy close. "You got a minute?"

Sin looked up from her toys and frowned. "Sure." Even while looking at him and getting off the floor in a single liquid motion, her hand automatically moved to cover the gleaming metal at her feet before she followed, the frown still in place.

He traipsed through the woods, noisy for him, but still far quieter than the usual human. Leading her about a tenth of mile, Lee decided he liked the fact that she didn't chatter, didn't ask questions, just followed.

When he stopped, he heard her breath suck in. "You didn't."

"I did. Happy Birthday, Cynthia Beller." He'd had to state her last name, her real last name, so she'd know it wasn't just a saying. He knew he'd given her the gift out of kindness, and had reminded her of her birthday as a way of letting her know that he knew who she really was.

She was walking around and through the standing poles. "They're the same ones from my yard."

"I packed them up and brought them in the trailer."

Sin sounded awed. Immediately, he regretted rubbing her face in his knowledge, both because it had been a little mean, and because it apparently had been wasted. She hadn't caught the slight. She was too busy rubbing her hands along the smooth trunks of the slim trees she must have chopped herself when she first set them up in Texas. She paced the distances between them, "Wow, you even got the dimensions almost exact."

He tapped his head, and couldn't help smiling at her wonder. "I memorized them."

Of course, he should have known Sin would point out that they were 'almost' exact and not dead on. But in her sneakers and stretch jeans she climbed them like a cat, leaping agilely from one post top to another until she stood, happy as he'd ever seen her, perched far over his head.

For a moment he wondered if she was going to jump down on him and strike a nerve bundle and go all way-of-the-ninja on him. But she didn't. She beamed down from high above.

Lee felt . . . he wasn't sure. He couldn't categorize it. It had been so long since he'd felt it. Felt anything. And that was what surprised him–he felt.

Owen blinked at his wife. Annika had just told the hostess that they'd look at menus and place an order to go. She smiled up at him, seeing, but not soothing, his bewilderment.

They sat at the bar not talking much. So it came as a complete surprise when he asked why they were getting the food to go and she'd replied with, 'we need to talk.' Why the hell they couldn't talk here confused him until he figured it out and realized he was in deep shit.

Keeping his feelings to himself, he stayed silent while they waited, and then paid for the huge bag of food. He followed his wife out into a day that was far too beautiful for what he was now certain was coming. She pressed the keychain button, setting off a short series of beeps on the nice car that she'd protested when he'd gotten it for her. Owen pulled at the passenger door and slid in, waiting for Annika to take the wheel and not liking the trapped feeling that was slowly washing over him. Even though he knew he deserved every ounce of it.

Annika had swung by and picked him up just beyond the front parking lot at the Bureau for a lunch together. He tried to manage one of these meals each week while Charlotte was in school. Just the two of them. Just to keep in touch with his wife. Now she looked at him sideways a few times on the drive home and he wished that his stomach wasn't churning, that he could really enjoy the smell of the food, because in his brain he knew it smelled wonderful. If only he didn't feel like he was going to vomit.

Pulling smoothly into the driveway, Annika pushed the gearshift into 'park' and started to get out. But Owen stopped her with a hand on her arm, not able to stand any more. He would have heaved but the deep clenching in his stomach prevented it. "Are you going to divorce me?"

Cold dread congealed in his gut and his eyes stared blankly ahead, his ears tuned for her answer. He knew she was going to say 'yes' and he also knew that he couldn't take it. He was horrible at showing it, but there was nothing in this world that was worth more than Annika and Charlotte.

Her hand passed in front of his face, forcing him to focus on her, on the here and now, no matter how certain he was that he wouldn't like it.

"I'm not divorcing you." Her head tilted and her eyes swam with pity. He didn't like Annika pitying him, but Owen figured it was about five thousand times better than what he'd expected, so he took it.

She spoke again before he could register his good luck and form words. "I knew what you were and what you did when I married you. I don't want to change you. I'd like to have you around more. But I'd rather have you a little than have you a lot and have you resent me for it."

"I wouldn't–"

Her hand on his arm effectively cut off his attempt to gush into an explanation. He was used to being calm and cool. He found dead bodies, the latest chain of cadavers had been killed in the most creative of ways, and rarely did he get worked up. But the thought of Annika leaving put his fear on high alert and his heart at risk. Owen wanted to tell her about his plan to quit the FBI. But he hadn't so far because he couldn't say when the ninja case would end. And he didn't want her and Charlotte hanging onto something that might be a while coming. He knew he couldn't live with himself if he left that one hanging.

"Let's go inside." Annika's hand slipped gracefully from his arm, and Owen was forced to find his legs and use them. Once inside it was Annika who gushed at him. "I didn't mean to scare you. I just wanted to talk about the ninja and we can't do that when we're out. I don't want to get you fired, but I love hearing about your cases."

She took the food from him and began setting it out on the table. Only the table had been draped with a linen tablecloth and set with a few candles and the nice china. She smiled at him, that wide, Russian, big-eyed look that had caught him deep in the gut years ago. He'd had a visceral reaction the first time he'd seen her, and while he didn't feel the punch to his chest anymore it wasn't because he didn't react the same way, but simply because he'd gotten used to it.

He was definitely leaving the Bureau.

She set out the meals, pushing them from their covered tinfoil pans onto the plates and frowning at the loss of presentation. Having missed his moment, Owen didn't try to grab her and haul her off to the bedroom. She wanted to hear about his work. Since she wasn't leaving him, what Annika wanted, Annika got.

He pulled her chair out for her, earning another big smile, and lit the candles, figuring she wanted the lighting that way if she'd set them out. They certainly hadn't been there this morning. He seated himself across the small table, all of its scars hidden now under the linen, and enjoyed the way the candles lit her face up. "What do you want to know?"

She sighed. "You said you were hoping to get more hair off the ninja. That would help prove she was female." Here she frowned. "Long hair doesn't prove the ninja is female."

"No, but double-X DNA in the hair does." He dug into the steaming plate of pasta, finally able to savor the smells wafting up to him.

"That just proves you have female hair, not a female ninja." She took a delicate bite of fish then continued. "I mean, I'm certain the ninja is female. I just don't get what the other hair proves."

He sighed. Then he was off and running, talking about the ninja even on his date with his wife. "That's the problem, none of it proves anything. But it would be damn circumstantial, because it would prove that the same woman was at two sites. If one is the campus rapist and the other is any mafia man, then the grudge ninja is the only link and therefore it must be her."

Annika nodded. "That's a shame you're not going to get any more hair then."

Owen stopped mid-bite. He'd twirled a forkful of linguini, but now it was poised halfway between the plate and his lips. "Why not? We got it once."

"That's the problem. You got it *once*."

She took another bite, and Owen took that as his cue to eat his own food, Annika was about to give up something good. He really wished he could have the FBI write out a portion of his salary to her and give her access to all the files. But they would never go for that. Instead, he chewed and waited.

Sure enough, Annika spoke when she finished the bite. "See, I've been researching your campus rapist online when I had the time. Reading police reports and the crime log from the campus paper."

Owen cocked his head and took another bite while he listened. He hadn't gone very far at all in that direction. The ninja had killed the guy, so good riddance. And he'd clearly fallen in her non-mafia pattern: bad guy hurting innocents. What else was there to research? But Owen was eating his nice lunch at home, so there had to be something. He took a moment to be glad he'd shown Annika how to research police reports.

"You don't have any other hair samples, because she's been very careful and knows what she's doing. You only have that one because she had to give it up to get the rapist."

"Continue."

"The rapist was grabbing his victims by the ponytail and cutting off their clothes. He preferred overalls, or girls in loose jeans. So that's how she dressed to bait him. Unless you want to send a rapist out with a similar M.O. you won't get any more hair, or probably clothing fibers, off her. She probably purchased the clothing for just that reason, and it won't lead anywhere."

Owen sat back. Annika was right. It hadn't been a fuck-up at all. The ninja had trapped the rapist, and who knew how long that had taken? The hair and the clothing fibers had been a calculated risk, a freebie. She wouldn't give them more. And Owen couldn't harm innocents, or let a criminal go unstopped just so they could bait her.

The more they learned about her, it seemed the less evidence they had.

"Besides," Annika spoke again after another few bites of her lunch. "Do you really need matching hair samples? You have the handwriting. It links most of the scenes, as does the M.O."

"No, we don't *need* it. We don't need anything in particular, just something that would give us proof."

"Seems to me you're going to be hard pressed to get it."

"Thanks, Anni." The wry tones had seeped into his voice, his comfort having returned after he believed she wasn't going anywhere. "If we had a fingerprint, that would be something."

"No, it's not." Annika laughed out loud at him. "It's like the hair. In and of itself it means nothing. You have to have a match to make it worthwhile. Do you really think this woman has fingerprints on file?"

Owen turned that one over, too. "For a long time I did. I've continued to delude myself into a little hope."

"Please." Anni gestured with the spinach pasta at the tip of her fork. "With everything else you've seen, you think she's going to let you match a fingerprint? She's either not on file, so you have the hair problem again–meaning you have to get her in custody and yank a hair physically off her head to see if it matches. Or, if her prints *are* on file, then I'd bet she's rubbed her fingers bare or something. It's never going to happen. You'll have to get her another way."

Owen swallowed the last of the pasta, his stomach happy and full. "So what do you propose we do, Sherlock?"

Annika laughed. "Got me."

"Then I guess I'm up shit creek without a paddle."

Her face changed again to a more thoughtful look. "You know, I've never understood that expression."

Owen's mouth twitched. It was very unlike Annika to need an explanation. English was her second language, but she spoke and understood it better than most of the people he worked with. "Well, shit creek would be a really bad place to not be able to get around."

She tossed him a dirty look. "I get that. But 'up' and 'down' the creek refer to the movement of the current. So if you're 'up the creek,' then you don't need a paddle, you should just float along to wherever you need to be. Now '*down* shit creek without a paddle' would be a really bad place to be."

Owen leaned over, putting his elbows square on the table and getting as close to her as he could. "Anni, I love you. Don't ever leave me."

Cyn ground her teeth, and then pushed the frustration to the back of her mind and ordered her jaw to stop working her molars together. It stopped.

But, while she had supreme control over her outward movement, and therefore appearance, she couldn't actually stop the frustration that was building inside her, only tamp it down a little. "Can I please drive?"

"I– . . . Well–" Lee paused. "You know."

Yeah, she knew. It was his baby, he'd practically built it, the 'kitty', and all that crap. "It has five gears plus reverse, it's not a fuckin' space ship."

He blinked, but didn't concede. "I have no idea what your skills are. I've never actually seen you drive stick."

"That's because you won't let me drive." She sucked a small amount of air in through her nose, trying to center herself. It didn't pay to be frustrated, and she so rarely was, but Lee worked his way under her skin easier than anyone had since Wendy. For a brief moment, pangs shot through her as she remembered the fights she and her two-years-older sister had been having before that night. Cyn shook it off.

"Can it wait until we unload the trailer?"

"Of course it can." It was his damn car and his damn choice. At least it would be until she snuck out in the middle of the night and put a hundred miles on it joyriding. But that would only prove that she actually was as immature as he seemed to think. She fought off the sigh that would sound like more of the same.

They were almost to Chillicothe, having just crossed the Kentucky / Ohio border, where they were going to return the trailer. Cyn had used the generator to fuel her hair dryer, and in an attempt to look non-lethal, curled her hair this morning as well. Lee had dried his hair, too, turning it into some big mass of curls and fluff, and rendering his face virtually invisible with the hair drawing enough attention away from any of his otherwise memorable features.

She'd had to hear this puffball tell her she couldn't drive his beat-up old car for almost a week now. She wanted her nice sedan back. The one she could park curbside, or at the mall, and have it blend in perfectly. She'd dented the back door on each side, just for that purpose, but Lee had taken that to a whole new level.

"You know," she started. "I need my own car."

Lee watched the overhead signs, taking the exit off I-75 for I-77, offering a slightly more direct route. "True."

"Let's get me one while we're here. Then I'll never have to drive the kitty." She pressed her advantage, trying to keep the tone of bribery out of her voice and only partially succeeding.

"Not in Chillicothe."

"Of course not. Jesus." She shook her head. "You know, I'd be long dead if I operated the way you seem to think I do."

The trailer was getting returned to Chillicothe because it was nowhere near Lee's cabin. Her cabin now. They'd set up the drop off point when they rented the U-haul in Boulder. Neither end was anywhere near either house. And, since it was just a pull trailer, it didn't log miles. Lee had discretely checked for a small odometer attached to either tire when they'd rented it, and found nothing.

"It may mean an extra day out. Or more." He eased onto the brake, swerving around a pothole in the road.

Even here there was evidence of the winters being colder. The road expanded and contracted with the seasons, wreaking havoc on the pavement. Cyn could feel the tug and sway of the now empty trailer as it was hauled along behind them. "An extra day doesn't matter. We need another car. I'm not going to last long if I need to ask for the keys all the time. And what would either of us do if we needed to get out while the other one was already out?"

There wasn't a bus stop, or even a good freeway close enough to walk. If Lee was gone and she went out to the closest road and hitched a ride, well, she might be there a damn long while waiting. In fact, it was likely that Lee would be the first one to come by. She needed her own set of wheels.

When they finally found the small U-haul center, it was only a fraction of the business done by Jed's Tire and Auto Body. Cyn smiled and batted her eyelashes and signed the paperwork in Cynthia Winslow's frothy scrawl. Lee had scratched his head and thanked the guy for unhooking the trailer. He'd played dumb, saying they'd had the thing on the whole time, when he himself had hitched and unhitched it on several occasions.

Cyn faked a smile at one of the cover-all'ed and greasy employees as they pulled away. "Let's blow this popcorn stand."

"You're serious about a car?"

She only leveled a gaze at him.

He sighed and accepted. Popping open the glove compartment he tossed a four state map into her lap. "Well then Cyn, where's your new car?"

She pulled open the large paper and looked at the threads of tiny red lines, running vein-like across the map. Lee was already heading south, so she checked that way first. "I think it's just north of Charlotte. Where the freeways cross." She tapped the spot with her finger, and held the map up to him.

Seven hours later they were at a used car dealership. Being lucky, they'd found a car in a shade that would blend into the forest. It needed some work on the outside, which wasn't going to get done. And it needed some work on the inside, which was going to be Lee's job. And that left them trying to barter down the cost, to something in the range of the cash Cyn had stashed. She always had large amounts of cash on hand, and extra while traveling. While she didn't have quite what the dealer was asking, it was enough to cover the car's value.

They'd dressed casually to return the U-haul that morning, with both of them in jeans and Cyn in a ponytail. She was slugging a liter of coke and worrying some slick pink lip-gloss off her mouth while she argued with Lee. He told the dealer they couldn't afford the car.

He was right, they didn't have enough cash on hand. Neither of them had a bank account so an ATM wouldn't cut it. That also meant no checks. And they sure as hell weren't going to leave and come back.

So Cyn played what she could. She looked up at Lee, as though he was just deciding against her. She gave him the puppy-dog eyes, and drew the word out to three syllables. "Dad."

His eyes narrowed just a fraction but he held it together. "*Cyndy,*" He returned, "we just can't afford this right now."

She played it for all it was worth, even pouting to the dealer, and getting him to come down a little, because 'Daddy' was being stubborn.

A half hour later she pulled out of the lot driving the old, pale green Toyota behind the kitty, and doing a little victory dance behind the wheel. She was out of cash, only the twenty stuck in her back pocket to save her, and that wasn't enough to get her either gas or food back to the cabin.

Lee didn't speak when they pulled over at the rest stop. But there was no need, they simply watched each others backs and the cars before they climbed back in and started off down the road again.

A half hour after that, she was flashing the high-beams at him as the engine sputtered and the car lost all power. Cyn fought the wheel, much harder to turn now without the power steering, and banked the car on the side of the road.

Lee sprayed gravel as he backed up and, leaving the cars nose to tail, he motioned for her to pop the hood. She was already out and watching as, with a paper towel to protect his fingers, he grabbed quickly at wires and swore softly as he looked under hoses and checked her oil level.

He was shaking his head as he headed back to the kitty and returned with a roll of duct tape and a quart of oil. "You're leaking. Not bad, or we'd have to stay over somewhere and fix it tomorrow, but we won't take it all the way in with us."

His fingers deftly ripped off a piece of tape and he wound it around one small cracked-looking hose a few times. He topped off her oil with the quart in his hand, speaking while he did it. "When we get close we'll park her around the other side, then you hop in with me and we'll go in the usual way."

Only managing to get some of the grease off his fingers, Lee pushed the hood back down into place. "That ought to get us home."

He turned back toward the kitty. But then he stopped and came back square to her, making Cyn wonder what was up.

"And, by the way, I am *not* your Dad."

Chapter 10

Lee tried not to swallow his tongue. Every time he watched her work, he was in awe. Although, given the hours she had logged since she'd arrived, it was no wonder she had mastered such inhuman looking feats.

The large cardboard box that had been delivered to her in Texas had contained another of the practice dummies. Lee had originally thought the cracked and broken one in her workout room had been old. But now he wondered if she didn't just keep ordering them. He'd seen the ads on TV, even remembered watching the whole thirty minute program that insisted that he call now. He hadn't been able to call as he'd had Bethy in his arms, happily slurping down a bottle. Nor had he wanted to. He'd had no need for anything advertised as 'tiger tough'. Sin had destroyed the old one. From the looks of her current workout, she had destroyed it at a much more rapid pace than he'd ever imagined. And the thing really did look 'tiger tough', there just probably wasn't a tiger alive that could take Sin.

Her focus was as intriguing as her movements. She clearly saw that he was standing there at the edge of her vision. She'd even given the one finger up sign between punches, indicating she'd be with him in a minute. But still she'd kept her eyes on the green plastic human form. Red lights flashed randomly, encouraging the fighter to hit them off. None ever flashed twice for Sin, even at 'master' speed, where she'd set it as soon as she'd pulled it from the box, before they'd hot-wired it to a car battery. Aside from its non-Sin-proof construction, the thing seemed to work perfectly. It was Sin's speed that ensured that the lights didn't finish the first flash before her knuckles or the heel of her hand or her elbow collided with the light, stopping it. A few times he'd blinked and realized he'd completely missed a hit. She was just that fast.

He was fast, too. Lee could have a gun on somebody and have them shot dead before they knew what hit them. He didn't sling wild bullets with fear or ineptitude. He practiced almost everyday. But at this point he'd been content with maintaining his skill and spending his time finding his next mark. Sin's concentration spoke of having mountains still to climb.

The dummy congratulated her in a synthetic voice praising her perfect score, and with a look that combined both her victory and the obvious irony, she bowed to it before slapping it off. A backward step brought her heel into contact with the edge of the gym mats they'd purchased a few days earlier. Her body shifted slightly allowing for the changing height of the floor, but she didn't falter. At last, she turned and gave him her attention even as she unwrapped thin cheap strips of gauze from her knuckles. Lee had initially thought they were there to protect her skin, but now he thought maybe it was to preserve the integrity of her dummy.

She didn't speak, but looked up at him waiting, much smaller than someone of her power ought to be.

"I threw all the knives. I suck." Lee stayed leaning in the doorway. He needed another lesson. And so did she. They needed to improve, to expand, both of them, and this was the easiest way.

"Fine." She slid past him, needing only the tiny sliver of space he'd afforded. Not changing from her workout gear of leggings and t-shirt, she pressed over to the end of a long run they'd cleared.

Looking over her shoulder he saw that her palms bore blisters, likely the result of the shoveling and construction they'd been doing. Again he thought of what they'd built, and how in a very short period of time Sin had dug some very deep roots.

A wide circle of wood, sliced from an old tree and about a foot thick, was propped up at the end of the run. A fistful of her unadorned knives stuck out from it at odd and varied angles. A few others lay on the ground in front of it having bounced right off. Lee wasn't proud of that, but he also figured if he hid his errors he wasn't very likely to improve.

Sin looked over the slab and picked up the fallen knives. "Your aim is good. Looks like you're hitting the wood, but you aren't watching your distance well enough. If you aren't an even number of revolutions away you'll hit with the back of the knife."

He frowned. "I thought you said these were back-weighted so that wasn't a problem."

"They are back-weighted, so it's *less* of a problem. But clearly you can still have it hit handle forward." She plucked one knife from the bundle she held loosely in her left hand as she casually walked a good distance down the run and, with only a glance, sent it flying at the wood. With a dull thud it hit square in the center and dropped, dead, to the ground.

Lee nodded. Yes, clearly you could hit with the handle. He pretty much had figured that out after he'd watched the first few fall to the ground. At least it had been due to bad pacing or whatever, not sheer stupidity.

Sin jogged him from his thoughts, smacking a blade into the palm of his hand, almost surgery style. Since these were point sharpened, he hadn't been in any danger, but there were still moments when he wondered. "Throw it."

Moment of truth, he thought: performing the art in front of the master. He felt as though he'd taken brush to canvas, copied Van Gogh's *Sunflowers*, then presented it to the earless one himself. Not the best feeling. He threw, and tried not to show how grateful he was that the knife landed with a *thwack* in a spot close to the center of the wood.

Sin probably hadn't seen it stick, she was all over him, hands on his arms, her feet kicking at his ankles, getting him into a proper stance whether he wished it or not. She frowned as she grabbed his hand and worked his arm like he was a giant doll, mocking the throwing motion.

That was enough. "What the hell are you doing?"

She shrugged. "I never taught anyone before. No one even knew I could do this. No one saw. I had some video tapes I watched and that was it." She had slipped into that teenager look again, this time perplexed. She shrugged a little, "I don't know, you just do it. You just throw at the wood until you get it."

He threw again, and again earned a satisfying *thwack*. But he didn't have her single-mindedness. "Is there anything else I can practice on?"

"Well, after the wood block, I started going for the trees. Lay out a plan," she pointed out several nearby trunks one by one, "then you lay a knife into the middle of each one, fast as you can."

Lee nodded.

Sin raised her eyebrows at him. "But warn me before you do that, okay? Because you suck."

"Thanks." But he sure as hell wouldn't want to explain that one to the hospital staff. So he offered a conciliatory nod and continued throwing the knives at the slab of wood.

Sin continued watching him and frowning. Far too often she grabbed one of his limbs and paced it through the appropriate motions, more than once modeling it on herself first. Whether that was for him or for her, Lee didn't know. But he improved.

Of course he improved. He couldn't *not* improve. Sin was watching him work with the same fierce determination that she applied to her own practice. She never smiled and her eyes never faltered. And she never tired of watching the knives hit the wood and get pulled free again.

Lee did.

"So if I have to be at a certain distance to know that I won't hit with the handle, then how do you use these in a fight?" He had mentally marked off a toe line where he knew he would have the correct number of revolutions to land the knives blade forward. It was the main reason he'd improved, at least by his own count. "I mean, I can't very well walk up to some guy in a fight and then pace back three steps before I turn and lay a knife into him. I don't think he'd stand still for it."

That didn't even earn him the slightest crack of a smile.

Nothing.

He sighed.

Sin responded earnestly. "You practice, you learn. The knife isn't that long, so you can easily adjust the length, and therefore the revolutions, by just stepping forward or back a little bit."

"Of course. But how do you know how far away something is to make the correct adjustment?"

"Practice." She reached out for the bundle of knives he held in his left hand and took them into her right. He'd already grown tired of watching her ambidextrous skills, and sure enough this time she threw left-handed. At least she didn't flaunt it, just stated it as a natural course to take given the nature of her needs.

Sin turned sideways to the cleared strip of land for throwing. With no warning, her left hand flew, lithely plucking blades from her right palm and laying a series of six of them into six different trunks all at different distances from where she stood. Unlike his blades which had pointed up and down like spokes gone awry, hers were all perfectly parallel to the ground, aimed straight into the heart of each tree. Each knife had landed square in the center of each trunk, no matter how wide, and unlike his, none hung by a tip or quivered. Hers aimed true and burrowed deep.

Her voice cut through his thoughts, his brain had been using his own skill as a reference and trying to back calculate how many hours of that single-minded practice had been necessary to achieve this. "When you can do that, then you do this."

Again her hand flew and she hit the same six trunks in the same order, not hitting a single of the already-sunk blades. And she missed every time.

Each blade hit the tree with a dull *thud* and dropped, lifeless, to the undergrowth beneath it.

"Yeah, I can already do *that*." Lee drawled.

That at least earned him a laugh. "Bet you can't." She was circling the area, knowing he wouldn't throw any of the knives he held while she was in range. "These are back weighted, that means the time spent with the handle forward is less because the knife's center of gravity, it's spin point, is in the handle. That makes it easier to sink the tip and even harder to hit with the handle."

She had a point.

But then again, she usually did.

So Lee changed tacks. "That's a great skill and all, but why would I want to hit with the handle?"

"Well there's the obvious practice-with-any-of-it-makes-you-better-at-all-of-it issue." And Lee figured out the rest even before she spoke it. "Then you can drop someone with a bump to the head. It seems to be just shy of a concussion, depending on the distance. But I had only one guy still standing after I nailed him right here." She lifted a hand and touched the back of her head.

She handed the knives back so he could practice his obviously inferior ability.

Lee lasted another twenty minutes before he was bored with watching a slab of wood take it for some unknown crime and with having Sin watch him like a hawk. He was afraid to scratch his nose, or god forbid, his ass. He polished off the bundle of knives he held in his hand, sending each one into the scarred wood and leaving them there. "Want to shoot?"

"Sure." Her face changed. Her concentration ebbed for just a minute, and again she looked like a kid. He could have offered Bethy ice cream out of the blue and gotten that same expression. Sin made him afraid for the state of the world. She lit up like the fourth of July because she was going to shoot stuff.

And she was shooting stuff so that she could use the skill to do murder when the time came. He waited for her to jump up and down and clap her hands. But thankfully she didn't.

She quickly made her way to the edge of an old cleared area that had been one of the selling points of the cabin when he'd first stumbled across it. Lee had plastic bottles strung from branches and hanging between the trees at the far end. A few were sitting on posts and upright cut logs closer in. Some of the hanging bottles he'd jury rigged with strings so that he could reach up and yank the cord over his head, setting his targets in motion.

Quickly, Sin focused again, that severe energy settling over her as she geared up. She donned the second set of earphones and glasses he'd bought this week as well, to protect her hearing and vision while she practiced. The two of them had traveled far and wide getting all kinds of crap he'd never had before but suddenly *needed* when Sin arrived. They couldn't–wouldn't–purchase too much at a single store. They couldn't afford to be remembered and didn't want to trip any homeland security flags with the combination of things they bought. The earphones and glasses were the least of it.

Lee sighed and pulled both of the Hecklers from the side holsters he'd sewn onto his jeans. Just about every pair he owned had the loops that looked like carpenter jeans to the outside world. But he was never without at least one of his guns. He handed one to Sin and watched as she pulled back to see the round in the chamber. She flipped the safety a few times, and Lee wondered what she was up to but quickly realized she was familiarizing her hand to the gun more than anything else. She knew how the safety worked–he'd shown her himself. She was simply creating a motor pattern, now pushing the lever that let the clip fall and sliding the bullets back in several times.

He motioned into her field of vision and spoke up, knowing his voice would be slightly muffled. “Now the other hand.”

She frowned, “Guns are right handed.”

“Not these.” He smiled and realized he was an ass, for getting tired of Sin’s two-handed ability. He’d worked his own just as hard, just in a different field, and they were on his turf now.

“Huh?” Sin flipped the gun over, and looked it up and down. She almost looked right down the barrel causing his stomach to flinch, but she moved the weapon out of range soon enough, seeming to realize what she had done. She’d only shot the thing once before and at that time he’d been worried more about keeping her from killing him in the process than introducing her to the machinery she held in her hand. But while Sin had developed a quick taste for firing off rounds, and an accuracy he would have guessed, she sucked at the timing so far.

He held the second Heckler 9mm in his hand out at arm’s length, touching it with only his middle finger and thumb so he couldn’t accidentally shoot it off. He rotated it, “These are ambidextrous.”

“Neat.” Again she rotated the weapon, this time instinctively mimicking his hold and making him feel a lot better.

He’d thought about getting Sig Sauers and retrofitting half of them to work left handed. He had been at the gun show in Nevada ready to order the conversion kits, but the man behind the counter had shown him these babies. Lee smiled at Sin, “You’re right, virtually all guns are right handed, and only a very few can even be converted to left handed. But what if you had two and your right hand got shot? You can’t reload well, so you’d need to be able to pick up each loaded gun and shoot it with your left hand. Or your right, depending on the situation. Enter the P-2000.”

He slipped his fingers back across the familiar skin of the gun. The Hecklers had turned out even better than he’d expected. He could hold two and drop the clips out of both with the same motion of each hand, something not possible with a regular gun. He’d tried it on a few Glocks at the gun show, and it was difficult to make one hand do one thing and the other do something different. Harder than he’d expected it would be. It wasn’t where he wanted to put his practice time. The Heckler and Koch model had been the answer to some very sick prayers.

Lee watched as Sin held the gun in her left hand now, clearly impressed with the capabilities available to that hand as well, and she repeated all the motions she had done with her right earlier. Only because he was watching closely could he tell that her left wasn't her dominant hand.

After a moment, she quit playing and sighted a coke bottle propped on a log. He'd filled the empty ones with a good bit of dirt to anchor them in place, and Sin hit it on the first try, spraying dirt in a wide cone out the back, but leaving the bottle where it stood.

"Try to hit it higher." He leaned one hand over and touched her elbow. Lee refrained from mentioning the jolt her arms had undergone when the bullet fired. She was strong, but no amount of strength would make up for good solid weight against a good gun kick. Her hands had flown a foot high from the recoil and, with that motion, it was a wonder she could hit anything at all. But she had proved that first time that she could. There was nothing she could do about it except recoup after each round, so Lee focused on her form before the bullet left the chamber.

She hadn't held her arms out straight in front of her like her natural inclination had been last time they'd tried this. Now she bent her elbows, supposedly to take some of the shock, but held her arms so stiff that he wondered if it was doing any good.

At his touch, she relaxed her arms a little, re-sighted and squeezed off another shot. This time the red cap flew up from the bottle and then disappeared into the tall grass a few feet away. Her face showed grim determination as she adjusted again, and on the third shot she nailed it dead center.

Lee didn't point out that she had taken a serious amount of time aiming each shot, and that she'd be long dead, riddled with holes, if someone had been shooting at her. It wasn't the time. He didn't squeeze the trigger on his own gun and take out the entire row before she could blink. Knowing he could do it was enough. He gloated in silence, even as he remembered how dead he'd be in a knife fight.

Then he corrected that thought. His opponent might sink a blade into him, but he'd squeeze off a few shots and the man would be dead. So it didn't really matter how well he threw that first knife.

Sin either didn't notice the throw or didn't notice his smugness. She was determined to master his field as well as her own, and that meant killing these coke bottles. Like before, she didn't waver.

After an hour, Lee went out into the grass and set up more bottles. Training Sin was going to mean more trips to more recycling plants. More theft from bins. Jesus, she was going through more bottles than he ever had. And she was only on her second day out. Given her propensity to look the weapon up and down when not shooting it, he'd taken her clip away from her before he set foot out in the field. He didn't want her trying out her surgical skills on him because she'd accidentally set the thing off.

He picked up one bottle only to find that it shredded as he lifted it. It had taken her a while to do this amount of damage to the thing, but there was nothing left. It was definitely dead. He set up extra bottles, putting two up where there had only been one before, knowing that Sin would go through them like water, and glad he had a stash of some already filled with dirt. He glanced up to find that she had slipped the earphones off her head and had the glasses in her hand, probably needing a break from the pressure against her head the same way he did after he'd been at it too long. But she was walking a tight circle and buried deep in thought.

She had the gear back on and was ready when he returned. Handing her the full clip, a sixteen round illegal conversion, he watched as she slipped it easily into place, checked the chamber and aimed. Her shot was true, and if her aim was a little slow, it was faster and more accurate than it had been just an hour earlier. She didn't look up again, just went back to murdering innocent pop bottles.

Half an hour later Lee tapped out and went inside to read the papers. They'd picked up so many while they'd been out tooling around, and they'd been so busy that he hadn't had time to read even his usual amount. He was back-logged. Yet another obvious difference since the arrival of Sin.

It was disconcerting to say the least, to hear the almost rhythmic blasts of gunfire just beyond the window. Having always been alone, he'd never sat and listened to the noise before. Never realized how every shot would tighten his chest just a little, cause a little tiny breath to suck in. Even though he knew what it was. That it was coming. That it wasn't for him. For a moment he contemplated that he would no longer be able to go out and practice at night if he wanted. Because Sin sure as hell wouldn't sleep through this. And he lamented the loss. Not that it was huge–he'd only gone out shooting in the moonlight once, mostly because it had been the one year anniversary of Sam and Bethy's deaths and he'd been alone–but the loss of the ability to do it if he so wished was disturbing.

An hour later Lee gave up trying to read and went outside to fetch Sin. He put the headphones and safety glasses into place before leaving the door, and saw her there immediately, feet planted apart, hips square, aiming and squeezing the trigger. He was pretty certain that she hadn't moved an inch from where he'd left her.

Deliberately making noise so as not to startle her, Lee came up beside her and into her peripheral vision before putting a hand on her shoulder to stop her. She looked up, moving only her head and not breaking her stance, but she didn't speak.

It was Lee who motioned for her to take off the protective gear even as he slipped his own pieces from his head and set them on the post he used as a small table. Recognizing what he saw in her face, he asked the question he'd wanted to ask since the first time he'd watched her practice. "What do you see?"

Her eyes flickered with something. He wasn't sure what the emotion was, but it was both darker and deeper than the color of her eyes. "Leopold, Janson, Robert Listle."

Lee frowned at her, and without her seeming to notice, or maybe she just didn't care, he slipped the gun from her fingers, automatically setting the safety and releasing the clip. "Leopold is dead. Who's Janson?"

"It doesn't matter that Leopold is dead. Janson and Listle are, too. You asked what I see. I aim at them."

"Who is Janson?" He asked again, wondering if he'd get a better answer this time.

"He was there with Leopold that night. He laughed when he shot my mother. He told my father they were leaving us alive so that my father would know we'd live long lives with the memory of watching them die always burned into our brains."

Night was settling around them, fireflies were coming out in droves, and Lee wanted to practice shooting them, but he didn't move, even as an elephant-sized mosquito landed on his arm. He just asked his questions. "So what happened to Wendy? Your sister?"

He knew she had died, but didn't know the circumstance.

Instead he got an answer that brought him back around to where he wanted to be. To where they'd started.

"Robert Listle." This time Sin's eyes filled with tears and he took pity on her and gathered the armloads of equipment thinking to lead her inside. Sin picked up several things herself, glasses, boxes of ammo, all needing to be put away and providing her something to do it seemed. She set it just inside the door where it had a new home, since she'd rearranged what furniture he had, and sprawled on the couch.

He set about fixing himself a sandwich, certain that she'd clam up if he sat down beside her and simply offered an ear. He was right, she began speaking as soon as he looked away.

"My mom had a few cousins, and the state contacted them, but none of them wanted two more daughters. Especially damaged ones who would need to see a shrink and what-not. We got shuffled off to foster homes."

Her hand rose to accept the glass of milk he held out to her, but her eyes didn't.

"At first we were together, then after the second home, they split us up. We had different problems and needed different help they said. We needed each other. I was angry and acting out on everything around me. Wendy pulled inside herself and didn't speak much at all. She was weak, and Robert Listle was her savior. Or so he said.

"He was a shrink who was also a foster parent and he was taking advantage of her weakness. He was raping her."

God, Lee thought, as if what those two girls had been through hadn't been enough. But animals were that way, and only some humans had risen above the animal urges that others still existed on. And no matter what the predator was, it always went for the weak.

"Wendy wouldn't fight back. She just slipped further and further away, and I wasn't there to fight for her."

He could see Sin, or whatever she had been back then, tiny and useless, but willing to stand up for her older sister. The police report he'd found of Leopold's attack on her family had said the girls had been bound and Lee knew now, without her having to say it, that it was Sin who'd stood first, who'd found a knife and cut her own bonds open as well as her sister's. It had been Sin who'd dialed 9-1-1 and talked to the operator and then the cops. Sin had come up fighting, and she hadn't quit yet.

"I told her to put a chair under her door knob at night. Listle didn't like it, and when he got the chance, he got revenge. On Wendy." She sucked in air, or a sob, and he realized that, even though it hadn't shown before, Sin felt. And right now she felt guilt.

"I reported it, but Listle denied it. Wendy wouldn't talk, and it was chalked up to my being afraid and trying to get back with my sister. I started learning some moves, taught them to Wendy in secret, begged her to use them. But she brushed me off.

"A few months later, she told me she was pregnant and it was his."

Lee had been eating the peanut butter and jelly sandwich he'd fixed to mask his attention, but he stopped now mid-bite. He'd wondered what happened to Wendy, and wondered now why he hadn't left well enough alone. Anyone could tell just by looking at Sin that there was some seriously bad stuff under the surface. But he'd started digging and he'd sure as hell hit something. He forced himself to chew calmly and not think about his own daughter that he'd brought into this world.

"I confronted him when I got the chance, I was fourteen by then, and had some basics under my belt. I'd been practicing in private so as not to draw any attention. Surprise was my best defense, and so I worked to keep any skills unknown. I felt confident I could protect myself if he came after me, so I spoke up, but he only laughed at me. A month after that, they found Wendy in the bathtub with her wrists slit."

Lee swallowed through the growing tightness in his throat, "Did he do it?"

"I don't think so." She had slid down from her original straight-backed position, and she shook her head, still talking to some space in front of her. "Wendy was tired, hadn't been anything above depressed since that night. The years had worn on her, and she saw nothing at the end of the tunnel worth staying for. Yes, Robert Listle did it, but Wendy took her own life."

He stopped chewing and shook his head, focusing on Sin now that the story was over. She looked exhausted from the telling. The fifteen minutes of speaking had drained her far more effectively than the entire day of practice.

At last he sat on the couch beside her, not knowing what to do. Humans should offer comfort, he knew that much in his brain. The certainty of whether or not anything human existed inside either of them was even further out of reach after hearing that. But he sat there, next to her, just being, while she re-couped.

So he was startled into slipping and drowning in the deep cold in her eyes when she fixed him with her stare. "I killed him."

He blinked. She'd been fourteen. Holy shit.

But she'd been made. All those things, she was a product of them. Everyone she'd loved had been ripped from her, painfully. Some quickly, one slowly, but ripped nonetheless.

Her voice was again a shock. "My foster family held a small service for Wendy, and one of his other foster daughters said she knew about Wendy and that Listle had been doing the same to her. I just–" She sucked in air, fueling whatever she needed to get off her chest. "I couldn't let him continue."

In that moment, he understood. Something shifted inside him. There was no light at the end of his tunnel, not without Bethy and Sam. But there was satisfaction. There was knowledge that he could remove *them* from this earth, even as they had removed his family. There was drive, if nothing else. And he understood.

Some part of him locked with Sin. As young as she had been, they were really no different.

"I would have shot him," She motioned to the guns now tucked safely in his waistband. "But a teenage foster kid can't get their hands on anything legal–gunwise, and even just getting caught with anything illegal like that would have landed me in juvie. So I used what I could. I bought videos with my money, trained in my room in the middle of the night. I went out in the woods and did push-ups and sit-ups. I ran like the devil was chasing me."

Lee wondered for a moment if maybe he wasn't.

"I picked a fight with a girl at school who was known for landing her punches, I needed the bruises."

Lee frowned, but knowing Sin, there was a method here. So he waited.

"I served my detention. I'd snuck out of my foster parents' house at night before, so I knew I wouldn't be missed. And I went to his house. I used a key I'd lifted from one of his foster kids. I woke him up, by accident, and he saw me. He fought, he hurt me, but I got behind him and cut off his air. I just held on until I was sure he was dead.

"I roughed the place up, stole money and some valuable looking equipment that I could carry. I'd worn gloves and covered my head. I can't believe I got away with it. I threw out the stuff, kept the money, even knowing it would do me in if I was caught with it. But no one questioned me at all. The bruises seemed to work, no one noticed there were fresh ones.

"They had a funeral for him. I went."

She'd spoken all of this in a calm tone, as if she were relaying her trip to the grocery store, but at this point she choked. "They praised him! They said he was a saint, and the world was a poorer place without him. They talked about Wendy and how he'd tried to save her, and the guilt he'd felt at her death when she was just some pitiful foster child. And I couldn't say anything without giving myself away."

Lee breathed. "That's why you leave the notes."

Sin nodded.

"I'd have given myself up just to be sure they knew. But I still had to get Leopold. I took the money with me when I went to the next foster home. They didn't give a shit about any of their kids, just wanted the paycheck. So I worked out, practiced until I was ready, then I hit the road. I suspect they kept collecting checks for me until my eighteenth birthday; there were never any 'missing' posters up with my face on them."

"What did you do?" He'd polished off the sandwich and milk and was fascinated that this tiny girl wasn't either truly tiny or a girl.

"I used the money. A few times people tried to mug me, but I fought back and I learned. I found a guy who made fake birth certificates and got all four of the ones I've been using. I got social security cards with those, driver's licenses, an apartment, a job. The documents said I was nineteen, so I could do all those things. I got the GEDs and got a better job and a nicer place and spent all my free time practicing. When I turned eighteen I showed up as myself to claim my parents' life insurance policies. Wendy was gone so it all reverted to me. It was the last time anyone's heard from Cynthia Beller. I got the house in Texas and started on the little guys. I was working my way up to Leopold when I saw you the first time."

Her eyes looked at him then–looked into him–and he saw the sheen of tears across the bottomless brown. But even as he felt some kind of connection, she blinked. As her eyelids lifted, they left shutters, concealing whatever depths had been there just a second before.

She yawned, and stood, stretching. “I’m tired.”

But she lifted her glass and went to the sink, washing it before setting it on the small rack on the counter to dry.

Lee watched all of this with a morbid fascination. She was pure Sin again. She was likely incapable of leaving the glass dirty. Just as she was incapable of letting anyone in. While he understood now why that was, it didn’t change that it was. It didn’t change what she was.

Riveted to his spot, he tried not to stare as she went into her room and fetched her supplies, taking them into the tiny water closet. She hadn’t balked at the hand operated pump that had been rigged into a mockery of a shower. He heard the water flowing in spurts as she went about the exact same routine he’d heard every night. She showered, washing away the day’s workout and probably the errors, too. She must have scrubbed them clean every night, because Lee had never seen her make the same one twice.

Sure enough, he could look at his watch, and she would emerge, eleven minutes later, just as she did every night. It was summer and there was no air conditioning here, so she had abandoned the flannels for linen button-front shirts that hung loose and square and below her knees. She hadn’t, however, abandoned her girly soaps and lotions. He could smell her, a deceptively sweet and young scent of lilies or gardenias mixed with baby powder wafted to him. And she hadn’t abandoned the whimsy she seemed to display only in her pajamas. This sleep shirt was yellow spattered with garishly green frogs wearing pink crowns and winking at anyone who got close enough to see.

Sin carried her dirty clothes tucked under one arm, her other hand curled around the handle of the travel case with her supplies. He didn’t know if that was the result of the fact that there was no space to leave them in the bathroom, or her fastidiousness, or if she simply felt the need to be ready to get up and flee at any moment.

She disappeared beyond the flimsy door to her room. The noises she made were ones he recognized, telling him that even alone she couldn't abandon her pre-set patterns.

Only when he imagined she was asleep did Lee pull himself off the couch and take his own shower. He stayed far longer than he'd intended, knowing there was no way to ever remove what he'd heard. Bethany had been brought lovingly into a world that allowed what had happened to her–that allowed what had happened to Cynthia Beller. He had the fleeting thought that maybe it was better that Bethy was gone. That neither she nor Sam would see what the world had become. Or really, what it had always been, lurking just below the shiny surface on which they'd lived.

He dried off and went to bed, stripped down to his boxers and a single Heckler that he kept folded into his hand. Tonight he wasn't quite ready to let go of it, to slide it under the pillow. It wouldn't be close enough there. He needed the weight of it against his palm, but with a thought toward sanity, he moved his thumb and popped the clip out. He shoved that under the pillow, hoping the feel of the gun would soothe him enough.

Lee knew, because he'd felt it before, but there was a nightmare coming on tonight. He'd always slept with the loaded gun in hand when he'd felt this pressure at his chest and fallen asleep begging for Sam and Bethany to claim him while he was under.

But now he couldn't keep it loaded. Because he was likely to come up shooting. And Sin would be both the trigger and the morbid result of him firing at someone he hadn't intended to. Her very existence here altered everything.

Not wanting to fall asleep, Lee stared up at the ceiling. Here there were only un-insulated beams above his head. They held up a tiny attic space beneath the tin roof he'd covered with branches for heating and cooling. More importantly the foliage obscured the house even further, and kept the roof from making gunshot-like cracks of pure sound when acorns fell from the canopy far above and bounced off.

The beams above his head now held up more than just the roof. The attic was full of the things Sin had brought in the trailer. Things that didn't fit in or out of the house, yet things she needed. She had a suit, still in the dry cleaning bag, up there. A few pairs of heels, a box that she said held the last of Wendy's things and a few odds and ends she'd gathered from her parents. The box was barely a half-foot in any direction and Lee wondered now why he'd begrudged her so little space for a family taken away so unfairly.

He had only three rings from his family. He'd had them around his neck when he'd cashed out his own life insurance and taken Sam and Bethy's payments and disappeared. He'd gone back for nothing. Not clothing, not mementos, not even a last look. Going to ground worked better when you truly disappeared. That first night, even as grubby and worn as he'd been, he'd still looked and felt out of place in the cheap motel he would never have set foot in before. He'd showered in a stall that was barely big enough to hold him and the spider he'd killed before climbing in. Only as he'd stripped had he found the rings, his and Sam's wedding rings along with a baby ring bearing Bethany's birthstone, on a chain around his neck. He'd worn them for a year, his own version of dog-tags, so that when they found him toes up, there'd be a means to identify the strange man who came in shooting and went down the same way.

But he hadn't gone down. By some weird miracle or erroneous twist of fate, he was still standing. And he'd stayed standing long enough to run into Sin.

He saw the similarities in their stories, and no wonder. It was the same reason they'd run into each other a handful of times. It wasn't coincidence. These guys weren't easy to get to. You struck while you could, and they were after the same people. They had been forged by the same hand, possibly even the same gun.

Lee also saw the disparities in their stories.

He'd come home to find his wife and child murdered. His family had surrounded him, offered solace and soothing. Even if he hadn't taken it, he'd known they were there. He'd chosen to leave them all behind.

Sin had survived what should have been the worst experience of her life, and come up fighting. Only to find that her remaining family, her sister, wasn't there for her, was now only someone who needed from her. The cousins had sloughed the girls off on the system, and the system had just sloughed them off.

He had been an adult, with solid foundations. He'd had the ability to feed and clothe himself. Everything he'd truly loved had been killed. But he'd still been his own man. Sin hadn't been formed, Leopold was her foundation. It wasn't that Lee hadn't suffered, but in comparison his story paled to glass. All he had to do to understand Sin just a little more, was to look at his own reaction to the relatively minimum insult he'd endured.

Many times in the beginning, when he'd been running off pure rage, he'd come into this very room and suffered the blurring of his eyes from staring at his targets for too long. His back had ached and his shoulders felt like they had been rattled loose from taking the recoil of the gun too many times before he was strong enough to withstand it. He had reminded himself that the fire would forge him into steel.

Before sleep claimed him, he wondered what in hell that made Sin?

His hand clenched at the gun, his middle finger nearly pulling the trigger several times as he twitched going into deeper sleep, then later with his dreams.

He awoke with a jerk, ready to shoot. He was coming awake as his left hand slid the clip into the Heckler, and he recognized the sound of gunfire. It took only a split second to know that it was coming from beyond the window, and he didn't even have to look to know that it was Sin, up and practicing already.

Chapter 11

Cyn walked into the restaurant with her computer bag slung over her shoulder. The ball cap hid her face, the ponytail and jeans made her blend in, and the gum and University of Tennessee logo on her sweatshirt meant no one was paying her any attention.

Choosing a corner table, where she could sit on the padded booth seat attached to the wall, she pulled out her silver, generic-looking laptop and began to swiftly set up the cords. She was booted up and online in a matter of minutes. Logging in under a numerical sign-in–one of many that she rotated in an attempt to not be traced–she began to look for acquisitions by the Shields and Krestev law firm in New York. The company was a front for the Kurev family, owning many of the houses they occupied, as well as several of the businesses that laundered the money they made.

The house they'd killed Svelichko in had been a Shields and Krestev owned property. It was one of the easiest ways to find the guys they were after. Lee was in a Kinko's using their internet access to find the same thing. The two of them were hunting their next mark. Maybe a little inefficiently, being in two separate places, but necessarily so. They couldn't afford to be seen much–and could afford to be seen together even less.

When the line at the counter thinned out, she popped up and ordered a panini and fresh squeezed lemonade, liking that the food was fairly wholesome and beat the hell out of the peanut butter sandwiches and protein shakes Lee made. Cyn sighed and missed her kitchen in Texas, and promised herself that she'd go back one day.

"I know," The voice came over her as she took the first cold sip of her lemonade there at the counter. "They make the best lemonade."

The voice had ruined it. She'd been enjoying the flavor, the act of drinking something refreshing that hadn't had a chugging generator behind it, keeping it cool but not quite icy.

Cyn didn't look up. Not all the way. There were Doc Martens planted about eighteen inches apart, and they were an intriguing shade of blue. The jeans were ripped, and not too baggy, almost but not quite clinging to a firm set of male legs. The waistband disappeared under a burgundy t-shirt that had surely started its life as a bolder color. The neck was muscled like the arms that had hooked thumbs into belt loops, and the jaw above it was impossibly square and hadn't been shaved for a while. Cyn didn't make eye contact. Her lips tightened and she offered that smile that said, 'sure, whatever you say'.

His head tipped, going after a glimpse of her eyes, and Cyn let him, only because to avoid him would draw more attention. Nonetheless, it was violating.

"I haven't seen you here before."

She shook her head. Not able to form words. But wanting to say, 'and you'll never see me here again.' She couldn't come back. Not now. Not if he might be here, not if someone might recognize her. Or worse, look for her. Heading back to her table, she gave him the same tight smile, then the back of her shoulder, upset at how the day had changed with that one brief encounter.

She couldn't bring herself to continue her search, couldn't in fact bring herself to move from the Ask Jeeves web page she'd left on the laptop in case anyone looked. She typed nothing of value, spending her time now looking up Italian or Hawaiian translations of various words. Just because.

His eyes had been green. The hair on his head curled slightly and had been dark, a rich shade foretold by the shadow along his chin. When she calculated, Cyn was certain he was a year or two older than she. Maybe a grad student.

She took deep breaths, wondering why that bothered her heart so much. Why she wanted to fight to breathe, why she had to.

The trouble was that she'd had to calculate his age–the guess wasn't instinctive. She figured he was a university student because of his attire. Grad student by the confidence in his shoulders and the way they had filled the t-shirt. It was an estimation that he was around her own age. Because she didn't know what her own age was.

Cyn remembered her birth date just fine. She hadn't celebrated it once since she had turned eleven, and that memory, of the slumber party and her mother walking into the darkened dining room at ten at night with a glowing white cake, was burned deep, never having been replaced. Turning eighteen had been the only time she had marked the day at all since that night, and that only because the state had forced her to, by holding her inheritance until then.

Until the other day, when Lee walked her out to her new/old set of ninja posts, and told her 'happy birthday' no one had given her a real present since her eleventh birthday. Even Wendy hadn't been up to it those last few years.

And this strange guy, who was making the initial moves at a pass in a small eatery where just about everyone was wired in, was just another chip in the wall. Because Cyn existed in a world where she moved freely among people, through them, around them, but she never made real contact. She wasn't allowed. She didn't know how. So there would be no birthday presents. No friends. No dates.

So she shut down every pass before it even got past the opening line. No you can't sit with me. No you can't talk to me. Don't even attempt it. She could kill the grad student in a heartbeat. As solid as he had looked, she could take him. She'd killed enough before, she could hide the body, make him just disappear. Not that she ever would. But surely he didn't see what she really was when he tried to crack open a conversation. He moved in a world through hers. Where families weren't shot, weren't sucked in to owing their very souls. She bet he'd never wondered if a contract had been put out on him.

He moved in the world she would have occupied if Leopold and Janson hadn't shown up that night. She would have been close to graduating college. Her smile could have been genuine. She might have dated him. Slept with him. Brought him home to mom and dad.

With the breath she sucked in at that thought, she gained a little insight into Wendy. Telling the story to Lee, she'd left out important parts. Like the rage she'd experienced when killing Listle, brought on by how angry she'd been at Wendy. Wendy hadn't loved her enough to stick around for her, with her. But now Cyn saw that Wendy had been older. Even at thirteen, she'd had a boyfriend of sorts. She'd always been the romantic type, but had gotten worse since getting into junior high.

Cyndy had never grown to that point, had never truly dreamed of the life in front of her, of a home of her own making, of creating a family, of building something like she had. But Wendy had. Wendy hadn't lost a nameless, faceless future, or the chance. Wendy had lost specifics. The dream of a wedding, of children, of dating a grad student she would meet in a restaurant over paninis one day and fall madly in love with.

Cyn closed her eyes and forced her breathing to even out, then she opened them and looked up the variations on the name Gwendolyn just for something to type, to look like she was working. She almost missed the name 'Wendy' over the loudspeaker, calling that her order was ready.

It was no shock that she'd chosen that name today. After what she'd told Lee last night, Wendy was on her mind. At the counter the Doc Martens were planted beside her own white sneakered feet. And the voice came again. "Maybe I'll see you next time, Wendy."

Her mouth was neither smile nor frown, just a sad pull to one side. Her shoulders simply shrugged and gave an I-don't-know of sorts as she lifted her plate off the counter and returned to her small table for one, all without meeting his eyes. That was because it was all a lie. He thought her name was Wendy, and he wouldn't see her here next time, and she couldn't afford to come to the surface anyway.

With the thoughts carried through to a reason for the clenching in her chest, she was able to put it away. Grabbing the sandwich, she attacked the work with renewed vigor, finding four houses purchased by Shields and Krestev since she'd last looked. She jotted down addresses, noting that they were all in different cities. One was exactly what she was looking for: a very expensive house in a very small town. That was where they would head next.

She went into the next assignment she'd set for herself, searching for any media references to her own and Lee's kills. She only found reference to the fact that Norikov had died, and that Svelichko, who was a suspected right hand man in the mafia, had died before he could stand trial for tax evasion.

Good.

No one was talking red ribbons and puncture wounds. No one was mentioning gunshot wounds that made the victims look like Swiss cheese.

Good.

She found a short list of mafia men on trial, and noted the where and when, thinking that they might be easy to follow when they got acquitted and released. She'd never done that before. Lee might have tracking skills that would make that possible. And he'd want a bead on Dmitri Kurev, due up to be tried for racketeering and fraud.

Cyn popped back up and placed an order for a cold coffee, an indulgence that she deserved after cracking her heart open just a little last night. Her body didn't need the chemicals, but her mouth could use the flavor. She shut down the laptop, and packed up her cords, shoving all of it into the right compartments in the bag as the name 'Wendy' came over the microphone again, calling her to get her drink.

This time she picked it up and went straight out the door. She freed the pale green Toyota from its curbside spot, throwing it into first gear and enjoying the give of the clutch under her foot. Her silver sedan had been automatic, but this time she'd gotten a stick, maybe just to rub Lee's face in it. Although she'd wound up doing no such rubbing. He'd put too many hours into getting this car running as smoothly as his kitty to have his face rubbed in the fact that he'd doubted she could handle a stick.

She sucked down the coffee, winding through the traffic in Knoxville, since this was the side of the Appalachians they had chosen to come out on today. Lee had probably duplicated a lot of her internet work. He'd probably climb in the passenger side and show her the trial information, or the house in the small town just outside Boise and say that he figured, given the price and the location, that it was a safe house for the mafia guys to go get out from under scrutiny.

They'd meshed well in the tiny house. But then again, they had more to go on than most marriages did. They each had the same singular vision, and no room for pettiness, jealousy, or infighting.

She pulled up to the curb at Kinko's, not seeing Lee anywhere, but sure enough he materialized on the sidewalk as soon as she stopped. He popped open the passenger door and slid in, and just as smoothly pulled the coffee from her hand and sipped down a good third of what was left. Cyn didn't get mad. She'd just remind him of it when he held something she wanted. And she'd remember to get him his own next time.

When he handed the drink back to her his eyes made contact. Not once had he made any reference to yesterday. "So, are we going on a road trip to see what's in Idaho?"

Owen stopped for a moment, and just sat at his desk, staring. He'd been doing that a little too much lately. But, then again, he'd slept in Annika's arms for several weeks straight now. That was enough to cause some daydreaming.

He'd also closed the last of his peripheral cases. Actually, it had been handed off to Agent Brandow once they'd seen the link. It was almost too fast. The first time he'd seen it happen–one case getting absorbed into another–he'd wondered why the agent who'd had it first had been upset about handing it over, but after these years he understood. There was a certain satisfaction to closing a case. To solving it and putting it away. Handing it to another agent meant you put in a buttload of time and got none of the final satisfaction. Just as a little added kick in the pants, it took some of the contentment away from the agent who absorbed the case as well, because suddenly it wasn't all his own work. But it made logical and necessary sense.

Still, it had been the last one. Now the ninja was all that was left. Owen hadn't yet told Bean that he intended to leave the Bureau, but if his Agent in Charge attempted to assign him another case, he would have to. The problem was he wasn't even certain he was capable of closing the ninja case. It might just hang open forever. The lack of evidence was seriously complex.

And this new crap was overwhelming him. The bullet lodged in the carpet at Svelichko's had turned into pillow talk for him and Annika.

It was Nguyen who'd said he was certain the ninja had fired the gun. Owen had been forced to bite his tongue to refrain from saying 'yeah, my wife said the same thing last night, once her brain started functioning again.'

With a shake of his head getting him back into reality, Owen lifted his perpetually empty coffee cup and went out to refill it.

With the coffee topped off, and knowing it wouldn't last long, he headed down to the lab. Nguyen was in his normal state, hunched over something, peering at it through magnifying glasses of some sort, and paying little attention to anything else. He looked up as Owen came through the door, the black rimmed Coke bottle glasses magnifying his eyes and adding that final little touch, just in case you weren't quite certain he was all nerd.

He didn't take the glasses off. "What do you need?"

"Wanna talk ballistics?" Owen settled in before giving Nguyen a chance to answer. Nguyen always wanted to talk ballistics. Dead bodies. Ninja. What was on the table in front of him wasn't going to crawl away, so he looked up, those magnified eyes appearing hyper alert.

"Sure. What do you want to know?"

Almost halfway through the coffee already, Owen set the Styrofoam cup on the counter, out of the way of anything precious to his friend. "The bullet in the carpet was fired from the doorway?"

Nguyen nodded.

"Then why isn't it embedded deeper?"

"Ah," The eyebrows rose, and he finally took off the stupid glasses. "Because it went through Svelichko first."

"Ouch. Where?"

"Ankle, from the looks of it." Nguyen started pulling up a chart. About fifteen by twenty inches, it contained an outline of Svelichko's body as it had been when they found it, with Nguyen's chicken scratch all over it in red. He pointed with the end of his pencil. "Most of the other bullets we found correspond perfectly to wounds. Here," He indicated a lung shot. "The bullet's embedded in the flooring, right behind the matching hole. That's a no-brainer. Same with these."

Nguyen indicated a kidney and the other lung.

Owen took it all in. "Shot point blank."

Nguyen nodded. "Likely standing right over him. He's already staked out when he's shot, or they wouldn't line up so damn beautifully. Given her estimated height and his girth, the gun was about two, two-and-a-half feet away. That matches the depth and drive of the bullets we dug out."

"All right." Owen tossed back another mouthful of the not bad/not good coffee. "What else? You said 'most of the bullets'."

"Well, we've got one here." He pointed to a spot just outside the line. "This seems to match with the kneecap shot here." Nguyen tapped the right knee. "Looks like it shattered the bone and glanced a little. The data's all consistent with that. There's another kneecap shot, that may match to this hole." He tapped a spot that would be a good foot outside the outline when scale was accounted for.

Owen frowned. "What are you thinking?"

Shrugging, Nguyen looked up at him. "I think she shot him when he was partially staked. Maybe hands tied down, then he disagrees about being killed and so she kneecaps him to make him more compliant."

It was interesting how easily they had switched over to 'she'. They had no real proof. But the female ninja theory just worked so well. Owen was about to stop calling her the 'grudge ninja' and switch over to 'black widow'. But they hadn't told many people–even other Agents–that the ninja was female, and that would completely give it away.

He soaked it all in. He wanted to take it home to Annika. "Can I get a copy of this?"

Nguyen nodded without looking up.

"So, what about the stray bullets?" Owen pointed to the one they had first found. Marked with a little red circle on the diagram it was a good four, maybe five feet beyond the body.

"Well, there are four wounds and five more bullet holes. There's one through the end of the mattress. Crime Scene Team found that one. It corresponds to some blood under the bed, and a drag mark–most likely made pulling that wound out from under the bed. That means limb, extremity–the man didn't get his torso wedged under there."

"Are you sure?"

Nguyen smiled. He was usually sure. "Of course. Aside from the size of him and the difficulty of doing that, there are no hairs under the bed, which he should have shed if he'd crammed himself in there. On top of that all the torso holes are pretty much accounted for with bullets in the flooring underneath."

"Could the bed have been moved? The holes lined up?"

Nguyen looked at him like he was nuts. No matter how used to Owen's every-angle questioning he was, he still looked at his friend in a way that told him first and foremost that idea was dumber than trying to pet piranhas. Then he proceeded to explain the stupidity. "The shot went through the mattress, so no, the bed wasn't moved later. Plus there are no dragging marks in the middle of the carpet. It would be virtually impossible to line the wounds up that nicely, *and* she would have had to shoot him somewhere else, then line him up. That would have left blood marks."

Satisfied, Owen nodded. "So we match up the remaining holes."

"Yup. Here goes," Nguyen pointed to the end of the bed. "My money says this shot was the one we found in his hand. There was a Glock stashed under the box springs, so it makes sense he was reaching for it. Two, the angle of entry on the ankle would mean that–if that were the ankle wound–he was lying face down when it occurred with his foot under the bed. And why would you shoot at that? You got a guy reaching under the bed, shooting at his hand makes sense."

Again Owen nodded, already getting ahead. "That means the one we saw first, in the middle of the room, was the ankle wound. And then the entry is from the back. He was running away?"

"Looks like."

That didn't sound like Svelichko. If she was at the doorway, then it was likely right after they saw each other. "What would make Svelichko flee? She's five feet six-ish! Not even heavy. What's so scary that Svelichko turns away?"

"Well," Nguyen started again, and Owen liked the sound of that. "There's a hole in the ceiling that doesn't match a wound."

"Ceiling?" That was news to him.

"Another Crime Scene Team find. They were thorough."

Nodding, Owen thought that was good, not all of the teams were.

Nguyen kept going, "So, the bullet in the ceiling doesn't make sense. There aren't any wasted shots here. Nothing else seems to have missed. And the ceiling is way out of range. Also the depth tells us it wasn't at full speed, so it went through something. *Or* it glanced off something. Like, say, a gun in Svelichko's hand."

Owen tipped up his cup only to find that all of the coffee had disappeared. He would bet that he had drunk the whole thing, but he sure didn't remember doing it. "So we're saying Svelichko's upright at that point. He's either up when she gets to the door or she waits there, toying with him."

"That's my guess." Nguyen's eyes were a little too bright. Owen was pretty sure it was glee in there.

He continued, "So she shoots the gun out of his hand, lodging the bullet into the ceiling, and explaining the lower number of wounds than shots, and the placement of and mark on the gun we found."

Nguyen agreed. "It also explains why he didn't get a shot off. Although, that would make me think he was up when she opened the door. Svelichko was a shoot-first, ask-questions-later kind of guy. Also, the last two bullet holes line up. One in the palm of his hand, then there's the slug in the wall by the bed, which would then go with the shoulder shot. Svelichko's on his knees, consistent with the blood smears we saw. Then she gets him down and staked out."

Owen laughed. "It's all great. We have the whole thing perfectly figured out and explained. We're just operating on this miracle theory. How the hell does a five foot six, hundred and twenty pound woman get Svelichko staked out? He didn't manage to draw *any* blood on our ninja. No one has. How the hell is that?"

"She's just that good, man." Nguyen sighed, and Owen began to get scared. Things were getting worse if Nguyen was starting to romanticize her.

"Maybe she's so disfigured it frightens them."

"Nah." Nguyen brushed the thought away faster than a fly, "No one's pissed his pants yet. Well, not until he actually died."

Owen just sat there on the edge of Nguyen's table absorbing all of it.

It was Nguyen who spoke again. "If we could just get another hair. Then we'd know it's a girl."

"We're not going to get another hair sample." He went on and explained, using Annika's reasoning and unhappily withholding her credit. He wanted to shout it to the rafters. None of these guys here had wives like her. Half were divorced, half of those because they couldn't stand their own wives and the other half because their wives couldn't stand them. And he spent half his own days wondering when Annika was going to wise up and realize she could do a hell of a lot better than him. Jesus, he was getting out of here. It was time to start thinking about what he was going to do for money after he left.

But not quite yet. Because he wouldn't be leaving if he didn't get this case solved and hopefully soon. "There are four other bullet holes that are plaguing me. The ones in the dogs."

Nguyen shrugged. "What's the problem? There are no stray bullets there either. Point blank, great aim. Each dog was down with one shot. And dogs don't sit still for that kind of thing." He shook his finger at Owen, as though the whole thing was wrapped up with one of the ninja's big red bows.

"It's bugging me. She's never shot the dogs before."

Nguyen shrugged and pulled a small piece of chocolate out of one of the drawers. A bag of them was under a photo of a naked Leopold, taken at the morgue when he was dead and holey. Owen figured that would keep everyone out of Nguyen's stash, himself included. That was a disgusting picture. Nguyen spoke around the candy, "She never had a gun before. Not that she used."

"Yeah, that's just it. She's clearly an ace marksman. Neither you nor I shoot with that kind of accuracy and she must be fast to knock the gun from Svelichko's hand. Why start using that skill now?"

Nguyen shrugged, but Owen kept at it. "It didn't look like Svelichko gave her any problems. He didn't draw blood or anything. It doesn't look like he even landed a punch on her, he's got no bruising, not his knuckles, knees, elbows, nothing! So why shoot him full of holes if she didn't have to?"

Nguyen shrugged. He started for another piece of candy then suggested lunch.

Owen hadn't eaten yet, but after seeing the drawer slide open and reveal that picture of Leopold, he didn't think he could. He begged off, suggesting that his friend ask again tomorrow when he hadn't flashed dead dick at him first. Then he went back to his desk, where he accomplished exactly nothing for a whole hour before giving up and deciding to ride carpool and get Charlotte.

After he dropped off her friends, he took her for ice cream, helped with her math homework, and hid his chagrin behind the black and white print of the newspaper while Annika helped her do English homework. They went out for dinner, played a game of gin rummy and tucked Charlotte into bed with a small light and a book. He enjoyed every minute of it. And knew he would enjoy it more when the ninja was gone from his brain. It seemed she was in there puncturing little holes in all his theories with her laser sharp sais. Bitch.

Anni turned to him from her spot on the couch where they curled up side by side like they always did when they were both home and Charlotte had gone to sleep. "What's bugging you?"

He smiled and opened his briefcase, pulling out the drawing that Nguyen had duplicated for him. Pointing out all the bullet holes, he let Annika draw her own conclusions. She asked all the right questions and came up with the same theory the two of them had. Owen waited until she got to the end and stated that the whole thing worked except for one major flaw: the size and weight of the ninja. But other than that it was all perfect.

"So," he sighed, "Why start shooting now?"

"Obviously she didn't. Start shooting now, that is. I can't imagine it's easy to shoot what you can't see with any accuracy."

"What do you mean?" His brows drew together.

She turned closer to him, tucking her legs beneath her as she did. "Well, the hand was under the bed. You said there was a dust ruffle."

He nodded, loving how she remembered, and grasped, all of it.

"So, she couldn't see the hand she shot. Just the arm going under the bed, and she shot through the mattress. Can you do that?"

"No."

"Exactly, and you have marksman plaques from Quantico hanging on our wall. This woman is good. So maybe she's shot before."

"Well, yeah." That much was obvious. You didn't just pick up a gun and pick off Svelichko.

"No, I mean maybe she's shot *victims* before." Anni's head tilted while she thought, and her eyes looked far away. "This is so much better than third grade English homework. Maybe she's been shooting at some scenes and fighting at others. Maybe she didn't start using the gun at this one, maybe she just started combining the techniques this time."

All the air left him. It rang true.

And it created mounds of research to do.

But he wouldn't do it tonight.

* * *

Lee sat arm to arm with Sin in the motel room they were sharing in a small town in the back waters of Idaho. They sure didn't need to spend money on separate rooms, lord knew they'd spent enough of it lately. A good chunk of that spent money was in each of their palms, broadcasting local news stations from all over. The tiny TVs could pick up satellite feeds from most anywhere. He was watching Atlanta, while Sin was tuned into New York nightly news at the same time. Nothing overly interesting was occurring in either city at that moment, except that he and Sin could watch them both at the same time.

At the half hour they each switched cities, then switched again with the six p.m. time zone change. Sin even watched TV with that same intense focus she used in practice. After three hours of staring at the two inch by three inch screen, Lee, however, was ready to fall asleep. The luster of his new toy had already faded, even though he knew he would use the thing religiously and bless the technology that made it possible every day. But his eyeballs were about to fall out.

The bed sagged where the two of them sat on the side. There just wasn't anywhere else to go. These days even the tiny log cabin seemed nicer than the dives he'd always stayed in. Sin hadn't batted an eyelash about the dingy motel, nor protested sharing a room. Two people not sharing would raise suspicions here. Still they would leave before checkout and move to a different dive tomorrow night, again afraid that they might get remembered.

Sin had started to suggest that she pose as his daughter, but he'd growled at her, having heard the last of that one, he hoped. Just what he needed, he finally gets someone to talk to and she needles him about his age. She'd suggested 'trophy wife' until he'd pointed out that any man who could afford a trophy wife didn't bring her here. 'Mistress' or 'cheap whore' was more likely given the atmosphere. Sin, naturally, balked at both of those. They'd settled on doing nothing, and letting the desk clerk draw whatever conclusions he wanted. Now they were just waiting for dark, until they could go stake out the house and see if anyone of importance was in it.

Sin was still glued to her little set, even as Lee paced the room, imagining scenarios that might occur. What would he say if they saw the cops? What if someone in the house saw them? What if there were dogs? A flat tire? Broken bone? Bleeding?

He pushed at her shoulder startling her out of her intense TV viewing. "Sin, it's dark. Let's get ready."

She nodded and shut the little TV off, stashing it deep in a battered old duffel bag before gathering a few things and slipping into the bathroom. The tiny door didn't quite close, but she managed. It gave him the advantage of being able to see when she was going to come out, so he slipped into dark, heavy denim while she was still inside. She came out in a white t-shirt that had a faded Corona logo and beach scene on it, just as he was pulling his shirt on.

Frowning at him, she shook her head. "You look like you're going to go stake out a house."

He rolled his eyes. Of course he did, he was in a black, long-sleeved shirt over the dark jeans. "That's why I'm putting this on."

He slipped a bright red t-shirt on top with a matching ball cap.

She nodded, until he said "wait" and took the cap off. With a grin he took it down two notches and settled it over her head, pulling her long hair out through the back in a sad mock ponytail. "Baby, you do cheap really well."

"Thanks." It was as droll as the look on her face, but she didn't remove it, just went about packing her red backpack. She threw on a denim jacket. It was acid washed and old looking and he didn't know where the hell Sin had come up with it. It didn't look like anything he'd seen her in before, and he'd gotten the solid impression that Cyndy wouldn't be caught dead in something like that, but it went miles toward obscuring the leather pants with all the loops and odd pockets.

They were down the hall and headed for the kitty in no time.

Forty minutes later they were parked a mile behind the big house. Being the price that it was, it had come with a chunk of land, not all of which was fenced. Surely they were trespassing, but Lee figured if they were ever brought up on charges even the judge would be laughing about 'trespassing'.

There were no dogs. No visitors. Lee peeled the red t-shirt, leaving only his darks, and pulled the tight knit watch cap down over his still blonde head. Sin traded out everything in the backpack, slipping sais and kamas into her pants loops while Lee added silencers to each gun and pulled more clips than could possibly be necessary from the bottom of the backpack where Sin had carried them for him. She shed the ugly jacket and braided her hair with quick efficient movements, then the Corona shirt came off, revealing a black leather top, cut like a sports bra, underneath. She immediately covered that with the leather jacket, and traded her shoes for boots. Then they sat.

After an hour looking through the binoculars and making slow creeping movements toward the house, they decided no one was home. Sin smiled. "Wanna go in?"

He nodded.

They were over the fence in no time, walking rather brazenly across the yard. It was pitch black with no moon out. Which was, of course, why they had chosen tonight to visit. Their eyes had adjusted rapidly enough, so Sin had no trouble tossing the rope over a branch of the tall tree they'd seen on the satellite photo. It was close to the house, but as they'd guessed, the lowest branch was too high to reach.

Sin tied the already knotted rope and scaled the trunk first, at last dangling her feet off the edge of the roof and giving him a thumbs up. Lee threw his weight against the makeshift device, giving it a good jerk and testing it with all he was worth. Simply because Sin had used it didn't mean it would hold him. But it did, and in just a few minutes he was beside her and they were pulling the rope up.

Clad head to toe in the dark leathers, she virtually disappeared against the sky as she went for the roof vent. Lee had realized a few break-ins ago that part of what made her so good was repetition. And now she dangled over the edge and popped the vent like she'd done it a thousand times. In truth, he wondered if maybe she had.

The house was cold and empty, they were certain even from the attic, which was cold and full of dust. They dropped into the top floor hallway, and Sin produced her yellow, car-wash chamois and dusted the two of them down, paying particular attention to their hands and feet.

For four hours they stalked the interior, memorizing it. They found the fuse box in the basement. The wiring around the windows led to the master command for the alarm system on a basic keypad in the front hall coat closet. The kitchen boasted full windows, as did much of the ground floor. Knowing their quarry, Lee figured these would be well covered when, and if, they needed to return. The top floor was a mesh of bedrooms and closets and a few baths. Nothing particularly unusual, but they committed the floor plan to memory, and paced each room a few times. Imagined where the master bed would go, where they would likely find their victim.

From the bottom up, they made a last sweep, doing the burglars rendition of the idiot check. They'd both worn gloves the entire time. They checked for footprints using small blue lights that wouldn't be seen from any distance, but found the floor clean as they'd been careful from the start. They blew in a few strategic places, sending up dust clouds from what had settled. In about half an hour, the cloud would settle again, leaving no trace of their passing. They went back out through the roof vent, not triggering any alarms and slung the rope over the tree branch for the descent.

Back in the car, they stayed silent while reversing all the clothing changes they'd done before. Sin peeled her leather jacket off and folded it inside out before pulling on the Corona shirt again, and undoing her hair. By the time she was done, Lee had stuffed all the unused clips down into the red backpack and was unscrewing the silencers. He loaded the guns and all his equipment into the backpack, letting Sin carry everything that might get them arrested.

She didn't protest that.

He would carry it next time, meaning only one of them could get detained, and the other would have a chance to free them. He felt better driving with that safety measure in place. In fact, he felt better, safer, with Sin around. She was a nuisance half the time, always wanting to shoot things or showing him up with her weapons. But he was a better hand fighter now, and he had someone to talk to. The amount to which he enjoyed that was simply embarrassing.

They stayed silent all the way back to the motel, where she threw the backpack over one shoulder and clung to his arm on the short walk to their room. Lee almost asked what she was doing, but then he noticed the other couple unlocking a door a few rooms down. Maybe he shouldn't feel so safe with Sin around. He'd grown a little lax, believing that she would watch out for them.

When they were inside Sin finally began to talk. "Well, with no one in it, I have to wonder who they're planning it for."

"Maybe no one in particular yet. Maybe it's a just-in-case house."

She nodded. “It’s huge, and it’s in the middle of almost literally nowhere. It will likely go to someone big who needs things to cool off for a while. We should keep an eye on it.”

Lee agreed. But there wasn’t much more to say. With the house standing unoccupied, they couldn’t do anything more than just sketch out how the hit would go if they ever got the chance.

Sin stood up, rifling through her duffel bag, probably just as much reassuring herself that it hadn’t been touched while they were out as she was gathering what she needed. Lee saw the purple cosmetic bag in her hand that she always carried, and while he couldn’t see the cut of the clothing she had picked up, he could tell it was pj’s by the pattern: psychedelic teacups danced across a lavender background.

After she disappeared behind the door, he heard the shower start and began changing himself. He stripped down to his boxers and gathered what he needed, waiting for his turn. Lying back across the bed he grew bored, wondering how the hell long she was going to be even as he saw the steam start to seep around the edge where the door didn’t fit closed within the casing. Of course she was taking her sweet time, she’d been used to hot showers when she lived in Texas and had been using the hand pumped travesty they had at the cabin. And without a complaint. Lee decided he could well afford to wait.

It was a good fifteen minutes before the water shut off. But another five after that, when she still hadn’t emerged, he called out.

“Hey!” Her head came around the edge of the already partially opened door, “Just wait a damn second.”

But the words went right by him, all thoughts that she had kept him out of his own shower for too long slipped right out of his brain. She was wearing the leather underwear.

On his feet in a heartbeat, he stalked closer even as she pulled back at his expression. “Jesus, Sin, what the hell is that?”

“What?” She stiffened, holding her ground and preparing for a fight, even though he wasn’t going to give her one.

“Leather underwear?” There was a zipper up the side that he could see and it had a two inch square of duct tape covering it, only the pull tab peeked out. The matching leather top she wore was closed the same way. He sputtered, unsure what was going on. The words that came out of his mouth weren’t quite what was intended. “What’s with the tape?”

She looked at him like they were talking about his sixteen-round clips for the Hecklers, like it was something illegal and cool that gave her an edge. “You can’t undo the zippers. Duct tape is the best zipper lock you can find.”

She was *locked* into her clothing? “Why?”

“No one gets in unless I choose it.” She shrugged at him as though it made perfect sense. Apparently in Sin’s world it did.

“You could just slice it.” Why he was even discussing this was a mystery to him, but he felt compelled to point out the flaws in her plan.

“No you can’t.” She almost smiled as she patted at the edges where leather met muscle. “You can’t get a knife under it, they’re too tight. Someone would have to slice from the outside, and it’s tougher than my own skin.”

This time he took a mental step back. This was Sin. She made certain that no one she didn’t pre-approve could get his hands on her. For a moment Lee wondered who would want to, but as he looked her from top to bottom he saw that, in the basics of it, she was really quite attractive. Remembering back, he figured she’d been stunning that night he’d found her picking up men in the bar. But no one would touch her since she looked like she’d just as soon geld you if you came near. Although apparently when Sin chose, she could just pull the tape and zippers and let some lucky guy in.

He shook his head. “Do you even own any regular underwear?”

“Of course!” She had balls to seem pissed at that.

“Because that is fucked up.”

Her mouth opened to a perfect ‘o’ and her brows slammed down, “Oh, but *you* are the picture of mental health!”

She slammed the door in his face, somehow getting it to actually shut for the first time.

There went his shower. Even if he was right. Problem was, she was right, too. Who was he to call anyone ‘fucked up’? He didn’t speak to anyone in his family. He knew they loved him and he loved them, and they probably all believed he was dead, and he was content to let it stay that way. He shot people and had no remorse. He pounded on the door, “I’m sorry.”

Maybe he was and maybe he wasn’t really, but he did want a shower.

"I'll be out in a minute." There was no responding 'that's okay'. Not verbally nor in her tone. Well, what had he expected? People didn't like being called 'fucked up', especially when they were. More surprising was the fact that that made Sin 'people'.

She stalked past him a few minutes later. Her leather pants and t-shirt were draped over her arm and her bag was clutched in her hand. Aside from the rigidity of her muscles and the steam that seemed to follow her like a lost puppy, she looked the same as she had every night.

Lee felt that same wet heat surround him as he stepped onto the now slick tile. Only a thin, lacking towel in a sad shade of over-used gray covered the floor to keep him from slipping and cracking his head. It was a wonder Sin had left it there for him. The shower, most likely running off a heater down the hall, stayed hot for longer than he was willing to stay in. His feet were wrinkled as were his fingertips when he stepped out, accompanied by a quick flash of memory. For a brief moment he could see Bethany's smile, clear as day, as she showed him her fingers and toes after lingering too long in the tub. Samantha stood behind her, holding the towel with the hood and kitty-cat ears tight around their daughter.

Then it was gone.

Once again Sam and Bethy's faces faded into the deep recesses of his memory, slipping through the cracks with the steam from his shower. He stepped into clean boxers and a t-shirt as the small room grew chillier around him.

Only after he put all his things away, and made a last check on the one club they'd locked into the window, the screamers they'd stuck on the glass, the bolts on the door, did he look back at the bed. Sin was curled up on her side, facing the wall, and apparently deep asleep.

Chapter 12

The ride home from Idaho was long, and Lee wasn't sure he liked all this new insight into Sin. To make things that much harder they were going to Tennessee by way of Wisconsin, not that any really direct interstate existed, but there were a hell of a lot of faster ways to go about it. Again, they didn't want to be seen, and didn't want anyone following them to know where they were headed.

Sin still hadn't forgiven him for calling her fucked up. The conversation was stilted, at best. So halfway through the second day he waved his version of a white flag. He drove through a Dairy Queen for Blizzards, something he knew she enjoyed, and surely hadn't gotten enough of as a kid. "You know, Sin, you shouldn't feel guilty over your sister's death. You did everything you could."

"Hmmm." It was mumbled around vanilla ice cream and frozen bits of m&m. For all the things the restaurant was willing to pack in there, Sin was a purist.

"You were just a kid. You didn't deserve what happened, and you aren't responsible for the clean-up."

She nodded, but didn't look at him. She even spooned up another mouthful and went to the trouble of finishing it before she responded to him. "That doesn't mean I couldn't have done more. None of us deserved any of it."

"Maybe." He used the red plastic spoon that looked just like the one he remembered as a kid to scoop up his own ice cream. He'd had his loaded with little bits of everything, and surely he would wind up with Oreo's stuck in his teeth. He was wondering how bad it would look, when Sin spoke again.

"You didn't deserve what happened to you either."

He swallowed. "That's debatable."

"How? The Kurevs aren't known for being just." Her head turned and she looked at him for the first time in over thirty-six hours. It sure wasn't how he'd wanted to open a real conversation. But she'd told him her side. He was living with a girl who'd murdered her first victim at fourteen, not a pretty sight. He couldn't afford to be held up as innocent.

"I was responsible." The ice cream had lost its taste and he wondered why he hadn't foreseen the conversation shifting this way when he'd opened his fat mouth.

"Then so was I."

"No. It's different."

She shook her head, but still managed to eat the ice cream. Nothing stopped food from going in that girl's mouth. He wondered if she would lick down an ice cream cone over a fresh kill if he handed her one.

Starting again, he fought through the knot in his stomach. "I brought on Sam and Bethy's deaths. Probably much the same way your father brought on what happened to you all."

"What are you talking about?" Her face hardened into stone and she stared at the road ahead, not seeing.

"I was an accountant. So was your Dad. I got a job with Black and Associates, which turned out to be a front. I didn't know it, but that's because I was stupid. The money they offered me right out of school was just too good. Seriously too good. With my cushy job I had the cash, so I married Sam. We bought the house. Two years later we had Bethy. Just after she was born I was asked to do some more serious work."

Sin hadn't looked one way or the other. But the Blizzard was disappearing one spoonful at a time, no longer a treat but a method of self preservation.

Lee kept going. "I was flattered at the promotion, and never really thought about it. I think most people are like that." He shrugged. "When I realized whose money I was working with, and what I was being asked to hide, I protested. Lord knows why I only then got a brain, but . . ."

"What happened?" Her voice was flat, but at least she was speaking.

"They put me in my place. Leaving my job was not an option now that I had figured out what was going on. So I thought I'd get them. I filled out their tax returns that last year, did everything the way they wanted, got all the signatures. I abused loopholes and hid all kinds of money in bad deductions. Then, after it was all ready to go, printed up and signed, I signed it, too, and I checked the box."

"What box?"

Good girl. As much as it twisted inside him to tell what he'd done to Samantha and Bethany, he needed Sin with him now. And she needed to know what he'd done, why he had to fix it. Not that he ever would be able to.

"There's a small box on every tax return that says something to the effect of 'check box to claim any illegal contraband'."

"Are you serious?"

"Yeah." He almost smiled. "The mafia is always getting away with all kinds of things. The government put it there to help them press charges of tax evasion when they couldn't prove the money was gotten illegally. If they can't get you for the contraband, they'll get you for not checking the box and paying the taxes on it."

"No way."

He let a small smile out. "Next winter, check out that tax return form. They all have it. So, I marked it. Figuring the government would be tipped off."

After a deep sigh, and no help from Sin, just the sound of her spoon scraping the bottom of her cup, he continued. "It was stupid, so arrogant, to think I could get away with that. They knew it was me, and they just took out Sam and Bethy to punish me. They came back after the funeral, tried to rough me up, but I was too drunk to feel it. It didn't matter what they did to me, without Sam and Bethany nothing really mattered."

He remembered sitting in the bar, feeling his eyeballs peel from the expensive whiskey he'd been drinking like beer. "My brother found me, sobered me up, slapped me around a little. But the Kurevs would come after me, so I disappeared. When I was sober I was . . ."

She nodded. "Mad isn't the word. It doesn't begin to cover it. When was that?"

"About three and a half years ago now."

Her lips pressed. "And what does that have to do with my Dad?"

Looking at her for the first time since he confessed to being responsible for the hits placed on his family, he wondered what she was thinking behind those pressed lips and serious eyes. Again her face looked far younger than her years, while the eyes staring bleakly ahead looked hundreds of eons old. If he hadn't looked it up, he would never have guessed her true age. "Did you never wonder 'why you'?"

"I try not to."

"It wasn't random, Sin. Your Dad was an accountant. Do you know who he worked for?"

"He wouldn't have worked for them." But after hearing his own story, she was clearly wondering and unraveling threads that must have been held together with denial for all this time.

Lee spoke what she was thinking. "Neither would I. And I bucked them when I figured it out. And look what it got me."

She sniffed–a sound he had never heard from Sin before. "At least you can say you are your own man. You stood up for what you believed."

His heart crushed inside his chest, and his lungs wouldn't fill with air. But he kept driving. He'd felt this before, and unfortunately he would survive it. He imagined this was what it felt like to be lung-shot, and that allowed him to enjoy the pain just a little. "I'd rather have Samantha and Bethany back. I may be my own man, but I don't exist."

"Well, what about me? I don't exist either!" Her voice rose an octave, and he wondered where all the emotion was coming from in the girl who'd been cool as an iceberg the whole time he'd known her. But maybe there was far more lurking beneath the stunning, glacial surface. "It wasn't my fault. Even if it was my father's!"

"I know. You're right. You were an innocent victim."

"I was eleven. What the hell does an eleven year old do to deserve that?" Her teeth pushed together, locking tight. Her eyes didn't blink, and her cheekbones were harsh slashes across her face. "Thinking it was my father's fault doesn't help. I prefer to remember him as a good man who loved us."

"Don't change. He was probably all that. But he was human, too." His lungs let in air again, although he wasn't sure why, and he hadn't wished it. "I'd prefer my girls think the same of me. But I brought it down on them."

Her expression unchanging, her words lacked inflection. "That doesn't mean that my father did, too."

"Think, Sin. Someone did. The Kurev family doesn't do random violence. They aren't out committing home burglaries. They hit your family for a specific reason. Someone triggered the attack on you. And I'll bet every penny it wasn't you or your sister."

She didn't respond.

So much for that conversation.

"When I'm done," He mused, telling her what he hadn't ever told anyone. Not that there'd been anyone to tell. "I'm going back to Black and Associates. There are a few key players there that I'd like to take out. But they'd recognize me, so I'd have to end it there."

Still she didn't speak.

"Dunham." The voice at the door was accompanied by a hand that held out four white tablets.

Owen stood, and thanked the other agent, before taking the Tylenol from her and popping it back. He swallowed it with coffee, the heat of the drink making the tablets dissolve into a powdery grit as they went down his throat. The bitter taste they left seemed appropriate, matching his feelings about marching in here a few days ago and announcing that he didn't think this was the ninja's first shooting kill.

Agent Bean had agreed with his/Annika's reasoning and put him and Blankenship right on it.

Owen had the mother of all headaches going on forty-eight hours now. He'd been sucking down Tylenol and alternating it with Motrin, a trick he'd learned from Charlotte's childhood fevers. The medications didn't attack the system the same way, so you could take both simultaneously. Taking one, then two hours later popping the other, allowed you to stay continuously over-medicated. He added his usual over-dose of caffeine by way of coffee to the cocktail in his bloodstream. Still the headache was merely reduced from jackhammer status to woodpecker.

He'd set Blankenship to work on finding other kills. But it had been too much for one person. So Owen had joined in, and looking through files of shooting deaths was like killing yourself with a safety pin. Eventually you *would* die from all the pricks, right?

Just the case numbers when he cross-referenced 'shooting deaths' were too many to look at. He'd even had to pull actual files with Blankenship, which they did randomly, until they could figure out what to search for and against. That had taken the better part of yesterday morning.

They'd opened folder after folder and flipped through killing after killing. But the vast majority had stray bullets. That, of course, wasn't noted in so many words in the Agents' documentation. Because damn near everyone had stray bullets. 'Ace marksman' wouldn't cut it either. Owen was certain, though, that if he saw a photo of his girl's handiwork with a gun, he'd just know it. In his head he could see the torso, peppered with clean shots.

He sighed out loud,

At least they'd realized they could have the computer sort out anything that said 'execution style'. The ninja did not give her victims the quick way out. She made them suffer. Unfortunately, the agents who reported the cases weren't required to mark a victim suffering scale on each case. If they had, he'd have his girl in no time. Instead he had about fifteen thousand files to go through and only a few things to cross off.

Blankenship appeared in the doorway already vacated by the Tylenol bringer. Agent Westin was a great agent, and she'd recognized his headache and taken care of Owen. She'd also made sure to take care of herself. Which meant, as soon as she delivered the drugs and a small smile, she'd gotten the hell out. Blankenship didn't look as good as Westin did in the doorway. In fact he looked like the file room had pulled a full out poltergeist attack on him. "We can get rid of anything with a 'domestic' or 'spouse' suspect."

"Yes." Thank you, God. These weren't domestic abuse cases. Blankenship was right. And when Blankenship was right, the world had gone to hell. But Owen typed in the order to remove domestic cases, and about four thousand dropped off the list.

Well, the computer said it dropped about four thousand. His screen still looked as full as it did before. And the woodpecker was still at it in his head.

He wanted to filter it for mafia, but that would be a last resort. He would lose about half the related cases if he did, because his ninja went after seemingly random side people, too. Owen was still looking for a connection there. Or rather Annika was. She dropped Charlotte off in the mornings and spent her day online, looking up the ninja's bad guys and trying to find the web that held it all together, however tenuous.

Owen stopped for a moment and wondered if Agent Bean didn't already know about Annika's side sleuthing for him. Surely the FBI could tap his home computer. Surely they had checked his Russian born wife, up and down, before letting him into the Bureau. He'd had more than one dream where she told him she was a double agent working for some Russian government.

He'd woken from that dream in a cold sweat each time. He would wake and watch Annika, as she rolled over and looked at him with concern because he'd roused in the dead of night. He'd had it about once a year after joining the Bureau. He'd been in the process of signing up when he'd met her. So she could be an agent. Not that that made any real sense.

But the dreams had stopped about three years ago, when she'd looked at him in the middle of the night with such love. Even though he'd refused to tell her what the dream was about, she'd comforted him, curled into him, and fallen back asleep. He'd decided then that, if she was an agent, he'd just have to pack up and follow her back to Mother Russia. He would play sleuth at home while she worked for the KGB by day. He'd drive Charlotte to school and cook dinner and ask to see her case files.

The dream hadn't come again.

And he was leaving anyway. It didn't matter if the Bureau knew about Annika's help. The only issue would be if they kicked him out before he could solve the ninja case. Because he desperately wanted to do it.

There had to be something.

Annika would find it.

Owen told Blankenship he was going to lunch. His stomach didn't need food. He'd fed it a full meal of pills and coffee. Next he would need ulcer surgery. What he needed was a break.

So he sat in the commissary, eating a tuna salad on wheat toast sandwich for no particular reason. Most of the other agents were doing the same as him: chewing and staring off blankly into space, cases churning through their heads. What a nest of anti-social freaks. No, this wasn't helping him relax.

So Owen decided it was time to choose a new career. He couldn't make a list of ideas, in case someone saw it. But staring at the middle space and not speaking to anyone was a perfectly acceptable way to spend your lunch at the Bureau. So by the time the sandwich was gone, except for the overly curly lettuce he'd dumped on the side of his tray, he'd decided to go into consulting. He just hadn't figured out how to get any consulting jobs.

He had visions though. Of a house in the suburbs. A picket fence. Maybe a tie, but no suits. Maybe he'd work in jeans and a t-shirt. From home. There was a certain appeal to it. Of course how he'd come up with this jeans-and-t-shirt job he still didn't know. That brought up an image of him printing up advertising flyers and putting them on car windshields. Or tucking them in front doors. Except of course where people had guard dogs. The vision of him and his flyers running like a scared girl almost had him laughing. And he'd have to run. He wouldn't be with the FBI anymore. He wouldn't have his Glock. If he had the gun on him he wouldn't be above using the barrel of his 9mm to stare down a dog.

He stifled his laugh until it hit him.

The dogs.

That was what they should search for. Executed dogs.

He stood abruptly, almost knocking over the flimsy table. But no one seemed to notice. The woodpecker in his head had stopped hammering.

Cyn stared through the window, feeling the burn building inside her. Lee hadn't moved, and she had told herself she would let him lead. But the burning was making that less and less likely. If he didn't move in the next two seconds, she was going to.

She couldn't watch anymore.

The window in the back of the church was clean and sparkly, someone had put some love and care into cleaning it. Shame they weren't paying as much attention to who they left their kids with. And this was one sick fuck.

She'd read an article about it in the Tempe Wrangler, several kids had accused the preacher of serious crimes. All she'd been able to do was hand the article to Lee. They'd packed the car within an hour. He hadn't asked any questions.

They'd found a motel, ridden bikes through the heat, drowning themselves in water just to stave off the dehydration that came so easily here even in the late autumn months. They'd found the man's house. They'd found his office. And they'd broken into both, installing cameras and recorders.

Though it was Cyn's first experience with the equipment, Lee had used it a bit before. He said he'd watched hours of footage of himself at his cabin in Atlanta, until he was sure he could install and operate it correctly. They had ridden the bikes again yesterday and eaten steak sandwiches at the mall, and Lee had forwarded through hours of tape while Cyn marked moves in the tiny space of the motel room, just to keep limber.

Lee's voice had cut through a very carefully mocked head kick. "He's guilty."

"What?" Coming closer, she'd stood behind Lee's shoulder, but he'd flipped over the tiny TV screen that he was now using to watch tapes.

"Don't watch, Cyn. Just don't."

Her stomach had turned then.

They'd come this evening to end it, thinking they might find him alone, but no. The church had been full, maybe not like Sunday morning, but a large number of people had been coming and going. So Lee and Cyn watched through the cameras as the man shook hands and thanked the church people for caring about him, for believing in him. For trusting him with their children. For their continuing faith in him. Her stomach had turned even then, but not like now.

He was alone in his back office with a little boy. And he was starting.

Lee still hadn't moved. Cyn did. She put her eye to the corner of the window and made certain that the office was otherwise empty. The preacher had locked it behind him, so there wasn't any real danger of someone coming in.

She pulled the mask down over her face, and quickly took out the pane of glass with her towel-wrapped fist. When she put her face into the hole she had created, both the man and the child looked terrified. Her eyes locked on the boy, and she realized it wasn't the first time he'd been here. "Leave. Lock the door behind you."

She'd whispered it, to keep her voice from getting recognized, but she wouldn't have been able to produce more sound if she'd tried. There were people still in the church. Many had left, but her heart pounded. She'd never done this before. And she wouldn't have done it now, except this man had to be stopped. Today. What she'd seen earlier on the camera had made it impossible for her to wait.

His eyes flew wide even as his hands flew into action. He adjusted his clothing, but Cyn leaned through the window and threw two knives, pinning his hands near his crotch, where he'd been straightening his pants.

The clicking of the tumblers caused her to jerk her head up to look at the door, but it was sliding shut, the doorknob lock clearly engaged. The thought went through her head, *Good boy*. Some part of that kid knew what was happening. And some part of him approved.

She slid into the room, followed quickly by Lee. He held out an envelope with the two tapes they'd collected. Already sealed, it held the words 'the good Reverend Deehan' in Cyn's left-handed writing.

The man whimpered but made no other noises as Cyn approached. She was ready to cover his mouth, kill him quickly if he gulped in air for a scream. She had yet to meet a single person who didn't give away their moves. You just had to know what to look for.

She took the envelope from Lee and pulled another knife from her jacket, this time she held it with the blade protruding downward from her fist, and she rammed it into his chest, deep into a lung, holding the envelope in place.

Although she wouldn't have thought it was possible, wide blue eyes got wider. The face was charming, friendly even, and he'd probably used it to his full advantage. Cyn wasn't into killing on hearsay, and she enjoyed the shock in those eyes because of what she'd seen.

But there was no time for more. Stepping back, she pulled the letter and folded red ribbon bow from under her jacket and let Lee finish the job. With a few fast sucking noises, bullets slammed into the man at close enough range to leave powder burns. His throat opened in a tiny hole, before blood filled it and marred the perfect circle. The crotch of his pants jerked then stained bright red. And silently she thanked Lee for that. Everyone should know. The man's eyes looked downward, maybe feeling what had happened, but not the pain of it, not yet. At last a bullet entered the chest, just a little left of center, and the last wobbling hold the preacher had maintained on being upright fled as he sank to the thick Persian carpet.

His eyes held a glassy stare in the face that had charmed too many children, as well as their parents. Some wouldn't believe. Wouldn't want to. But the tapes would be there to speak for those who couldn't. Cyn sure as hell didn't want them.

Even as she tacked the bow and the note to him, Lee went around the room removing the two cameras they'd installed. Lipstick sized tubes, they caught enough of the happenings that no one would doubt what this man was guilty of. Lee undid the screws as carefully as he felt they had time for, and had reclaimed both the pieces even before she was partially out the window. He followed quickly.

They kept to the bushes, sneaking out, then they had walked almost brazenly into the space behind the building. Tempe offered very little in the way of tree cover, which was Cyn's preferred method for changing after she left a scene. But here she settled for the back of the green Toyota. She was in a t-shirt and low side pigtails in under two minutes, one of Lee's ball caps planted firmly on her head. Even as she popped the car in gear and pulled out from behind the buildings where they'd stashed it, she slapped a garish pink lipstick across her mouth.

In her passenger seat, Lee had slipped out of his long-sleeved shirt and was sliding into a tee. Just the warmer clothing alone would have been suspect in Tempe at this time of year, and he balled it up and stashed it under the seat. He used a spritzer bottle she now kept stashed in the glove compartment to put water on his hair and keep it from sticking out in all directions, from looking like he'd just pulled a ski mask from over his head.

Fifteen minutes later they were walking into the motel, Lee holding her hand, her shoulder pressed to his arm. Partly it was for show. Partly it was because she was threatening to shake.

She wasn't used to this. Cyn felt her brain churn with thoughts that it had been too fast. It was quick by necessity. There was no real way to get to this man otherwise. His apartment had been less of an option than the church, as he had another minister staying with him. The cameras there had yielded nothing, and she and Lee had taken them out this morning, posing as repairmen.

They'd been seen.

She'd had blonde hair, and he'd put embroidered ball caps on both their heads, so no one got a good look at their faces. Except for one little old lady whose glasses were so thick that Cyn had looked right up at her and smiled a big grin, knowing that even if this woman was put on the stand as the only eyewitness to their 'crime' no one would believe her. Then Cyn had petted the little dog and made nice.

To add to that, the speed with which they'd dispatched the preacher to the hell he lectured on had not been what she wanted. The slow death had its purposes, one of which was suffering, and in that respect this man had not paid enough. The note and the tapes would make certain that no one would praise his sainthood when they buried him. The Robert Listle scenario had not repeated and Cyn would not let it.

But the other reason for the slow death, was simply to make sure that everything had gone right. That fuck-ups had not occurred, and that you hadn't left hair or objects behind. Surgery was a slow and painstaking process for the same reason, and she wished to stay in this business. Not behind bars. That meant no errors.

For the first time, she'd let her emotions, her feeling for those children, push her to hastiness. If this didn't kill her then she needed to learn from it. It couldn't happen again. No matter what the forces pushing her. She said as much to Lee after he finished stashing the things in the spaces around the room. Even in a two-bit flea bag room, the two of them could hide an arsenal for an army. Even the cops would be hard pressed to find all of it.

Grey eyes looked her up and down, as Lee seemed to realize for the first time that she was still standing in the middle of the room. She wasn't shaking, but only the control she'd fought and trained so hard for ensured that.

He didn't speak, but opened a mini-fridge that was doubling as a bedside table. It was covered in dark wood veneer contact paper and would have been too tacky for words if it hadn't blended so well with the rest of the bad décor. Pulling out a can of Coke that he must have stashed there earlier and a fifth of Jack Daniels, Lee divided the soda into two squat plastic cups and topped them with the Jack before handing her one.

As a rule, Cyn didn't drink. There'd been no need. She didn't want dulled senses. But now she rescinded that decision and slugged the soda that, with the Jack in it, was a little flat, a little hot, and had a strong over-sweet aftertaste. It didn't kick as harshly as she had thought it would, though.

She was almost done when Lee spoke, and she had to wonder if she was drunk because she hadn't expected what he asked.

"So where the hell do you keep all that stuff in your jacket?"

"What?" She swished the drink, suspecting that she'd had enough, but then slapped the rest of it back, enjoying how it pushed her thoughts to the side and beginning to finally understand alcoholism.

"Every time I see you wear it, it's like watching someone pull a rabbit out of a hat. I know there's a logical explanation, but I don't see it." He kicked back the end of his own drink, but the effects weren't anywhere near as strong on him as they had been on her. At least not visibly. Aside from the smell in the cup, he looked like he'd been drinking soda. "I mean, you throw a knife then another just appears in your hands, then stars come out of nowhere."

She smiled. She loved that jacket, had designed and sewed a good portion of it herself, altering a basic design she'd found in a chain store years ago. With a flourish, Cyn crawled under the bed and hauled out the backpack, in turn pulling the jacket from the bag and slipping into it to demonstrate.

If anyone came to question them, and saw her in the leather coat, they were toast. But no one had followed them. No one likely even knew the preacher was dead yet. And no one was going to knock on the door to offer maid service or to chat, not here. So she ignored the possibility and showed off the pockets.

"See, down the sleeves?" Cyn held up her arm showing both the underside and back of the forearms. Small squares of matching leather were tightly stitched on and held about five stars each. "I took apart another identical jacket to make all the extra pieces, so it would all match."

Lee nodded and reached out to feel the pockets. He watched closely as she pushed a finger under one tip of a star and rotated it quickly out of its slot. "Slick. How do you keep the pockets from curving with your arm?"

Again, the grin smothered her face. “At first they did. I had to cut little metal squares and stitch them in the lining to keep them flat. Otherwise they bent and the stars got caught.”

She shrugged out of the sleeve and pushed it into his hands, watching while his fingers felt the metal backing she’d put there.

“Hey, the knives.” His fingers traced the long compartments inside the body of the jacket.

Slipping the sleeve back on, she opened it and showed off her stash the way a street vendor sold cheap knock-off watches. The throwing knives were in slim pouches that ran vertically along her ribcage under her arm.

“Why so far back?” Lee reached for the fridge again.

“Well, there’s a story there.” She sighed, “I put them in the front, thinking they’d be easier to grab. Practiced with them there. Then went out one night to perpetrate some crime. I didn’t make it to my destination. I leaned over the top of a fence and punctured myself with my own knives.”

“No way.” He sat up and looked at her.

“Yup.” Lifting her shirt hem she showed off a small v-shaped scar along the right side of her belly. “With my breasts in front the tips were already aimed at me. So when I leaned on it, in they went.”

Lee looked at the scar again, then shook his head, even as he offered her the refilled Jack and Coke.

This time she sipped it. “I moved the pockets after that, and did much more thorough testing on all the additions afterward.”

“No more scars?”

“Nope.”

His drink was half done, but the cup was small anyway. So Cyn didn’t worry about the effects too much. Lee helped her out of the jacket and searched it again before folding it and stuffing it into the backpack and shoving the whole thing under the bed.

Worn out from the night, and certain that they hadn’t been followed, Cyn reassured herself that they wouldn’t be caught. She shucked her leather pants, leaving them on the floor, before she pulled back the covers and curled up in the bed.

She woke to a smell she wasn’t familiar with. Her eyes didn’t open, even though she knew it was early morning, that she usually woke at this time, but she felt a little fuzzy, and wondered what could be wrong. Almost without her input, her chest heaved a deep breath, re-equilibrating her system, and the smell came again. Half of it wasn't smell at all, but heat. The other half was comprised of something male with a hint of something sweet.

The muscles at the back of her head tightened, and from behind her eyes she remembered the Jack and Cokes she'd drunk the night before. That was the sweet part of the smell. The male part was familiar even though she wasn't used to it.

Forcing herself to blink, Cyn saw that she had slept in her t-shirt and leather underwear. Her nose was almost pressed into Lee's chest, and when she looked up, through slow heavy blinks, he was looking at her much the same way. Like 'what the hell are you doing here?'

"Hmmm." It was all she could manage before she rolled away. Her feet found their way to the bathroom easily enough, and she climbed into the shower, breathing deeply and letting the steam open her lungs. She was reminding herself not to drink again, when she realized she'd come in without anything to change into. Cyn re-reminded herself why she hadn't drunk before, and sighed.

In a moment, she'd figured out what to do. After finishing washing off with the one cheap bar of soap the motel had provided, she called Lee to bring her some clothing. His feet shuffled uncharacteristically beyond the doorway and his hand reached in through the open crack where she was holding a towel around herself and wondering why she wasn't more concerned.

His voice was a little mumbled, but Cyn didn't comment. Surely he could hold two cups of Jack and Coke. So maybe it was her brain that was mumbling. "I brought your leather undies, too. But where's the duct tape?"

"Ha ha."

She changed quickly, and by the time she had emerged into the room, she'd made certain she looked like a college kid. "Your turn."

Lee didn't respond, just sat staring at something on the wall behind her. Only then did the sound penetrate. A woman spoke from the television in serious tones, and the words "minister, here at this church," caused Cyn to stop and take the seat next to Lee on the end of the bed.

She watched as the over-made up woman in the red suit gestured to the scene behind her, a view just outside the church they'd broken into last night. The camera pulled back and showed the growing crowd at the edge of the police tape, trying to get a glimpse of . . . what, Cyn wasn't quite sure what she was looking for.

Another woman now stood beside the too-bright reporter, and was introduced as a cleaning lady in the church. Her thin gunmetal gray hair was wound repeatedly, directly on top of her head, and she had that look on her face that said she was going to call everyone she knew and tell them she was on TV. She explained in excited but serious tones, and poor grammar, how she had found the man who had given her a job and saved her. A tear, maybe even real, rolled down her cheek as she talked about what a good man he'd been and how kind he'd been to her and so many others. She would miss him.

Smiling her pity and condolences, and placing a hand on the woman's shoulder, the reporter effectively ended the sob story and turned her attention to informing her audience that there were tapes, and it was speculated that they would provide proof for the accusations that had been leveled against the man.

"Even more concerning is the way the body was found. Apparently he was wrapped in a large red bow and sported a note resembling a gift tag."

Cyn smiled.

"That's not good." Lee's voice cut through her thoughts.

"Yeah, well, he's dead, and that's good."

"True enough." He stood and shuffled into the bathroom.

An hour later they were long gone.

Owen's head pulsed at jackhammer speed, and until he took enough medication to kill himself he wasn't going to be able to make it stop. Since he wasn't sure he was going to heaven, death might not even be enough.

From the crowd gathered beyond the yellow tape, and the sheer numbers of officers whose sole job was just to hold them at bay, it looked like he might already be dead. If he was, he was definitely in hell.

Owen stopped for a moment and prayed again that he was dreaming, nightmaring more like, but the image didn't fade when he opened his squeezed eyes. So he probably wasn't dead yet.

The three of them had taken off their suit jackets and ties, having gotten the warning of the gathering mob only after they were already in the air. That the cleaning lady had found the body was bad enough, but the growing crowd was a thousand-fold worse. There was also the problem that the Phoenix office had been on site for a while now. Their crime scene team had already reported that they had tapes and had found screw holes in the plaster of the walls where the cameras that captured those images had been mounted.

That the victim had been very guilty was of less concern to Owen than the fact that he'd been tied and tagged like a used car. The bow alone told of his guilt, at least Owen believed that with all his heart. His ninja was in no way indiscriminate. And she had excellent timing. They'd been onto something with those dogs. The files that search had yielded looked like pure gold. However they were still sitting on his desk waiting to be sifted through. While instead of sorting files, he was here, and here was bad.

He didn't mind having another dead body on his hands. It was the crowd. Because, as the three of them stood at the perimeter without their suit jackets and ties, they weren't recognized as the feds. So it was required that they flash their badges, which brought on a swarm of reporters.

"Sir, you're with the FBI?" He'd no more than clamped his teeth together than he heard Blankenship say 'yes'. Owen felt his eyes roll back.

"And why are you here?"

Not the most eloquent of questions, but it got the job done. He pinched Blankenship's arm this time, and his partner gave the same tight non-smile that he and Nguyen passed out like candy. He tried to remind himself to be grateful that they'd just been lucky the media hadn't fallen on them like a soggy blanket before this.

He pushed past and made his way into the crime scene, thinking that his desire to get into the church without being recognized as Bureau had been as short-lived as it had been stupid. Inside, he and Nguyen donned their paper suits while they sent Blankenship out to stand perimeter. All of it a vain attempt to keep the media ignorant.

The minister lay inside, slipped down to a seated position against the solid front of his desk. His hands had leaked blood around the familiar knives that pinned them to his lower abdomen. The same kind of knife entered deep into his chest and held an invitation sized manila envelope. The envelope had been sliced open by the cops, who'd been told not to remove it. Whether that was an act of defiance or just plain stupidity, Owen wasn't certain.

They'd already reported that the tapes were a serious batch of child porn. Owen found himself looking at the body and being grateful that the man was dead. But not knowing what to do with the holes that had leaked red onto his clothing. Three knives. Three bullets. His little ninja wasn't reverting back to hand and weapon combat only. She'd moved forward, continuing to combine her weapons with ballistics. And from the stack of files that was waiting on his desk, she'd been trying her hand at ballistics for a while. Going on three years now. At least.

And here was the latest, the broken window showing entry, shards of glass littering the carpet under the window as well as the sill beyond. People had been in the church when the man had died, the ninja had come and killed and gone, all with parishioners nearby.

She was escalating.

Owen knew that meant his time was coming.

The bullet holes were in perfect alignment. One through the trachea, surely just for pain. One in the crotch, meant as a punishment, and maybe a warning. One in the chest, just a little left of center. His ninja was no dummy. From the kidney and lung shots he'd seen in the past, Owen knew his ninja knew her organs. But Annika had been reading up, and found that was what ninjas studied: anatomy. They made low impact blows to highly sensitive nerve clusters, taking their enemies down by making their own bodies work against them. It was the first explanation he had heard that offered a decent reason for his little ninja to be able to fell the large mafia men.

He talked with the local homicide dick, who explained that the camera made no attempt to hide the angle from which it was shooting, and the screw holes had been obvious once they looked in that direction. But the cameras themselves were gone. Owen withheld his comments about the tapes having been removed and viewed when the FBI had specifically told them not to touch the scene.

His girl was entering the technological age, too.

The bow was the same as they'd seen before, the gift tag just like all the others. Owen recognized the handwriting immediately. He'd found himself looking over shoulders in the grocery store, checking out shoppers' lists, waiting to see that handwriting, anywhere else but tacked to a dead body.

Unfortunately, there was nothing really new here.

Nguyen shone his fluorescent lights around, then his halogens. He picked up hairs that he could see. A brunette strand, pinched tight in tweezers, was held up to the light and examined by sight.

Owen had started to get excited, but Nguyen shook his head even without looking away. "It's not hers. Too short, and looks too young. The end is cut, so this hair was worn at this length."

Of course it wasn't hers. Annika had said they weren't going to get another one.

They left three hours later, not surprised to see that more people had gathered, more news crews had arrived. He pushed his way through, Nguyen trailing him with his mouth shut tight, his baggies of evidence concealed in his shoulder bag. He looked like any other businessman heading off to work. Blankenship brought up the rear, his smile less clamped, more open.

Reporters ditched their current interviews to turn on them, and Owen imagined he could drown in the sea of them, the rhythm of the pounding in his head could have been the slosh of tall black waves breaking over him.

There was nothing he could say. The horses were out of the gate.

Chapter 13

"There were dogs chasing me. Big black Dobermans and Rottweilers. I have nightmares all the time. But they're usually the same thing. This was new."

This *was* new. Lee listened to her frown her way through the disturbing dream from the side of his bed. That Sin was curled into the other side of the bed was enough to make him wonder if he was still asleep. He frowned back, but she remained oblivious.

"I'm not afraid of dogs. Not dogs that look like that. I'd never run. I'd face them. But in the dream I'm running from them, and I'm so scared. The dogs are about to catch me. I just know it. And I'm not afraid they'll eat me or kill me. I'm afraid they'll take me down."

"Hmmm." He responded. Not sure if he should respond to her fears or to the fact that she must have come in his room and crawled into bed with him. He'd woken with her nose pressed into his chest now for the third morning in a row. He found words and let them loose, "That sounds like one of those symbolic dreams."

"Surely." Sin was still curled there, on 'her side' of the bed, never mind that the entire bed was 'his'. "I just don't know what it symbolizes."

Neither did he. He didn't know what this new development meant either.

It was one thing in Phoenix. She'd been shaken by the preacher. Truth be told, he had, too. He'd never killed with people just beyond the door. That had not been on his terms. But when Sin had handed him the article, her fingers shaking just a little even then, he'd known she was going whether or not he went with her. And that's what this crap with them working together was all about. He had to be there, especially when she was likely to do something stupid, like kill a man in his own church, with potential witnesses nearby. There hadn't been a question.

Then he'd given a twenty-year-old, who'd probably never drunk anything in her life, two reasonably laced Jack and Cokes. So it was no wonder he had woken with her nose in his chest and her t-shirt the only thing covering those ridiculous leather undies. She hadn't showered, hadn't pulled the ponytails from her hair, hadn't changed into her whimsical jammies.

Then she'd done it the following night. But again, they'd been in a bad motel, with only one bed, so no wonder. But now . . . this was his bed, in his room, and she had her own of both of those. "It's probably from watching the news last night. They haven't been trailing me before."

"Clearly they were. Or they wouldn't have shown up now." He wanted to laugh out loud. He'd wondered more than once if maybe they each had an entire task force assigned to them.

The news last night had been unsettling. One of the reporters had refrained from harassing the FBI agents that had scoped the scene. Only one agent had shown up on screen and he didn't say much. Just that they were checking out the situation. This reporter had a clip from him, but more importantly she had research. She'd found other police reports of victims with red bows and tags, and put two and two together. She asked point blank, "Given that there are other victims like this man, and that the FBI is on the scene, are we dealing with a serial killer?"

The agent had given nothing away. He'd looked like there wasn't anything in him to give. That made Lee feel a little better, that the agent tracking them had the brains of the cocker spaniel he resembled.

But that had been short lived. As soon as the agent had walked away, the reporter had faced the camera and delivered her line, "While the FBI won't speculate, at least not for us, the local police believe that we do have a serial killer on our hands, and have even gone so far as to dub him 'the Christmas Killer'. Back to you, Jason."

That had been the kicker. That 'back to you, Jason', so that they could do a piece about which local plastic surgeons did the best boob jobs, the Christmas Killer all but dismissed.

He scrubbed a hand through his hair, hoping that would be the end of it, but certain that it wasn't. A serial killer in the hands of the media wouldn't go away. Not unless he and Sin did. And he wasn't sure they could.

He left her there in his bed, trying to ignore the woman who wasn't supposed to be there. If he'd begun to achieve it, the frog jammies would have made it impossible. She didn't roll back over though, but climbed out after him, making him want to climb back into the bed now that it was vacated. Instead, he headed into the living room, wearing only his boxers and t-shirt, and flipped on the small screen TV tuning it in to a Phoenix station, as they were about to cue up their six a.m. news, and more actual news was reported at that time than in the later broadcasts. Sin turned the second one on and hooked into CNN.

For a while they just watched in silence, then he pointed and Sin pushed flush against him to see the tiny screen he held. Phoenix was reporting that they had found at least three other murders that could be linked to the Christmas Killer and that the police had clamped down on information.

When CNN offered a small aside to the Phoenix murder, they mentioned that the tapes were being considered conclusive evidence that the preacher had committed many of the crimes he'd been accused of. Sin's lips curved, and Lee caught it from the corner of his eye. It was a true smile. He blinked twice, almost missing the anchor's mention of the FBI's involvement.

They were fucked.

Pushing the power button on her TV, Sin pushed up and left the room. She returned, fully dressed, not more than five minutes later. "I need to shoot something."

Owen sat on the edge of Nguyen's desk, coffee cup in his grasp. But he didn't so much as sip from it. Instead, he fidgeted with it, needing something to do with his hands. He didn't speak.

He'd set files on the counter next to Nguyen. This time Nguyen was looking at charts he'd prepared. One was the old chart of Peter Svelichko. The second was the same black ink outline of the body and the room, but of Reverend Deehan. The third was of Leopold – but that was just a body outline as he'd been found in the water. Even the outline looked bloated to Owen. Small marks, circles and x's, covered the bodies in red ink, clearly marking wound points. Nguyen was deep in comparison and Owen didn't want to interrupt that. On more than one occasion before, Nguyen had blown a case wide open with his lab sleuthing.

He'd probably been sitting there about three full minutes when the scientist looked up, but Owen couldn't be sure as he didn't want to move, even to look at his watch. It might have been an hour for how it felt, but his brain told him he was over-reacting.

"Dunham!" It was exclaimed as though he'd just shown up. "What can I do for you?"

"We finally got to those files. The ones we sorted for the executed dogs." It had taken quite a while, what with all the clean-up on the preacher man's death and the sudden swamping of media. Blankenship had fielded it with his usual talk-a-lot,-give-away-nothing answers. The reporters weren't a problem except that they existed, and they were like ants. You could crush them, but there were so many. You could stomp them out, but more would surely come. And they were digging. Who knew what they might find? But, as of yet, no individual one had been a problem.

"And?" Nguyen prompted. He hated being interrupted unless there was a point. So Owen always gave him one, just not always as fast Nguyen would have liked.

"We got a lot. Mafia hits. Centering on the Kurev family." He pushed over the top three files and waited while his friend took a quick flip through.

That was all that was needed. "No martial arts weaponry at all."

"None. Just bullet holes." That had been disturbing in and of itself. "And dead dogs."

"Weird." Nguyen looked at the photos that had been taken at the time. He checked out the documentation at too rapid a pace to get the details. But Owen knew he'd gotten the major points. His words confirmed it. "So she had two M.O.s?"

"Two entirely separate M.O.s. There are no notes, no gift tags. And these guys are as dirty, and some dirtier than, the ones where she did leave notes. She killed the dogs. Broke windows, shorted the security systems, and shot with the skill of a marksman the likes of which I don't think I've ever seen."

Nguyen nodded. All of it was true. "So she did that until she was up to par with the weapons, and devised the new method she's using to get into the houses."

Owen nodded. He hated that one. "It still seems to be 'transform into vapor and flow in through the vents'."

"Dracula method." Nguyen smiled.

Owen didn't.

Nguyen tried another tack. "Just mafia guys? Or were there external kills as well?"

"We're pretty sure there were externals. It's hard to say, and harder to sort, as everyone and their brother has bullets. We've got a pimp taken out with knee-capping, bone shattering shoulder shots, and a slew of symmetrical wounds to the abdomen. A few others."

Not having bothered to slip out of his white paper coat, Nguyen finally pushed the even stupider looking surgery cap off his head, and looked at the files again. "So that's all the same."

All Owen gave was a nod.

Nguyen filled in the blanks. "So she's doing the same thing, tormenting them, taking out the same kinds of people, but with an entirely different M.O." For the first time he met Owen's eyes. "Dunham, are you thinking you have a multiple personality disorder person here, and both personalities are after the mafia?"

"Now that's funny." Owen finally unclamped his hands from around the coffee cup, which he'd almost worried a hole into, and shook his finger at Nguyen. "Because I actually had that exact thought go through my head. It does explain a lot, except that this case is already so out of hand, and there's no way we could take that to the media."

"But if it's the truth . . ." Nguyen re-stacked the files. "It would explain her proficiency."

"What?"

"Well, MPD is usually the result of a trauma, a really severe one, often repeated. Severe child abuse, repeated rapes, that kind of thing. The personality fractures, leaving one persona to handle the abuse and the other to live a life free of it, often with no knowledge that it even occurred."

"Because that personality wasn't there for it. But how does that make her proficient with those weapons and the guns?"

"It usually happens at a young age. The personality splits while it's still forming. In adults it's already cemented and we can compartmentalize it that way. That means she's likely been out for blood since a young age. Lots of time to practice."

Owen frowned and thought that one through. He'd already dumped the theory of MPD, but there was a nugget here he needed to hang onto. He just had no idea which one.

Nguyen spoke again. "It's too much, though. It also has holes: like there should be one psycho-killer personality. The other should be trauma free. Why two traumatized and vengeful personas? We need to go Atcham's Razor here: the simplest explanation."

"It's not simple. None of it will ever be simple." He shoved the remaining two files at Nguyen.

With a quick upward glance to see if Owen's face would reveal anything, which it didn't, Nguyen tackled the remaining two folders. Only, very quickly, he realized he knew one of the cases. "This one's part of the ninja file already."

They were older murders. Owen had been buying into the multiple personality disorder theory until he saw these. He waited.

Nguyen read, his brow furrowed. He skimmed, knowing the other agent held out a link and not knowing just what it was. After a minute, he spread the papers out across the desk so he could scan them as a whole. Nguyen was always fast like that. Owen could see the exact moment Nguyen found it.

"Holy shit. The dates are the same."

Of all the files he had – and Blankenship was still looking for more, periodically finding them, too – these had been the most disconcerting. "Sure, two personalities could have plotted two separate murders, down to this degree of detail, and carried them out separately on the same day."

Nguyen pointed. "But these are in separate states."

"They're across the country." He clarified. "There's no way one person did both of those. Unless we have our times mixed up."

Nguyen shook his head. He knew the labs. He'd done a lot of the work himself. "There's no way we're far enough off to get her from one of these to the other. There's just not time."

Owen nodded. "Not to mention that everything has always appeared flawless, and that means planning. There's no point in planning two at once. With different methods. Just the tools alone would be hard to gather."

Nguyen didn't speak for a moment. When he did, it was with a question in his voice. "So these were committed by separate people? Same grudge, same ideas, different methods?"

Owen nodded, then asked his question. "What I need to know is: was Svelichko alive when the bullets went in him? Was Reverend Deehan?"

Nguyen nodded 'yes' to both of those.

Owen felt his heart shrink. He'd been so hoping Nguyen would say 'no'. That there'd be an alternative. But there wasn't. "And those two people are now working together. The Christmas Killer is two people."

"Damn." Nguyen almost lifted his hands into his hair, but stopped himself. He didn't touch his head, his face, didn't scratch anything while he was doing his lab work. So even just the beginning of the gesture was a sign that he was shaken.

"I need you, bud." Owen set the cup down. "I've got a stack of files on this grudge gunner, and I need to know everything I can about her. Or him."

Nguyen put his hands in the air, peeled his gloves, and motioned for Owen to bring on the paperwork. "You win, I'm fuckin' hooked."

With a heavy heart, knowing that his caseload had just doubled, and the likelihood of solving the thing had just cut in half, Owen looked into his coffee cup. He didn't like seeing the thin ring of brown at the bottom and decided to remedy that immediately. Not to mention the muscles at the back of his head were tightening. Whether that was due to the fact that he hadn't had caffeine in a good two hours, or that his grudge ninja had a friend and he had a mountain of work to do just to get up to speed, he couldn't say. But a full cup of coffee would soothe, if not solve, some of the ills of the world.

He left Nguyen and went to re-fill the dark liquid from the break room. Then sent an aide back to the lab with copies of all the grudge gunner files. Blankenship fielded calls from the media off and on throughout the rest of the day, and handled Agent in Charge Bean. Bean was pissed about the media, but Owen was grateful for the way it went down. The cleaning lady had told all the sordid details before the Tempe cops could shut her up. So none of the people who knew better was at fault. There was always an air of suspicion when leaks occurred, always the background murmurs wondering if the agent had let out some of their own info just for the notoriety. So, no matter the trouble, Owen was glad that he wasn't coming under scrutiny for that, too.

But he could still practically hear Bean from all the way down the hall yelling at Blankenship. "You two close this down and close it fast!"

By seven, Owen's stomach was grumbling, and he knew if he didn't high-tail it out of here, and fast, he wouldn't even get to see Charlotte today. So he closed the files and headed home. Thinking while he drove, he mused that, with the very recent death of Reverend Deehan, and the obvious planning that went into each slaying, the world was probably safe from the grudge ninja for a while. But was the world safer?

That was a tough question.

He hadn't answered it by the time he pulled into the driveway, although he was ready to concede that he likely never would.

He ate quickly and read to Charlotte when she was tucked in. His mind wandered during the chapter, thinking that his daughter and wife were safer with the ninja and the gunner out there. Lord. He needed to quit.

He said exactly that to Annika when he walked into the living room. She was sitting on the couch with the remote in her hand. She didn't even acknowledge that statement. He would have thought she would be jumping up and down, but no. She just wanted him to come sit by her. Pushing her arm out straight, she punched a button on the remote, "Watch."

He could see by the recording bar, registered at the bottom of the screen, that she'd recorded something for him and rewound it.

Tickers sprung to life across both the top and bottom of the screen, streaming far more information into the human brain than even the sharpest of people could keep up with. But it was the talking head that got him. She was rattling off bits of information about the Deehan tapes and what had been on them. About families stepping forward to sue the church, the organization, whomever they could get their angry legal hands on.

Owen didn't see much point, but the woman did say that, under their own investigation, it appeared at least five other murders were tied to the Deehan murder. Specifically, she mentioned, the campus rapist in Kansas eight months prior.

Blinking, Owen wondered where she'd gotten her information, and realized that it hadn't been any of his people, when she used the words 'interrupted an attack in progress'.

Still it wasn't much more than he had been seeing over the past few days. Little bits were filtering out to the public here and there. But he'd expected that. There had been a dam, and it had sprung a leak. It would continue to leak, no doubt.

He watched all the way to the end of the brief report, when the woman closed with "FBI agents have been tracking the killer, but so far have no solid leads and remain baffled."

She went on to her next story as Annika paused the program again, leaving the woman with her eyelids half dropped and her mouth hanging open in what looked like a drunken slur. He was glad she looked horrid between frames, he didn't like her.

"Well, what do you think?"

Huffing, he turned to his wife. "We are not *baffled*. We have plenty of info."

Her wide mouth turned into an even wider grin. "That's not what I was talking about. But you should ignore that."

"I'm tempted to go hand her all our stuff and tell her to crack the fucking case wide open herself."

This time Anni flat out laughed at him. "That's exactly why she said it. She's hoping one of you will come prove her wrong, and she'll have the scoop. But has anything else leaked?"

He shook his head.

"Then what is it?"

"There's two of them."

She nodded. "A shooter and the ninja, working together."

Only his eyes moved to look at her. He loved her, and sometimes he hated her, just a little.

Lee was getting more and more afraid that he'd need to see a doctor if he didn't learn how to unclench his jaw. A month after the good Reverend Deehan had been put down, Sin had held another article out to him. Lee had said 'no' in no uncertain terms.

They couldn't afford another fast job. They couldn't afford another job out in the open after the last had been so iffy. The media coverage had died down fairly quickly, although there was still the occasional report of another old murder tied to the Christmas Killer. The online rooms were full of all kinds of stories, and Lee printed some of it out when they traveled the next time. They had been off gathering supplies and info in Florida when he'd brought the pages back to her at their hotel room and held them in her face. "Did you really do all of this?"

True to form, Sin hadn't batted an eyelash, she'd just taken the printouts from his hand and said, "yes, yes, no, no, no, yes, no, no, no, yes . . ." right down the list. Then she's handed it back and said what a shame it was that Robert Listle wasn't going to make the list. She shook her head the way most girls would about the first boy who'd dumped them. His jaw had clenched a little tighter.

Only then had Lee realized that she was sitting in the middle of an orgy of shopping bags. "Did you knock over the mall?"

"No." She had the nerve to look put out. There went the jaw again. They'd gone out to do research and it looked like she'd spent her time shopping. "We're finally staying someplace nice enough that this doesn't look suspicious."

That was true. She'd pulled out a fake ID and a credit card to her account still in Texas. It was risky but, they decided, worth it.

Sin smiled. "Besides, it's Christmas time, everything's on sale."

"Thanksgiving was three days ago, it isn't Christmas time yet." Not that they'd celebrated Thanksgiving. Lee was pretty certain that they'd had banana and protein shakes from the blender he'd run off the generator, and ham sandwiches for dinner. He'd been thankful that no one could hear Sin shooting at the pop bottles as though they would fire back any second.

Her aim was much better these days, but that meant that she ran through ammo like water. At least water came up from the well, ammo was getting damned expensive. It was one of the things they were buying while they were down in the panhandle. He also had thought to train her on the rifles, but now he wasn't sure he wanted her to be that deadly.

Given the glut of purchases she'd made, holding his tongue until they started back home had been difficult. Only, when they packed her old green Toyota full of all they had stocked up on, some of the gear had overflowed the trunk and had to be packed into the back seat. Sin had raised one eyebrow at him, then proceeded to cover all the exposed gear with tissue-papered and puffed-up shopping bags. Two were from *Victoria's Secret* and one from *Frederick's of Hollywood*. She'd placed those where the labels were visible and Lee had to agree that no cop in his right mind would go looking through that.

It still felt odd to have her driving him around, and he took the wheel more than once on the way home. It was more than a full day of driving, and coming up from Florida the weather got consistently colder as they went. The day stretched long on the drive. Still they made it home without incident, and for Christmas all Lee really wanted was for their luck to hold.

But he knew it couldn't last much longer.

The cabin was cold when they arrived, and Sin stayed in the thick coat she was wearing along with her gloves and some sherpa-looking boots. They unpacked quickly, keeping warm until the generator could power the space heaters enough to warm the place up. Sin's bags littered the living room and she began unpacking from there.

Lee stopped and looked at her, his head tilted to one side. "Did you just get things to get the bags or did you actually buy something at Victoria's Secret?"

The girl had nerve. She looked indignant. "I bought things."

"Those jammies? They sell those?"

Again her eyes flared. "I bought underwear."

"I didn't think they sold leather."

She huffed and hauled her bags off into her bedroom to unpack them, which was really all he wanted her to do in the first place.

Aside from ammo and supplies, the trip had yielded knowledge. Most importantly, while they'd been gone, they spent a good deal of time in the room watching the three hundred satellite channels they'd paid good money for. That gave them three TV feeds instead of two. Because they were watching for the decision on the Sandoval case.

Sandoval had been acquitted.

The TV stations had caught it all from every angle. He'd left the courtroom, amid much fanfare, a free man. While Lee and Sin weren't present to see his walk into the sunshine, friends had been there to shake his hand and slap him on the back. And, given all the camera coverage, there was no doubt that Kolya Kurev had been one of those men.

Lee and Sin were placing their bets on Idaho.

If they went and Sandoval wasn't there, then so be it. Nice trip, gather more evidence, apparently Sin might shop, go home.

They also had seven other names of men they would take out if they found one of them occupying the house. A few would be dealt with in slightly different ways, each according to both his crimes and what danger he might pose to them.

So they'd hightailed it back to the cabin and turned the generator on. While jackets were eventually peeled, the two didn't really stop moving for the entire four days they were home. There was too much to prep. It was a long drive to Idaho, they knew from experience. And a roundabout route was the best, just in case they were followed, or if later someone came around with photos. Nothing like a straight line of people recognizing you, right down the interstate, to point exactly to where you were.

Sin worked out as much as she worked. At one point Lee found her atop the ninja poles, looking like she was asleep. On two feet, she was only hanging by her toes, because that was all that would fit. There should have been a little sway up that high, but Sin was perfectly motionless. Still, he'd interrupted her. "Do you want a gun for the trip?"

"What!" It wasn't a question so much as a curse word. And while he watched, the great Sin toppled. She hit the ground in a graceless thud that made him feel bad about how much he'd enjoyed it.

Standing over her, not admitting her pain any more than she would, he asked again, "Do you want a gun for the trip? You're barely proficient enough, but I trust you not to shoot me, so . . ."

She pushed herself to standing with more bruising to her pride than anything else. She'd rolled when she hit ground. Of course she rolled, it just hadn't altered the fact that she'd hit the ground. Lee shook his head.

"No, I don't want a gun. What I want is to know if you intended to damage me by sneaking up on me like that?"

"No." That much was honest, and he hoped he'd conveyed that in his voice, rather than the glee that was still singing in the back of his head.

"Why the hell do you sneak up on me like that?" Even before she finished the question, she was asking another. "Why the hell *can* you sneak up on me like that? I have to move out. I've gone soft since getting here. I'm going back to Texas to play with the big boys."

Lee laughed outright at that. "You didn't play with *anyone* in Texas, if you recall, and you haven't gone soft. At least I hope you haven't." He ignored the fact that she was rubbing at her knee, and prayed it didn't mean she'd be injured in Idaho. "I assume I can sneak up on you for the same reason you can sneak up on me." He didn't add that that seemed to include into his damned bed in the middle of the night. What with the traveling and all he'd woken up with her nose pressed into his chest more mornings than he hadn't. "You've filtered me out. That part at the back of your brain that listens still hears me coming. But disregards me as 'safe'."

"You believe that?" She would have looked more menacing if she'd been taller. But as it was she was three inches from his chest and practically looking up his nose.

"It's the only explanation that allows for the fact that I can hear that there's a large cat just off to the north of us right now, but not hear you when you come up behind me."

She leaned over and rubbed the knee again, "Yeah, I heard the cat, too. I was hoping it'd come up for a fight. I never fought a cat before, and I've got some energy to burn."

Lee shook his head. He wasn't gracing that with an answer. He didn't know which was more concerning: that she had energy to burn, that she *wanted* to fight the cat, or that he had thrown in his lot with her. Leaving her there rubbing her knee, he was grateful that she didn't want a gun. What the hell had he been thinking?

Maybe he'd just wanted to know what his chances were that she'd grab one off him during a key moment and maybe use it on him. Those pop bottles sure had paid for the crime of bearing high fructose corn syrup to sedentary children.

Two days later a cold snap came in, unfortunately it was preceded by a wet snap. People remembered the beautiful pictures of the Appalachians softly blanketed with snow. Singers had praised its glory, but after several winters here, Lee was waiting for the country tune about grandmamma dying in the ice storm.

The abrupt change in the weather didn't stop them, it only delayed. Still they'd started out at four a.m. as planned, the world dark and glassy around them. They'd lifted heavy duffels, and Sin had tucked her teddy bears into bags and under her coat, and Lee had considered telling her to leave them behind, but they served a purpose far more useful than Sin's comfort.

They were both loaded to the gills, like usual. But the climb was uphill, and given the ice, they literally slid back every time they tried to go up. After a handful of attempts, and wet gloves from the number of times he'd gone down and used the palms of his hands to save himself, they'd tried another tack.

Using an old piece of plywood and sturdy rope, they rigged up a piss-poor sled. But they climbed one step at a time, anchoring themselves as they went, and handing the sled up, bit by bit. The path leveled out about a quarter mile up, and the trees grew denser the further they got from the cabin, which cut back on some of the wind that had been biting at them. But it was also narrower here. That meant they had to unpack the sled thing and haul their own bags. And the ice was no less here than it had been earlier.

The rain that had come before the snow had puddled, and frozen over as such. Pine needles and fallen leaves were trapped in white or black glass panes under their feet. The debris trapped in the ice were sometimes the only thing that kept his feet from going out under him, and sometimes even that wasn't enough. His ass would have been as wet as his hands if he hadn't invested in a good long coat.

Sin, of course, walked the icy path like the damned ninja she was. Footholds apparently spoke to her, and she stepped with purpose, her feet finding flat on clear spots and setting straight down, her body gliding from position to position as she went. She admired the beauty of the landscape along the way. Distracting Lee from the taxing job of just walking.

"Wow. I don't think I've ever seen anything like this." Her voice came out on a breath that he could see.

Lee had finally wised up: he put Sin in front and stepped where she stepped. While it still wasn't perfect, it was a huge improvement, and he didn't go down or fight to stay upright nearly as often. He also quit answering her and focused on his feet rather than his side of the conversation.

Sin didn't seem to notice. "I wonder if this is what *Winter Wonderland* was written about."

Lee snorted and thought about composing *Grandmamma Died In The Ice Storm* himself. But Sin kept pointing to icicles and trees with clear glass casings, having frozen when wet and dripping. "Look, every needle is covered."

She held out a branch for his inspection, snapping the ice in several places as she moved it.

This time he did respond. "And Idaho is getting further away. We're likely driving on icy roads for a while. So get your butt in gear."

The little TVs had saved their hides. He couldn't remember the last time he'd watched the weather channel, but he knew he'd been dressed in a suit and tie with a steaming mug of coffee in his hand and concerns about the cream colored carpet. But he'd watched for all of five minutes this week, then traipsed out to each of the cars and put chains on the tires. Once he unfroze them, he'd be glad they were there.

It took forty-five minutes to get to the kitty, Sin ooohing and ahhhhing the entire way. He really wished she'd just complained. Instead she volunteered to drive so he could get out of his wet clothes.

"My clothes are fine." The coat had literally saved his ass. He picked at the lock for a minute on the driver's side, finally getting the key in and watching the button pop up. He threw his bags into the back seat, before leaning in to start the engine.

Sin waited patiently on the passenger side, watching him, probably wondering when he'd help her out. Her hands were full of bags, her jacket bulged in lumps from the bears she wore underneath it, made worse by the straps criss-crossing her torso. Her eyes peaked out from under her burgundy knit cap, which didn't match a damn thing she was wearing. She only blinked at him and waited, pressing her lips together to ward off the cold or get rid of the strands of hair that had blown and stuck to her mouth. Even while she waited, little gusts of wind turned wisps of it into phantoms dancing around her head.

Lee decided that it would be easier and better if he crawled across the driver's seat and pulled the lock up himself. He'd worried about damaging the mechanism when he broke through the ice. So he shucked his coat and stuffed the too-puffy-to-be-manly garment into the back. When he stood up straight, he promptly slipped and fell on his ass.

Sin cackled. She threw her head back. She grabbed her belly. She traipsed around to his side of the car still loaded with heavy bags. All the while unable to keep it together, yet somehow able to keep on her feet. Bitch.

He felt the wet seep through his pants as the word seeped through his brain. For a moment he wondered if he deserved it. While he attempted to find his feet, and failed once, Sin stuffed her gear into the back, even artfully arranging her bears across the tops, so they could watch out the window. She peeled her coat and stuffed it down into the foot well. "What do you need?"

"I'll get it."

Even shoving her aside didn't knock her off her feet. But at least she didn't say anything. He pulled sweats and boxers from his duffel bag and tried not to stomp angrily around to the passenger side of his own damn car. The last thing he needed was to go down again.

Sin's face glowed. She'd been itching to drive his kitty from day one. And here it was in the worst possible conditions. Lee amended that pretty quickly, ice wasn't sleeting onto them at the moment. Although he thought his wet ass might be freezing over.

Slipping into the driver's seat, Sin motioned for him to get in, wind was whipping away all the heat the engine finally produced from the car. He blinked to realize that she'd already folded a towel and laid it across the seat for him, and he slid in managing to just restrain his huff.

She was backing slowly out of the 'garage', her hand on the back of his seat, her head cranked around. Lee couldn't look. He waited for the car to shudder from impact, even though he'd ridden with her time and time before. But that was in her own car, where she was fearless. He wasn't sure he wanted her to be fearless with his kitty.

He didn't change his clothes yet. Not wanting to be found dead with his pants around his ankles was a strong enough motivating factor to keep him there with his frozen ass until she made it to the highway. Sin looked for other drivers, unwilling to pull onto the road in front of anyone. But Lee wasn't surprised that no one else had ventured out in this. It was shameful to think they might have better weather in Idaho. But he wasn't counting on it.

Once they were a few minutes down the road, the chains clanking through a light dusting of snow and Sin's pace just above what he himself would have done, he stripped his shoes off and peeled the offending garments down his legs. Sitting bare assed on the now wet towel was no picnic, but Sin politely kept her eyes on the road. Which was a good thing, because he was hanging in the breeze.

He tugged at the front of his sweatshirt thinking he might stay covered and only then realized that there was a huge wet spot on the back of it as well. At that point he gave up. Lee peeled it, too, and sat buck naked in his own passenger seat blessing the heater while Sin's mouth fell open.

"We're going to get arrested. And it's going to be for *nakedness*?!!?"

He gestured to the surrounding area, devoid of any life besides themselves. "No one's looking." Hell, even Sin wasn't looking, her eyes were glued to the road ahead. "Close your mouth."

For once, she did what she was told.

He slid the dry pants up, slipping the towel out from under him as he did, and settled his dry ass into the cold seat of the kitty with a sigh of relief. He threw the wet clothes into the back and dug out another sweat shirt. Idaho was going to be a fucking barrel of monkeys.

He clicked into his seatbelt and managed to unclench his jaw each time he found it locked from Sin's driving. An hour later, they'd gotten all of twenty-five miles from the cabin, but he was able to get out and take off the chains. He didn't slip and fall on his ass either, which was another blessing. And he demanded the driver's seat back.

Picking up speed, he even laughed as Sin hollered. "Lock up your daughters and hide your hookers! The Christmas Killers are coming!"

"I'm not the Christmas Killer. You are."

"*We* are." She amended.

He kept his eyes glued to the road. Just because they'd taken off the chains didn't mean the driving was safe by any measure. "By the way, I take offense at that. I've never killed anyone's daughter or a single hooker."

She nodded. "Me neither. But I feel I ought to, what with the label 'serial killer' and all. Isn't that who they kill?"

Lee sighed and pushed emerging thoughts of Bethany back from where they'd come.

Sin's voice was soft as she saw something, "Sorry."

Lee didn't grace it with a response, but his brain latched on and wondered where this sensitivity had come from. Wasn't Sin made of granite?

He merged onto I-40 and kept heading west. They went straight through Knoxville, which was awakening to rush hour. The roads were ice free, as Knoxville was used to this, so the residents might slip and fall on their asses getting to their cars, but once there, they didn't even need chains. Lee and Sin were only in the crush because it had taken so damn long to get out.

They drove with just bathroom and food breaks until they called it a night in Little Rock. And damned if he didn't wake up with her nose in his chest again. He'd thought of her as a girl, but that was a mistake. It took a woman to exasperate a man that bad.

She compounded it the second day when she declared herself bored halfway through the drive and simultaneously produced a sci-fi novel and a CD player from nowhere. The novel was already partially read, much to Lee's surprise, and the CD player had some volume on it, so she could share Aerosmith with him. He paused for a moment to be grateful that he liked Aerosmith.

It took four days to get to Idaho. Even though he was used to logging time in the car, Lee was worn out from the hours of heavy pop she played. Even more because his sleep was disturbed by the fact that the girl who had once clung to the edge of the bed could no longer seem to stay on her side.

Each day he'd tapped out a little earlier and handed her the wheel. Each day she smiled and accepted. So he was asleep in his own passenger seat when they passed through Boise in the dark of night, only vaguely aware of the thick blanket of snow riding the rooftops of anyone who dared build a house out here. The roads were clear of all but the lightest of dustings, something done better by northern cities who knew what snow was about. Lee only truly woke when Sin pushed at his shoulder, "Lee, look."

He blinked and did as she commanded. The house in front of him loomed large and softly dreamy-looking, glowing a sweet melted butter color through the hedge of snow. He blinked again, realizing that not only did he know the house, but it was *the* house. And it was occupied.

Sin turned the wheel and smiled, not saying anything more as she headed away to find a motel in Horseshoe Bend, just beyond the house, and further from the city.

Lee stayed awake and useful through check-in. Letting Sin hang on his arm and chew loud gum, moving those pink-glossed lips she always did up in public. They made their way around back, Lee having made his usual insinuation about noise. As the clerk was male, he just smiled and gave them a key, even as he looked Sin up and down. She hid her face beneath the ball cap but otherwise played it up.

Once inside, they set about unpacking, hiding weapons, locking up the one window with the club. Sin stuck a screamer to the upper corner of one pane, then tapped the glass before sighing and yanking it back off. "Damn thing's not glass. We've finally gotten so cheap the windows are plastic."

Lee had braced an extendable rod under the door handle and locked it in place before unloading the bags of guns and ammo. Sin ripped stitches on her teddy bears, then sat in her jammies with the dancing teacups and sewed the butts back together. She'd been sticking the weapons in that end for a few trips now, which of course had raised Lee's eyebrows and invited a slew of comments, all of which he managed to hold back. Sin thought the necks were getting a little too much wear and tear from all the opening and closings. If you didn't notice the wicked looking blades behind her, that Lee knew for certain had dripped blood on many occasions, then she'd look like any female sewing, repairing a teddy bear.

By the time she was finished, he'd already crawled into bed in his t-shirt and boxers. She plumped her bears, and stashed her blades around the room, she set all but one of the bears in a cute array on the tacky side table that probably cost less than the stuffed animals. The last bear she hugged tight while she turned the switch at the base of the lamp. Lee didn't know what to do when he felt the bed move beneath her weight, then shift as she settled into him. But somehow he fell asleep.

He woke with her in the same position, grateful that he'd found some sleep after all. Sin seemed to wake with the motion of his eyelids, and she was up and pacing forms before he even managed to throw his legs over the side of the bed.

He figured that by now he'd be used to the sight, but he still had to hold back laughter at the forms she mocked with deadly accuracy in those damned ridiculous pajamas. Every movement spelled her skill. He got the impression that he could yell 'freeze' at any minute, and she would–could. He entertained fantasies that it would work if she was midair and she would just hang there until she decided to move.

When she finished, she pulled the kamas from beneath the mattress and bowed to an imaginary partner before she silently ripped him to shreds. Lee was reminded of the first time he'd seen her handle the weapons, they had danced in front of her, even left her hands, but never her control. He'd had the opportunity to pick them up again and give it a shot in recent months, but he'd always failed miserably, still more likely to injure himself than someone else if he let go of his death grip on the handle. Once her imaginary partner was summarily dispensed, Sin bowed again, and looked at him once before heading off to the bathroom.

He changed while she was in, an old routine by these days, and was in dark heavy jeans and woolen socks when she emerged. He found shirts and layered them while she added a few more to her own outfit, then pulled on a cap she picked up the night before with a local logo on it.

Her hair hung down her back, and she was getting antsy, being over-warm for the room. She charged out into the day, only the dagger and throwing knives accompanying her, and so well hidden under the clothes that no one would know they were there. Sin spun in the parking lot, admiring the fresh blanket of snow that had appeared while they slept. Lee worried about the tracks they were going to leave, and whether Sin might just lay down and make snow angels.

They grabbed drive-thru breakfasts and sat outside the house watching through binoculars. The snow was too heavy, and the wind too high for Lee to use his listening dish, but still, by ten a.m. they were certain that Sandoval was indeed the man inside.

They left mid-afternoon, knowing what they needed, and returned just after dark, Sin for once without her usual leathers. They'd had to dress in whites, jeans and thick jackets, with an under-layer of thermals. They both wore fleece caps in a creamy color, and Sin had wrapped her hair up under it. For once her coloring was working against her. Still she had no doubts and no fear. The white color may look more angelic, but she was still Sin.

Armed to the hilt, they crept in closer to the house, following the path they had decided on before. Sin let Lee take out the dogs, since she hadn't been able to get close enough earlier to make friends. They were kenneled unless someone came out with them, so there was nothing for it but to take them out of the equation. She made that same sign that he'd seen before over each of the bodies, and they headed up to the house.

Using the rope, they climbed in, thankful that it had been cold enough here to snow consistently, not rain then freeze. They skimmed the roof, watching for ice, and leaving footprints that told everything anyone would need to know, then popped open the vent.

Inside, they stayed silent for nearly an hour before moving further. The house was closed down for the night, Sandoval having turned off the lights hours earlier. On silent treads they made their way painstakingly to the bedroom, and slowly opened the door.

Lee hung back, just outside the frame as Sin positioned herself to throw the first knife. Wanting to stake the man to the bed, and do what she'd intended to do with Svelichko, she'd been hoping to catch Sandoval in bed like this.

What she caught was a hail of bullets.

Chapter 14

Later Cyn would realize that Lee had been right. Her instincts were still functioning. It was just him who got by them. Because when she opened the door she saw Sandoval asleep in his bed. He breathed in once, and while the front of her brain couldn't detect a single thing wrong with it, the back of her brain told her it looked funny.

She was diving to the side even as he sat up, a gun in each hand. The black barrels were pointed right at her, and later she would still be able to see the orange-red flare of bullets leaving the chamber. For some reason there was no sound. Just the feel of heat ripping her skin. From her position where she was pressed to the floor, she watched as deep red blooms appeared on the white of her clothes.

And, God, if that didn't just piss her off. Somewhere in her mind she realized she'd been shot. But since it didn't hurt, probably due to shock, and since she was mad that he'd shot her, and mad at herself that she'd gotten shot, she sat still until the bullets stopped.

Then she lifted her head. With knives in hand, she looked at Sandoval at the same time she let fly. The blades were already airborne before she was consciously aware that he was sitting up, and watching her, an empty gun in each hand.

Lee appeared in the doorway just then. To Cyn it was only a movement of Sandoval's eyes as he glanced over her shoulder and up. The movement behind her registered in her brain, but she didn't turn.

In Eduardo Sandoval's eyes Cyn read too much. They were bright and clear–he hadn't been sleeping at all. They had narrowed when they saw her standing in his doorway, his brows had pulled down even as he'd come upright with guns firing. He'd been expecting her, if not her small size or the fact that she was female. Now, his eyes widened just a little as they looked in the doorway again. He hadn't been expecting Lee.

Her knives found his shoulders, and she was throwing another even as she registered that his arms had gone limp. Sandoval's mouth opened, and his pupils dilated, as the knife found his throat, but it was already too late. Small round burns already littered the center of his chest, the seventh, eighth, ninth, whatever, appearing even as the first began its red spread across the button down shirt he wore.

Almost too slowly, Sandoval slumped back across the bed, his head falling onto the pillows, his body leaching fluid and making macabre designs on the sheets. For a moment his throat burbled blood, but after the first initial spurt even that satisfaction was gone.

Sitting on the floor, Cyn had to blink twice, the thick plush of the carpet was the same creamy shade as every other damn carpet she'd seen in these stupid safe houses. Not that they were safe. Not for the men in them, she'd made sure of that. And this one hadn't been safe for her either.

There were spots on the carpet, small red spots, and another appeared as she stared. From behind her, hands reached around and clasped her waist, lifting her to her feet. Cyn hung limp, until finally her legs caught and locked. She felt Lee's hands on her shoulders, turning her. Only as she faced him, still feeling out of sorts, did his hand move. Pain shot through her arm and up to her spine, but Cyn only clenched her teeth.

"Son of a bitch" were the only words out of his mouth.

She shook her head, certain she could clear it of the fuzz that was derailing her thought. With a few blinks Cyn re-entered reality and noticed Lee's mouth held in a tight line. His shoulder had blood on it. Her eyes widening, she reached for it, only to have him jerk back, the line around his lips growing whiter with tension.

His voice was a whisper, as always in these situations, in case Sandoval had been prepared with more than guns. "First we tie off the wounds. We can't be bleeding on everything. Then we sweep for cameras and bugs. Then we clean the blood."

Lee reached under the ivory colored sweat shirt he wore, Cyn shot her gloved hand out and stopped him. "Don't rip your shirt. You'll leave evidence. We'll use one of his."

She turned and went to the closet, aware that blood was seeping down her arm, but thankfully not dripping. She chose several white button-down shirts much like the one Sandoval had died in. Even walking back to Lee, still in the doorway, watching over Sandoval as though the man might just get up, she tried to rip the seams. But pain shot through her arms and she swore.

"I need scissors." Uncertain if there even were scissors in this barely occupied house, Cyn tromped downstairs into the kitchen. Luckily there was a pair in the knife block, so she stole those, then turned to find Lee behind her in the archway.

He searched under the sink, pulling up several garbage bags and a large bottle of bleach. By the way he held it, the jug looked heavy and therefore full. Cyn was grateful.

The curtains on the ground floor were all closed for night, she didn't have to look. She'd checked before they entered. Although now she thought maybe they'd been closed in anticipation of their arrival. "Let's do this here."

Careful not to move her arms too much, she began peeling the sweatshirt over her head. Thinking to warn Lee, she looked up at him, and saw that he was already making sure not to bump the cap he wore as he pulled his own shirt off. Spilled hair could be damaging evidence.

She peeled down to her bra, stuffing the clothing into the garbage bag along with Lee's shirts, not letting anything touch the floor.

"Holy shit!"

Lee's voice caused her to jerk, wondering if she was wounded far more seriously than she felt like. It was entirely possible with the adrenaline coursing through her system. She almost asked 'what?' but he must have seen it in her eyes, because he answered.

"That's a real bra!"

Her breath huffed out of her, and her chest loosened. The feeling of being annoyed by Lee was the only familiar one she'd had since she'd opened that door, and that felt like it had been a thousand years ago. It had in reality been less than ten minutes.

Shirtless, and ignoring the blood that oozed slowly from the wound at the edge of his shoulder, Lee pushed a finger into the waistband of her once-pristine white jeans and pulled. He looked down, "What the hell did you do with Cyn? You're wearing lace and bullet holes!"

He just looked confounded. And bleeding.

She rolled her eyes, hoping her face didn't convey the comfort of the exchange.

"It's from Victoria's Secret." She said it as though that would explain everything, when in fact she knew it explained nothing. Instead of continuing, she grabbed him and turned him to where her eyes were even with the wound.

Entry in a small neat hole, already red and swelling from the trauma. No exit wound. "Good news, bad news."

"Lay it on me, then it's your turn."

With a deep breath in, wishing it wouldn't ever be her turn, she told him what she saw. "The bullet's embedded. That means no nasty exit wound, but I'm going to have to dig it out."

"Later. Bind it." He tilted his head away and Cyn did just that. She folded fabric and paper towels she pulled off the roll, thinking they'd be cleaner than the towels in the kitchen. Then bound the bundle tight against the wound with strips she cut of the fine fabric of the shirt. Then she rubbed at the blood down his arm with a wet paper towel and threw that into the garbage bag as well.

He started to move, but Cyn held onto him for closer inspection. Something in her heart pounded in an unfamiliar rhythm. Nothing could happen to Lee. Even though she wasn't sure why, as she'd been alone all along before this, she simply couldn't let anything take him out. So she checked every inch of exposed skin and looked at his pants for holes and blood that he might not be feeling.

She had left blood on the scene at Robert Listle's house. The only place she'd left blood before tonight. It had been cleaned up, along with Listle's blood, and never noticed. She'd never been suspected. But here . . . she didn't want to think what her blood here might mean. Cyn pushed aside the memory of the red spots on the carpet upstairs, uncertain what she could do about it now.

Lee now grabbed her and began cleaning her up. He pushed reddened paper towel after reddened paper towel into the garbage bag, and had her hold a few pads over the wounds that were still seeping. "You got grazed." He said about her right upper arm.

"Grazed again, deeper." About the blood coming from the left side of her rib cage.

"In and back out again." About her left arm. Followed by, "You lucky little bitch."

Cyn didn't begrudge him the term. He'd only caught one bullet, but she was going to have to excavate it. Her breath escaped her as his pronouncement sunk in. If she was a lucky little bitch, then she was going to live and be relatively unscathed.

Lee tied off the wounds, using the same padding of fabric and paper towels, and strips of Eduardo Sandoval's shirts. At least this way, if the FBI collected fiber evidence it would lead no further than the upstairs closet.

Cyn picked up one of the shirts off the floor, and pulled it on over her bra and bindings. It was way too big, and it grated to be wearing that man's clothing. Her gloves stayed on the entire time, making the buttons hard to work, but she wasn't about to take them off. Tucking the too-long tails in required her to open the front of her jeans and push the smooth fabric down the front of her legs. When she was put back together, albeit uncomfortably, Lee was ready, looking even dapper in the fine fabric that fit his frame. Aside from the lumps of the makeshift bandages, Cyn realized this must be what he'd looked like in his old life. She wondered if she should have grabbed him a tie or two and a jacket.

With barely a head nod to each other, they worked in concert to clean up. Cyn triple bagged their shirts and the used paper towels, while Lee found a mop. They poured a good quantity of the bleach in the center of the floor and spread it as far as they could. They debated scrubbing down the cabinets, the bleach would destroy the evidence, but it would lead the investigators to everything they touched.

"We had gloves on." Cyn looked down at their hands. No blood on the fingers of the gloves. There was a spot at the edge of the cuff of her right hand, but she and Lee decided it was worth the risk to not highlight with bleach everywhere they'd been.

There was about a quarter of the jug left, and Cyn suggested they bleach the spots in the carpet upstairs. “The chemicals would destroy all the cells right? All the DNA?”

Lee nodded. “But it admits that we bled. They’ll go looking for other sources of evidence. And they likely won’t stop until they find it. We’re serial killers.” The words sounded harsh in the whisper she was growing familiar with. Without another sound, which they’d tried to keep to a minimum, just in case the place was bugged and they were heard, Lee reached out and plucked a freshly washed tumbler from the dish rack.

Unsure what was happening now, Cyn carried the bleach jug and the bagged clothing up the stairs behind him. The ache in her arms slowed her, and by the time she reached the edge of the room, she found Lee using another of Sandoval’s shirts to protect his gloves while he tipped the body and spilled gooey blood into and over the cup.

That’s disgusting. She almost said it out loud, but instead watched, mesmerized, as Lee brought the cup of blood to her, and proceeded to pour it over the few spots where she’d dripped her own blood.

That’s brilliant.

She’d have to remember to say it later.

He created new spots, re-doused the originals that contained her blood, and when he finished he looked around the room. Her eyes followed where his led, seeing bullet holes peppering the walls all around the doorway. With a breath in at what she’d missed, Cyn went back to work, and into the closet to bring Lee another several shirts. She left the hangers on the rack and carefully wrapped the glass so they could carry it out without incriminating themselves.

Setting the bundles in the hallway, they did a quick sweep of the bedroom, hoping that if there was a bug or a camera that they’d find it. But they found nothing. They had no detecting devices, no scanners, nothing any more technologically advanced than the guns that Lee carried, or the laser sharpened edge on her weapons. They were operating on prayer. Cyn just wasn’t sure who to pray to.

Lee took the bag, and slung it over his shoulder, looking like a sinister white-clad Santa Claus, and left Cyn to carry the cup. They’d have to get rid of it later. They made their way back onto the roof, being very careful not to leave evidence of their passing.

She was pretty certain that from inside no one would suspect they had gone out the attic vent. However from outside, fresh tracks appeared on the rooftop, and that would be a dead giveaway to anyone who stood back far enough to see. She let Lee and his sack of evidence go down first, while she used the bundle and her hands to move the snow around, hopefully obscuring their tracks while she backed down to the corner.

She did the same thing as she backed away from the house. Under the cover of trees they spent another half hour making tracks in every direction they could find, then finally gave up. Once they were in the car she cranked the engine to a soft purr and pulled out of the spot where they'd left it hidden for hours now. In the distance she heard sirens and wondered what they were for. But she decided to ignore it, and took them, and her thoughts, to the nearest paved road, where their tracks completely disappeared amid all the others.

Only then did Cyn find relief. And in her relief she felt the burn from her arms as she steered, and wondered what Lee must be feeling in the passenger seat. He was finally able to sit still, as he should have from the moment they'd discovered he had a bullet lodged in him.

He stayed that way for the hour it took Cyn to find an open and empty looking campground. At this time of year, with snow blessedly beginning to fall, the grounds were cleared. They pulled spare clothes and the first aid kit from the back of the car, and hiked to a wooded spot at the edge of the water. Most of it was frozen, but only thinly, and a current passed visibly under the layer of ice.

Cyn peeled her gloves for the first time in hours, and pushed her fist through the surface, the shock of cold water far more painful than breaking the half inch thick ice. Still she reached back in and handed a chunk of it to Lee to hold against his shoulder.

She was shocked when she opened the kit. He had syringes and anesthetics, long forceps and small suture packs. "Did you rob a doctor's office?"

"No!" He looked offended. "I paid someone to rob a doctor's office."

She just had to laugh. It felt good, too, especially considering that Lee expected her to sew him up.

It seemed he preferred to do the injecting himself. "I paid really close attention the last time I got stitched."

"Why?"

He shoved the needle into his arm and depressed the plunger several times while he talked, clearly already somewhat numb from the ice. "It was after the Kurevs roughed me up. And I knew what I was going to do. So I paid attention."

She frowned while he touched his shoulder a few times before pushing the syringe in again, this time further back. He seemed to not notice that he was shirtless in the cold air. "Why did they beat you up?"

He stopped with the needle and handed it back to her, "Same reason they killed Samantha and Bethany. To get me to cooperate." He shrugged with his good shoulder. "Problem was, after that, there was no reason to cooperate. There was nothing worse they could do."

He touched at his shoulder again, as Cyn realized there was nothing she could say. Her mind wandered, to wonder what her father had done to get himself killed. It must have been something unredeemable, and apparently turning the Kurevs in to the Feds was considered redeemable if they'd left Lee alive. Or maybe they'd simply discovered that killing their accountant wasn't the best way to go.

Lee's voice pulled her back to the present, which she wasn't sure was any better. "You should get to it, I have no idea how well this stuff works since it's a few years old."

For the first time she looked at the bottle. Xylocaine. That part sounded good, but, "This expired a year ago."

"Then get cracking." He closed his eyes.

With cold fingers operating cold forceps, Cyn prodded and poked at the wound. She could feel the bullet in there, and he winced when she tapped it. After eight tries that made her as tense as he was, she grabbed it and managed to pull it halfway out. Swearing a blue streak, she went after it again, then threw it into the unfrozen section in the middle of the lake. It landed with a small satisfactory plop.

She cleaned and stitched him with clumsy fingers, and re-bandaged him with more ease. He even thanked her at the end, then demanded that she strip down and subject herself to the same stinging torture she'd just put him through. But he extracted no revenge.

They climbed into the clothes they'd worn out of the motel that night, jeans and shirts, ball caps and sneakers. Setting three smaller bundles into the stone circles nearby, they burned the evidence and later washed the glass in the spot where she'd opened the ice before breaking the tumbler on a rock and scattering the pieces into the water.

Cyn reopened her wounds when she showered when they got in to the motel. But she made sure all the blood went down the drain. Groggy as the sun came up beyond the curtains, she let Lee re-bandage her before she slipped into her frog pajamas and curled up against him.

Owen had jerked awake as his pager buzzed, knowing instantly what it was. But, then again, with all his other cases closed, solved, or absorbed into someone else's investigation, what else could it be?

The ninja had been out again. Or the gunner. When his pager went off in the middle of the night these days he could be assured of a dead body with one of two things accompanying it: a big red bow or executed dogs.

Randolph in dispatch informed him right away that he only had the dogs.

And that pissed him the hell off.

That simmer of anger, for a fugitive he had previously admired if not liked, had kept him awake on the long flight–another thing he was relatively assured of when he was summoned in the dark. In fact, he'd kissed Annika and a sleeping Charlotte good-bye and was in the car with his packed bag slung into the back before he even returned the call.

Now, in the middle of Idaho, of all places, his body was threatening sleep. Owen was threatening back with large quantities of low quality coffee, even though he was mostly immune by this point. Maybe he'd switch to soda. But out here it was too damn cold to think about enforcing that one any time soon.

A quiet snowfall belied the importance of the night. The Christmas Killer had struck in time for her holiday, even if she'd come without ribbons or tags. And Owen, for one, hoped that meant that she'd sit still and be quiet for December 25th, and just maybe he'd get to spend it with Anni and Charlotte.

That meant clamping down on media coverage. The only way Owen knew to clamp down was to keep them entirely ignorant. Once the cops had called it in to the Bureau, they'd been informed in no uncertain terms to put the lid on it. According to the looks on their faces at the scene, they'd been offended that someone thought they needed to be told.

Good cops, Owen thought to himself, and he hoped his smile conveyed his appreciation. The local blue had traipsed through the house, destroying a good lot of evidence. But they'd backed out once they saw the body, and called in the feds. Not so much because of the dogs they said, but because they recognized Eduardo Sandoval from the case on TV.

Good enough.

The body was going on twenty-four hours old according to Nguyen. Judging by how the blood had congealed, and the lack of rigor mortis, and a few other things that Owen didn't want to know about.

He'd read on the flight over that the local police had been tipped off by a neighbor who didn't like all the activity at the house next door. Out here though 'next door' was barely in within sight. But she'd heard something suspicious the night before and then nothing. So she'd called Ray, the Sheriff, because she'd helped his mama some when he was little, and he radioed Jeff, his cop friend whose jurisdiction it was in, and Owen got a headache with all the degrees of separation that had somehow put him just outside of Boise staring at a dead Eduardo Sandoval at eight a.m. two weeks before Christmas.

He shot the last of his coffee and worried the cup in his hands.

Blood was in random places around the room. Even though Nguyen had turned on the fluorescent it didn't show anything that wasn't already visible to the eye. Sandoval had died laid out on his bed. The lower half of him was still under the sheet, although when they looked they saw he was wearing khakis and shoes.

Nguyen raised his eyebrows, "He was waiting up for them."

Owen had had the same thought.

The lab man smiled, his paper form giddy with energy Owen didn't feel even though he knew he should. "Dunham, Sandoval shot at least one of them. That means blood and that means we've got more DNA. Finally."

Owen agreed in theory. It looked like Sandoval hadn't left the bed. So he couldn't be responsible for the blood by the closet, the window, or the door. There were even three small drops over in the corner by the TV. Those were the ninja's. Or the gunner's. Or, if they were very lucky, both. Owen didn't expect them to be that lucky, though.

The body sported no bow. That irked Owen as much as anything. But again he agreed with Nguyen. "Looks like he shot her, or them, and they just took him out."

"If the knives in the shoulders are any indicator, she disarmed him–"

"Funny." Owen responded dryly.

"Gotcha." Nguyen only nodded. Maybe not that much was funny when the house was warm enough that the body was starting to let off a little odor. Owen considered going to get another hit of coffee before he suited up and joined his friend. But Nguyen wasn't finished talking. "And the gunner just killed." He held up the edge of the shirt placket, "Looks like between five and fifteen shots here, clustered right into the heart, a little left of center."

Nguyen took a moment to admire the gunner's skill. Owen did, too. He looked at the pristine wall behind the dead man, at the headboard of the bed, which had blood splatters, but not a single nick. When they got the body into the lab and counted the actual bullet holes through the heart, then they would know exactly how many shots the gunner had fired.

But there was no bow. No tag. No articles condemning the already dead.

Owen turned to go. Let Nguyen play with the body some more. His brain needed space to digest. Sandoval was clearly dead. So why no fluffy ribbon? Had she come without it? Had she lost that feminine touch? This man hadn't suffered, not because he didn't deserve it, but because he knew what he was in for.

Given the nice clothes he was wearing, Owen guessed he had been hoping to call his boss with the Christmas Killer ready for delivery. Although if that would be alive or dead, Owen didn't know.

He figured that Sandoval hadn't counted on what he himself had only just discovered: that there were two of them. Had they met on the internet? In some sort of "I hate the mafia" chat room? He'd set the profilers on both the gunner and the pair of them, to see if they could glean more supposition for him. The problem was that profilers worked off of past evidence, and previous female serial killers were rare. Very rare. Duos were also very rare. All the recorded cases seemed to involve a dominant personality and a submissive. A girlfriend who helped her man bait the unsuspecting. A husband who brought the wicked playthings to his sociopath wife.

And not one damn little iota of it applied here. None of the Christmas Killers' victims were kidnapped or taken anywhere. They were all killed in their own homes. Strike one against known history. There was no dominant personality here. Strike two. The two killers seemed to have been working entirely separately and met up, either by chance or design, and decided to go it together. Strike three-damned-thousand-four-hundred-and-fifty-fucking-two.

Owen wanted to rip his hair out and scream to the heavens. Not that the Christmas Killers would hear him because they were damn long gone by now. Snow had fallen and obscured any tracks. Although *something* should have shown. *If* they'd left tracks that is. And he just bet these guys didn't.

He stepped outside, feeling his ass freeze as he ducked into the small tent the locals had set up in the front yard. He refilled his coffee and grabbed a rice crispy square, then made sure he saw at least one other cop eating one before he took a bite of it. The taste threatened to transport him back to childhood. The situation threatened to get him transported to the looney bin. For a moment he gave psychiatric care careful consideration. Annika would visit him every day. But there would be no conjugal visits. Oh well, that was a deal-breaker. So he wandered the lower floors, trying to figure out how these lethal creatures of smoke, who apparently did bleed, had gotten into these damned houses in the first place.

He tried the basement, with no luck. Other cops and local agents were looking through the area, but it appeared that the killers hadn't been down here at all. Owen wandered the ground floor next, not finding much more to go on, until he hit the kitchen.

Just beyond his senses lingered an odor he recognized.

Quickly swallowing the last bite of the crispy treat, he sniffed again, and stepped further into the room. It was a local female cop who held out an arm to stop him. All she said was "Bleach," followed by "Look."

She turned out the light, then pulled her flashlight from her belt, shining it on the cabinet directly in front of them. Her voice was too sweet to have seen any real action on the job, but she wasn't vomiting, so Owen listened. "My Mama was one of those white gloves people. And she'd check if I scrubbed the floor well enough by putting the lights on dim. It shows all sins."

When Owen looked at the floor, he realized her Mama had been right. The floor was shiny clean, even streaked, in a wide, irregular patch in the middle of the room, but the edges weren't touched. It had to be the killers. No way Sandoval did this. When Owen leaned over the smell was much stronger, someone had poured straight bleach onto the floor and pushed it around. But why?

"Dunham!" Nguyen called from upstairs. And momentarily Owen was pulled from his thoughts. "I'm going to have them pull up every patch of carpet with blood on it. But you've got to get up here. It's all random, and get this, Sandoval has no shirts."

Owen was halfway up the stairs by that time. "What?" His face contorted with the total lack of reasoning involved.

"Yeah," Nguyen met him halfway out the door. "He's got pants, jackets, ties, sweaters, but no shirts. Just a batch of hangers."

"Son of a bitch!!!" This time Owen did scream it to the heavens. His head tipped skyward and Nguyen moved like the waves of sound had blown him back several feet.

When Owen gathered breath to speak again, it was at a slightly lower volume, which was still too loud for even impolite company, and with no less anger. "He shot them! Sandoval shot one of them!"

"Yes?" Nguyen had already said that.

"They bled. They took the shirts to the kitchen and bandaged whoever was shot and they bleached the floor. There are fibers pushed to the edge of the clean spot and every goddamned one of them is going to be from an over-priced designer white button down!"

"But there's blood!" Nguyen pointed at the spots littering the room.

Owen was still in his impotent rage. "Who the fuck bleeds a little over here and then a little over there? What in God's name would they be doing by the TV for just a second?" He took a fortifying breath in and started up again, "They *knew* they were bleeding. They bleached the kitchen. You think they left you drops in here!?!? Ten grand says there's nothing in here that's usable!"

Nguyen looked taken aback, and Owen couldn't think of any time he'd let his anger get the better of him in front of his friend. He stomped off muttering, "We still don't even know how they get in the god-damned houses."

Lee had jerked awake that morning at three a.m. according to his watch. Then again at 5:30, although he'd barely been able to see the face of the watch that time as Sin had been lying on his arm.

She didn't even pretend to go into her own room anymore. Somehow, since Idaho, he'd found it vaguely comforting. That could be because the nightmares he had involved her diving through a rain of gunfire. When he jerked awake with her limp body in his arms, he always had a moment of panic, but then she moved, stirred, in some way letting him know that she was alive. His brain would recount the hours after Sandoval opened fire on them, and he would turn his face back into the pillow and fall back to sleep, only to have it happen all over again.

The reporters hadn't flocked to the scene. The TV stations didn't tell tales of the Christmas Killer racking up another body in time for the holidays. Only two days later had CNN confirmed that a body found in Idaho had been identified as Eduardo Sandoval, recently acquitted of a long list of tax evasion crimes and suspected of much worse. No one seemed to miss him much. And no one breathed about the Christmas Killer.

So the FBI had found him. Lee had hoped that maybe the Kurevs would get to him first and dispose of him. No one would complain if Sandoval went missing. But he'd been reported, so no luck there.

The holidays came and went with him and Sin scouring the internet, traveling to three different states to do so, and not turning up much of anything. Lee prayed every night that Sin's blood didn't incriminate them, that it didn't even show. It would mean they could lock her up forever, or fry her if she was ever caught.

He'd told her that he thought maybe someone upstairs was watching out for them.

Sin had replied, angrily, that she would have fucking appreciated it ten years ago.

That he understood.

New Year's had passed with a couple of Jack and Cokes. Lee had gotten just buzzed enough to remember kissing Sam that last time, over at her mother's New Year's Eve party. He'd barely made it, late from work, and he was so glad now that he had.

His shoulder still stung if he shot too many rounds at once. Sin still punished the pop bottles, and had added cardboard boxes with ketchup and mustard packs she'd taped to them just for the fun of watching them bust.

The fact that Sin had done anything 'just for fun' had amazed him. Even her silly shopping spree after Thanksgiving had seemed to have a purpose. He itched somewhere deep inside, what with the passing of the holidays, or the fact that they'd nearly been blown to pieces. With the weather cold and often dark, he was lacking in good outlets for it. "Come on. We need a good fight."

He stood across the mats from her and stared her down. He crouched low, ready to go after her, but she stood with her hands on her hips, just in front of the practice dummy. It stood silent behind her, knowing better than to disobey, as she'd already beaten two of the lights into an early grave. "I don't need a fight."

"Your practice dummy says otherwise." He pointed. But she didn't rise to the bait.

"You need to take it easy on your shoulder."

He didn't buy that one either. "But you don't? You took three bullets."

"Grazes! One shot in the arm for Christ's sake." Her voice rose, and Lee had trouble with what was before him. Something was simmering in there. He'd be more comfortable if they could just beat the crap out of each other. She huffed. "Why didn't he kill me?"

"Did you want him to?" He got closer, figuring if he tackled her, she'd have to fight back. And he needed something, some good physical exertion, to get his feet under him.

Sin had to see him stalking her, but she didn't respond, not even to his question. She just steered the conversation a different way. "I just don't understand. He fired two guns to empty and I got three grazes and you got one bullet, because you were stupid enough to step in the way."

He stood up straight. Fuck this. "You're welcome. Next time I'll let you take all the heat."

"That's not what I meant." Her hands gestured into the air in front of her, no language sufficing for the frustration she clearly felt.

His shoulders slumped. "You could have asked me that weeks ago." He rubbed at the back of his neck. "We didn't get any mortal wounds because he's mafia. They kill by their willingness to empty an entire clip into a person. Not by any finesse or accuracy. Did you see where some of those bullets went?"

She nodded. "Some went out into the hallway."

"Uh-huh. He was aiming with prayer and not talent." Some of her worry started to dissipate, so he continued. "And your reflexes are fast. By the time I realized what was happening, you were already on the ground."

"I knew something was wrong when I opened the door. You were right about my instincts."

There wasn't going to be a fight.

Never mind that he was on edge. The winter hemmed him in every year. Mostly he read, but this time he was watching Sin do katas–martial arts forms. He'd had her teach him a few, but they felt like Tai Chi to him, almost slow and peaceful. It had been much more fulfilling to learn how to grab a wrist and strike against the forearm up near the elbow disabling an opponent for at least part of a second. She'd demonstrated on him, and by god it worked.

She'd asked about his shooting techniques, using his third finger as a trigger finger and lining his index along the barrel of the gun. In the living room, with non-firing practice rounds in the Hecklers, he'd showed her. She'd easily gotten the hang of it, and liked it as much as he had when he'd first discovered it. You just point at the thing you want to shoot and squeeze your middle finger. It was virtually impossible to jerk the trigger accidentally, and made two-handed firing much more feasible, as you no longer had to sight the barrel.

Unfortunately, the first time they got out for her to try it, she nearly lost the gun. On the recoil, which she usually managed to control, the weapon threatened to fly out of her hand. The butt of the gun was too big for her smaller hands to grip well with her strongest finger now on the trigger. Any aim she gained was well and truly lost and Lee took the gun away from her, fearing for their safety.

But that had been over a week ago. He was healing, and had no vent for his agitation. He had no intentions for his future kills, and didn't want to know what Sin was planning. Having Sandoval pop up, armed to the teeth, was enough to make him think they needed a new M.O.

And he had no idea what it should be.

So when Sin came up that night right after he finished his sandwich, he was already restless, and not up for whatever she might have in mind. When her hands pushed him forward to the edge of the couch, and she crowded in behind him, he wondered what the hell she was doing. When she began kneading his shoulder and back muscles, you could have knocked him over with a feather.

"Sin, what are you doing?" He tried to keep his voice even. But it was so hard to do. His brain was warring between worry about what Sin was really up to, accepting the back rub for what it was, and sudden, day-bright memories of Samantha doing exactly this after he'd been at work all day. He almost laughed aloud there in the small cold cabin. You didn't know what tense was until you'd been underground for almost four years, killing hit men for sport, and living with another killer whom you were only recently certain wasn't truly sociopathic.

Lee tamped that thought down. Sin had always had a conscience. It was a little overzealous maybe, but she wasn't a sociopath. That thought didn't make him worry any less when her uber-deadly hands were rubbing at his shoulder blades, no matter how good it felt. Still he tried to relax. He leaned back into the pressure of her fingers, not asking what had inspired this, because he was in knots, and if he pissed her off she'd stop. He could analyze it later, after she finished.

She worked with motions that should have been surprisingly strong for her size, but Lee didn't think twice. Aside from sneaking up on him, there wasn't much she could do that did surprise him anymore. Then he reminded himself that she was giving him a backrub, and realized he didn't know half as much as he thought he did about her.

Her hands worked down to the base of his spine, then started back up with slow, heavy, sure motions. By the time she hit the area around his shoulders and neck he was positively loose, and it was only as the blackness was closing in around the edges of his vision that he realized he'd been had. But he couldn't pull out of it, and he sunk deep into the abyss.

"Lllleeeeee."

"Llleeeeeeee."

The voice came from so far away, and he was shaking. Or rather someone was shaking him. As his eyes fluttered and light strobed into his brain, he realized it was Sin. The momentary relief to see her was blindsided by the sudden realization that she had been responsible. His tongue found action by sheer force of will and he spewed at her. "What the fuck was that?!?"

She smiled.

That bitch had the nerve to smile?

Then again, he'd allowed Miss Umpth-degree Black-belt to give him a back rub. That was class A idiotic if anything ever was.

Her voice worked just fine. All of her did. Lee was flexing his fingers even as she spoke. "Vagal nerve. It runs along your carotid arteries, just to the side of your neck. If you push it you can slow the heart."

"Thanks for the demonstration, Lizzie Borden."

"Hey, I had to practice. It's hard to find."

He stood and rounded on her. "And I'm sure slitting my throat would have been just too crass."

She looked put out. What right did she have to look put out?

"You would be dead if I had slit your throat. I wouldn't do that." Forget put out, she looked hurt. "Besides, you got a nice back rub."

"And a nice trip to the netherworld." He stood and paced the room.

"Well, we need something new. Something to occupy us until the media coverage dies down and we can go after the next one."

"Newsflash, sweetheart," He was still mad at her, even though she had artfully changed the topic, "It isn't the media that made Sandoval fire at us."

She frowned, and Lee felt some of his anger fade at being the next replacement for her used-up practice dummy. "The media didn't cover a damn thing about mafia hits. Just because some of their guys came in bows didn't mean we were after Sandoval. Not only is the FBI after us, but the Kurev family is, too."

With a deep breath, he waited while that sank in, then he went at it and hammered the point home a little further. "The Kurevs have thought one of the other families got themselves a nice ninja hitman and came after them, and they might have retaliated, which I have no issues with. But they put it together a while ago. Svelichko had a gun in his hand and another under the bed. And that was before the Christmas Killer got named."

His hands went into his hair, and his heart sped up, and he had a fleeting thought to be grateful that all of him worked properly and that he was going to pay her back. "By my best guess, none of them knows there are two of us. But I don't know that for a fact. I'm hoping they weren't able to get DNA from the blood you dripped. And I'm hoping I didn't drip any, because we sure as hell didn't find it, but the FBI will."

Her voice sounded like she was at a tea party, it was only missing a good English accent. "So your plan is: lay low and beat up on each other for a while?"

He felt his mouth quirk. "I was actually ready to give up on the fighting, and the back rub was nice. But I'm really ready go ten rounds in the ring now." Consciously, he unclenched the fists that had formed at his sides.

"I'll give you a real back rub?"

"Like I'm going to fall for that shit?"

She shook her head. "No ninja stuff."

"Bite me."

"You can learn it on me."

At that, he turned back to her.

Sin babbled like she was trying to cover for something, but Lee wanted to see where this went. "See, I learned on you, you can learn on me. You should know how to do this, too."

She motioned to the couch beside her, then tugged him down. With his hands in hers he let himself be led, although he wasn't sure why, other than good old-fashioned curiosity. Sin placed his fingers around her neck in several different ways before deciding that it would work best if he used a choke hold and crossed his thumbs, so each was hitting the nerve on the opposite side. "Now press. Gently!"

Lee stared at her. He had his hands wrapped around her pretty little neck. Now, he had no illusions that if he actually tried to cut off her air–which was really tempting to a good portion of his brain–that she would fight back with all she was worth and inflict some serious damage. But he pressed his thumbs in where she showed him. "There's something very satisfying about this."

She was going to nod, but her eyes were turning glassy. Her mouth started to work, and the sounds she produced were faint. "I think you found it." She made as if to push his hands away. "Hhhheeeyyyy."

Lee smiled as her eyes rolled back, and he laid her down on the couch, certain she was still breathing, and denying that there had been something vaguely erotic about it. He'd never gotten off on something like that before, and he sure as hell wasn't going to start now.

He enjoyed the three minutes of peaceful silence he got before she came to, sputtering. Lee simply lifted an eyebrow at her as she attempted to glare at him from where she was spread out across the couch. Between the backrub and getting to choke Sin, he'd lost the desire to hit something.

Chapter 15

Owen looked up as Nguyen popped his head into the doorway Owen now purposefully left open all the time. He was afraid that, if left alone, he might give serious thought to piercing his neck with the Excalibur-from-the-stone letter opener Charlotte had given him for Christmas. He'd placed it prominently on his desk, a symbol of how he hoped she saw him. Although at this moment he was afraid he wouldn't even be worthy enough to get this reproduction letter opener out of the Lucite block it rested in. And he was contemplating the poetry of dying with a tiny Excalibur through his jugular when he spotted Nguyen coming in and he decided to hold out for another day.

"I owe you ten grand." Nguyen looked like someone had popped his party balloon.

Owen knew how his friend felt, his own party balloon having popped weeks ago. "Told you."

They had gotten nothing from the carpet samples they'd taken. And Nguyen had lorded over the blood lab. Hell, he'd hands-on done part of the work himself. They extracted all manner of things from that carpet. None of the blood had been identifiable as anyone's other than Sandoval's.

Nguyen sank into the chair across from Owen, his shoulders slumped. He looked defeated and unkempt without his paper coveralls. Hell, somehow the man actually looked worse in a three piece suit. Nguyen eyed the letter opener and Owen thought, *whoa buddy, I got dibs on that one*. But Nguyen didn't reach for it. "That weird stain off to Sandoval's left? I think they tipped the body and collected blood. Then they poured it randomly around the room. Thus triggering that little dance you did there."

Chagrin climbed his spine as Owen watched Nguyen mimic his anger.

"Who the fuck bleeds a little over here and then a little over there?" Nguyen quoted and waved his hands side to side in what looked far more like a hula than any motion Owen had ever made. He hoped.

With a deep sigh, the lab man continued with their failures. "Whatever blood they dropped, they covered with enough of Sandoval's to thin it out enough that we'll never ID it. And they made it so we had such a glut of samples that we didn't go looking for any more. I really thought that maybe they'd just made so many spots thinking that we wouldn't know which ones were theirs. But we took *all* of them. Every last sample we saw. Cleaners have been in the house already. I called and checked, just in case. But no, we are well and royally fucked. And I don't have ten grand on me."

"I'm not collecting. I'd rather have evidence."

Nguyen shook his head. "That ain't happening anytime soon. Blankenship find anything?"

Blankenship had been hunting and gathering with a team outside the house. All he'd found were indentations in the fresh snow that might have been tracks, and might have been made by the killers, and seemed to lead both everywhere and nowhere.

"No, he didn't find anything."

"I do have one thing."

Owen's head snapped up. Then why did Nguyen look so glum?

"It's only trivial. Interesting, but of absolutely no value whatsoever."

Of course. "What is it?"

Resting his head in his hands, Owen sought to open his brain to all possibilities, in hopes that he would see the connection and solve the case or, more likely, throw a clot and have a stroke. Which would just as officially end the case, for him at least. But again, that would mean no conjugal visits with Anni. He prayed for insight.

Nguyen leaned forward. "I opened the chest and counted holes. Looks like twenty two."

"Okay."

"All fairly straight in, all at least grazed, if not dead center into, the heart."

"Okay."

"Well," Nguyen held one hand up flat, palm facing the other, which he made a gun shape with. "Ten bullets, through the heart, and the body starts to fall back." As he tipped the flat hand back, Owen realized that was supposed to be Sandoval. "Pop the clip and reload and you're shooting a reclined body."

This time Nguyen pointed at his own chest, to the heart, but aiming up, from under the ribcage. "Our guy doesn't look like that. So no reloading. All twenty-two shots fired before he falls back. That's real damn quick."

"We knew that."

"There are only ten rounds in a legal clip. So he has to be using illegal extendeds. Pretty much anyone can get their hands on those. But it does give us a few places to look. Also, even with the extendeds, eighteen rounds is the highest I know of. So he's firing two-handed."

Owen nodded. "Of course he is." That would just make things peachy.

Nguyen stood. "That's all I've got. Well, that and the mother of all headaches."

Owen opened his drawer, having wised up after Idaho. "What do you want? I have aspirin, ibuprofen, Tylenol, Aleve, ketoprofen, and two Tylenol with codeine."

Leaning over the desk, his friend looked at the display of loose, mostly white pills that filled the built in pencil tray. "Damn, that's half a pharmacy. Any Demerol?"

"Sorry, bud. Codeine's the hardest I've got."

"Excedrin?"

"Yeah," He handed over twice the usual dose at Nguyen's request and told him good-bye.

Leaning back in the chair he laced his fingers behind his head. He couldn't be a consultant. He'd spend too much time finding work, like all the time. It would be freelance. At this point, factory work–maybe making happy meal toys somewhere in Taiwan–was sounding right up his alley. The thought of snapping the heads onto plastic cartoon figures all day was soothing in a sick way.

No, he needed a real job, where he showed up and did his tiny part, and wasn't the boss. Someone else did the paperwork and accounted for the profits and losses. He'd be his own man at home. Which would be okay, because he'd be home so much more often, and he'd *be* there when he was. A small smile sat on his lips as he savored the thought.

That was how Agent in Charge Bean found him. "What have you got on this Christmas Killer?"

"A whole lot. But none of it points at anything we can apprehend."

"So tell me about him." Bean referred to the case in the male singular until he closed the door. "Anything back from the profilers?"

Owen shook his head. "Only that they can't really profile what they haven't seen before. There's not enough history to do anything more than a good Psych 101 guess."

"Tell me what you do have." Bean sat back in the chair Nguyen had vacated earlier, and Owen excused himself long enough to wash down his own handful of ibuprofen, then he started talking.

Lee's bout of stir-crazy hit him again right before the cabin froze over for two weeks straight. Sin, of course, thought it was fantastic. The girl seemed to know every way there was to ratchet him up and increase his tension.

She sat backward on the couch, facing out the window, her sherpa-like boots hanging just off the seat, while she watched snow fall out the window for something like two hours one day. She commented on its beauty, and Lee didn't have the heart to remind her it was deadly. It covered the ice patches, and people were dying on the roads. He'd been watching the local news programs on his little TV when the white-out didn't block the signal.

They had both chopped wood the one time the sun had shone, the two of them swinging axes side by side while split logs flew. Lee worked up enough of a sweat to actually peel his shirt, which felt supremely odd while he was standing in the three feet of snow that had drifted and stayed in their little valley. Sin had commented on the fun of it, as she'd never split logs before and apparently was immune to blisters. She wrapped his hands that night, not flinching at his glare, and told him he looked like a boxer. Lee braved the old drifts and newly falling snow the next day to take it out on her practice dummy. He decommissioned one light and sent the plastic body toppling three times when he couldn't hold back a punch. Then he was glad he hadn't said anything untoward when he turned to find Sin in workout gear, stretching across the floor behind him.

The well had frozen at the beginning of the storm and they ran out of drinking water at the end of the ninth day. Sin rigged up a pot over the stove, in which she melted snow while she practiced forms. Their supply of fresh fruits and vegetables had disappeared the first week. The cars were likely encased in solid ice given the cycle of snow / thaw / freeze they'd been enduring on almost a daily basis. Even if they dug or chopped one of the cars out, the roads back here were impassable.

Although Lee thought his half-mountain-goat partner might be sure-footed enough to hike the fifteen miles to the nearest mini-mart, he certainly wasn't. Given that it was locally owned and not part of any chain, there was every possibility that if they didn't feel like opening they just wouldn't. So there wasn't a point anyway.

While Sin watched a soap opera, Lee took stock of the cabinets and began to think they would likely start to get really hungry in the next few days, if something wasn't done. The emptying pantry didn't yield any answers either. They did, for some reason, have thirteen cans of creamed corn. He grabbed one and heated it to go with sandwiches that used the last of the bread.

When he entered the living room, which meant he turned a small corner, Sin was cross legged in the center of the room staring into the fire. They were sending up a smoke signal that they were here. But they couldn't run the generator, not often, not on what they had stored. So they had fire for heat, and when they wanted cold they opened a door or window. Lee and Sin hoped there were enough other random families still out here in the Smokies that no one thought much of another patch of smoke in the mountains.

That night they slept on the floor in front of the fire, just like they had for most of the week. There weren't enough blankets to save his back, and Lee didn't dare drag the old mattress out. He'd thought of it once, then was immediately engulfed in visions of a stray spark sending the thing up in flames. Followed quickly by the house, then the outbuilding, then half the Appalachians. While he and Sin fled. They'd be barefoot, but they were both pretty hardy. No, Lee was certain they wouldn't die of exposure–they'd be shot by well-meaning mountain folk, threatened by the half-naked crazy man and the witch in the electric blue pajamas with the creepy big-eyed lizards.

Sin woke with a cheer that told him her spine wasn't suffering at all like his. Of course her spine had been pressed against his front most of the night, not the floor. She sat up with an ease that Lee didn't feel. He liked to believe it was due to his position and not his age. She rubbed it in by stretching. "It looks almost sunny. Do we go hunting today?"

So she'd seen the empty pantry.

It was either hunt, hike, or starve. So Lee voted for 'hunt', too.

Two hours later Sin was stalking wild things in her sherpa boots. Lee followed her, picking his way through high drifts, one silenced Heckler in his hand at his side, another in the left side loop he'd sewed into his pants. Sin had stars and knives with her, and he figured they were in some age-old cowboy versus Indian contest. He didn't really care though, he just wanted food, and so far they hadn't seen anything worth killing. Squirrels were out in abundance, but there were eleven cans of creamed corn to get down before he sunk to that.

One large cat, probably a neighbor, slunk by also out on the hunt on the first sunny day in a while. Lee didn't think cat meat would be any good.

"There's a lake south of here." Sin pointed. "Can we get ducks?"

"No."

"But I saw ducks there."

He shook his head, "Did you sleep through high school bio?"

She stiffened, the knife she'd held at the ready showing the tension of her grasp. "I didn't take it. I left at sixteen."

Not knowing what to say, he didn't respond to that part. "They flew south for the winter. If we're lucky we'll see a deer."

"We can't eat a whole deer!"

"Eventually we can. The other option is wild boar. I've never had it, but my money is on 'gamey' and 'tough'."

Sin agreed and they stalked the wild deer for another two hours before heading home empty handed. They saw a young buck just before they got to the cabin, and Sin chucked a knife into its throat even as Lee was lifting his gun.

One point, Indians, he thought.

The deer convulsed, and turned its head, looking square at them, at which point Sin turned into a total girl and started . . . what? crying wasn't really it. Her mouth was open and her lip shook. Her eyes went wide and wet with regret, and you'd think she was four and she'd killed Bambi. Lee put a bullet in its head to end its suffering and his. One point, cowboys.

Only his suffering didn't end. Sin got upset while he was dressing it. Lee figured there was a better way than the royal mess he was making, but he was making it up as he went along. Sin's issue, though, had been the deer's innocence. Lee's issue was his hunger. And the deer was already dead. Not much he could do about it now. They scattered the entrails, noticing two large cats circling before they even tied the carcass up and left. In exchange for her not helping him gut the damn thing, Lee decided to not help cook it.

Of course that meant he found Sin making venison ka-bobs over the fire after he showered. Her eyes sparkled at the way she'd over-prepared simple deer meat. She seemed to have lost all compunction about killing Bambi. She served him up with creamed corn.

Instead of feeling better, Lee's urge to fidget upped another notch, though he really wasn't sure why.

He was sick of creamed corn and venison by the time the roads thawed a week later. They dug out her green Toyota and got fresh food. Lee drank a quart of milk under the awning outside the store while Sin stuffed two HoHos in her face with a smile and a shrug.

A week after that, they left town with an idea where to strike and a very well thought out plan for how.

Owen hated Tampa. He hated Idaho. And he hated Tempe. He hated Wichita, Kansas. And any number of other places he'd been dragged to at a moment's notice.

Here, young and old flocked to Florida's West Coast to get away from the snow wherever it was that they called home. The young flocked in the streets and outside the clubs at night. The old flocked to the buffets at four p.m. for the special. And everyone just flocked. That meant his crime scene was in a house that was all of five feet from the neighbor on either side. Which made it nearly impossible to keep people out or away.

And they all wanted to talk to him. That sweet man, the dead one, had been so kind, returned old Mrs. So-and-so's Chihuahua, tipped the lawn boy really well, and on and on. No one mentioned, in fact no one seemed to know or even care that he'd earned that nice house and tip money by offing people who didn't agree with the Kurevs.

Reporters hovered at the edge of the yellow tape night and day. One even recognized the agents from the coverage of the Reverend Deehan killing and asked point blank if this was another Christmas Killer case?

It was Blankenship who flat-out laughed. "This was mafia related."

Good one, Owen thought. His partner made the reporter sound stupid without even lying.

They all watched as that knowledge rippled through the crowd of neighbors and lookie-loos like the waves lapping in the bay directly behind the big house. Then Blankenship had given the reporter a look that condescended in a way he had no claim to, and told her, "Ma'am, we handle many cases at a time. Just because you see someone you recognize doesn't mean you've got the Christmas Killer on your hands."

Owen wouldn't have been surprised if his partner had raised his hand and patted her on the head, so complete was the picture. Then he and Blankenship ducked under the tape and opened the front door to a wide white screen that had been set up for the express purpose of keeping anyone from seeing the big red bow on the body or the articles tacked to the chest with throwing stars.

Of course, just when he thought the MO had changed, she reverted back completely. Aside from a nifty, almost bloodless bullet hole in the windpipe, and one in each knee cap, the gunner had stayed out of it. This man had been bound like a pig to his coffee table, after the glass top had been shattered out of it and left lying in sharp pieces around the floor. Owen made a mental note to never get an iron coffee table. The man looked strong, he might have struggled enough to break a wooden table, but no, not here.

The only real new addition to the scene this time was that, while the articles had been photocopies as usual, they were taped together end to end and rolled up. They were tacked with a throwing star at each of the top two corners and left to unfurl down the length of his body and across the floor, as though he was the sole recipient of Santa's naughty list.

The team was anxious to check it for fingerprints, since there had certainly been work done on the pages. Owen wasn't holding his breath, didn't even think it would be worth the time to call the lab later and find out that they'd uncovered, oh, not a damn thing. He was bored with the scene. It yielded nothing except the idea that he had no idea where they were going to strike next, or even how.

What made his blood pump faster as he slowly walked the scene in his paper suit, was that he was on a peninsula. His body was here in Tampa, taking in the sights filleted out before him, but his brain was surveying the map he had up in his office. The thumbtacks had progressed in color through the yellows. This guy, Pyotr Kurev, was firmly in the oranges and heading to red, a.k.a. fucked.

But the map was finally proving useful.

The two may walk away from a scene, but that only got them so far. If they existed in society, then they were very well camouflaged in fake ID's that were dug in deep. But no matter what their alter egos were, ninja weapons and 9mm's with silencers and illegal clips didn't grow on trees. Weapons also didn't travel on planes. That meant that these two drove everywhere.

That made them central. No fucking way they did the Idaho and Tempe jobs from here. Owen finally had his radius. Once he made that realization, he saw he could tighten the noose even further. The campus rapist, hitting schools in and around Wichita, hadn't been caught in a single effort. No way. That meant the ninja had visited several times. Which meant she lived close enough to do so. No more than an eight hour drive. There was also the issue of the gunner learning to shoot like he did–wouldn't someone that good draw attention, even at a low key range? Maybe he'd trained with a militia, knowing they'd keep their mouths shut when the feds came around. Hell, they'd probably even do the research for killers taking out the mafia. Except for that whole trend toward over-conservative Christianity.

With where his mind was racing, nothing about Pyotr Kurev interested him anymore, so Owen walked away, leaving Nguyen and his geeky forceps to glean whatever tidbit he could from here. Owen wanted to be in his office. He wanted to see the map himself, look at the pins again, even though he had them memorized.

He shed the white paper suit as he exited out the back, staring at the bay for only a second before he turned his eyes away from a family in a boat that was lookie-looing from this side of the house. He ducked into the gazebo that Pyotr had thoughtfully enclosed for them and Owen handed a twenty to the cop who knew of the nearest bookstore.

In fifteen minutes he held a detailed road map of the state of Florida, and a three-foot fold out of the entire US interstate system. He'd called Agent Bean and gotten the manpower from the FBI for research and permission to commandeer forces from various Florida Police Agencies.

Pyotr Kurev's body wasn't even cold yet, and that meant his Christmas Killers were still in Florida, right now. Not very far away.

Owen hedged his bets that they weren't above-ground citizens. It would be difficult to keep even a part-time job and keep up the work they did. If he was right, then they were in a cheap motel that didn't require ID or a credit card and wouldn't look too closely at their guests or think anything of a cash payment. He sent cops out right away, phoning in all out-of-state plates they could find at low-rent motels. He had agents waiting to find the unregistered car. A handful turned up, not surprisingly. Owen had them cataloged.

He calculated the speed with which they might have been able to get out of town and set up teams of officers to be in place and wait off to the side of the roads. They would visually check out passengers and radio to teams uproad which cars to pull over and search. The northern flow of traffic was luckily not heavy at this time of year.

Owen instructed them to look for a man and woman together, no kids. Brunette hair on the female–he just hoped she didn't disguise it. Out-of-state plates or stolen Florida plates. Non-descript car, older model, likely sedan, although maybe hatchback. Owen thought harder–it would be brown, dark gold, any shade of green, or silver to true gray. Those would blend with surroundings best. He could narrow the colors down if he knew or had a better guess what their normal surroundings were, what color it was where they lived, green, gray, or brown. But this was the best he could do for now.

Of course all this was a huge waste of money if the two were camping out and biding time mid-way, but Agent Bean had okayed it. The higher-ups were antsy about catching the Christmas Killer. Owen thought maybe they were just as pissed as he was about being constantly outsmarted. And they didn't even know it was a woman. A *small* woman. He started to entertain a fantasy about dragging her, cuffed, before his superiors, but he squelched it in favor of doing something that might actually catch her.

He was banking on I-75, because it would get them out of the state the fastest, and was the most direct route to the central states. State Road 19 was too small, with stoplights even, and I-4 would lead them horribly out of the way–through heavily populated Orlando to boot. Owen clutched the map, called his office, and headed out to catch a plane so that he could sit just off the interstate, with binoculars in hand, just south of Ocala.

He wanted to see their faces.

Cyn enjoyed the drive north on 75. It was one of the few roads they drove often enough that she could know it and feel at home on it. Almost like she had with the barely-two-lane road that led to her house in Texas. But somehow this was more. The cabin that time forgot was far more comforting than the sturdy house with the hot shower ever had been.

She ate better. She felt better. She slept better. She could sleep right here, right now, in the passenger side of the car, going down the interstate. She could fold into a tight ball without the taut tug of the leathers she'd always worn. She didn't need them. Didn't have a straight backed chair in her bedroom now. Didn't even really have her own bedroom now.

It seemed once she'd gotten a taste of safety she'd kept moving in for more. Although she was certain that Lee was going to call a halt to her invading his space one of these days, she kept pushing it. She curled into him at night and fell asleep almost instantly, she woke feeling fresh. It was what she'd always read sleep was supposed to do for you, and couldn't remember ever feeling before.

Lee was rope, net, life preserver. Shelter from the wind. So when he didn't like the way the kill had gone, Cyn disagreed, but only to a point. She did promise they would map the next one out better.

They had rented a boat on the cheap, due to the off season, and cruised the shoreline of the gulf all the way down to Tampa. On the way back they had hit storms, and tied up in both Cedar Key and Destin for a day or so each to wait them out. Lee hadn't liked that much. They arrived back in Mississippi later than they'd planned, still within their rental time, but only by a day. That had also made Lee nervous. He didn't want anyone thinking about them or looking for them, even if it wasn't really them.

Cyn didn't care about that. They had booked extra time, and figured they'd sail around to use it up if need be. They had banked on a contingency and had used it. So what? But Lee cared. So Cyn cared. She liked her new safe little world.

They'd docked in and out of Biloxi. And on the return trip they'd taken a scenic, if wet, ride up state road 49, which Cyn had enjoyed immensely, never having been that deep into Mississippi before. Everything was better now that she had that core she could depend on. They'd hooked into I-59 and she'd pulled out a Beatles compilation she'd bought for Lee and popped it into the portable disc player while she drove. He had slept through the whole second disc, giving her the satisfaction of his trust.

They even discussed who to go after next, and decided to focus their efforts on Ling Mai Na. She'd been brought up on trafficking charges too many times to count. The Kurev lawyers always found a way to get her acquitted or a mistrial declared. Never mind that dozens of drug mules were dying or going missing under her care.

If Cyn had her way, Ling Mai Na was going down, the faster the better.

The element of surprise, which had been their best defense, was clearly gone. Well, Cyn amended, part of it was. The Kurevs knew someone was after them. The way Sandoval, then Pyotr Kurev, had reacted, they knew some *one* was coming for them–the second player had still been a shock.

She had baited Pyotr out into the living room, calling to him in her whispered voice. He'd fired silenced shots into his own walls while Lee positioned behind him. When Pyotr had turned, startled to see a gunman behind him, Cyn had hit him with a flying blade. The handle nailed him in the back of the skull and dropped him like a tree, thank you very much. She'd even pointed it out to Lee, who'd responded with only 'yeah, yeah' and 'let's get him trussed'. Pyotr had come around already tied down to his own iron coffee table and Cyn had been able to have her fun.

Lee would get to play with Ling Mai Na. She would die full of bullet holes. Cyn would just add the wrapping. And the very thing that had made her their next target was because she was on trial again. In Dallas.

Cyn smiled at the thought of getting to see her little house again. She'd take a long hot shower and turn cartwheels in the back room.

That was, if the house hadn't been found. Wasn't being lived in by derelicts. Wasn't staked out by the FBI. If, if, if. Lee had pointed out that getting back into her house was going to be a serious endeavor, but Cyn was up for it. Besides, it was winter, and winter in the Tennessee mountains was telling her she should get the hell out.

Lee was ready. They'd stayed in four different motels around Dallas. They'd driven out to the house each day, taking first his car then hers as they'd brought them both.

With Na on trial, it would be easy to keep tabs on her. Too easy. Everyone else would have tabs on her, too. Including the government agencies that were making sure she showed up each day. Because the Texas business woman, who ran a series of small clothing stores and pizza joints, had enough cash on hand to post the multi-million dollar bail the judge had asked of her. The news had twittered for several days about the disdain with which she had whipped her checkbook out right there in the courtroom, offered the signed slip to the judge himself, and asked if she could please just go now?

So Lee and Sin would have to wait their turn. Since Lee preferred to wait for it in her house, they'd scouted. They'd walked up and peered in the windows. They'd staked the place out from where he'd parked in the woods the first time he'd followed her home–and that stakeout had convinced both of them never to go into law enforcement. Watching the empty house in Idaho for activity had been far more fun than watching this empty house for *in*activity.

It seemed no one was there.

Lee was tired enough of watching nothing happen that he was about willing to just say ‘okay, you got me’ if someone did show up to haul them in. At this point, he figured they’d only be guilty of abandoning the house. Since Sin had set up automatic withdrawals from her account before they left, there was no reason for anyone to be suspicious.

With cautious hands, Sin worked the key in the back door and pushed her way in. Entering behind her, Lee realized the house even felt abandoned, as though somehow the buildings knew when they’d been left. But nothing was out of place. Nothing gave the feeling of trespass. The dust hadn’t been touched.

He sighed, and watched his breath kick up fibers in the air. “We’re in.”

“Let’s stay here tonight.” Sin seemed to meld with the surroundings. Of course she did, they were *hers*. Lee remembered seeing her here before and thinking that this was ‘hers’ in a way nothing had been ‘his’ in years.

They flipped up dirty covers and let the few pieces of furniture they had left here breathe. Sin pulled sheets and bedding down from the attic, shaking the layer of brown dust off the garbage bag she’d thoughtfully stored them in, and Lee wondered if she had a plan, had thought ahead, for everything she encountered.

He wondered if she had a plan for him. Then promptly decided that he didn’t want to know.

She made up the bed and, without talking about it, they both slept there. Sin with her nose pressed into his chest every night. She’d later gone shopping in one of the smaller towns where she was sure she wouldn’t get recognized and turned up one evening in a long red thermal nightgown with matching socks. Lee had raised his eyebrows, but hadn’t said anything, thankful to be rid of all the creepy, acid-trip creatures she’d been wearing into his, now her, bed.

His sleep was solid, but his days were fitful. His mind processed everything they could find out about Na, and replayed Tampa in his head. Pyotr Kurev had turned and aimed the gun at him, after the man had shot up his own living room hoping to take out Sin. But he wasn’t dumb, and he’d popped a new clip in, quickly too, as he turned to the whispered sound of Lee’s voice.

Lee had stood frozen, two guns aimed at the bastard's head, half a heartbeat from pulling both triggers and making the body unidentifiable, when the eyes popped wide and rolled up. Kurev collapsed from Sin's carefully thrown blade. But Lee hadn't liked the wait one bit.

He also hadn't liked the part where Sin laid low in the living room while bullets peppered the walls at flesh-ripping speeds within inches of her skin. That wasn't acceptable. Then there had been the storms and delays getting out.

They had gone so far out of the way on that one, Lee wondered if it had been worth it. Then again, they didn't even take the same route to and from the mini-mart, or go to the same store twice, if it was avoidable. He'd have enjoyed the boat ride if they hadn't been running late–or running from a fresh murder scene. It would be something he'd like to do in the future–just rent a boat and go for pleasure. He and Sin could go out on the open water and hunt nothing more dangerous than a tuna or two. Sin would likely throw blades in them, but as long as she didn't go all Bambi over the fish, it would be fun.

He pulled his brain back from the tuna and the blue Gulf waters that he hadn't been able to enjoy and asked Sin how they were going to keep Na from killing them while they killed her.

Sin forked another piece of the chicken she'd baked up for dinner, but spoke before she put it in her mouth. "Ling isn't a killer. Not a hitman. I expect she'll be armed, but not very proficient. She usually just watches while her mules die at her feet. I've heard she's more upset about losing the coke that kills them than the person."

Lee had read that, too. An interesting internet blog by an anonymous Columbian claimed Na had gotten him and his sister into the country as mules, then got them deported and used them again. His sister had died the second time and he had fled. The blog had mysteriously stopped after a handful of postings in which the writer stated he was certain Na and her thugs were looking for him.

"What if she's got a guard with her?" Lee wanted to think through every angle. Every time. Thinking on his feet wasn't anything he intended to do. That, he figured, was bound to get him knocked off his feet.

"Then we wait until she's alone." She waved the now empty fork around at the house. "We've got a place to stay, hot water, no freezing rain–we can wait her out."

That was true enough, he thought. "I want to get into the house."

"Of course."

Three weeks later it was done. They'd been thwarted twice by rain, not willing to go in and possibly track mud or leave footprints even in the area outside. As disturbing as it was, and even though they were able to get around so much, a little water could still stall them. But twice they'd gotten in. Sin was now best buds with Na's dogs. And Lee was familiar with the layout of the house, knowing which open doorways would provide cover if necessary and where someone might be able to come up behind the unsuspecting, which no longer included him. They had drawn sketches of the layouts and talked through bullets and a fighting Ling Mai Na, along with several other contingencies they'd thought of. And the creepy jammies had not come back to bed. Sin had traded out the red gown for a blue one, also with matching socks. All in all, Lee thought things were looking very good.

Owen stood with his hands on his hips and looked at his map. His eyes strayed to Ocala, Florida and to the reddish-orange pin that stuck out of Tampa, marking the death of the second Kurev grandson. Those had been some nasty men, and Owen was happy to have them out of the picture. They would be replaced, of course–the mafia just worked that way. If they didn't give birth to enough to keep the family going, more could always be recruited with the bait of easy money and a rich lifestyle.

He'd been disheartened not to have caught the ninja and the gunner with the road survey. He'd love, just love, to arrest them in a grocery store, or somewhere mundane. But then again, he was glad no one else had snagged them either.

His eyes circled back to erasable black circles he'd traced in various spots on the map. Places he'd chosen for his Christmas Killers to call home. The Wichita Campus Rapist case was very helpful when narrowing things down. I-35 was the only major freeway through the area and, although a spur–135–connected the city to Interstate 70, access was limited.

Owen's black circles were now on the map rather than under his eyes and for the first time in a while he wore a faint grin. He wondered if either of them could feel him breathing down their necks. The grin expanded to full width as he realized the woodpecker in his head had flown the coop in Tampa. It hadn't come back since.

Des Moines, Iowa was in range, as was Omaha, but they were northerly. Probably too cold. There were good militias nearby for the gunner to train without public notice. But these guys clearly could get out in the middle of winter, as Pyotr Kurev's cold body could attest to. Des Moines was a possibility, but not with the best score.

Kansas City and Topeka were better bets. Closer for easy access. Multiple freeways running through. Again, the possibility of snow, although not as bad as Iowa. St. Louis was workable, and very central. But Owen thought maybe it was a little too central. Living underground meant living with no ID and while you *could* do that in the city, it was difficult.

Boulder got way too much snow. And he knew for a fact the city had been under three feet of it, enough to shut the airport down for days, just prior to Pyotr Kurev eating his last supper of bullets. Albuquerque was close enough as the crow flew, but no cars could go that way. The two paths by freeway system went too far out of the way to get to Wichita and back in any reasonable time. And the more direct paths were too small to be fast. Owen scratched both those cities off.

Which left the southerly cities.

Amarillo, Oklahoma City, Dallas, and possibly Little Rock.

But Owen Dunham was able to gamble with government money, and so this time he was betting the cost of a plane ticket and some hotel fare on Dallas. Because even if his Christmas Killers didn't live there, they should.

Ling Mai Na was on trial in the city. As she was one of the Kurev family's best traffickers, she was overdue for a hit.

Chapter 16

Lee crouched in the attic amidst the dust and boxes he was now familiar with. Sin, next to him, was as silent as he, and they communicated that they were ready to move with nothing more than their eyes.

Not surprisingly, Ling Mai Na had been acquitted of the crimes she was tried for. It was almost more disappointing than if she'd never been brought up on charges. This meant that those atrocities were wiped from her slate, never to be heard again, due to the American Legal system's insistence that no one be tried for the same crime twice. However, once the hoopla had died down, and she'd gotten her pat on the back from Kolya Kurev himself, she had settled down in the house to operate some border business from her living room. Tonight, she'd already gone to sleep, probably believing she'd destroyed enough lives for one day.

The trap door into the house was well oiled and it opened into a dark hallway without a sound. They dropped in as quietly as they had done everything else up to that point, and stilled for a moment as one of the dogs let out one good bark. It was silent after that so they moved. Down stairs, around walls, through arches, they swept every room, looking for traps that might have been set, making sure that their information from outside the house–that Na was alone and in bed–was correct. They ended in position as planned.

Sin was in the living room, crouched behind the end of the large, expensively upholstered couch, when she motioned to Lee to get into place. He took up point in the dining room, just beyond the grand open doorway. No one coming into the living room from upstairs would see him, but he would see them.

A crash sounded in the space by Sin, but Lee didn't move. He heard her swear a blue streak, then something else knock over and clang on the highly polished hard wood floor.

So far so good.

Not a full minute later he saw *her*.

Ling Mai Na, in jeans and a red sweater, stalking past the open archway where he waited. Gun outstretched, she held the black Glock in two hands, and kept it in front of her, sweeping the living room with it, forefinger ready to jerk the trigger at a moment's notice.

Good, she wasn't a proficient marksman.

However, the jeans, sweater, sneakers and gun told that she'd been waiting up–so while she wasn't a crack shot, she wasn't a fool either.

While he slowly came out behind her, two hands aimed, fingers pointed down the barrels, both at her, Ling Mai Na spotted the fallen lamp and tipped end table. With cautious steps she went over to check it out, placing herself exactly where they'd wanted her, directly between him and Sin.

Slowly, Sin stood up as Ling turned, facing Sin. For some reason the woman raised her gun and pointed it at Sin, and Sin didn't react. Lee didn't like the tightness in his chest that kept him from breathing during that half second. Sin had a knife in each hand and a look on her face that told Na she might get a bullet out of the chamber, but she wouldn't live to tell about it.

Lee was less than three feet away, the end of the silencer only five inches away from brushing the tips of Na's neatly bobbed hair, and he spoke in a whisper that was more guttural than he had intended. "Right behind you."

He expected her to swear. From the deadly look in Sin's eyes Lee could tell she was staring down Ling Mai Na, and the other woman was also vying for alpha dog. She didn't capitulate as he had hoped she would. At least he hadn't been stupid enough to expect it.

From the name, and silky black hair, even the neat, clean lines of her clothing, he'd expected someone more Asian sounding, but no–it was all cultured American, with a little bit of killer cool. “Well, I guess we have a problem here. You shoot me, and even if I die I jerk the trigger here and kill your little girlfriend.”

It was Sin’s voice that answered. “Yes, but you’re in the middle. Sucks to be you.” She even smiled.

Lee was sweating bullets. Sin had a gun trained on her at very close range, by someone who obviously wasn’t that familiar with the weapon. That was more dangerous than . . . well, just about anything, and she didn’t seem to have the sense to be frightened by it or to even tense up just a little.

Na must have smiled, he could almost see it reflected in Sin’s eyes, and he could certainly read it in the subtle quirk of her brow. Ling’s voice was still modulated and cold. “But see, I’m not alone.”

Lee saw it as she said it. A shadow appeared to his left, large, with arm outstretched. He guessed that would be a gun aimed on him. The guess was an easy one to make, because another bulky man stepped through the open space behind Sin, his .357 Magnum aimed on her. Her eyes didn’t move from Na’s, but Lee could tell she knew what was going down.

Ling went so far as to lower her own weapon, taking one deadly possibility off Sin, but there was another pointed at her now. To Lee’s practiced eye, the mafia man’s one-hand hold, steady grip, and casual air all spoke of skill, and that worried him as much as Ling’s ineptness had.

For long minutes no one breathed except Ling Mai Na, who almost seemed to be enjoying herself. Lee quietly seethed, the one thing he hadn’t expected was to find himself in a fucking Mexican standoff. Slowly, and with infinite patience, he rotated his left wrist to point the gun at the man behind Sin while keeping his right aimed at the back of Na’s head.

Ling spoke again. “You two should set your weapons down. I promise not to do anything with you but take you to Kolya. He’s anxious to meet you. *Both*.”

The last word told Lee that she had two goons brought in for the one killer she had been expecting. The extent of their reputation would make him smile later. If he survived this.

Sin’s eyes met his, from beyond Ling Mai Na, and he hoped the drug queen and her goons couldn’t read in them what he did. Although there was nothing he could point to that had changed in his partner's expression, to Lee it was plain as print: Sin was going to make a move. In three, two . . .

Lee moved too, but he saw Sin through the perfect clarity of his fear. With no motion to wind up, to gain speed, knives flew from her fingers as if large magnets had been turned on and she'd simply let the blades go. Somehow the knives rioted into action from normal standing height, when Sin wasn't even there anymore. One had gone short range into Ling Mai Na, and another flew past him to the goon with the gun aimed at his back. He prayed it was enough. Lee hadn't blinked, but his partner was on the ground, fresh blades in her hands.

Bullets had fired from each of his guns, one into the back of the righteously smug Na's skull. His neurons registered her hair parting and shattering for the close range shot, her body accepted the lead and Sin's blade at almost the same moment, and if he'd been watching it in real time, he'd have called what she did a 'jerk'. As it was, he saw it as more of an awkward dance.

His left hand put three bullets into the man behind Sin, two into his face, which Lee aimed exactly where the man's forehead and nose were, and the third into his chest, which Lee put a little low, knowing that the body was already beginning a slow fall.

His ears heard other shots, more than the four he'd fired, and he was thinking through putting another bullet into Ling who seemed to still live for the less-than-a-second that it took him to think all this. Lee didn't fire at Na again, as she was falling to the ground, Sin directly behind her, and the trafficker was too far gone to be a threat.

Sin's feet swept Na's out from under her, helping the woman in her rapid descent to earth and aiming her fall to crack her head against the edge of a nearby table. Lee watched as the black hair spurted blood and fell in a now direct line toward the sharp furniture corner.

The other bullet sounds he had registered in his ears became feeling as one ripped into the right side of his chest, another hit him square center, and he staggered backward from the force.

Sin looked up at him, wide-eyed, even as more bullets hit him and the guns dropped from his grip. Lee managed to plant one foot behind him and he went down, seeing only the ceiling, and not able to direct his gaze much of anywhere else.

A beefy hand appeared at the left of his vision, the gun aimed down at Sin even as a knife flew toward it. Red sparks flew from the tip as another bullet left the chamber. He prayed Sin was out of the way, as he couldn't even turn his head to look.

The floor smacked him in the back, knocking the wind from him, although he didn't think that was his major concern right now. He heard more bullets hitting flesh and a grunt from Sin, who never grunted.

Lee closed his eyes.

Voice escaped Cyn as she grabbed the gun Ling had dropped when she fell. With a firm grip, Cyn used two hands and rapid, wild fire to make certain the man off to Lee's side was dead. She slipped one sai loose from her pants and pushed it into the heart of the fallen mafia man beside her, yanked it free, and drove it through Ling Mai Na's heart as well, although it was impossible that the woman still lived.

She watched as Lee furtively grabbed the guns he always kept stashed along his calves. Before she could blink he'd sat up, hands full, weapons aimed at the person who was moving–her.

With a breath in and a relieved sigh, he melted back, guns slipping away from their aim dead center of her chest. His voice was slow and hollow. "Did you take any hits?"

She nodded. "Two in the back."

With swift movements he found his feet and spun her to look, his fingers quickly finding the holes in her clothing and locating both bullets. One was in the center of the shoulder blade, the other had nearly missed her entirely, hitting at the top of her right shoulder nearer to her neck.

As anxious as he was, Cyn turned back and traced her fingers along his chest, finding a series of burned holes, one on his pec, several at his abdomen, and one at the exact middle of his heart that made her breath suck in. "We have to go."

Without worrying about the noise they made, they fled, this time through the back door. There was always the possibility that the FBI was listening in. Fast was more important than furtive. Aside from someone guessing their size, no identifiable traits would be distinguishable given the dark and the distance.

They skittered through leaves and debris that littered the ground through the man-made copse of imported trees and along the equally man-made lake. They burned a trail right to where the kitty sat, waiting patiently for their return. The FBI and the

Kurevs would know which direction they had gone, where they had parked, and what road they had connected onto. With research they would know what tires were on the kitty. Cyn didn't care about any of it.

They spent only a moment changing out of bloodied clothing. Jackets were shed with ease. Lee groaned to make his arms work, and Cyn barely bit her own grunt back, although she wasn't sure quite why, as they both worked the thick Velcro at the sides of the Kevlar vests Lee had insisted on.

The Tampa job had not gone to his satisfaction, too many bullets had flown in their direction, and he had insisted on being prepared. Cyn had whined. They'd be fine. They didn't need Kevlar. All the way up until they had gotten out of the kitty. The damned vest was uncomfortable, she had been afraid it would hinder her movement.

Lee had pointed out that bullets in her chest would hinder her movement more. And he wouldn't go in if she wasn't wearing it. End of story. She was too shaken now to even tell him she was sorry she'd whined.

Lee had peeled everything, including the cotton t-shirt he'd worn underneath, as it was sweated into and plastered to his skin in the shape of a Kevlar vest. Bruises were seeping under his skin in places where the bullets had slammed into him, but she didn't get a good look, as the fresh shirt he had stashed under the seat was already out and over his head.

With a quick perusal of her, Lee's hand followed his eyes. A baby wipe in his fingers, he rubbed at her cheek and along her neck. When he pulled the white cloth away, Cyn saw that it had red patches, most likely of Ling's blood. Thanks to the Kevlar, none of it was her own.

Focusing back on himself, Lee shucked his jeans at the same time she did, and they changed quickly. Not touching his dark socks, Lee shoved his feet down into loafers and started the car. He grabbed a comb and pushed his sweat-slicked hair back even as he pulled forward out of the spot.

With only a minute or two of bumpy dirt road before they hit open space, Cyn took a quick stock and peeled her own t-shirt, and even the sports bra, off. Still bending over to shove them under the seat, she pulled out a sweet, long-sleeved pink shirt that read 'Angel' and yanked it over her head. She sat up and untucked her braids, letting them fall down her back, and pulled out the bright pink lip-gloss she'd stashed in the pocket of the jeans she was now wearing.

Content that she was as different looking as she could be, she reached across Lee and plugged in his seatbelt for him, before doing her own. She was not going to risk damage to either of them in a car accident after they'd walked away from *that*. Nor was she willing to get pulled over for violating seatbelt laws, when they had a car full of incriminating evidence, and she wasn't able to draw a real breath to speak.

This was unlike her to be keyed up.

After Robert Listle, and the attack of nerves that had come with killing him, she'd found serenity. She'd calmly walked away from each kill. Knowing the world was better, and not caring if she was caught. She'd have happily spent years in jail. She'd have confessed all on the stand, or pled the fifth and bided her time. But she didn't do this. She didn't need to fight to control her breathing. And she didn't understand it.

Cyn looked down to find her hands were shaking, and quickly she clasped them together. Her jaw, too, tightened to stop the sound she only now recognized as her own teeth chattering.

Her eyes straight ahead, she saw only the road slipping under the front of the kitty as Lee wound them through surface streets and up the ramp onto the freeway. Only when he'd shifted into high gear did his hand slip into his hair, destroying the tiny rows made by the comb. He slid back into a more relaxed looking posture, even as his eyes moved too quickly from one mirror to another, making sure they weren't followed.

Not participating, Cyn sat still while he parked the car in the woods behind her house, and only when he shook her shoulder did she come around and find herself. With her usual steel attitude finally in place, she pulled her clothing from under the seat and carried it inside. She climbed into the tub fully clothed and washed the blood from her leathers before asking for Lee's clothing.

He brought her bleach and she practically swam in it. The shade of the leathers and his dark jeans practically faded before her eyes and the room reeked of the chemical smell. But Cyn kept working. As she finished scrubbing, she wrung out articles and handed them up to Lee who produced scissors and promptly shredded them into small pieces, distributing them among seven different trash bags of varying brands that he'd lined up along the floor.

He left her there in her tub, and headed to the hallway bathroom for a quick shower. Then gathered the bags she had tied still wearing the two layers of latex gloves she'd donned upon getting in the tub. He looked clean and fresh, and darker haired when he came back into the room to gather the bags. "I'm going."

She heard the voice from beyond the dark shower curtain and over the noise of the sprayer as she showered away everything she could. Smiling to herself she called out, "Don't get caught."

He left then, and she wished she hadn't said it.

She smelled like freesia when she emerged, and she slathered on the matching lotion as a way to eat time. She blow dried every inch of her hair. Changed into her nightgown and watched TV. Doing deep breathing exercises, and keeping her heart rate lower than it felt like it ought to be, she found the three a.m. re-run of Oprah and left the channel there. She tried to enjoy the feeling of the cushy couch and the clear picture on the large TV she had always kept more for show than anything. Not that anyone had ever appeared to show it to.

Cyn repeated to herself that Lee had seven places to go. Four large apartment buildings, two junkyards, and a metal works with car-crushing facilities. He had all the bags to drop or hide and wouldn't be back for a while.

Oprah was long over before Cyn heard the back door open. She didn't move from the couch, just watched as he came into the room. Even from her vantage point she could see that he finally let all the tension seep away. The Na job was finally over. If any of the trash was found, it couldn't be traced to either of them, and likely it would never be found, or identified as what it was, the way they had washed and distributed it.

Standing, finally, she let fly. "What the hell was that?"

His eyes blinked, and he stepped back, startled.

Cyn didn't stop. "What did you do in there? I saw you! I watched your face! They pulled guns and you got scared!"

He looked at her like she wasn't right. "Of course I did–"

"No! You–" She sucked in air, preparing to yell maybe loud enough for someone outside to hear them. So she cranked it down to a heavy hiss. "You were afraid when it was only Na with a gun! What the fuck were you thinking? Since when do you get afraid in the middle of a damn job!?"

It wasn't a question. She was pacing so harshly she was surprised the carpet didn't combust where she stepped. "You do this all the time! Her gun wasn't even pointed at *you*!"

It hit her full force, ripping through her outer shell, slamming into her like bullets. She felt her mouth and eyes go wide, and lost all control of her heartbeat as it bolted away from her. Three breaths later she was finally able to form words, to answer the question in Lee's eyes, as he seemed to need to know if she would be okay. Cyn wasn't sure. "You were scared for *me*."

No one had been afraid for her, not since the night her parents had died, not even herself since she had made it through her first kill. Cyn hadn't given a second to fear for her own mortality in years. She made plans to live, but didn't care if she didn't.

She launched herself at him before she knew what she was doing. Her mouth found his, her arms locked around him, her body pressed full length down his. Fear for him, for herself, that she had never admitted she felt, joined the relief to still be standing, the deep gratefulness that he had forced her to wear the Kevlar, and all of it rolled off her in waves.

Her hands ripped at the t-shirt he wore, abiding the drive within her that needed skin contact, and she pulled it over his head. Cyn was pressed into the wall, her feet not touching the ground, the pressure of Lee's body holding her there, while his hands sought to rid her of her clothing as well.

Something animalistic within her took over, and her nightgown was gathered in a bunch around her waist when he drove into her.

Owen had been lifting his bags out of the back seat of his sedan, and looking forward to seeing Annika and Charlotte again after a long and painful absence, when his pager had buzzed. He'd wanted to stamp his feet and have a temper tantrum and cry, 'No, no, no!' He railed against the thought that he wouldn't see his daughter at all unless he woke her for a few minutes.

Instead he'd gone inside quietly, and thought to wake his wife, but she had been waiting and first plucked the pager from his belt, not knowing that it had already gone off before he'd gotten in the door. Anni tossed it into the laundry and threw the belt after it, then his shoes, and his shirt, and Owen didn't care for a good long time that he'd been summoned.

The summons meant there was a dead body. And dead bodies would keep. He had a naked, writhing Anni that wouldn't. He made love to her with the cold seeping into his heart that he had to tell her he was leaving again, and he didn't yet know where he'd be going or when he'd be back.

For long minutes afterward he lay next to her, content with her contentment. When he found his breath again he asked, "Anni, if I wasn't a government man, what would I be?"

She laughed, filling him with that deep richness that made everything okay. "You'd be a college professor. You always loved to teach."

They both heard his pager, buzzing at the bottom of the hamper. Her eyes found his. "Can it wait?"

"It already did. It went off once before I even got in the door."

"Oh, baby." She sighed with sadness. But it was regret for him, and not against him, that filled the sound. "Then you'd better answer it."

Owen dressed hurriedly into a different suit, which was ridiculous since he'd just stepped out of one, and it was three a.m. Then he called, while he and Annika both waited to see just how wrong he'd been when he'd predicted Ling Mai Na would be the next hit. Anni had looked over his maps and analyzed his thoughts, and agreed they might be onto something. So she sat beside him, naked, but as curious as he where he'd be going next and who the victim had been.

It was again Randolph on the other end of the line telling him his destination, and again Owen wanted to howl with impotence. He told Anni and she cringed. But she helped him repack his bag.

An hour later he was back on the plane, Blankenship nodding at him and giving a bleak, sarcastic "Long time, no see."

Nguyen joined them this time, looking more awake than either of the other two agents. Of course, he wasn't going back to the place he'd left less than fifteen hours earlier.

Blankenship looked worn and a little defeated.

Owen was certain he just looked mad. He couldn't believe he was going back to Dallas and wondered if the hotel had even changed his sheets yet.

They'd had surveillance on Ling Mai Na until the previous morning. Agent Bean had cut the funding at that point. While Owen had been warned twenty-four hours in advance that they would pack up if they didn't have anything, he'd still been convinced he was in the right place. He'd fought tooth and nail to stay. He'd been denied in no uncertain terms.

So sure that he was right, he knew he'd finally seen something predictive. Even though there were no previous cases like the killers he was hunting, and the profilers couldn't work with it because they had nothing to go on, Owen felt he was finally getting in the Christmas Killers' heads. At last he was getting his brain wrapped around their pattern, maybe even the way they thought, the way they planned. He'd been sure they were driving to their kills, and he had no idea why he hadn't caught them coming up I-75 out of Florida, but he was still certain he'd been close there.

And now, he'd been so certain they'd hit Na.

His only satisfaction was that he was right. And 'well, I was right' wouldn't mean a lot to the bosses upstairs when he didn't produce any killers. Even when it was the bosses and the funding that thwarted him. Owen understood the Bureau couldn't very well go to the media and say, 'Well, we knew where they were going to be, but . . ."

At that moment he decided that as soon as he got home he would tell Annika he was leaving the Bureau. They would also sit down and map out an end date. He would resign by that date whether or not the Christmas Killers case was closed. He would at last put his family before his country and his agency and the idea that it was all right to play God, simply because you believed you were in the moral and legal right. Maybe he would even leave by fall, some time corresponding with the start of university classes. Even as he sat there on the too familiar plane, the idea was growing on him.

He didn't read any briefs during the flight, just caught whatever sleep he could there in the uncomfortable airplane seat and only truly woke up as he left his bags in the company car and donned a sterile paper suit outside of Ling Mai Na's home.

Because he hadn't allowed himself to be updated or read any of the paperwork, he stepped into Na's living room expecting a dead body. Instead he saw what looked like the shootout at the OK corral.

"Fuck." It was the only word that Nguyen spoke. And he'd read the briefs.

They walked the perimeter of the scene, sending Blankenship on his usual inspect-the-outside mission. Half of Na's beautiful face had been blown away by what appeared to be a nasty exit wound. Her one remaining eye was dark and glassy and looked heavenward. Her face revealed she'd been shot in the back of the head, but they'd likely never find the entry wound as she seemed to have split the base of her skull on the sharp corner of a once pretty end table. Definitely not child-proof. Or ninja-proof for that matter. The killers seemed to use whatever was at hand and use it well. As familiar as he was with their other scenes, Owen seriously doubted they'd simply gotten lucky and Ling had happened to crack her head on the way down.

Blood pooled in several places, sliding carelessly across the slick hard wood flooring. Na's head wound was a source for a lot of it, but there were other bodies and they had spent some time bleeding profusely, too.

The two dead men were clearly mafia. Their dress–formal and pressed–and their guns–.357 Magnum–still gripped firmly in their right hands identified them as nothing else could have. Yet despite their skill, their background, and the fact that they had been prepared to face their killers, they were all cooling in pools of their own blood, and the ninja and gunner were nowhere to be seen.

Evidence of the killers was everywhere. Again there were no bows or tags. Again the work was fast, if not sloppy, and evidenced the make-do situation the ninja and gunner had found themselves in. This was not what his Christmas Killers had planned to do. It did not go down as they had intended. From the looks of it, not as any of them had intended.

A Glock lay on the floor under the archway to the kitchen. Bloody footprints in the size ten Skechers tracks Owen was so familiar with, along with other, larger prints led straight out the back door.

The prints were flat. The steps regular if far spaced. Once they'd crossed the threshold to the kitchen, they had run. A few overlapped prints showed they paused, just the smallest amount, to get the door open, but they didn't even take each of the steps. Deep impressions in the dirt beyond showed the speed at which they'd pounded out of here. Hale and healthy. Upright, and not bleeding. At least not dripping.

All the blood that led out this way was tracked blood. Owen went back to check, and sure enough, nothing indicated that either the ninja or the gunner had gotten themselves wounded again.

That, of course, matched with everything he knew. They did *not* make the same mistake twice.

"They went out the back!" Blankenship's voice carried in to where they stood.

"Thanks." He and Nguyen hollered it at the same time, and Owen, at last, found something to smile about.

Lee stepped back, snapped his pants, and gritted his teeth.

"It'll be better next time."

He blinked, and couldn't believe he had heard that. He couldn't believe that moment of insanity had happened and that was her response. He couldn't believe . . . hell, any of it. He pushed his voice out through clenched teeth. "There is nothing about this day, nothing that has happened since we first left the house, that should be repeated."

He didn't look at her, although he could see Sin adjusting her nightgown to cover herself. Normally under tight control, his emotions were wreaking havoc when finally let loose. Not knowing where the words came from, or why they fell out of his mouth, Lee let the rant take him over. "I have only had sex a handful of times since Sam died. It's been nothing but an empty need. I picked up women in bars and didn't give them my real name. Once I even got slapped with a bill afterward. I was surprised, but I paid it." He watched as Sin's back got straighter with every word. Still the words tumbled out. "I have never desecrated my wife's memory like I just did. If I ever hate myself that much again, I'll–"

He turned to glare at her as he spoke and only too late saw the fist. It made contact somewhere behind his nose by the time he even registered it was coming.

"Aaaagh!" Whether it was in pain or a battle cry, he didn't know. Maybe both. Staggering backward, Lee caught his momentum even as his hand came up to hook the arm that had thrown the punch. Ducking to lower his center of gravity, he missed a second swing from Sin, and came up, palms front, the heels of his hands connecting with her shoulders and shoving her backward.

The heavy thud of two bodies slamming into the wall reverberated through the house. She looked shocked, as though she hadn't expected a fight, but Sin kept her head from hitting the wall behind her and found the strength to snap it forward and crack her skull against his own.

He took the blow, not feeling the pain he knew radiated outward from his forehead, and planted his feet solidly before bringing one elbow up against the side of her face. A duck and a well placed arm took her out of contact's range. Stepping to the side, she threw a punch to his midsection that he sidestepped. Probably as she had planned, the sidestep brought him directly into contact with her other fist. Right in the kidney. But he was moving away from her even at impact, and it greatly lessened the blow.

Pulling his fist back, he watched her find her stance as her eyes tracked his knuckles with a meanness he'd only previously associated with mother bears. Lee swept his right foot out, knocking her left out from under her. Sin toppled, but redirected it so she fell into him. Taking her weight, he adjusted and took her down under him.

She fought for dominance, a furious flurry of fists and knees, a hellcat scorned, and she aimed for his face and gut. He never knew where she was going to strike next and he spent his time deflecting her blows, until he finally got lucky and managed to capture her wrists.

Pinning her to the ground, Lee took a deep breath that hurt each of his ribs and found a moment to be grateful that she hadn't gone for any of the nerve clusters she knew how to find. Then again, neither had he. It seemed they'd both been content to strike at the bruises that already covered each other from this hellish day. Although Sin had seemed to want to go for his face, too.

His relief didn't last for long. She bucked against him, almost throwing him off, then screamed loud enough to bring in the cops. Startled, he let go of one hand to cover her mouth, and she instantly stopped screaming.

He figured out why when the side of her freed hand made fast, hard contact with the side of his face, right in front of his ear.

"Aaaagh!" He toppled off of her, and lay panting on the floor, waiting for her to go for his neck, or take her sick pleasure in finding his vagal nerve blacking him out, or just stopping his heart completely.

His eyes focused on hers hovering above where he lay, "Do your worst."

Instantly deflating, Sin sat back on her heels. Her voice was small. "I'm sorry I desecrated your wife's memory. You may have only had sex a few times in the last several years. I haven't had any in nine. I'm sorry."

She stood up and walked off with a dignity she shouldn't have been able to find in the dimness that was lit only by the muted and flickering TV. The sun had risen a while ago, but the blackout curtains had obscured all of it.

Lee lay on the floor where she'd left him.

He shouldn't have worn the Kevlar.

He should have died killing Na. He shouldn't have fought with Sin. Or done any of the rest of it with Sin. He should be man enough to get one of his Hecklers out and eat the bullet that surely already bore his name.

But he didn't have the energy.

Battered and bruised beyond recognition, he gave in and fell asleep there on the floor.

Chapter 17

Lee awoke with plastic over his face. In a moment's panic, he jerked, his nerve endings only then registering the cold, and the fact that the plastic only covered part of his face.

He'd slept poorly on the floor.

No surprise there. His back was stiff. His bruises screamed at him. And he felt like shit, both inside and out, both physically and mentally. Soft hands touched him, and he knew instantly that it was Sin. He just didn't know why. Unless she was searching for nerve clusters again.

"You're awake." Her voice was soft and sounded battered.

When he opened his eyes, he saw that she looked battered, too. Deep shadows resided under her eyes. And her eyes looked hurt. She didn't look like Sin. This girl looked wounded, and Sin was incapable of that. He wanted to frown at the thought, but the very idea of expression made his face hurt.

"You should go sleep in the bed." Her hands plucked at the bag, lifting it, rolling it, and placing it against his face again. Only not before he'd been able to discern that what she'd set on him was a zipper bag of frozen peas to help ease the swelling she'd caused.

Turning to look at the window, Lee figured it was only a few hours after he'd crashed there on the floor. The light at the edges of the blackout curtains didn't come into the room, but looked bright and far too cheerful in its desperate attempts the breach the barriers Sin had so skillfully erected.

Lee didn't answer her. Just blinked and watched as she shifted other bags of peas, and a few of corn and even mixed vegetables, against his chest. He stared at the ceiling, and lay still, in only his jeans. His torso was a mass of bruising, and every breath hurt. Sin had clearly had to raid every last corner of the freezer to tend to him.

Between the bullets and the hard hits Sin had delivered, his body matched his state of mind.

Everything was wrong.

Nothing was as it should be.

Finally, he found his voice.

"We're done, Sin. Finished. No more."

She pulled back a little at the words. It assured him she was the Sin that he knew–she wouldn't want to hear that.

But her answer made no sense.

"I know. I'll sleep on the couch."

This time he did frown. And it hurt like a mother-fucker. "No, both of us should sleep in the bed. You must look as bad as I do. We need rest."

Her smile was slow and sad. "But surely you don't want to be near me. We're finished."

Oh.

He wanted to shake his head at her. He wanted to sit up and shake her. He wanted a lot of things, and wondered where the iron will that had served him so well these past years had fled to. Lee searched and found just a little of it. Using his elbows, he pushed upright, forgetting the vegetables that adorned his chest until they slipped and fell haphazardly into his lap.

In the only kind gesture he knew to make then, he lifted one of the still cold bags and pushed Sin's nightgown off her shoulder. Sure enough, large purple stains marred the pale coffee colors he was used to seeing. He settled the bag over the bruise and heard her breath hiss in at the sensation.

Doing what was necessary, Lee pushed himself to standing and held the bag against Sin's skin while he helped her to her feet, too. He searched her knuckles, wondering if she sported bruises there, too, from turning his nose inside out. But, no, her hands were used to hard hits. No one would suspect anything from looking at them. He tugged her into the bedroom while she looked at him with big wary eyes, and he motioned for her to lie on her stomach so he could place the bag of frozen corn he carried onto the bruise she'd gotten across her shoulder blade.

His bullet wounds hurt the worst, and aside from his nose, they looked the worst–he'd gotten a glimpse of himself when he walked past the hall bathroom. Which meant that Sin had pulled every punch she'd leveled at him. Just as he had. Even furious, they didn't seem to be able to do each other real harm.

Her eyes drifted closed, and her breathing was too even to be anything but forced. She very carefully stayed on her side of the bed. Her bed.

"Listen, Sin. There're two separate things here." He sighed and remained on his feet. She only nodded slightly, but it was enough, and he continued. "First, you should have told me you were a virgin."

"But I wasn't."

"You were."

She frowned at him, and he knew that behind her eyelids she was looking at him like he was nuts.

"Sin, there's making love, and there's sex, and there's screwing and fucking, and what happened to you wasn't even on the chart. The way you talked, I thought you'd been with other men in the meantime."

He huffed, angry at himself for his own stupidity. The leather underwear? She hadn't let anyone in. And in hindsight, of course, it was all perfectly clear.

"Oh well." Still not opening her eyes, she offered a small shrug beneath the frozen foods. "The next time I'm a virgin, I'll be sure to tell whoever it is."

Why? Why did he just want to hit her so much of the time?

He took a leveling breath. "I'm sorry about what I said. You were so hot for it. Or at least I thought you were, until the last minute. I've never had a woman grit her teeth with me before. It makes sense now."

"Hmm." Was all she offered.

That was all he could handle of it right now, too. "The other thing is: we're out of the business."

"What?" Eyes opened wide, revealing the Sin he knew. "We walked away! We'll get better at it."

"We didn't walk. We *ran*. Out the back door. Not knowing who was coming down the stairs or going to show up at the front door in the next few minutes. We left tracks–clear tracks–straight to the car. I have to change the tires today and get the others out to the dump."

Her breath sighed out of her. "We should put them on someone else's car."

That was a good idea, but he didn't address it. He wasn't in any shape to change tires, or even to flee if the Feds showed up at the door. "The Kurevs know about us. They're waiting up at night *with backup*. Backup that we didn't find when we swept the house." That had been the really disturbing part.

Sin looked at him, but didn't deny anything.

Lee kept talking, pacing the room with an agitation that hurt his arms, ribs, and face. Although, after the shootout last night, the pain was reassuring in a way. "The FBI is after us from the other side. The fact is that we have no idea how close they are. But it feels pretty damn close. We're either getting our asses killed, hauled before Kolya Kurev, or thrown in jail for a long, long time."

"I thought you didn't care."

His chest seemed to get smaller. "I didn't. I do. I do now." Lee shook his head. "I don't mind continuing. But we can't do it safely–"

"Yeah, not if you're going to get scared like a little girl in the middle of it." Her mouth quirked up on one side, even though she hadn't moved, hadn't disturbed the ridiculous looking veggies on her back.

"*You* should have." He was near to yelling, and only wasn't louder because his ribs protested to remind him every time his volume got too high. "Na came up with a gun aimed at you!"

"At my chest! I was wearing Kevlar!"

"What if she'd moved it just a little higher? Did you have Kevlar on your head? I think maybe you have it *in* your head!"

"Hey, bullet proof brains!"

"It's not funny!" His ribs protesting weren't enough to stop the yelling. "You could have gotten your head blown off!"

Her eyes blinked, the same comprehension he'd seen before. "And you would have cared."

"Hell, yes, I would have! God help me, I don't know why!" But he stopped pacing and peeled his jeans before stretching out beside her. His hand plucked at the bags of vegetables, tossing them across the room just to get rid of them. With movements that were neither rough nor gentle, he moved Sin around, until she faced him, with her nose pressed into his chest. Only then did he really begin to breathe easily.

Her voice carried up to him. “So what do we do?”

“I don’t know. I was thinking maybe we could just start over.” He let his voice follow his thoughts. “What if we show up at FBI headquarters and demand immunity? Can we go into Witness Protection?”

He didn’t like it even as it left this mouth.

Neither did Sin. “I’ve killed three men who were in WitSec. The Kurevs will still find us.”

Lee finished. “And when they do, they’ll kill us. And we’ll have no idea when it’s coming. Yeah, we don’t even really know anything worth trading. We killed all our bargaining chips.”

He felt her nose move as she nodded. “Can we just stay underground?”

“I’ll go crazy, just hanging out. What will we do?”

A small laugh escaped her and he wondered what she thought. “Kill each other? Shoot deer for food? Become really well trained so we can do nothing?”

“The Kurevs will still eventually find us. They are pissed. We’ve taken out a lot of their best people.”

“What do you want?”

That was the sixty-four thousand dollar question, wasn’t it? But suddenly he didn’t have to think about it. An answer came immediately. “A life.”

“What? A house? A wife and kids?”

He shrugged, “Maybe. I was happy as an accountant before I knew who I was working for.”

“You still miss them.”

“I’ll miss Sam and Bethy every day for the rest of my life. And I don’t know how I’ll ever not blame myself for the fact that I wasn’t watching out, wasn’t paying attention to what I was doing. I got them killed. But I’m still here. And I’m not really willing to do myself in. I want . . . something. Don’t you? Do you miss your job here? Your friends?”

Her head shook against him, he could feel it. “I didn’t have friends.”

“Do you want any?”

“I don’t know how to have friends.”

“But do you want any?” Lee waited.

Sin didn't answer.

Somewhere in the spaces, in the middle of the pain, the open ends, and the questions that neither of them could answer, Lee curled closer to the only living thing he knew and fell asleep.

Owen was looking at the resume Annika had edited for him when Nguyen came into his office. Quickly shuffling the papers so his friend wouldn't see what he was holding, Owen looked up, "Got anything?"

"Got all kinds of things." Nguyen pasted on a wide smile. "And just like before, none of them add up to crap!"

"Well, then, have a seat and share it with me." Owen motioned to the open chairs, noticing Nguyen looked as rumpled as always. You'd think the scientist would have invented a way to press his suits by now. The man could jury rig Rube Goldberg contraptions in his sleep, and back figure murder scenes like no one Owen had ever worked with before. But somehow he couldn't keep the wrinkles out of his suits.

"Well," Nguyen took a seat and folded his hands formally on his lap. That did not bode well. "We have blood."

Owen felt his heart kick up.

"From three sources."

Of course. His heart slowed again.

"Ling Mai Na, who is O positive. Vladimir Miskevet, already ID'd, AB positive. And unknown male, early thirties, A negative. It was very kind of them to all have different blood types. There doesn't seem to be a drop from either our gunner or our ninja."

"But, of course." Owen folded his own hands.

"We have the footprints leading out the back door. First, the prints themselves: given the treads and the size and weight, it remains our best guess that the gunner is male."

Owen nodded. "That's the one thing the profilers thought. Males are more likely to take up firearms. For mental reasons as well as biological ones."

"Testosterone?" Nguyen's brows rose.

"Larger arm and back muscles. Able to support the weight of the gun and handle the kick easier."

"Hmm. Makes sense. Especially for our two-handed shooter. Which is pretty cool, I have to say." A real smile emerged on his face. "I've been shooting things myself, trying to figure that one out."

"And?"

"Aside from the fact that I always forget just how much I love shooting things? Two handed is a bitch. Especially getting the clip out and reloading left handed. Some of the old scenes that are just his–assuming it really is a 'him' and not a two-hundred-plus pound bruiser of a chick–"

Owen grimaced at the thought.

"Given that the bullets are 9mm, I'm guessing he's either using Sig Sauers retrofitted for lefties, or Heckler and Koch. They make an ambidextrous gun."

"Interesting." Owen wasn't sure what importance that was, but every little thing helped.

"Well, it builds a case when we find the guy. I doubt he's got Glocks or Colts or anything of that sort." Nguyen continued, and Owen jotted notes, just to help keep it all in his brain. "Okay, both sets of footprints go right out the door, into the trees and right up to some tire tracks. They're Goodyears–"

Owen just raised his eyebrows. Everybody and their brother used Goodyears.

"It narrows down the car a little." Nguyen protested, and he was right. Although Owen thought he already had a pretty good grip on the car. If they were operating on the outskirts of Dallas, it would be brown, and a little battered looking, but run like the wind.

"Fine then," Nguyen started on a different tack. "Both the .357 Magnums had been fired. Multiple times. Although the clips weren't emptied."

Owen sat back for that. "So that means what? These guys died before they could fire all their shots?"

"That's my guess."

"What about Na's gun?"

Nguyen shook his head. "Fired once."

"Hmmm." That he hadn't expected. "So she took the knife to her throat and the bullet to the brain and she only got off one shot?"

"There was a 9mm in the ceiling. I'm thinking she didn't get a shot off before she took it from both sides. Her finger jerks as she dies and she kills the plaster work overhead. Our gunner doesn't hurt harmless ceilings. And the thugs are firing .357s. Very well I might add–there were no stray .357 slugs."

"Well, it did look like they were all at real close range." Owen pictured the way the bodies had fallen. "It actually looked like Na and her two goons were all shooting at each other. But that wouldn't make any sense. So I'm guessing there was a gunner and a ninja somewhere in there, who somehow got up and walked away."

"Oh yeah, and get this:" Nguyen's eyes actually sparkled. Owen thought of the resume buried under the papers on his desk. He loved his friend, but it was time to get the hell out. Nguyen's voice ratcheted up in speed with his excitement. "They walked away with seven bullets! We can't find *any* of the shots fired by the thugs. I mean we could have done ballistics. But they were using .357s, so we don't have to. There isn't a single round in the house from either of their guns."

Nguyen's hands fidgeted and he kept talking up a storm. "There were missing bullets from the clips. I suppose they could have been fired earlier, but . . . Na was dressed, and so were they. That most likely means they were waiting up. Somehow they even got behind or around our guys, and our guys are *good*. You wouldn't go into that without a full clip, not unless you were flat out retarded. So it doesn't make any sense that the rounds were fired earlier. Plus there was recent powder on the muzzles of the guns: they were each fired *recently*. That all makes perfect sense. Until you get to the part where the Christmas Killers walked away without leaving any blood behind, but taking seven bullets with them."

Owen sighed. Yeah, that kind of mystery was par for the course these days. He was wondering if he could set up a meeting between them, offer the Christmas Killers immunity, just to ask them how the hell they did it.

Nguyen stood. He stretched. "That's about it for now. Oh–except the fact that there was no hair, fingerprints, or fibers that are likely theirs."

"But, of course."

Owen suffered out the rest of the day. He watched his map as though it might move, dance, or fold itself up and tell him to just give up and pack it in. His brain hurt by noon, but at least the woodpecker hadn't come back.

That afternoon he picked up Charlotte, reveling in the expression on her face when she saw him at the edge of the schoolyard. Annika had a similar smile on when he showed up at home then took Charlotte to gymnastics that night. Of course, he'd left Anni buried under a load of FBI files to read while he watched his daughter do handsprings and flinched as she fell off the bars several times before finally spinning all the way around the high bar and letting go in a feat of inhuman flight to get to the low bar and then swing effortlessly back up. The damn bars were further apart than she was tall. It must be the Russian genes, Charlotte sure as hell hadn't gotten any of that from him.

He'd read her another chapter in her book before tucking her into bed that night, and then faced down Anni on the couch. With no preamble, he asked, "Where are they going next?"

His wife shook her head. "I don't know. I'm still hung up on how they got out of Na's house without leaving blood."

"Me, too."

"I mean, they fled out the back door. They must have been in a bad hurry."

He hadn't thought of that. This time they might as well have left an arrow pointing which direction they'd gone.

Annika opened her mouth and closed it again before she was able to form words. "They must have been injured. Or heard someone coming."

"But who? If it was mafia–Kurevs or any other family–they would have cleaned the scene long before we got there. If it was the neighbors come to check out the noise, they would have left evidence."

"So they were injured. You said they took bullets with them."

"So how come they didn't drip? Any bullet they took would have been fired at such close range, it should have gone through and left a nasty exit wound to boot. Like Na's face. But . . . nothing." How come he wasn't bald yet? Either from pulling on his hair, or just from stress. How come he hadn't stroked out?

Owen had driven by the post office with Charlotte that afternoon. She'd enjoyed putting the letters in the drive-up mailbox. His resume had gone to five different universities.

He just had to hold on until September.

*   *   *

Lee had sat in the driver's seat of the kitty on the long drive back to Tennessee. Alone.

For nearly two months, he and Sin had laid low in her house in Texas. They had healed, waiting until the bruises didn't hinder movement. For two weeks they didn't emerge at all, just ate the food they had stocked, watched the TV, and spent far too much time wearing cold zipper-bags of vegetables.

They had made plans. And cleaned out the house. They destroyed evidence. Patched holes in the wall of the practice room. Cut down the barb wire perimeter and tossed the trash into the landfill themselves. They reset the sprinkler heads to aim water only into the yard. Removed all the weapons from their spots in and on the walls, and peeled and cleaned away the Velcro that had held them there. They cleared the attic, driving hours on end to dump things in different landfills, hopefully never to be seen again. They cashed out Sin's accounts and put it in lock boxes in different banks in three different states under three different names.

After five weeks, when his face finally looked normal again, and the house was scrubbed from attic to flooring, Cynthia Cooper Macey called a real estate agent and put her house on the market. Lee stayed out of the way for the walk-throughs, although Cynthia chattered with prospective buyers about how she had taken work in Oregon and had to leave for her new job soon.

It was as good an explanation as any for why the house had been priced low enough to move it quickly. And why she wanted only two weeks in escrow.

Just that fast, the house was gone. A family with five kids was moving in. Five boys, who would occupy the large extended back room that Sin had practiced in. To Lee it seemed a sign. The house had sold with little fuss and few visitors. Sin had dropped the keys off with the realtor on her way out of town. They had effectively dissolved her connection to Dallas, and ultimately to Cynthia Cooper Macey, easily.

But he was uneasy on the trip.

Lee had taken interstate 20 out of town going through Shreveport and then cutting north to arrive in Knoxville. Sin had started north on thirty-five and would connect into forty, taking her through Memphis and Nashville. She should arrive at the cabin later than he did.

They each carried their own clothes and weapons. Sin's were stuffed in their teddy bears, far more camouflaged than his Hecklers stashed under the seat and at the bottom of his duffel bags in the trunk.

Eating nothing but Coke and Doritos, Lee stopped only long enough to pee and get more chips and soda each time. His stomach couldn't take anything else.

There was no music, as Sin had her CD player with her in the green Toyota, and Lee was surprised to find that he missed it. He hadn't thought he'd ever miss anything other than Samantha and Bethany. He had thought that if they started to fade from his memory he would go insane. And yet they were fading. So many times recently he'd thought of one or the other of them with only fondness at the pictures it brought to mind. There was none of the hatred for the Kurevs that blinded him to enjoying memories of his family. None of the bitterness at the unfairness, or anger at himself for bringing it on.

He arrived and parked the kitty under the weeds and kudzu that had overgrown the 'garage' since he'd left. In the deep dark that came in the mountains at night, he'd almost missed the spot. With grim features, he slung his bags over his shoulders to hike the almost-mile back to the cabin. It was cold, but not icy, and the land had sprung up green in his absence. Almost a year since he had first brought Sin here.

He waited outside the small house thinking to scope the place out, but lacking his usual patience, he was inside within an hour. He started the generator and prepared what food he could, planning to finally eat something while he waited for the place to warm up–for Sin to show.

They had no cell phones, not having real identities, or even anywhere to send the bill. She wasn't following him, like she had on the way out to Texas. He only hoped she was okay. He'd gotten far too tied to Sin. But the thought that he shouldn't care didn't mean that he didn't, and it didn't make the food go down.

Five hours later he was still sitting on the couch, staring at the glowing coils of the space heater in front of him. In spite of the huge drain the heater placed on the generator, he'd fired up another one in his bedroom. The food sat, waiting, untouched and drying on the counter.

The old heater had only 'on' and 'off', so it cycled itself through phases of 'heat' and 'let cool' to regulate temperature. It had just clicked off, leaving Lee in utter darkness, when the door pushed open and Sin let in a blast of cold air along with the warmth of her smile.

"That was long." Even through the grin she looked tired. It was more than a full day's ride but, going separate ways for security's sake, they'd decided not to stay over. She peeled her jacket in the heat of the room, going about unloading her bags in an animated fashion, but quickly began to fade. Sin opened one duffel bag, identical to his, and pulled out a nightgown he hadn't seen before, in a vivid pink. She brushed her teeth and her hair and had crawled into bed, asleep before he even realized that was what she intended.

Nothing could have convinced him more that they needed to get out of the business. They had both become lax. Feeling safe with each other, they weren't taking the proper precautions, not maintaining any decent level of awareness. He had sat on the couch while Sin came right in the door. Of course, there was every possibility his sub-conscious recognized that it was her. But his forward brain sure hadn't. He'd have been on his feet, thrown the door open wide to greet her, had he been aware. Even now, her teddy bears were scattered across the couch, still stitched tight. What was in the room with her to have at hand? Nothing. She was counting on him to keep her safe while she slept. A deeper, more satisfying sleep than she slept without him–where she was less likely to rouse in the face of real danger. They'd both admitted that one to each other a while ago.

Was that what had gone wrong at Na's? Had they been lax and under-prepared?

No. They had swept the house, searched every room but Ling's looking for anything out of the ordinary. His eyes had been sharp, he'd been expecting something. But they just hadn't found it. They'd had Kevlar vests, for which he was supremely grateful. And they'd come within millimeters, milli-seconds, of getting themselves killed. In his brain he could replay the scene and almost see bullets flying from chambers, rounds slamming into him. So many, with such force, that they toppled him backward, leaving him to pray for Sin's safety but, in the half second he was down, not able to actually do anything about it. It had all gone down so quickly that, even as fast as he'd been able to get back up, it had been over by the time he regained his footing.

Finding the very last of his energy, as it seemed he'd used up almost all of it on tension waiting for Sin to arrive, Lee got up and pulled out his Hecklers. He loaded three of them, slipping one under the mattress at the end of the bed and the other two under the pillows. Sin didn't rouse as he tucked the loaded weapon beneath her head.

No, they couldn't work like they had been. Not anymore.

They had each lost that drive–inertia, instinct, fear, whatever it was–that had kept them alive. If they wished to stay that way, they had to stop.

He didn't remember curling up beside her and falling asleep, but he remembered waking with her plastered to him. Light streamed in through the thin curtains, making him blink even as he grit his teeth and pushed her away from the morning wood he was fighting, even though by the light it was clearly afternoon. Already awake, she tensed, and he wished she hadn't felt his response to her. Until her mouth found his neck and placed the smallest of kisses there.

Only human, and wondering when humanity had been bestowed upon him once more, Lee pushed her further away. "Sin, I told you back in that alley that you can't do that to a man and not expect him to want something."

Sin pushed back. Her mouth again on his skin, "I know."

"Jesus."

He let himself react and let her feel that reaction, figuring he'd scare some sense into her.

It didn't work.

Cyn erased the whiteboard where she'd sketched the plan. "No. Not good enough."

Somehow their roles had reversed. Where Lee had browbeaten her into wearing the Kevlar to Na's, she was the one who this time had trashed option after option as not secure enough.

Her sense of purpose had been renewed. At a level she'd not experienced before. She had a plan. A long-range one. And she had a job to do as part of that plan. Deep inside her, the drive she had felt when practicing writing left-handed, or working forms, falling and getting bruised, or throwing knife after knife, had returned. Her goal now was less the taking of someone else's life and more the securing of her own.

Lee shook his head. "We won't know how to take them out until we see the place. Until we get inside. Right now this is the best we can do."

She was keyed up. She had smiled at Na as the woman had raised the gun to her, because she had believed herself invulnerable. The expression on Lee's face when she had fearlessly faced the barrel of a loaded gun had changed all that. "Then let's go."

He blinked. Looked like he hadn't expected to just pick up and leave. "Two more weeks. There are more things we need. And we should just practice more."

She didn't like it. Cyn wanted to go now. To get in and get the job done. But she capitulated. Lee had kept himself alive through some seriously dangerous situations. Even more, at Na's he had come up, guns in hand, because he didn't know what had happened to her. He also didn't know what he was facing, but he'd stood up anyway, when it would have been smarter to stay down and act wounded. She trusted him.

So she shot at the bottles as though they were Kolya Kurev with guns pointed at her. She had Lee throw things into her line of sight, and she shot them down. She made him work with the throwing stars and the knives. Moved his arms and corrected his form and ignored the feel of his skin beneath her fingertips.

They drove great distances, and she shopped with the same focus, knowing what they needed and making sure all of it worked. They had mock knife fights with sheathed weapons and practiced holds and slices, feints and jabs, and readied themselves for as much as they could. At night, she locked the doors and stashed her weapons within reach, making her fortress as secure as possible, before she gave herself to him with the same blind drive.

At the end of the two weeks, when they had everything on their list, they drove through Oklahoma and removed large quantities of cash from one of the safety deposit boxes where they'd stashed part of her inheritance. They continued to Nevada, and gave all of it to a hacker who placed new names for them into the Social Security system. Then they headed to Chicago.

It was two weeks to the day from when they left the cabin that they arrived. Cyn felt she had been in the car the entire time. But still, they first drove around the edges of the city and found a handful of cheap places to stay before settling on one. They located spots in and out of town where they could easily change clothing so they didn't look out of place either scoping out high end spots in the city or slumming it in motels on the outskirts.

She felt out of her depth casing a place in the heart of a big city. In the past she had waited until her mark showed up somewhere with the right requirements for an easy break-in. That wouldn't be possible here. They had to hit this building, and the only reason they thought they could pull it off was that it was in Highland Park, and being a wealthier area, there just weren't as many people around the building at night. Well, late at night. As Lee had suspected, it was well after midnight before the lights went out signaling the end of each workday.

On the seventh day, they waited just beyond the parking structure in their rented car, and followed the last man home. But they did nothing other than look.

Two days later he was mugged in the most embarrassing way. The small girl had approached him, asked for cash, then hit him when he said 'no'. He woke up in the nearby alley when she kicked him awake, flashing the three hundred in cash she'd pulled from his wallet and taunted him. "Shoulda given me a buck or two."

Shaking her ass as she walked off, she tucked the cash into her bra, but somehow managed to take him down again when he tried to tackle her.

He didn't file a report with the cops. He thought he'd only lost money and some pride. Robert Graff had no idea that his wallet and pockets had been very carefully searched while he'd been unconscious, and photos and impressions had been taken. He never saw the man she worked with.

Job done, they'd returned to Tennessee.

Three weeks later, Lee and Cyn were in Chicago again. They wore sweats and ball caps and checked into one of the motels they'd seen earlier. They mugged three other people in much the same fashion as they had Robert Graff, Cyn stealing and flaunting cash each time. Only one of the three filed a police report. The person he reported as attacking him and taking his money was larger and beefier than Cyn. And male.

Lee had laughed about that one.

It took six days, although they had been ready each evening, before there was a night when everyone went home early. Then they walked into the building as if they owned the place, flashing the forged badges they'd had made. The security guard smiled at them. "Do I know you?"

"Are you new?" Lee spoke through his teeth, as Cyn flashed a sideways glance at him. In his sharp gray suit and power tie, he looked irritated at being checked, which was just how they planned on playing it. "We just got in from New York."

"How long will you guys be working tonight?" The guard checked the IDs and, finding no flaws, handed them back. Cyn tucked hers carefully into the expensive leather wallet in the expensive leather purse she carried.

Lee held his hands out, sharp briefcase dangling from one, "I don't know."

And truly they didn't.

With a sigh that didn't reveal her voice, and her position carefully monitored to obscure both her and Lee's faces from the lobby cameras, Cyn gave the guard her best irritated and haughty look, and started heading toward the elevators.

They were certain there weren't cameras elsewhere in the building. Partly because there had never been any, and partly because recording the goings on here would have been stupid. Not wanting to break character, she didn't reach out and enfold her hand in Lee's, even though they were the only two in the closed elevator.

Instead she looked at the odd reflection staring back at her. The woman had midnight black hair, which Cyn decided went well with her new skin tone, the result of a dark shade of makeup. It was made more striking by the long cream coat and gloves she wore against the chill of the night. The khaki-colored pantsuit underneath was expensive and shot through with Lycra, one of the few she had found that wouldn't rip if she had to kick something. She'd had it tailored so the hem of the pants would break low, nearly obscuring her shoes. And the shoes looked good. The toes that peaked out from under the edge of the pants were fashionable enough that no one would suspect the squat, sturdy heels that had easily removed the last bit of life from her practice dummy.

The eyes that looked back at her were grey, although a darker shade than the other pair that glanced her way for just a second in the reflection of the highly polished elevator door. Lee's were a paler shade than her own, although his were green, his hair auburn from temporary color and wavy from her hand and a curling iron. His rough beard grew around his chin and connected into a new mustache above his lip.

It would be gone tomorrow.

The ding of their floor startled her from her reverie, but Lee didn't do anything other than grip the briefcase and head for the opening doors. What he saw when they parted, she didn't know, but something subtle settled into his bones at being here again.

They scoped the building, finding the emergency exits had all been locked in the non-alarm position. Cyn imagined they could simply be keyed to the 'on' position before inspections, allowing the owners to look like model citizens, yet be able to leave their building by the back way any time they wished.

Together, she and Lee used the keys they'd made from the impressions they'd gotten during the muggings to open a handful of the doors. With gloves on, they settled at desks and let themselves into the computer system. Cyn watched as Windows opened, and pulled as many files as she could. They hadn't gone after anyone randomly, and she knew what she expected to find. Lee's description of the programs was very accurate, and she had to assume that in four years the system hadn't changed all that much. She wrote files to disks, then electronically scrubbed her trail as best she could before she stood up and went into the second office.

When she finished with three offices, Lee was still working on his first. Robert Graff, the first employee they'd mugged, was an accountant. His computer held the files Lee was most familiar with. He was also the highest up in the Black and Associates hierarchy.

For long minutes, Lee didn't acknowledge she was there, standing just inside the doorway, looking every inch the business woman, even if she wasn't. At last, when his fingers quit flying, he looked up, sharp green eyes meeting her own. The contacts gave her a moment's start, which she didn't betray with physical movement, even though her heart jogged each time she didn't quite recognize him.

Fifteen long, quiet minutes later, he stood and stretched before handing her a shiny disk. Scrubbing the computer memory the same way Cyn had on the other computers took a few more minutes and was far from perfect, as neither of them were seasoned hackers. But all it needed to do was get them out of the building without the company knowing they'd been breached. And they had to go. They'd been here long enough, if they stayed much later, someone might get suspicious.

The two of them re-checked all the doors, turning locks with the illegally gotten keys, leaving each office as they had found it. Then they rode the elevators down to the lobby and exited the front doors, both of them making motions as though they were just now pulling on their gloves. Looking straight ahead, and carrying on a pre-planned conversation about sushi, they responded to the security guard with a wave and a 'goodnight' only after he'd spoken first and as though even that was an imposition far beneath them.

Cyn's heart thudded within her chest, the evening far from over.

They climbed into the expensive rental that waited all alone in the parking lot. They didn't even glance at the attendant as they pulled out, all the better if he never got a good look at their faces. He wasn't the same one that had checked them in.

At one of their locations where they couldn't be seen, they pulled out hats, wigs and shirts and changed their clothing as well as the plates on the car, quickly putting the rental plates back on. Next, she dropped Lee and their stuff at the green Toyota and returned the car to the airport lot, leaving the keys, and knowing that if the car were traced, Cynthia Ellen Winslow would likely be identified as the culprit. But as Ms. Winslow was blonde and very blue-eyed with a complexion much more toward peaches and cream, there was every possibility that the connection would be lost. Also, no one would be able to get a hold of her at any of the numbers connected to the credit card that would never be used again.

The shuttle bus drove her out to long-term parking, where she got off at the first stop and walked out to the road beyond to hitch a ride with the pale green sedan that pulled up just then. They drove to another spot they had picked out previously for privacy and assembled what they had.

Entertaining thoughts of sleep, they let themselves back into their motel room but were too keyed up to rest. Neither of them had ever pulled a job like this one before. At least it seemed it had gone well. It was two a.m. and they talked themselves into following the original plan, which was to stay through the remainder of the night and leave in the morning.

Cyn showered and brushed her teeth while Lee washed the color out of his hair. He shaved the goatee completely off, finally looking like the Lee she knew again. He crawled into bed after her and stared at the ceiling for five full minutes before groaning and pulling her into his arms. Hands tugged at flannel pants and nightgowns, desperate for contact. Residual fear was channeled into lust and they came together clinging to the belief that they had made it out the other side.

They lay, entwined and breathing heavily for a while, still neither of them able to find the peace of sleep, when Lee finally said, “Fuck it. Let’s just go.”

Chapter 18

Owen sat in traffic, like he did every morning when he hadn't been called out of state to view a slaughtered body. So really traffic was a good thing. It might be composed of different cars every day, but it was always the same thing. It was only the cares in his brain that truly seemed to differ.

This morning one thing kept tumbling in there, like laundry in a dryer, softening as it went. While he and Charlotte had been discussing the latest developments on her favorite cartoon over raisin bran, Annika had casually mentioned an article she had found. It seemed the drug trade through Texas had remained significantly low these past months, having dwindled from huge movements of cocaine to merely a trickle with the unexpected death of Ling Mai Na.

If the courts hadn't been able to pin anything on the woman while she was alive, the correlation when she died was enough to know she'd been guilty. The authorities had gotten smart and jumped. Having seen their chance, they managed to plug the hole, fill the gap, whatever, before the next head sprouted up to take Na's place.

Interesting.

The Christmas Killers, who'd again left no bows or tags, or anything other than dead bodies and footprints, had done something the DEA hadn't been able to do for years.

Wanting to close his eyes and absorb some of his thoughts, Owen thought better of it. *FBI Agent Closes Eyes During Rush Hour, Causes Pile-up* wasn't the headline he wanted to read from his hospital room. Still with his eyes open, he could imagine himself throwing open a door, gun trained into the space, and finding them . . .

What?

Mid-kill? Would he stop them if he found them, say, putting the final touches on a barely breathing Kolya Kurev? Owen's sworn *job* was to stop them and get an ambulance to help the man. But Kurev's lawyers would surely get him acquitted and he'd go free again.

No, that didn't sit well.

Maybe Owen would find them sitting in a room somewhere, plans in front of them. And then he'd know how they did it. How they got inside, how they got around the Kurevs' alarm systems, and beyond the dogs the times they had. But again he couldn't picture himself slapping cuffs on either of them and hauling them in. Even in his own head the image got away from him. He saw his hand come out as he introduced himself, his head leaning over their shoulders to look at their plans, and his voice saying, 'what happened to the seven slugs from the .357s at Na's? Where did they go?'

He couldn't even *imagine* himself arresting them at this point.

He was beginning to wonder if he just had to keep them from getting caught before he left in September. He pulled into his parking spot, not remembering the trip, but able to recall every thought he'd had along the way. Apprehending the Christmas Killers would make his career. He'd get an Agent in Charge position most likely. He'd be free of Blankenship. But he didn't really want all that. He didn't want to be a budgeteer, didn't want to have to tell his men that their surveillance was cut short. Even if he went off to teach, he'd have a remarkably better salary, and a lot more options, as 'the Agent who caught the Christmas Killers' than as Owen Dunham.

But Owen Dunham had a problem climbing high on the backs of those who didn't deserve to be stepped on. It was why he'd gone into the FBI in the first place. He would have been a cop if he could have gone straight into homicide, but knew he didn't have what it took for the climb through the ranks.

His cell phone rang even as he entered the front doors. Of course he dropped it, like a bumbling fool, because it was difficult to answer the phone and press his thumb to the glass pad and his magnetized ID to the reader while looking into the camera all at the same time. A smarter man wouldn't have tried it. Wouldn't be looking at the tiny screen at his feet that read "Agent Bean", which it didn't need to say, because the phone had popped open when it hit the ground and Owen recognized the voice yelling up at him.

The beep of the machinery meant he'd been cleared and he swiped the phone up even as he passed through the opening doors. Talking over the dressing down he was already getting from his superior, Owen inserted a false note of cheer. "Good Morning, Agent Bean, what can I do for you?"

"You can answer your phone without a hammer–"

"I dropped it, my apologies." Summer. University. A roomful of young faces wanting to learn about crime scene investigation and research. He promised himself this and breathed deeply.

"Regardless," Agent Bean's voice was rough, but the one thing Owen knew was that it wasn't about a dead body, and it wasn't like he was late for a meeting or anything. Or was he? In a panic he pushed buttons on the phone to call up his schedule. But Bean's words stopped him. "There's a package here for you. Where are you?"

"Downstairs. I'll get in the elevator when it shows up. Package?"

"Just get the hell up here."

A click in his ear signaled the disconnect, leaving him staring at the calendar that showed, no, he didn't have a meeting today. Apparently he did have a package. But from whom? And what the hell would give Bean that tone?

It seemed someone had to get off at each floor, and Owen almost bolted at ten and ran the rest of the way up. He talked himself out of it, thinking that arriving sweaty and at a dead run wouldn't look good to his superior. Even if the man wouldn't be his superior that much longer.

When the doors finally opened on his floor, he pushed through and managed a fast walk down the hall, bypassing his own office entirely, going all the way to the end, where the door was open into the office. He could see Agent Bean at the desk, the wall of windows behind him displaying both the city and hills, as well as the importance of rank that the man had achieved.

In a blink, Owen saw that he was the last to arrive. There was an assembly for the opening of his package, it seemed. Blankenship stood to one side, hands clasped behind his back, looking every inch the junior agent out of his league. Nguyen waited in a chair, in a full sterile paper get-up. Three other agents that Owen didn't recognize at all waited at the periphery, although one carried a large metal kit with him. He didn't have to read the letters on the side to know what they were about.

Words fell out of his mouth. "Someone sent me a bomb?!"

Bean didn't react much. "Doesn't look that way. None of the sniffers found anything, not in DC, and not here."

"DC?" Owen was at loss. Confused, he simply stayed on his feet, unable to make any decisions at the moment, even the small ones.

"It went to D.O.J." Bean gestured at the FedEx box on his desk.

"For *me*?" Yeah, that stroke was going to happen . . . any . . . minute . . . now.

Figuring the bomb squad hadn't suited up, and the box hadn't exploded on the trip to or from the Department of Justice, Owen leaned over to look at the innocuous looking tag.

From: The CKs

A Chicago address followed, one he should have recognized, but it didn't get further than tapping on his brain, because he was busy reading the rest of it.

To: The Agent on the Case, FBI, Department of Justice, . . .

That address he recognized. Pennsylvania Avenue, DC, yada yada. But that wasn't what was important. It was filled out by hand on a standard FedEx air bill. It was the handwriting that made Owen's breath stop. "It's from the Christmas Killers. That's her handwriting. From the tags."

Bean just nodded. "It was sent from a Highland Park drop box. Two blocks from the return address, which is for Black and Associates. An accounting firm who handles –"

"most of the accounts for the Kurev family." Owen heard his voice take over, not that he'd really willed it. He wasn't functioning on all cylinders here. "The Christmas Killers sent this to me?"

Bean shrugged. "It says 'Agent on the Case', that's you."

"Holy shit." He said it two more times. Killers contacted newspapers, tried to publish manifestos, left taunts at the scene. He couldn't think of the last time an Agent had been FedExed by their quarry. Maybe they'd sent him an ear. A finger. He shuddered. A tip? He wouldn't get so lucky. His fingers itched. "Can I open it?"

Owen looked at Bean. Bean looked at the bomb guys. Blankenship looked wide-eyed with equal parts fear and excitement. Nguyen's eyes held none of the fear–the scientific, bomb-squad check had likely been enough to convince him it would be exciting rather than explosive.

When no one protested, Owen grabbed the pull tab and ripped open the end of the box. A small black case emerged into his hands. It sported a big red bow and a handwritten tag.

Owen's mouth hung open.

He blinked a handful of times before being able to read the tag. "Perhaps the most effective way to kill Kolya Kurev.–The Christmas Killers."

Bean looked at him from under partly lowered lids. "Does that mean anything to you?"

Owen shook his head, but his hands were ahead of his brain. They slipped off the three inch wide red velvet ribbon, the same stuff Owen knew was untraceable. He didn't worry about his fingerprints. There was no way they'd left a fiber or even a hint of a breath on this thing. From the note they clearly weren't turning themselves in.

Bean started to protest his handling of the package, gift, whatever. But Owen heard Nguyen, a soothing sound like ocean in the distance, telling the Agent in Charge all the same thoughts that had been slamming through his head. Owen unzipped the edge of the case, finding it was a CD case, just as he'd suspected.

Inside were five, unlabeled, shiny, silver discs.

Spring was in full swing and Cyn was unable to keep her nerves down. It had been five weeks, and nothing–*nothing*–had surfaced on the Kurev family.

The FBI wasn't taking them down–quietly or noisily. They didn't seem to be mounting a case. And her heart was beating a little faster each day. She was anxious now. Ready to get out. Itching with the desire to be done.

That, in and of itself was dangerous.

Previously she'd enjoyed the job. The act of killing Leopold had been a very satisfying experience. A pleasure in many ways. Not just a means to an end. Now the end was all she was in it for. Her brain wasn't on the present, but somewhere in a nebulous future she saw. A future that held Wendy's dreams of an ordinary life.

For the first time she wasn't angry at her sister for giving up and leaving her. She wondered if Wendy had been afraid of getting pregnant the night Leopold and Janson had come. The thought had never crossed her own mind. Cyn wished she'd been old enough, or understanding enough, to feel more for her sister when she'd told of Robert Listle. Cyn had only ever been able to rail at the injustice of it. She'd never been able to feel or even think of Wendy's pain and fear. She wished she'd been knowledgeable enough to demand testing. To prove that Wendy's baby belonged to the man, to maybe bring him down alive.

Cyn also had new respect for Lee.

He had achieved Wendy's dream, then had it ripped away from him. And would never believe that wasn't his fault.

She hadn't felt anything other than drive and anger since she was eleven. Cyn had forgotten she knew how. So now she shuddered under the deluge that threatened to drown her, the sweep of softer, simpler emotions making it that much harder to think about going back in and doing another job.

"Lee?"

He shook his head, looking up from the small screen TVs he held in each of his big hands. He spoke even as she pulled away her ear protectors and holstered the Heckler she'd been killing the trash with. "Nothing."

Her heart slipped into the bottom of her belly. "Do we go back?"

They'd been talking about it for three weeks. Each day deciding to wait.

Lee had written everything he remembered of Black and Associates encryption programs on one disk before they had gone into the building. They knew all the files they would need were coded, and that it would be easier if the FBI started with the code in hand, rather than trying to break it. Lee had given them everything he could. But maybe it wasn't useful anymore. Maybe it wasn't enough. Even though he said the code hadn't changed in the five years he worked there, maybe it had in the four since he'd left. There was no reason to change it. They thought he was dead. They didn't know they had a rogue accountant running around with a good part of their encryption system in his head. But then again maybe they did.

He was looking at her face, seeing the resignation, and making decisions. "Let's go into town first. Do more online research. Dig a little deeper before we decide we have to go back."

She nodded. He didn't want to any more than she did. "What town?"

"Asheville?"

"We've been there twice."

"Charlotte's beautiful this time of year."

Cyn nodded. And by nightfall they were checked into a sleazy no-tell motel beyond the borders of the pretty southern city and she had spent an hour and a half in a café with wireless access.

Having learned nothing, Cyn wound the cords and pushed her new laptop down into her old carrying bag. Necessity had dictated that she throw the old computer away and purchase a new one, in cash, by walking into a big store that wouldn't remember her at all. The new one was silver and non-descript just like the last, and it too was going into a landfill as soon as she was finished.

She waited at the corner, chewing gum and keeping her face tucked under the bill of her navy blue ball cap. Her Duke University sweatshirt and loose cotton pants made her look athletic and would keep anyone who wanted to remember her from being able to describe her weight or shape accurately.

After an interminable two minutes, Lee pulled up in the kitty and reached across, swinging the passenger door open for her. She slid in and saw his face immediately. "Nothing?"

He shook his head.

"So, Chicago then."

"One day." He combated her resignation. "We get up tomorrow morning, pack everything in the car, and tool around for the day. We eat a nice sit-down lunch. Take the day off."

Cyn nodded.

She woke the next morning, brushed her teeth, packed her gear, and stashed it in the trunk. She climbed into the passenger seat while Lee dumped the keys at the front desk. Then she didn't know what to do.

She hadn't had a day off.

Ever.

The last time, she'd been a kid, and she'd had nothing but days off.

Lee knew what to do.

So Cyn followed along. They walked around downtown. They window shopped. They shopped with money and bought things. They ate a lunch at a small café where a girl in a white apron offered them steaming bread and asked what they wanted to drink. Lee ordered crab cakes and Cyn practically moaned while she ate them.

He had laughed at her, and kissed her there in public. Still keeping the old façade in place, she managed to keep her eyes from flying open. Then she distracted them both by suggesting that if they were going all out they ought to get wine. Lee laughed as he shook his head at her. "No IDs. Besides," he leaned over close to her ear, "you're not legal 'til next month."

They walked further, ate ice cream in the middle of the afternoon, and her head swam with memories of being a kid, things she'd shut down a long time ago. Things she'd forgotten she ever knew. He bought her a t-shirt that said "Charlotte" across the front and laughed at her when she held it up.

They got up the next day and packed for Chicago.

Lee drove most of the trip, once again missing the music that Sin played. She wasn't playing it this time. Instead they were planning. They went down lists they had memorized, debating each possibility.

Of the people they'd mugged, Robert Graff was the highest up in the organization. They knew where he lived. His route home. They knew they could get him. Cyn liked the idea. Lee was afraid the man might remember him. Although the possibility was slight, the risk was probably too much to take.

He shook his head. "If he recognizes me, then they know exactly who they are looking for. They can use photos. Best case anyone probably has right now are those police artist sketches of us. And we both know those are worth crap. But if they know who I was . . ."

Sin put in her two cents. "Besides, he has a family. I'd rather hit someone single. Especially if it's in their own home. I'm not going to have his wife, or god forbid, kids, find him. They don't deserve that."

They both mentally scratched him off and went to the next name on the list.

By the time they reached the edge of the city and checked in, they had a victim chosen and knew where they were going.

Taking the biggest gamble he ever had, Lee walked into Black and Associates the following night, Sin at his side again. They pulled the same don't-pester-me routine they had the first time. And this set of badges passed inspection just as the first had.

They went into the elevator with Lee's knees shaking.

He'd been afraid that they would be stopped right there in the lobby. That the company would know they'd been breached and have pulled the tapes from their previous visit. They wouldn't have seen his face, but they would have heard the whole in-from-New-York thing. And they would know that a man and a woman had come after the rest of the employees had gone home.

But this wasn't the same guard–something he and Sin had waited for. And the man had let them in.

Part of Lee's brain argued the entire time that this was ridiculous. Unnecessary. They didn't have to come back, but the other part was afraid of not finishing the job. They needed every bit of evidence they could gather. That part won.

He let himself into Graff's office and sat at the desk while Sin worked down the hall, hacking more files. They had to work from the same desks as before as they didn't risk getting more keys. Lee pulled documents from other sources. He worked at cracking passwords to get into other places he hadn't even tried before.

Then he realized that the footsteps coming down the hallway weren't Sin's.

His head snapped up, his ears alert, listening for long enough to realize it didn't sound like the heavy-set security guard, either.

There wasn't time to do much of anything. But a moment later he was ready.

When the doorknob turned, Lee knew things were going down. He would have alerted anyone who was walking by if he'd flipped the light off. So he hadn't, and he'd prayed the person would pass. It hadn't been enough.

The key twisted in the lock, and the door swung open obscuring Lee from view.

"What the–?" Robert Graff walked into the room like the accountant he was. He had no street savvy, hadn't even thought to look behind the door, or simply leave. Clearly, someone had been in his office. Lee felt some kind of sympathy. Especially when the man's stupidity put him right back at the top of their list.

With a Heckler firmly in his grip, Lee stepped out from behind the door. Knowing he made an odd picture, in his suit and the dark ball cap he'd pulled out to cover his face just a moment ago, Lee used the look to his advantage. He didn't look right. And that would make Graff wary.

Lee raised the gun into the man's line of sight. The silencer stuck out from the muzzle long and menacing, every inch of it very out of place in the rich office. As he watched, Graff's entire body tensed. Lee whispered. "You shouldn't have come back tonight. But now you're going to help me."

Graff answered in a whisper, unconsciously mimicking the man in power. "What do you want?"

"Open the accounting files where you hid the laundered money. Pull up any offshore accounts you have access to, show the series of deposits and withdrawals as far back as you can go. Save it all to disk."

"No!" The man's spine jerked. "They'll kill me."

Robert Graff wasn't as stupid as he looked. He was smart to be more afraid of the Kurevs than of anyone else. Unfortunately, Lee was the immediate danger.

With the gun not aimed directly at him, Graff made a play. He turned and grabbed for the muzzle, managing to get his hand fisted around the silencer only because Lee wasn't willing to shoot him. But Lee wasn't above hurting the man.

Yanking back on the gun extended Graff's arm, and Lee's left fist came down on the nerve cluster just below the elbow. The man's hand lost all ability to grip, and Lee regained control of the Heckler. Which was a good thing because Graff was already swinging his right fist to connect with Lee's face.

Not smart.

Like most non-fighters, he pulled back, alerting everyone around him what he intended to do, and he swung wide, hoping to gain momentum as his fist careened around.

With no wasted movement, Lee flicked his wrist and brought the long nose of the Heckler down across the tendons near Robert Graff's neck.

As the swinging arm lost all form, Graff opened his mouth to howl. Lee had moved by the time the gathered inertia brought the limp arm to its original destination. Another quick snap of a movement brought his left hand slapping over the man's mouth, his own harsh "Shhhh!" drowning the start of the man's cries.

Wide blue eyes darted to the doorway, alerting Lee that someone was there. He glanced up to see Sin standing against the frame, her own ball cap pulled low to cover her face, and easily identifying her as his partner. Graff stepped back, flexing both hands to be certain that they still worked. The man looked like he was about to piss his pants, and for all their sakes, Lee really hoped he didn't.

Sin gave a quick nod from the doorway.

They would have to take Graff.

Sin's voice was an even harsher whisper than Lee's had been. "Do you know who you work for?" She didn't look up from under the cap. Her short strawberry hair flipped out from under the edge, making her look like she was spending the day out at a game until you looked at the neat suit.

Graff nodded. "Black and A–"

"Who you really work for." She didn't let him finish the half-truth. She was pissed and Lee wondered where she was going with it. But he'd always enjoyed watching her work.

Graff's voice was little more than a mumble of concession. "The Kurevs."

"Exactly. And do you know what they do?"

"I prefer not to think about it."

Lee smiled. That was a great reply, it wouldn't get Graff killed if they were Kurev's men come to extract some kind of revenge, and it answered Sin's question. Perhaps the man would be useful after all.

Sin didn't smile. She went for the jugular. "You work with us and we'll save your family."

"How?" Graff was shaking, standing in the middle of his own office, probably regretting he'd ever come back for whatever had seemed so important.

"You tell me what to tell your wife. Where they should run. Where the Kurevs won't find them. I'll get her the message before you're found." She closed the door softly behind her.

Lee saw his own eyes in Robert Graff's. Suddenly knew what the man's family was worth to him. His heart went out, but at the same time he shuttered it–no one had given Lee the chance to save his family. His voice was harsher than he intended it, but never left a whisper. "You're working now to save your wife and daughters. Your pretty blonde wife, and three little girls, the youngest who is still in diapers and has red curls."

Graff stiffened at the mention of his family. With lead feet, he sat himself at his desk. "What do you want me to get?" Even as he asked it, Lee was positioning the Heckler along the man's spine to remind him to do as he was told.

Trust me, he thought, *you don't want to find out what the Kurevs will do to your girls*. But he bit his tongue and didn't issue the warning. He had worked with Robert Graff, only a little and a long time ago, but he couldn't give the man that much warning about his identity. Because he wanted out.

Graff stank of scared sweat an hour later, but he'd opened all kinds of files the two of them would never have been able to.

Grateful for that, Lee motioned the man out of his own seat and stepped in to scrub his trail. Fifteen minutes later they had cleared out both the offices they had been in. They had better decrypting software that Graff had loaded for them, and offshore accounts with deposits going in.

Still afraid but resigned to his fate, he only nodded as Lee talked him through the next step. "You realize you are in serious trouble here?"

Graff nodded again.

"We're going to save your family from the Kurevs. Where should we tell them to go? Someone not connected with your family in any way that can be traced."

Graff thought on that for a minute. After he told them, he acted like the model prisoner, staying with them as they used the back exit to the building. They all climbed into the rental car, with Sin in the back, holding the Heckler on Graff, and drove out of the parking structure looking like the best of friends. There was no traffic to speak of, as it was nearly midnight by that point. But that meant no one would see Graff with them or remember the three of them in the gold sedan.

Lee thought as they drove along, that they absolutely could not go back to the building again. The guard would likely look for them when they hadn't returned in several hours. The accounts Graff had tapped into might very well show the activity. Things would blow soon–they'd lit the fuse, even if they hadn't intended to.

He pulled up in the alleyway behind the pretty house in a nice Chicago suburb.

Graff looked at it longingly and even moved for the handle of his door.

Sin's voice carried on a sweet whisper from the backseat. "Goodnight, Mr. Graff."

Her hands expertly located the bundles of nerves in his shoulders and he slumped just a little, the sensation not the same but not all that different from pain, Lee knew. When he was disabled, her hands closed around his throat, her fingers searching. Even as Graff regained use of his limbs, he blacked out.

"Go." Her word reached Lee, and he nodded only once before pulling the ski mask down over his features, the only thing showing were his lips and blue eyes. He used Graff's key to let himself in through the back door, the alarm pad there blinked at him, and Lee popped open the panel and cut a wire, then quickly taped two others together. Graff hadn't lied about the system. So far, so good.

The hard part was sneaking into the bedroom–violating this woman's sense of privacy and her space. But it was the only way he knew to save her. She was sleeping on her back, and Lee wondered what Samantha and Bethany had been doing when Leopold had come in. He shoved the thought aside and focused.

He brought one gloved hand down across the woman's mouth. his finger found his lips, motioning her to be quiet even as her eyes flew wide in fear. "Shhhh! Don't wake your girls."

She nodded under his hand, her motions controlled by abject terror.

"Listen, Robert sent me." He didn't move his hand, no matter how confused she looked. "His firm works for the Kurev family. He's in trouble. They'll come after you if you don't take your girls and leave now. Now. Nod if you understand me."

She did. Eyes wide. Breath came heavy against his hand. She would never forget him. He was grateful his eyes were blue tonight. As always, just in case.

"Robert said to go to your fairy godmother's. Do you understand?"

She frowned, and her chest moved with the deep need for air. He wasn't cutting it off, but she was still fighting for it. Lee watched as her eyes changed. He knew the nod was coming before she did it. She'd figured out what Robert meant, which was a damn good thing. Because Lee sure didn't get it.

"If you do not leave in the next hour, the Kurevs will likely come after you. Do not contact anyone. Throw your cell phone in the water. Take only what you need, whatever money you have on hand, stop and get as much cash at an ATM as you can before you leave town. Use your credit card to fill up on gas and leave the card at the gas station. You want it to get stolen and used. Take the little car, it uses less gas. Take any jewelry you can pawn. Do not contact anyone. Anyone."

She nodded again and again while he talked. And Lee hoped she was getting it all. One slip up, one credit card receipt in the wrong place could bring the Kurevs down on them. He tried again to give them every advantage. "Buy hair dye, make your girls look like boys. Don't do anything to be remembered along the way."

Her breathing had ratcheted up, but Lee stayed calm. "I'm going to remove my hand. I'm going to leave. Do not scream. Do not call the cops. The Kurevs can get to you through the police. I'll be gone in one minute and you'll never see me again. Then get up and leave."

His hand had slowly moved from her mouth. He stood upright and walked backward out of the room. He heard no movement from any of the other rooms, until he was at the back of the house.

A small blonde girl in a ruffled nightgown held a glass of water with two hands. She looked up at him with questioning eyes. And, God help him, he saw Bethany.

Her mother appeared in the doorway behind him and he was bracketed by the two females. "Hey, sweetie." She said to the little girl, who docilely walked within inches of him, more worried about spilling her water than she was about the strange man in the ski mask. Mrs. Graff looked up at him one last time. "Robert?"

Lee shook his head and whispered. "I don't know."

Then he slipped out the back door. Mrs. Graff punched buttons to re-set the alarm system, he was too far gone to tell her he'd disabled it. He spotted Sin in the driver's seat and Robert Graff in the back, already trussed up and ready to go. He only awaited the red bow and tag. Lee looked back at the house as Sin pulled away and was grateful to see what appeared to be a flashlight bobbing in one of the upstairs bedrooms.

Owen was a bundle of sweat and nerves.

His pager had gone off at three a.m. Again he was dressed and in the car with his bag before he placed the return call. He'd come fully awake to hear that no, he did not have a dead body on his hands, but a live one.

It had taken a while for the feds to locate the man yelling into his cell phone, as he hadn't known his location himself. Once they arrived they'd done nothing. The agents had left him right where he was. They worked with the local police after being alerted by a passerby who had called 9-1-1 describing what she'd seen. They set up barriers around the man, the high fabric kind they used to keep people from staring at bad car accidents. They were saving the scene for Owen. Not a cop in the U.S. wanted to touch anything that came with a big red bow.

Owen got a call from a police officer on the scene halfway through the flight, updating him. Armored trucks had been driven in as barriers, and other bullet-proof shields were being erected around the man, unless Owen wanted them to move him? There had been shots fired ten minutes earlier. One officer was on the way to the hospital but would live. The barriers had provided enough of a shield that at least the shooter had missed his mark.

Agitation poured down his forehead in liquid beads. Owen fought to take a breath. Who was trying to take out the live man the Christmas Killers had left? And why? "Who is he?"

"Robert Graff, sir."

"That means nothing to me." God, people were stupid. "What does he do? Why him? I need info!"

The cop took it all in stride. "He's an accountant with Black and Associates."

"Get him out of there!" He heard the barked order repeated at the other end of the line to the agents already on the scene and Owen just as quickly rescinded it. "No! Wait! What does his tag say?"

"I'm not looking right at him, gimme a sec."

A 'sec' felt like a year, but he waited, praying he didn't hear shots ring out in the background of the call.

"It says: 'To the Agent on the Case. From the CKs.' I'm guessing that's the Christmas Killer–"

"Yes." He wanted a teleporter, although if the first thing he would do upon appearing at the scene was examine the man or wring this cop's neck, Owen wasn't sure. "Anything else?"

"Yes. 'Will tell all in exchange for immunity'"

"Take him down!" Owen practically screamed it into the small cell phone. As it was, between the force of the words he was expelling and how slippery his hands were with sweat, the phone was likely to go flying right out of his grasp at any moment. The thought didn't calm him. "Protect him with your lives!"

Why didn't the plane go faster? He was grateful it was only to Chicago.

The order was issued. "One more thing. We're going to have to cut some rope to get him down, and he's got some CDs he's wearing on a string like some kind of tribal necklace. He's not gonna blow if we move him, is he?"

"The Christmas Killer has never used explosives before. He'll be fine." Owen didn't mention that there were two Christmas Killers and that they just kept changing their M.O. Case in point. So explosives wouldn't surprise him one bit. Them killing an accountant would. He spoke into the receiver again. "Be sure he's protected from the top as well as the sides from gunfire."

"What? Someone's coming after him in a chopper? Or up in a tree?"

"The Kurevs are after him."

That shut the cop up real fast. In Chicago, the Kurevs were big business. The cops either worked for them or feared them. This guy had called Owen, so he likely wasn't on the payroll. Owen prayed Robert Graff stayed safe.

Five minutes later he got a call from the Chicago field agent. "Sorry we couldn't get in touch before, we were securing the scene. I think it was an officer that fired the shot earlier. With that tag, the Christmas Killer might as well have just dumped him in a piranha tank with some raw meat. We didn't get here in time to keep it strictly feds. But we are removing cops as more agents are answering the call."

"How is he –" Owen didn't know what to ask. "Is he tied up? Staked out? What?"

The agent actually laughed. "He was tied to a tree. His arms were wrapped around the trunk and secured with some knots that take me back to Eagle Scouts. His feet were also tied and secured to nearby trees."

"Let me guess," Owen scrubbed a hand over his face finally feeling the descent of the plane, and noticing for the first time that Nguyen and Blankenship were gleaning every ounce of the conversation that they possibly could from his side. "He was tied up with rope that could be bought at Home Depot, OSH, any of a handful of stores."

"Try Wal-Mart."

"Fuck."

Nguyen looked up at that, and Owen mouthed 'Wal-Mart' to the scientist who then uttered his own 'fuck'.

"We took photos. Lots of photos. And we've got Graff in the armored truck now. What's your ETA?"

"Twenty minutes."

Chapter 19

Owen leaned back in the chair. It belonged to the Chicago Field Office; it was FBI issued. That meant it was nearly identical to his chair back home. Maybe just a different model year. It was close enough to feel comfortable at first sit. Enough to lull you into putting your ass there and thinking you'd be okay. And enough off that after a few hours you needed a chiropractor. He would have stood up and walked around the office, but it wasn't his office, so there was nothing of interest–nothing helpful–to see. Also, to stand would be to admit he'd been stupid enough to sit in the bad chair and get bent out of shape.

Owen sighed.

Robert Graff was in protective custody. Although how secure he was remained to be seen. Owen prayed for him.

Agents had come out of the woodwork to interview the man. His disks had showed some of the pathways where Ling Mai Na had brought in money through her cocaine imports. The FBI now had access to offshore accounts and better, more updated decryptions than the Christmas Killers had left the last time. The first program they'd sent looked like an earlier model of the codes the programs were written in. It was far better than starting from scratch, but the feds hadn't been able to read everything. Some of the best agents were hard at work trying to crack the rest of it but Graff's disks had been the glass slipper. The files all opened as if by magic, clear and in English, and everything was suddenly better.

Agents were hounding the Black and Associates accountant, even now, about the Kurevs. There was an entire sector of the FBI designated to the mafia family, a whole slew of Agents and their superiors with that one major assignment. As a high level, loyal employee, Robert Graff had his hands in quite a bit. Blood money flowed freely amongst the Kurevs and Graff had been showering in it on a daily basis.

By the time the agents could get to his house his family had completely disappeared–Graff would only say that he didn't know where they'd gone. Owen was pretty certain the man was lying. But, given that he'd lie too in the same situation, he didn't push it. He didn't think the other agents were going to either.

Owen had spent hours with the man, pissed in the extreme by his lack of knowledge. This was the only person who had knowingly been in the presence of the Christmas Killers and lived to tell about it and still he knew so little.

Graff had given them what he could.

There was a woman.

Petite, seemed to be in good shape–she'd been in a khaki pant suit, so it was hard to tell. She'd had on a navy blue baseball cap and kept her face low. She had no identifying marks on her chin or neck that Graff could see. She had full lips. She was obviously strawberry blonde with a short cut that stuck out under the edge of the cap.

Owen hated that one. As the only thing they had known was that she was brunette, and her hair was long.

Fuck!

The second was a man.

Finally! Confirmation on that one.

He'd also worn a suit and navy baseball cap. He'd also managed to keep his face obscured for the entire time. He'd stood behind Graff while the accountant had worked on the computer, so there had been very little time to see what he looked like. Was there a reflection in the monitor? No. The monitor was low glare. Of course. The man had dark hair, maybe black or brown from the few pieces visible from beneath the cap. He also had no identifying marks on his chin or neck.

Graff had never seen their hands. They'd worn gloves the entire time.

And apparently they were very good at keeping their heads low, in the literal as well as figurative sense.

The local agents thought they were wearing wigs. Nguyen guessed hair dye. Owen expected it was a combination of the two. It was what he would do. That way no one would really know where to look, or what to expect.

Owen expected to finish the bottle of Excedrin he'd started that morning.

He shot the fistful of pills down with his usual coffee and leaned back in the chair waiting for them to take effect. He told himself that, come August, he'd jog every morning. Give up coffee entirely. Play Parcheesi with Charlotte in the evenings. And not worry all day about finding bodies, both live and dead, waiting for him at various locales around the country.

He called Annika just to hear her voice. Wanting to tell her everything, but knowing he couldn't, and certainly not over the company phone, he held back. They talked about Charlotte's fourth grade science fair and her weather project. Anni said she missed him and he heard her bite her tongue at the last minute from spilling the beans about his leaving the Bureau in the summer. Instead she asked if he thought he might get the Christmas Killers before August.

All he could say was 'maybe'.

Anything more certain would be a lie. Anything more certain would invite the ninja and the gunner to laugh to the heavens at him.

He told her he loved her and hung up, and Owen watched as Nguyen came in to the office, sullen faced. "Kicked out again?"

Nguyen nodded, offering explanation for the expression. Used to ruling his own lab in addition to a handful of peons, he hadn't taken well to being in the back. The local lab hadn't taken well to Nguyen's natural assumption that they should do as he told them, or maybe just get their asses out of the way.

The words only added to the expression. "We got nothing on the package they sent either."

"Nothing? At all?" Owen knew he shouldn't be surprised. Hell, he wasn't. He'd put his own prints all over the thing, knowing there wasn't going to be any evidence to destroy.

"We got a smattering of greasy fingerprints–all yours. Two fibers, they matched your suit by the way. And a blond hair–yours. Seriously, in the two minutes you held that thing you managed to shed on it."

Owen shrugged. Clearly he was not cut out to be a criminal. As Nguyen had said, he left evidence everywhere.

The findings continued, although Owen wasn't sure why. "FedEx was the perfect shipping company to use. They give out the boxes, air bills, everything. So none of the supplies can be traced. This box had been wiped clean, probably with alcohol, both inside and out. The ribbon is the same make as all the others, although none of it appears to be from the same batch. We can't match a single cut end, and there's always the most minor variation in the threads. The CD case is also from Wal-Mart, Target, Best Buy, Guam, you name it–the most generic small case in the world. Same on the disks. No prints on any of the disks. Likely also wiped down. Because there is not a spare cell, partial print, smear, nothing."

Nguyen's shoulders slumped.

"And that took how many hours in the lab to find all this nothing?"

"I hate you, Dunham. I really do. I hate them, too."

Owen laughed, his headache vanishing. He enjoyed the respite, maybe because he knew it was just for the moment.

Lee watched the windows. Maggie Leftson had arrived home an hour earlier. To the best of their knowledge she had no plans for the remainder of the evening. The jammies, eerily reminiscent of Sin's old cartoon flannels, were a good sign.

The woman ate dinner in front of her TV. Sat at her computer and hopped online to thumb through what appeared through the binoculars to be personal email. She visited an online dating site.

Of course, Lee thought, she left work, went right to the supermarket to buy a prepackaged dinner at the deli, then went straight home and got into her jammies. She was a prime candidate for online dating.

Or really, she *had* been. Maggie Leftson was about to get in some serious, deadly, trouble.

He and Sin watched while she talked to someone on the phone for about an hour, a small smile on her face. Then she went out of view, behind closed curtains, and turned out all the lights.

Three cramping hours later, they pulled down the ski masks and Lee popped keys into the two remarkably poor back door locks. He looked for the wire to the alarm system and found it quickly. He sighed. Damn thing wasn't even turned on. There was every possibility this would be the easiest job ever.

The small house had a circular path leading around a central fireplace. Lee and Sin took separate routes meeting just outside the woman's door. With every step Lee had felt the weight of the woman's series of mistakes weighing heavily on him.

Maggie Leftson was a fool to work for Black and Associates. But Lee could forgive that one, he knew just how easy it was to make that mistake. And how much it could cost you. Maggie Leftson also hadn't reported that she'd been mugged a few months ago. That was just stupid. Of course, she'd also have to report that she was felled by a single chop from a girl smaller and shorter than she, *and* that she'd been taking a shortcut through a back alley. That was so stupid Lee couldn't begin to fathom it. He was grateful Sin was never that retarded, even though *she* could defend herself. Maggie Leftson had also made other, less obvious, mistakes. Like buying a house and not getting a roommate. She didn't use her alarm system and the locks looked like the ones that had been installed when the house was first built. There was no telling who had keys–like, say, Sin and himself. If she'd reported the mugging to the police they might have realized she'd been unconscious briefly, and they just might have found traces of impression material on her keys. She just might have changed her locks.

Maggie Leftson had done not a single one of the things that might have saved her.

So Lee was shocked as hell to open her bedroom door and find the woman holding a shaking Smith and Wesson revolver at him. He hadn't worn Kevlar for this one.

His heart raced just a little, but he'd walked out of far worse situations than this. He'd faced down Kurev's killers more times than he'd like. And after looking in their eyes, he could easily tell from Maggie Leftson's that she wasn't going to pull the trigger.

She did manage to squeak out a few words in several different octaves. "What do you want?"

It was Sin who whispered to the woman from over his shoulder. "You're going into Witness Protection as soon as you tell the FBI everything you know about the Kurev accounts. You'll help them get into the files they need."

Maggie Leftson jerked her hands to aim at Sin, and even as she did it, Sin's hand came down across Maggie's forearms, startling the weapon loose and dropping it into Lee's outstretched hand. Lee examined it. Damn safety was still on. He didn't feel so bad for Ms. Leftson anymore.

Maggie backed further into her bedroom, "Please don't do this. The FBI can't get into the files. I can't help."

She didn't ask what files or why the FBI would want them. She knew exactly what she did at work, and she continued to show up everyday. The last of Lee's regret vanished. He wanted to pistol whip her.

Sin's whisper mocked the scared woman. "The FBI has the encryption programs. They are probably in the building reading the files as we speak."

Lee figured that was as good a guess as any given the information they had handed over with Robert Graff just that morning. The agent on the case was going to get another present in just a little while.

Sin kept talking, "You can help us and gain the FBI's protection, or you can fight it and go down with the rest of the firm."

Maggie Leftson resigned. She held her hands out in front of her and whispered "Please, don't hurt me."

Lee was debating telling the woman that they wouldn't and Sin was reaching for the rope, when the docile hands flew upward, catching them both off guard. He deflected most of the blow but still took a tap on the chin as part of his attention was directed at Sin. His small partner managed to entirely escape the flying fist by grabbing the hand that came at her even as both of them spotted a foot sweeping out for their legs.

Ms. Leftson had clearly taken a self defense class. And she was using what she knew. Unfortunately for her, she was out of her league.

Lee braced, letting Maggie make contact. As he absorbed the blow rather than going down, she lost momentum and managed to topple herself instead. Sin yanked on Maggie's arm and placed a well-aimed sucker punch in the woman's armpit.

Ms. Lawson collapsed.

A small driving tap was all that was necessary to the nerves there, and Maggie looked up at them with pain and real fear in her eyes. But, though her mouth moved, she made no sound. And Sin's hands came down around her neck.

They left Maggie Leftson trussed up in her own living room. She was tied with cables and router cords from her computer. The laptop was set up next to her, the link to Black and Associates already opened.

The woman was still unconscious when Sin dialed the number for the FBI field office. She held the phone out a little distance from her ear so Lee could listen. It rang three times and the operator for the office answered the line.

They waited through a few 'hello?'s, then Lee saw it coming. And there was nothing he could do.

Sin sneezed.

Then she swore.

"Damnit!"

His breath sucked in and he was grateful in that instant that it was only a whispered curse. He sent up every prayer he knew asking that she hadn't cursed them.

Her eyes registered her error, even as her finger snapped the 'off' button. Taking the phone receiver with her, she marched into the bedroom. As she emerged, a second receiver in her hand, she dialed the FBI again and left the phone line open in Maggie's lap.

Sin was shaking her head as she walked out the back door with him in tow and the sneezed on phone in hand. At least she was doing everything she could about it. She quickly yanked out the batteries, ending the soft glow the phone had emitted, and waited until they were in the car to ask him to run her by Lake Michigan. Even if the phone was ever found, all traces would be washed away.

Instead they managed to pitch it into a waterway off a small bridge just south of Deerfield Rd. It wasn't a great lake, but the water would wash it just as clean. They continued out of town and changed their hair and contacts.

Lee was pulling the rental car out of the obscured spot even as Sin was blinking at the tiny handheld mirror she looked into. She snapped it shut and smiled up at him. A sweet smile that didn't relay any of what they were up to tonight.

Tonight they were getting out.

He could read it in her clear, green eyes.

An hour and a half later they were parked in the dark alley behind Papi's. The New York Style Pizzeria sold big thick slices that had been so good the day before that Lee could read real regret in Sin's eyes for this one. But they were both willing to sacrifice even the best pizza for their chance.

They pulled the masks down and approached the small building. Not part of any chain, it was perfect as what it was. A small glass front offered pizza, salads, and calzones to paying customers. The back opened like a garage door to allow cool air in or deliveries out. Tonight the smell of dough and cooked cheeses came out the open garage door with the light that showed the last delivery boy getting into his beat up Civic and Papi himself putting the day's take in the deposit bags.

Letting the delivery boy drive by first, they stalked up on either side of the open door. Papi, actually Reynoldo Casto, continued to count tens and ones in the glare of his own store light. He was a beefy man, certain of himself and just as certain of those around him.

Lee appeared first, Heckler out and aimed at Papi's heart.

Casto glared at him and he must have read the truth–that Lee suspected the pizzeria owner had been suckered or dragged into working with the Kurevs and that Lee felt some sympathy. That meant Lee wasn't willing to kill. He wasn't willing to pull the trigger, and he'd violated the first gun law.

Papi saw it, and he went for the gun.

Lee used it to block the hands coming at him, just as he and Sin had practiced for hours on end. Still Papi came, and the man's weight alone was an advantage Lee couldn't match. He made up for it with skill.

Sin came up behind the man and kidney punched him–once on each side. But his girth absorbed too much of the blows, and he was wounded, but not down. Sin went after the man's shoulder, chopping at her favorite nerve bundle, and Casto went limp on his right side.

But only for a moment.

Lee turned the man's attention from Sin and planted a fist into one dark eye. Papi's head went back with the force of the blow. Lee had put his hips and shoulders into the throw, he'd carried through, giving the man no choice but to fall back or have the fist tunnel into his skull.

Sin already started searching the racks in the back of the joint. Knowing they were all illuminated by the same light Papi had been, she searched quickly shoving aside delivery boxes and large cans of sauce with an ease that spoke of her strength. She shook her head up at Lee even as he saw Casto plant himself to throw another blow.

He sidestepped, not wanting to take the weight Papi had channeled into his fist, and simply stayed out of the way for the half moment it took Sin to position herself behind the surprisingly agile man. With the swings he was taking, Casto put his hands right into Lee's grasp, and Lee twisted the wrists together holding the man tight.

When a large foot shot out behind him aiming for Sin, she simply grabbed it and held tight. They were both reaching for rope when Papi moved. Like everyone else, he gave fair warning of what he was doing before he lifted his other foot–the only thing keeping him off the ground.

His weight fell to the hard cement floor, and Lee and Sin adjusted, neither willing to let go simply because Papi had decided to smack himself against the earth. But in the split second where he realized they weren't even going to even try to hold him up, that all his weight was going to hit down, Casto jerked.

And the jerk brought his free foot against Sin's arm.

They all heard the crack of bone.

Lee knew his face registered far more than hers did. Hers registered nothing.

Sin's hand let go of Papi's leg. And hung limp.

The rest of her reacted with speed. With nothing more than flat-out irritation showing on her face, she marched over to Lee and pulled a Heckler from its holster.

Lee didn't let go of Papi's hands. Because Papi was desperately trying to get away. If he'd read in Lee's face that Lee wouldn't shoot him, he certainly read in Sin's now that she had every intention of doing just that. Before Lee could say anything, she'd put a bullet in one of the man's shins, the recoil of the heavy gun traveling up her left arm.

"We were going to play nice." Her tone, whisper though it was, let it be known in no uncertain terms that they were no longer being 'nice'. "Where's the cash?"

"In the drawer."

Casto had flinched at the bullet going into his leg, but managed to look pissed still.

"No. Kurev's money."

That got the man's attention. Only a few people knew that Papi's New York Style Pizzeria was a way station for Kurev drug cash. Robert Graff had known. Apparently Papi wasn't innocent either.

Sin aimed the gun at his chest as a warning, then put a bullet in his other leg. "Where?"

Grudgingly the man gave directions and Sin used her one good hand to pull out two non-descript black suitcases full of small bill cash while Lee tied Casto. He put a rope right around the leg wounds Sin had put in the man. It was to help staunch the bleeding and also to inflict extra pain. Lee pushed Sin's broken arm to the back of his thoughts.

With one hand she pulled out her gift tag and kneeled on the edge to hold the page still while she wrote. Lee was grateful she'd been writing the tags left-handed. She made him pin the tag and bow with stars she produced from the right sleeve of her jacket. Only the tic of a tiny muscle in her jaw told of the pain it was causing her.

He propped the suitcases open while Sin dialed the FBI from the phone on the wall.

They ran, then. Into the dark of the warehouses. The only thing behind Papi's, they were all closed up at this time of night. It was the only reason they'd been able to hit the place like they did. They argued in heated whispers all the way back.

Lee wanted to find a hospital quick.

Sin thought they needed to pack up first and get their stories straight.

The only thing they didn't argue about was the need for a physician.

Owen's pager had gone off.

Fool that he was, he'd counted on the old M.O. and stayed up late thinking he wouldn't get another middle-of-the-night call for at least a month. They needed that long to plan a good hit, or for one to present itself.

So he'd just crawled into the hotel bed when the damn thing had buzzed on the table. The sounds of the vibrations of technology against wood were the only familiar things in the room. He'd called in, fairly pissed. "What? I'm in Chicago. I already saw the damn scene."

"There's another." Randolph's voice was almost cheerful. In the time it took Owen to wonder where the hell he could be flying to now, the operator told him it was a mere twenty blocks away, and it was another live one.

He'd gotten a lot of the specs before he'd arrived. So Ms. Leftson was quite irritated that he only asked her questions about her attackers and hadn't helped her at all. She hadn't been untied. She hadn't been asked if she knew why she was assaulted in her own home and she was pissed.

"They almost killed me!"

"That's bullshit." His voice was calm and orderly if his words were not. "You got hit by the Christmas Killers. See that nice, pretty bow you're wearing? That nifty tag? If they'd wanted you dead, you would have been dead. And you would have suffered immensely. As it is, they saved you. The Kurevs are going down. Black and Associates is going down. We've got a warrant and our people are over there opening files even as we speak. The lucky few who wear big red bows are going into Witness Protection, *if* they cooperate. The rest are going to jail."

She quit her litany of complaints after that.

Maggie Leftson answered every question in precise English.

Owen wasn't surprised that the female attacker had been auburn-haired. It had hung in a thick braid to about the middle of her back.

She'd had on a ski mask.

That had excited Owen.

The ninja was described with the same full lips, and her eyes were a soft shade of violet.

A redhead with violet eyes? Owen didn't buy that for a hot second.

Her eyelashes? Maggie Leftson didn't know, and clearly didn't like being asked about it.

The man?

Blue eyes and long, chocolate brown hair that hung out from under the ski mask.

The masks had very small eye and mouth holes. So she couldn't talk about brow lines or wrinkles at the edges of the eyes. Owen thought about getting a damned artist in here to listen to Ms. Leftson and produce a very expensive rendering of absolute crapola!

Every other part of them had been covered. Maggie could estimate heights, but weights were difficult because their clothing had appeared bulky.

Blankenship came up just then, reporting that the other extension for the phone was missing. Owen had expected no less. The operator had reported, indeed–like every incoming call–had *recorded*, a sneeze and a whispered 'damnit'. Likely they threw the missing phone into the lake or one of the branches of the Chicago. It was an easy way to get rid of that kind of evidence.

He went back to questioning Maggie Leftson. Had she seen what they drove up in? No. Did she know which way they were headed? No. Did they threaten her? Not really. She'd held a gun on them, but they'd quickly disarmed and embarrassed her.

Owen asked the next question because he had to.

"Had you ever seen them before?"

Maggie sighed. "The girl, she might have been the one who mugged me a few months ago."

"What!?"

Maggie just nodded.

Owen was compelled to point out, at high decibels, that she hadn't filed a report.

Leftson filled him in on her supreme stupidity. The girl who mugged her had only taken cash. Although she'd knocked Maggie out fairly easily, Maggie had come right around, and everything was as it should be.

Owen felt a simmering rage, as well as some admiration bubbling up. That, at least, explained some of it. "You have keys to Black and Associates? Your office? Your *HOUSE*!?"

Maggie nodded.

Owen had already seen the lobby tapes from the firm the night before. A man and a woman had shown seemingly valid IDs to the guard and gone into the elevator. The cameras had caught nothing useful, as the two had carefully kept their faces averted. They had never come back out. The guard was still working with the sketch artist, who said the guard had about the worst memory of anyone she'd ever worked with. Those lucky sons of bitches.

"Blankenship!" He called out to where his partner and Nguyen were combing the house for any stray evidence. Never mind that it was an exercise in futility. "Call in to the office, see if Graff was mugged a few months ago!"

He turned back to Maggie Leftson. "When, exactly, was it?"

"Can I have my day planner?"

He still didn't untie her. Didn't like her attitude, and thought about throwing her on the mercy of the courts. He made an agent rifle through Maggie's purse and call up the planner feature on her electronic calendar. The surly woman had nerve. She stared at the agent, "Let me see it. It's not like I added in 'get mugged' on that date."

Owen was ready to clip her with his Glock. But he held back, there were just too many witnesses.

Maggie and the agent fumbled through and she produced a date that was three weeks prior to the arrival of the CD case at DOJ. Son of a bitch.

Blankenship got a call just then, stating that Graff had been mugged the month before Leftson had, and that he, too, had been unconscious for only a short piece of time. But it had been by a 'blonde Latina girl, who could not have been the same one in the office'. Owen would bet the farm that Graff couldn't be more wrong.

He was growing more frustrated by the minute, when the only thing that could make his evening worse happened.

His pager went off.

Owen called the home office. With no questions he started his rant. "This is Dunham. What the hell are you calling me for? I am *already at the damn scene*!"

Randolph kept his cool. He just said, "Yes, sir."

And followed with, "There's another scene."

"What!?"

Nguyen and Blankenship looked up at him. So Owen repeated what he'd heard to them. Leaving the other agents with Maggie Lawson still trussed up like a Sunday pig in her own living room, and looking utterly ridiculous in that bow, the three of them hopped in the black Bureau sedan and started off for Papi's New York Style Pizzeria down by O'Hare. Nguyen hadn't bothered to remove his stupid paper suit.

At three a.m. no one fought them for road space. They arrived in very little time. Agents were already on the scene. They'd learned with Graff that once the Kurevs found out their people were singing, the mafia family was glad to take their pound of flesh themselves. Bullet proof barriers had been erected around the back of Papi's almost from the moment local agents had answered the silent call. FBI medics were already there and caring for Casto's wounds. They were stitching him by the time Owen squatted down to examine him.

Owen decided to leave the man trussed up.

It would turn out to be a mistake.

Reynoldo Casto was every bit as pissed as Maggie Leftson had been. He agreed to spill everything only in exchange for the FBI going immediately to his home and getting his wife and three sons out of the very nice house. Too nice for the owner of a very good, but not very high traffic, pizza joint.

Only after he'd spoken to his wife on the phone held to his head did he answer Owen's questions. Seriously pissed off, he answered only what Owen asked. The first question this time was 'had you ever seen them before?' But Casto's answer was a clear 'no'.

He spoke of the man and the woman. They wore dark clothes from fingertip to toes. All he could see was some hair and eyes. They were both blonde, the man's a gold color and hers platinum. Her eyes a clear green, his black as night. Owen knew now it was all shit. They'd hit two places within hours bearing different descriptions each time. They whispered through the whole exchange.

Papi had fought them. The man fought back with the guns and the little girl using her fists. No, he couldn't estimate weight, yada yada yada. They made him tell where the Kurev money was–hence the open suitcases. Apparently with every last dollar still in them.

It was only after Owen had been sitting in the cool night air in the back of the pizza joint for an hour and a half, about three hours after Casto had been trussed and left for the feds, that the man narrowed his eyes. "They tied me up. They dropped me on the ground. But I got back."

"Yeah, what'd you do?" Owen was almost bored. He was thinking of the four interviews he'd scored with his resume.

"I broke the bitch's arm."

Casto's black eyes glittered.

"What?" Owen's voice held the silent edge of predation.

Casto repeated the line word for word, and sent every agent around him into a spin. Owen was calling the field office, demanding they check every hospital within a five hour drive radius of Papi's.

"Which arm?" He demanded in Casto's face.

Papi thought for a moment. "Right."

"Where did it break?"

"Wrist to elbow." There was glee in the older man's eyes.

Within fifteen minutes the hospitals were on alert for any woman of any age with a break to the right forearm.

With nothing he could do until a call came, Owen took his frustrations out on Papi. "Did she write the note in front of you? Which hand?"

"Not the broken one." Papi looked at him like he was stupid.

Maybe he was. He'd been trained to catch flies with honey. He had confirmation now that she was, indeed, a lefty. And if something came through, he just might catch up to her, if not both of them.

The question was: would the gunner stick with her?

Five hospitals reported within the first fifteen minutes. But two of the women had been in the hospital before Papi had been assaulted. Two others had shown up late enough, but doctors declared the wounds old–one had only been a sprain anyway, and Casto swore he heard bone snap. The fifth report belonged to a tall ten year old girl there with her mother. She'd fallen out of her bunk bed. Owen didn't even think of following that one up.

Two hours after that, he got the call. The nurse at the front desk in the Trauma Unit at BroMenn Medical Center, one hundred and thirty miles away, had been reading charts and saw the FBI directive. The patient was still there. Twenty-three year old female. Broken right radius and ulna. It hadn't pierced the skin, but was clearly a break. They'd already x-rayed her and casted the fracture.

Owen told them to get the cops and hold the patient.

Glory be, the nurse asked if her boyfriend should be held, too.

Owen, Blankenship, and Nguyen were already in the car before he finished the conversation. They'd driven the hundred plus miles in fifty minutes, sirens blaring all the way.

They abandoned the car in the ambulance bay and entered the ER with guns drawn. Although Owen doubted they could–or should–shoot either of the Christmas Killers, the two were definitively lethal. They'd only carefully chosen deserving targets in the past. But no one knew what they would do if cornered. He hated it, but Owen kept his Glock in both hands.

The nurse at the front desk had relayed a lot of info in that first call. Owen knew what room she was in, knew the basic layout of the trauma department, knew which way to go when he got in. A plump nurse decked out in cat scrubs followed them at a bit of a run.

Owen hissed for her to get back.

But she walked right up. “They’re gone.”

He couldn’t believe it.

Then again, he could. He didn’t say anything, just fixed the woman with a stare. She started talking real quick. “They walked out while I was on the phone with you the first time. They were gone before the cops went in. Some of the people in the waiting room saw them leave.”

“The cameras?” That was Nguyen.

The nurse shook her head sadly. “We’re not that big, we don’t get the kind of trouble we’d need cameras for. Not before this.”

Owen let his head fall back. They’d left almost an hour ago. The nurse had tried to call back, but the agents had all been on several lines apiece the whole time. No telling which direction the Christmas Killers had gone. He tried every question in the book that might yield anything. Were there cameras in the parking lot? Did the cops see them leave? Did they mention anything about where they were headed?

No, no, and no.

Owen was ready to give up. He was about to hand his badge and Glock to Nguyen and catch the next flight out of O’Hare, but as he turned he realized Nguyen wasn’t there. Having conceded that they weren’t going to catch up to the killers, the scientist was already searching for evidence. And Owen realized his capitulation had been premature.

Nguyen looked puzzled. “The bed is clean. No evidence. No way.”

The head nurse in her kitty cat top explained. “We had an overzealous orderly change the bedding right away.”

“But I need it.” Nguyen sounded like she’d taken away his lollypop. Maybe in a way she had. “Where did it go?”

She gestured to the bedside hamper. Just a sturdy wire frame, it held up a lidded, red, biohazard bag. Nguyen ignored the red flower warning and started digging.

Owen sighed. “We need their paperwork.” He sent Blankenship to fetch it and to find out who filled it out. He turned back to the nurse, “I need her chart.”

Even though all this was for shit if they didn’t find some evidence that proved–or at least proved to him–that this was the ninja and not just some other chick with a broken right arm, Owen got to work. He cornered the physician and the nurse while the other two agents tracked other paths. The man had blonde hair and green eyes and he'd looked to be about thirty. The woman was younger, said she was twenty-three, with long brunette hair and brown eyes.

"But they looked like contact lenses to me." The nurse added. "I saw her up close and you know how the colored contacts still don't look quite right? That was what it was like."

All Owen could conclude was that his ninja didn't have blue, green, brown, grey, or violet eyes. What the hell that left, he didn't know. Maybe she was god-damned Orphan Annie.

The hospital staff said the two were very loving to each other. He took care of her. Sweet to the point where the nurses had suspected domestic abuse. The head nurse shook her head. "She said she was a gymnast. That that was why she had other, older bruises. And how she'd gotten the broken arm. I can't tell you how many times we hear 'gymnastics' from grown women whose boyfriends and husbands are doing it. But she wouldn't press charges. They never do."

Owen wanted to laugh. What the nurse suggested was serious, but he couldn't think of any female less in danger of domestic abuse than his ninja. Besides if the gunner abused her, it wouldn't be with his fists. He'd just leave her gut shot. Then Owen startled, and wondered if they'd planned it to look that way. They wouldn't look any more suspicious than your garden variety girlfriend-abuse case. The nurses probably wouldn't even remember them.

The physician talked about her chart. He'd paid no attention to the interaction whatsoever. Except to press her to press charges. Which he'd done because the nurses told him to. "But look at this."

The man clipped the x-ray onto the lighted wall board. "This is why I think she just might have actually been a gymnast."

It looked like an arm to Owen. You didn't have to be a doctor to see that the two arm bones had been snapped. And, if you followed the thin line tracing the edge of the arm and hand, they hadn't poked through the skin. The injury, at least, was consistent with Reynaldo Casto's story.

But the physician pointed something else out. "See these bones?" He traced the broken ones with the back of his pen. "They're too bright."

Huh?

The question must have shown on Owen's face, because the man very quickly reached back and pulled another x-ray from the charts he'd set on the counter when Owen had stopped him. He popped this one onto the light box right beside the first. It was a foot. Owen was lost.

"These aren't hers, but see how the bones are paler? That's normal." He tapped his pen against the wrist x-ray again. "These are brighter, that means the bone is denser. Significantly denser. Stronger." The doctor shrugged. "You might build that kind of bone strength doing gymnastics."

Nguyen's voice came from over Owen's shoulder. It held a world of wonder. "Or Karate."

Even as hope bloomed in Owen's chest, Nguyen held up pinched fingers. "Look what I found."

Owen had to squint to see it. But he did.

Nguyen held up two long brunette strands of hair.

Chapter 20

Owen had handed in his letter of resignation. He was done with the FBI. He had a very low level professorship awaiting him at UCLA. The University was big enough to climb the ranks if he so decided and had a big enough name to get him to the next place if he didn't like it there. There would be a world of opportunities for Charlotte in Los Angeles. Annika could do whatever she wanted. Everything awaited.

A change awaited.

That was maybe the most important thing. This last run-in, putting him so close to the Christmas Killers, had left him so drained. As the three agents had driven away from the hospital, with evidence in hand and a slew of agents still combing the place, Owen had found a moment to be grateful that he hadn't come muzzle to muzzle with the gunner. Not one of his men could shoot like what the evidence said the gunner could. And none of them could go hand to hand with the ninja. They would have had power in numbers, but Owen didn't know if even that would be enough.

These two wanted out, it seemed. This last round of firecracker activity, where no one had gotten killed and the FBI now held the documentation it needed to put Kurev, and most of his cronies, away for a damn long time, had been a final bid. That meant they likely wouldn't appear again. Not unless Owen's pager went off and went off damned soon.

Had they all met face to face, it would have been a bloodbath. And Owen was more and more happy it hadn't happened, because he sure as hell didn't know if he would have walked away or not.

He leaned back in his chair, in his office, and looked around. Four more days.

The map still hung across the back wall. The pins had made it all the way through the colors, the last dark cluster in Chicago, from three weeks ago. The small plastic heads were all deepening shades of true red. A.k.a. fucked. But Owen didn't feel fucked. He felt empty.

He stretched and walked down the hall to visit Nguyen, stopping for his coffee along the way and having the nerve to already feel nostalgic about it.

Nguyen looked up, his paper coveralls far neater and more pristine looking than any suit had been. "What now?"

"Nothing." Owen perched on the edge of the desk. "Anything new?"

"Same old, same old."

The hair had matched. The two strands from the hospital had been identical to the one from the campus rapist scene. They'd run DNA analysis then, and bingo. But Nguyen had done that almost three weeks ago.

Nothing much else had turned up. There were no new scenes.

Owen had artist renderings from anyone who had seen their faces. The BroMenn Medical Center employees had seen both of them. The physician couldn't recall either with enough clarity to make a sketch. The nurse could. As could the guard at Black and Associates on the first night they'd entered.

The problem was, it had rendered several entirely different drawings for each of the killers. They *could* all be the same person, he supposed. But the descriptions were for different nationalities, hair colors. The eye shape and nose width was different enough in each drawing to make certain that not a single one was believable.

Nguyen left the file out and went back to work.

Owen watched for a few minutes then thumbed through the hefty folder. There were pages of Nguyen's typed notes, baggies of evidence. In particular, two–clipped together–with matching long brunette strands. There was also a small silver recorder. Owen picked up that baggie. "What's this?"

Nguyen looked up from across the room and smiled. "Listen to it."

The recorder itself wasn't evidence, according to the label on the bag, so Owen plucked it out and hit the play button. He heard the FBI operator answer and identify herself, followed by a long patch of silence, then a sneeze and a whispered 'damnit'.

It was female. Even through the whisper he'd bet his salary on that. It was the ninja's voice, or as close to it as they were going to get. Owen listened again.

"You know," Nguyen interrupted the small joy he was feeling at hearing the sounds repeatedly, "it seems there are people in the Bureau who are on the Christmas Killers' side."

"What do you mean?"

Nguyen shrugged. "Just that the initial recording got deleted from all the base files."

"Huh?"

"No one can find it. What you hold in your hand is the only copy we have."

Owen's brain was running with that one when Nguyen reined him back in.

"I haven't copied it." He waited until he caught Owen's eyes before continuing. "And there you hold the only recorded evidence in your hand. On a little recorder that you can buy at any Radio Shack around the country."

Was Nguyen suggesting . . . ?

He didn't say, but Owen's gears were churning. He had four more days.

With only a nod to his friend, he wandered back out into the hall, feeling more out of place than he had in decades. When he arrived at his office, seemingly by his own two feet, Blankenship was waiting in one of the guest chairs.

Owen sighed. Only four more days of Blankenship. He seated himself and put his coffee on his desk, directly on the ring he had first made years ago. When Blankenship stood and closed the door, the day just got weirder.

His junior partner seated himself, looking nervous and excited all at the same time. Owen wondered what was going to blow up, and if it might be Blankenship.

"So, I had all the paperwork from BroMenn Med Center, from when the killers visited."

Owen had seen it. It was typed in by the night check-in girl. The ninja had claimed to be right handed and therefore unable to sign. She was to do her best once the cast was dry, but left the hospital before she could. It was a useless batch of info and that was why he'd sent Blankenship crawling after it.

"Okay, the gunner gave all the info to the night clerk." Blankenship flipped through papers, "He said they were from Chicago, and he gave 1067 South Washtenaw Avenue as the address."

Owen had seen that.

"But, that address has been occupied by a Mrs. Margaret Landley for over forty years."

No surprise.

Blankenship was up to a mile a minute, "But more interesting is that four doors down is a daycare. At 1055."

"So?"

"It became a daycare four years ago after the house on the lot wouldn't sell. And it wouldn't sell because the wife and daughter of the happy family that lived there had been shot to death. The job smacks of Sergei Leopold, by the way."

Owen leaned to the edge of his seat. Holy shit.

"Yeah," The junior agent smiled. "I just followed Margaret Landley and found it. Thing is, the murdered mother is the daughter of Mrs. Landley. Who lived at the address the gunner gave us. And the father, who found his murdered wife and child by the way, was a Mr. Lee Maxwell, no middle name. He was an accountant with Black and Associates until he disappeared shortly after the demise of his wife and daughter."

Blankenship smiled like a maniac.

Owen almost fell out of his seat. "Are you serious?"

The junior agent nodded like a well performed puppy.

"Do we have photos of Lee Maxwell?"

"Well," Owen could see it all falling apart. "We have his high school photo. There's nothing else on the web. But I already have calls in to the family. I just can't figure out why he gave us that address."

Owen was having trouble absorbing all of it. His head was spinning and his partner wanted him to think. All he could think was that sending Blankenship on all those stupid paper chases had actually turned him into a good researcher.

Jesus.

He shrugged. "I guess he needed an address and that one made sense. He probably wasn't thinking clearly."

"But why not make one up?"

"The med center's computer program will reject it if it doesn't exist or if the zip codes don't match. You need a real address. Maybe that one was handy." His world somehow still on its axis, he dismissed his partner. He needed breathing room. "Good work, Blankenship."

Owen hadn't seen any of that coming in a million years.

He hovered around the office looking up what he could on Lee Maxwell in a haze until he went home for dinner. Annika knew something was up, but didn't question him until after Charlotte was in bed. Owen spilled everything.

At last, when he'd divulged every piece of information he knew, she gently asked, "What are you going to do?"

"I don't know."

She nodded. "Well, just in case, I'm going to invite Charlotte's little friend Jessica over to spend the night this weekend. She's got the most beautiful long brown hair. You can decide any time between now and Saturday."

Cyn turned the key in the lock and swung the door from the garage to the kitchen wide open. It was late, but Lee would be up still. So she hollered out, "Hey, honey, I'm home."

It still felt like a bit of a joke, but far less than it had when they'd moved in three years ago. The place had been damned expensive, but there was a lot of money from her parents' deaths and from Samantha and Bethany's insurance policies still left over. And she felt she was finally honoring their memories, that their deaths had been avenged.

"In here!" Lee sat in the dining room, his laptop on the table. He wouldn't emerge from tax season for a while, and they'd decided to go on a real vacation then. That alone was exciting. Cyn was hoping to go shark diving or bungee jumping. A bag of Doritos was open at Lee's side and he looked up as she came into the room–he'd slid so easily into being a husband.

Not that they'd ever gotten married. But they'd bought rings, because their hacker had put them in the system as married. They'd also bought Lee's CPA license and an excellent test score along with their new identities.

Cyn had retaken the damned GED. High school records were a bitch, apparently. And she hadn't really been old enough for a college degree to be forged. She was half a term away from earning a real one now anyway.

Lee stood up and stretched. "How did it go?"

"Great. Like always." Only now was she beginning to feel secure enough to make friends. Not many, not really good friends. But it was a start. "Was that your dinner?"

He nodded.

Without talking much, they put together a very late meal and sat on the couch eating. Halfway through Cyn started in on him. "I want a baby."

"I know."

"Now."

He rolled his eyes. "You don't just pick one up at the store. We said we'd try in the summer."

It made him nervous. The house, the job, the wife–he was fine with all of that, but the child still scared him a bit. She pushed. "I want to try now. Maybe it won't work until summer. But we've been here a while. We're settled in. Nothing's happened in three years."

She tried to look her most pleading and her most motherly all at the same time. She was probably too young to be a mother. But who wasn't? She was definitely already too old in too many ways.

Half his mouth quirked. "Okay."

That was all it took. She smiled the grandest smile she knew, and went back to eating her dinner.

A few minutes later she broke into his thoughts, as he was obviously already getting concerned about this future child. "You know, I stopped by the ATM on the way home tonight."

"Uh-huh."

"The light was out where I was walking back to the parking structure. And this guy came out of nowhere."

"What?" His fork stopped midway to his mouth. He stared at her. "What did you do?"

"I tried to just run, really I did. But he was too close." Words flew out of her mouth in an effort to explain. She'd asked about the baby first on purpose. "He mugged me!"

"You mean 'he tried'."

"Yeah." Cyn attempted to sound apologetic, and didn't quite make it. She really needed an outlet these days. "I let him have it."

Lee's voice was strained. "Is he dead?"

"No!" The nerve of him! She tried to conjure up a little hurt at the offense, but didn't quite muster that either. "He was just a mugger."

"Where is he?"

"In the bushes under the burned out light."

Lee stared at her.

"He's tied up. He can get out, so he won't wind up with the cops, but he'll be damned embarrassed."

"Sin. You fell off the wagon! After three years." He sighed. Lee was trying to be mad at her, she could tell. After about thirty seconds he broke loose and laughed.

Owen took the walkway back to the parking structure. The light was out. It would just figure. His hand still automatically felt for the Glock at his side, but it wasn't there. It hadn't been there for several years.

He was finished with Los Angeles. It hadn't been the bastion of opportunity he'd wanted. And he'd come to some hard conclusions. Mostly that he'd been a fool. In those first days, he'd lied to himself, believing that the ninja hadn't factored in at all. But LA was where he would have gone to surface, if he'd had a history like she did. He had harbored a useless hope.

But it was time to cut his losses and pack it in. Charlotte was in junior high now and they all needed real roots. After three years out of the Bureau, it was finally time to leave it behind. Owen breathed in the night air of his last spring in California.

The sidewalk cut an alleyway between the backside of the classrooms and the cement parking complex. Tall trees had been added for shade during the day and probably for looks as well. But all the people with night classes, like the associate professors, had to walk down a tree-lined and fairly dark path even when the lights were on.

He kept his ears alert. The Bureau guys would find him and mock him mercilessly, even from a distance, if he got himself mugged. Owen moved his bag from his hand to over his shoulder.

He liked the weight of it. Teaching agreed with him, and more, better opportunities awaited him in North Carolina.

Much of it was as he'd expected: young faces, some older, looking to him at the front of the classroom. The students seemed to like him. He'd taken real pride in his evaluations that first Christmas. The night classes cut into some of his time with Charlotte, but he saw her far more than he ever had before. He even got to have lunch with Anni several times a week now.

He was smiling right as he heard the sound. The bush to his right shook. Owen tensed, waiting for whomever was hiding there to pop out and try to get his bag. He figured he could take a mugger.

But no one popped up. He would have thought the attacker had seen him and decided not to come out. So why keep shaking the bushes?

Cautiously, Owen walked over and peered down into the underbrush where the non-working light was anchored. A young man in only a t-shirt and jeans squirmed against the pole. A moment's assessment showed that he was tied to it, his arms and legs held in front of him, wrapping around the post. He'd squirm himself out of it in a few more minutes.

Ever skeptical, Owen just looked.

"Dude," the kid called up, "Can you help me out?"

"I don't know." Something didn't ring true.

"I got mugged!"

He saw the piece of paper then, and clearly this guy wasn't going to attack him while he leaned over. Owen picked up a bank slip. "This your receipt?"

"Yeah."

"Mugger got your money?"

"Uh-huh." Still the kid struggled against his bonds. Owen could see now that he'd been tied with a sweatshirt. Probably his own, he looked a little cold.

"How much money did you take out?"

The voice faltered. "Forty dollars . . ."

There was almost a question at the end.

"Nope! Wrong–you took out eighty!" He squatted down with his elbows resting on his knees. "Let me guess, you mugged the person this receipt belonged to and they taught you a lesson."

Owen felt everything gel as he said the words. The kid had barely nodded before the next words were out of Owen's mouth. "Brunette? Slim? Pretty brown eyes?"

The kid had nerve to look at him like he was crazy. "I didn't see her eyes."

But Owen was already gone. *Her* eyes. His fist clenched the slip and his feet pounded the pavement, he had slammed through the building doors and unlocked his office before he could think rationally.

Still in his coat, his breathing heavy, Owen called up his computer program into the school directory. He found white pages online and jotted down the address before searching and printing a map. He almost forgot to lock the door on the way out.

As he walked back to the car, he reached for his cell phone and called Anni, ignoring the rustling in the bushes as he went by. Over the sound of the kid calling out to him, he told her he'd be late, but he'd need to swing by the house. He gave instructions for the small silver recorder he kept in his desk, and she was standing at the end of the front walk with it when he pulled by.

He took a deep breath, "Thank you. I'll be back within the hour."

Anni had smiled at him, as understanding as always, and didn't ask for an explanation.

Owen hadn't needed his records to know the name. Diana Kincaid had run through his mind before.

Blankenship had found even more paper trails in those last few days before he'd left the FBI. Owen had packed everything in and handed off the dead file to the next agent. But not before his partner had pointed out that the hospital record was for a Cynthia K. Wiggs. He'd also found a rental car–a gold Acura sedan–returned to the rental lot at the airport, keys left in the drop box forty-five minutes after Casto's assault. Blankenship had scrounged up the parking lot security tapes. A petite female with blonde hair turned the car in and walked to the edge of the lot to climb into a small, non-descript, older, brown car. The tape was fuzzy and there was no way to distinguish faces, but it appeared she hadn't used her right arm at all. The car had been rented to Cynthia Elizabeth Carrol.

So they had a good idea what the car looked like. And Owen still felt some gratification for having pegged it. Blankenship had dug further and found nothing. The same kind of significant nothing they'd always found. There was a driver's license from Arkansas and the one credit card. And not a damn thing else. Cynthia Carrol didn't exist.

It was Annika who suggested the ninja used 'Cynthia' both times because it was what she answered to. Owen hadn't shared that with anyone at the Bureau. It was also Annika who had gifted him with a printout three days after they'd moved into their new house. Knowing it still ate at him, she'd been doing research. And she'd found a family from Chicago who'd suffered a horrible home invasion. Both the parents had been killed, and the daughters left alive. The report was well over ten years old, but the father was Claymore Beller, an accountant for Black and Associates. The younger daughter was Cynthia. The last known picture of her was her sixth grade school photo. Owen had seen it. Nguyen's damn DNA had been right. Cynthia Beller was only now twenty-four.

He hadn't needed any suggestions to make his brain wander. He couldn't help it. At first all petite brunettes had caught his eye. It could be her. He might dismiss the woman for some reason–too young, too old, too fat, too weak–but he looked. He'd wondered where the Christmas killers had gone. He wondered if he was right and they had come to LA.

Both his first two quarters he'd had a class with a Cynthia in it, and he'd watched the first day as students filed in, his eyes on the brunettes. The first Cynthia had been blonde with blue eyes. That he could work around, but the fact that she was nearly six feet tall and far too heavy meant it wasn't his ninja. The second Cynthia had been African American. The third quarter had produced no Cynthias at all.

Owen settled for using his criminology classes to see if anyone could offer reasonable explanations for unsolved cases. Because they were unsolved, and FBI property to boot, he'd had to give hypotheticals. But he had a handful of papers about breaking into houses and getting into the criminal mind.

This term he'd posed a situation that still ate at him after three years. A dead body in a small room by itself, recently fired gun in hand, four rounds missing from the chamber, two rounds are in the body, only the dead man's blood is found. He'd started the discussion in class, and the group had figured out fairly quickly that a second person had been involved. They'd wondered if the dead man had fired then moved into the room.

Enjoying the banter, Owen had followed that through: you're holding a gun that you clearly know how to fire, it has bullets left in it and you let someone shoot you? The man didn't put the bullets in himself, and his own bullets aren't to be found . . . He'd left the class with an assignment to write their suspicions in a paper.

He'd spent over a week reading all kinds of weird ideas, and writing lengthy replies and asking for re-writes. It was a big workload for him. But it was fun and Owen had enjoyed it. He'd even shown one to Anni. The student had suggested that the other gunner had worn Kevlar.

Anni had agreed, it was the best explanation to date, and she knew what he'd been digging for. He was still digging. Even though he'd sworn to himself he'd leave it behind. He kept looking for missing pieces from other, older cases, and trying to fill a wealth of gaps regarding the Christmas Killers. He hadn't had all the papers graded by the next class, and he'd started into another discussion on the ballistics reading he'd assigned.

His eyes had strayed repeatedly to one girl in the room. Her shirt read "Charlotte". Owen knew he kept looking at it because it was his daughter's name. But, because the girl was attractive and he didn't want any harassment issues, he'd tried not to stare. But before the end of the class, his brain had told him he was looking at a petite brunette. And in his bag was a paper suggesting that a person could walk away with bullets and leave no blood by wearing Kevlar.

He wanted to dismiss it. It was ridiculous.

But this time when he handed the papers back, he paid attention. The brunette had raised her hand for Diana Kincaid, the writer of the Kevlar paper. This time he looked at her on purpose. She wrote her notes with her right hand. But still he wanted to see her handwriting.

She'd asked a question after class that night and–with three other students standing around–he'd pulled the klutziest move he could think of. Making a wild gesture, Owen knocked his coffee cup off the edge of the desk. With lightning reflexes, Diana Kincaid had caught it. She'd set it back upright, without a spilled drop, and kept talking as though nothing had happened.

Unable to stop digging, and certain that he'd find proof that she *couldn't* be the ninja, he'd stalked her as best he could. He looked her up in the school records. She was listed as 'dropped out of high school'. She'd been accepted on a GED she'd obtained in northern California two months to the day after Reynoldo Casto had broken the ninja's arm.

After that, he'd looked for more solid evidence. He was a logical man, and there was every possibility that he still so badly wanted to find the ninja that he'd conjured one up. He'd given out blue-book exams at midterm, forcing the students to hand-write their essays. He figured he'd probably seen Diana's handwriting somewhere before, but what if he hadn't? And he was so close to convinced. He'd wondered.

But no. It wasn't the same writing. And Diana Kincaid wasn't a lefty.

He'd dropped it.

But now, as he tore through the streets of Los Angeles, he wondered if she could choose to be.

Heart pounding, Owen pulled up to the curb and took a moment to look at the cute house. It was small and, like his, had to have cost far too much money. But it looked cozy and inviting. Like a home.

He grabbed the bank slip and checked his pockets, then climbed out of the car before he could change his mind. The short walk up to the front door was made of stepping stones with large dragonflies impressed on them. He wondered if they'd come with the house or if Diana Kincaid and her husband had picked them out. He steeled himself to knock twice on the door.

She opened it, "Dr. Dunham?"

"Hi, Diana."

A tall man stood behind her, his hair a shade between blonde and brown, his eyes a warm grey, and full of puzzlement.

Owen found his voice. "I was leaving class and I found this on the walkway by the ATM." He handed over the slip. "I think you dropped it."

"Oh!" She looked at it and seemed to recognize it. Even though there was no name on the small paper. "Thank you." Her brows quirked, showing a series of emotions–confusion and bewilderment–as they crossed her face in rapid succession. "I hope this wasn't out of your way."

"Oh, no." He smiled, hiding the mental score he tallied. Diana Kincaid had confirmed she was at the scene. For half a second, all he could afford really, Owen stood there, memorizing everything he could about the two of them. “I just figured you’d want it, so I dropped it by.”

She nodded and waited, staying where she was in the doorway. The man still standing guard behind her.

Owen decided to go for broke. “Well, goodnight then, Cynthia. ‘Night, Lee.”

“Goodnight.” She smiled at him as she reached out to close the door, and then her face changed. Her body stilled and her eyes went empty. They stalked the scene in front of her, ready to make a move. And Owen knew she understood what she’d admitted.

His voice was soft as he pulled the recorder from his pocket. “You’ll probably want this. It’s the last piece of real evidence.”

Slowly, she reached out and took it. Tied to the cord was a large, red bow. With wariness in her eyes now, not fear, not his ninja, she pressed the ‘play’ button and listened to the FBI officer answer the call, herself sneezing and saying ‘damnit’.

She looked at Owen with a question in her eyes.

But all he said was, “Goodnight, Diana. Will.” He tipped his head, and started down the walk.

It was Lee Maxwell’s voice that said “Thank you.” It was the first time Owen had heard the gunner speak. Or maybe it had been Will Kincaid.

Diana called out, “I’ll see you in class next week, then?”

“Of course.” He waved and climbed into his car. He was going to sleep his first good night in forever.

Read the first four pages of AJ's next novel

He pushed his way through the synapse between the spaces. It required more energy than he possessed. It always did. Still he always made it. For now, he paused and breathed the searing air deeply into new lungs, holding it despite the pain. His teeth clenched and his hands grabbed for the edges even though they offered no purchase as he forced his way further through.

He stopped again to rest and wait . . . and feel. A small breeze from somewhere brushed his fingers. It didn't matter where it came from, only that it touched him, and that the sensation produced a euphoria like a drug high. All sensations did. Taking another gulp of air, he exalted at how the fumes trailed into his lungs and produced a raw, not unpleasant scream in his tissues. He pushed further through the tear in reality he had fought so hard to create. It would last only as long as he needed, the fissure would seal itself behind him as he fell the last part of the way. But he wasn't there yet.

He inhaled again, taking in the acrid scent of his own burned flesh. He always forgot just how painful it was. The edges sparked tiny friction fires as he forced his way. Tracers of smoke and greasy lines of soot followed his path and marked his passage as he clawed into the abandoned subway station from somewhere most humans only imagined existed.

Gabriel didn't notice. He was too busy watching the changes in himself, and besides, he'd done this enough before. He knew about the black ash just as he knew that there was nothing he could do about it anyway.

As he altered, his eyes watched the human skin of his arms knitting into a smooth, pale color that made him smile despite the pain. The color showed just how far he had come. When he pulled a short lock of his hair forward for inspection, it, too, was light - a translucent honey color that went with the skin and the mind-altering agony. He would bet on his eyes being blue or green, again without the depth of blacker tones. He took immense pride in having earned the pale features he would display on this visit.

With effort, he turned his newly minted brain back to the task at hand and gave the final shove, birthing himself into the human plane. He looked for all the world like he was of it. Appearances were often not just deceiving, but downright dishonest. He wondered what his boss would think of the thoughts in his head. He wondered if they were up to snuff. Then Gabriel pushed that thought aside, too. His deeds would be what he was measured by. He needed to get to them.

Katharine didn't have a cat. So she doubted her sanity as she chased the sleek black creature on its dash into her bathroom.

Her bare feet padded softly, but the noise was ghastly when compared to the ethereal cat that made no sound whatsoever. Since that realization only added to Katharine's disturbing conclusions, she chose to ignore it. She also refused to question why she was running after a creature that she wanted to believe wasn't real. Without thought, her body followed.

Her long bare legs halted, toes digging into the plush carpeting for purchase as she came into the open doorway. The cat had darted in here. Katharine caught just a glimpse of the flick of a midnight tail as the creature slipped behind the toilet.

Her breath stopped, her nose crinkling against the smell she did not want to identify as familiar. But her brain, usually so adept at ignoring what she disliked, was hard-pressed to deny the odor that tickled at her senses.

Ash.

Cautiously now, she stalked her way around the toilet. It was the latest in plumbing innovations, a sleek, low-volume flush model that sat clear back against the wall. There was no room for the cat to duck out when she stepped around, no outlet. She should have the cat trapped - but knew she didn't. The smell told her what she'd see when she peered around to the once pristine carpeting on the concealed side of the toilet.

Still Katharine stepped across the expanse. Blinking slowly, she forced a breath to fortify herself, then immediately wished she hadn't. The remnants of fire burned her lungs, but she pushed on.

As she had suspected - known - there was no cat. Katharine would have been grateful to chalk up the experience to a bad dream. But dreams ended when the dreamer woke. That was when hers had begun.

The small cat had been sweet, rubbing his unbelievably soft head against her hand, demanding the petting that was surely a cat's due. Katharine had obliged. Half-asleep, her fingers had stroked ears and spine, all of it overwhelmingly real, even after she woke fully to the knowledge that she had no cat. That she had closed and *locked* all the doors and windows because she had feared something like this might happen. Because she had convinced herself that it had been her fault the last time. She must have left something open. Her fault meant her fix. So she had sealed the condo before bed.

Tonight when her brain had recognized the cat, she had sat bolt upright, her nose already detecting the faint scent of fire that accompanied her visitors. Her lungs had gasped for air with the final piece of knowledge that told her things were wrong. Her waist had bent, bringing her straight upright in the bed and startling the cat into its mad flight.

Katharine blinked now. Her eyes might be deceiving her, but she had begun to doubt even her doubt.

Slashed across the bathroom carpet was a dark stain of soot. Wide enough for the creature, it was about a foot long, lighter at the end of the streak closer to her and thick enough near the wall that there was actually a tiny pile of burnt ash.

She didn't want to touch it, but some part of her was compelled. She had believed she was hallucinating all of it until once her maid had asked what created the black mess. Katharine didn't know, and had therefore been of no help whatsoever in the art of stain removal. The maid, however, had been instrumental in notifying Katharine that she wasn't the only one who saw it. It wasn't her brain that needed soot removed, it was the pale, deep carpeting.

That was more disturbing than the thought that she was going crazy had been. If the things she had seen were real, then she was playing a game where she had no idea of the rules or the stakes. Real meant that the cat had not been within the confines of her definitions. That she could pet and stroke it meant it wasn't merely a ghost cat, the likes of which she was pretty certain she could deal with. No, this was worse.

From what she had seen before, and the way she had deliberately cornered the cat behind the toilet tonight, she had to believe that the creatures could at least pass through the walls. That would mean the large black dog of two weeks ago had passed through her closet into her living room, then somehow escaped from there. But she hadn't found him in her living room, or the common hallway. Nor had her neighbors complained. There had been just enough time between the last visit and this one to make her believe maybe it had simply ended. The black ash on her floor now said otherwise.

If her previous ideas had been correct, then this cat had dropped through the bathroom floor into the unit below. The soot was a tracer as the beings went through - the carpet or wall or barrier remained unchanged once the mark was washed away. But she didn't believe the dog had passed into the neighbors' unit and she was certain the cat had not dropped down on the condo one floor down, which meant that she didn't know where they went. Katharine didn't want to know. Taking a deep breath, she let the smell be a reminder that she was no longer allowed that luxury. Her only recourse was to learn what she could. So she knelt down and stuck her finger into the soot.

God's Eye

About the Author

AJ Scudiere lives in Nashville, TN and holds a Bachelor's Degree from New College and a Master's Degree from UCLA. A seasoned educator, AJ has taught math, science and writing at every level from junior high through graduate level. These days AJ is mostly found in front of the computer at work on the next novel.

Readers can visit AJScudiere.com